A Cold Flame

AIDAN CONWAY

KILLER READS

A division of HarperCollins*Publishers*
www.harpercollins.co.uk

KillerReads
an imprint of HarperCollins*Publishers* Ltd
1 London Bridge Street
London SE1 9GF

www.harpercollins.co.uk

This paperback edition 2018

First published in Great Britain in ebook format by
HarperCollins*Publishers* 2018

A catalogue record for this book
is available from the British Library

ISBN: 978-0-00-828119-9

Set in Minion by
Palimpsest Book Production Limited, Falkirk, Stirlingshire

Printed and bound by CPI Group (UK) Ltd, Croydon, CR0 4YY

MIX
Paper from
responsible sources
FSC
www.fsc.org   FSC C007454

To the Memory of
Matthew Francis Fadden
1929–2016

One

The few flowers left in the chipped vase had withered to dry brown stalks in the searing August sun.

"You're still sure this falls within our brief?" said Carrara as they stared at the cold, charred remains of the ground floor flat. All the bodies had now been removed but their presence lingered.

"It's another fire, isn't it?" said Rossi. "Probably arson. Why not?"

It was not the first fire in the city to bear the hallmarks of foul play, but it was the first fatal one since they had been moved off their normal duties.

They were standing in the welcome shade of the elevated section of the *tangenziale* flyover, on a side street off the busy, grimy Via Prenestina. It was hot, cripplingly hot. Thin rivulets of sweat were meandering down Rossi's neck despite the shade.

"Even if there's a file on this one already?" said Carrara. "A file that's as good as closed."

Rossi shook his head and continued to gaze into the blackened ruins.

"It's August. You can get away with murder in August. Who was on it again?"

Carrara leafed through the case notes.

"No one I know. A guy called Lallana. Had a racial homicide's brief. Seconded to us in June and then transferred out again, at his own request, now buzzing all over the place with Europol. I got hold of him by phone but he wasn't keen on talking. Says it's all in the reports and he's got nothing more to add."

"Giving you the brush-off?"

Carrara shrugged.

"He had it down as a hate crime – seems the victims were all foreigners – but not a single, solid lead. No witnesses, just the one guy who survived it."

"A survivor?" said Rossi.

"Was. Dead now. Had 60 per cent burns. Should have been long gone but somehow hung on for nearly a week."

"And all while I was on holiday," said Rossi.

"You can't be everywhere, Mick," said Carrara glancing up from the notes. "I mean a break was merited, after Marini."

Rossi's thoughts turned then to the events of the previous winter but as his shoes crunched on the ash and scorched timbers he was still struggling to comprehend the present horror. Shooting, strangling, stabbing – that was one thing – but *burning* to death. They must have been locked inside when the fire started. Some might have woken but had been unable to get to a door or a window, the security grilles put there ostensibly to keep them safe from intruders thus consigning them to their fates.

"But why wasn't anyone able to get out?" said Rossi. "Because they locked their room doors every night?"

"Correct," said Carrara. "Normal practice in bedsits, but no keys for the security grilles were found, not even after a fingertip search."

"What about the front door?" said Rossi. "Couldn't they have got out with their own keys? They all had one, right?"

Carrara took out a blown-up scene-of-crime photo.

"The lock. Tampered with, the barrel and mechanism all

mangled up. Some debris was found inside. It could have been someone forcing it – an attempted break-in – or it could have been sabotage. The occupants might have been able to open it from the inside to escape, if they had managed to reach the door, but the bolts were still in place. Nobody could get in until the fire guys arrived and then it was too late."

"And their forensics?" said Rossi.

"Well," said Carrara, "significant traces of ethanol – one version of the facts is that there was a moonshine vodka operation – and they did find the remains of a timer switch next to the burnt-out fridge. Lallana maintained it could have been foul play, or just as easily some home brew electrical set-up that shorted. He didn't exactly go all out for the former theory. In the absence of a clear motive and witnesses the coroner delivered an open verdict. Have a look for yourself."

Carrara handed Rossi the relevant report.

"Open?" said Rossi noting now with near contempt the irony. "Someone locked those poor bastards inside."

"Like I said, no keys for the window bars were found but no one lived long enough to tell any tale."

Among the scorched masonry and fallen timbers, one of the grilles lay across the small desert of debris, like the ribcage of a once living and breathing being strewn across a bleak savannah.

"Any names?" said Rossi.

"Just the one," said Carrara. "The tough nut. Ivan Yovoshenko. He was found in the communal bathroom and had dog tags from his conscription days. But for them he would have been a zero like the rest. It seems he had at least tried to get out, got severely burnt in the process and maybe finally sought refuge in the bathroom. He could have struck his head and collapsed. Judging from the amount of alcohol they found in his bloodstream, he had to have been blind drunk and wouldn't have realized just how hot the flames were. It was enough for him to survive as long as he did."

3

"And nothing on the others?"

"Nothing," said Carrara.

"Well, they can forget checking dental records," said Rossi. "These guys could probably just about afford toothpaste."

Carrara pulled out another sheet for Rossi.

"Presumed missing persons in Rome and Lazio for the last six months, but no matches with this address. The word on the street is that they were five single men, probably illegals, but anymore than that ..."

"Sounds familiar," said Rossi. "But no friends, no workmates?"

Carrara gestured to the desiccated blooms and a brown, dog-eared farewell note or two.

"Paid their respects then made themselves scarce, I suppose," said Carrara. "If it's a racial hate killing they were probably thinking 'who's next'?"

"But a landlord?" said Rossi, sensing an opening. "Tell me we have an owner's name." But Carrara was already quashing that hope with another printout from the case folder.

"Flat sold to a consortium two months ago as part of a portfolio of properties, a sort of going concern with cash-in-hand rents through an established 'agent' who hasn't been seen since the fire."

"That's convenient," quipped Rossi.

"Says here they always sent an office bod to pick up the cash in a nearby bar and the go-between got his room cheap as well as his cut. No contracts. No paper trail. No nothing."

"And no name for the agent?"

"Mohammed. Maybe."

"That narrows it down. And the bar? Anyone there remember him'?"

"*Nada.*"

"A description?"

"North African. About fifty."

"Great," said Rossi. "Well, it looks like the late Ivan's our only man, doesn't it? Let's see what the hospital can give us."

"And then a trip to the morgue?"

"You know, Gigi, I was almost beginning to miss going there."

Two

"Yesterday was yesterday," the checkout girl declared as Rossi, making one of his regular top-up shops, tried to pay the ten cents lacking from the previous evening.

Time to forget.

Time to move on.

After lunch and a short siesta he'd spent an hour in a bar, leafing through the papers thinking things over and watching the more popular TV channels to see their take on the Prenestina fire. The mayor had shown up, looked contrite, made a bit of a speech. A local priest was more outspoken, calling it ethnic cleansing. But it wasn't as if there was any great rallying cry to get to the bottom of it, to trace and compensate the victims' families, whether it was racially motivated or down to some underworld grudge. While the space being dedicated to the story was rationed after the initial reports, it was almost as if some sections of the media were giving the tacit impression that it had been, if not a necessary culling, then almost an occupational hazard for "illegals".

As he left the supermarket a figure flashed past in the crowd. Was it? It couldn't be. She was dead. He stood and watched as the dark-haired, athletic silhouette melted into the crowd, and then shaking himself back into something like rationality he proceeded homewards.

But the *doppleganger* had set him thinking – thinking about *her* again and the fallout from the Marini affair. It was almost unimaginable now to think that this same baked, arid city had been wreathed in snow and thrown into chaos while he and Carrara pursued a serial killer dubbed 'The Carpenter', trying to halt his murderous crusade against the city's women.

It had been dubbed 'The Carpenter' case, but Marini had been at the centre of everything, playing an ambiguous role on the fringes of a coterie of obscure, occult power brokers in the Church, the state, and big business. For her own ends, she had played them both like violins almost all the way, before coming on board with him and Carrara as they made a pact to use her secret service skills to nail the killer. Her contorted rationale had been a part of a broader strategy, so she could control everything. They discovered that Giuseppe had had a history of working for the services and her cronies all along, and even if in a ragged way Rossi and Carrara did eventually get their man, the circumstances and the consequences still rankled.

He knew that the work of the dark, deep state, the powers-that-be, was not finished. It was an ongoing concern.

And then a decomposed body had turned up in the spring. Hers presumably, in the car she had escaped in through the snowstorm following that last encounter. The corpse had been buried in an unmarked grave, and Rossi and Carrara alone remained the custodians of the whole complex secret. But with no one having stood trial for either The Carpenter's crimes or Giuseppe Bonaventura's own murder and no one looking likely to, and while a file remained technically open, the case was considered as good as closed unless new evidence came to light.

All despite the misgivings and rumours that rumbled on in some quarters.

There was no shortage of paranoid speculation on the more

radical fringes of the political world and within the world of crime investigation itself. No one but Rossi and Carrara knew the guilty truth. *The tangled webs we weave,* thought Rossi. They wouldn't even believe it if he ever did try to come clean. Either way, he would go down for malpractice, perverting the course of justice, you name it. They would make sure of that.

But the dominant, accepted narrative was that the evil had been exorcized, the murders had ceased and The Carpenter had met a justified violent end.

One day perhaps it would all come out. One day.

The domestic political upheavals remained largely on hold now as the MPD faced up to its being so near yet so far from obtaining anything like real power. A general election was far off, unless the government were to fall, but that seemed unlikely. So little had changed in the city in terms of its politics and the penchant for corruption at every imaginable level. On the park walls, on the apartment blocks, the far-right graffiti, however, was fresh, with new variants and vile, resurrected favourites.

HONOUR TO THE FATHERLAND.
DEATH TO PERFIDIOUS JEWRY.
GYPSIES TO THE INCINERATORS.

The comments too that Rossi might hear from disgruntled older citizenry could be strikingly un-PC. "It's an Islamic invasion, mark my words," was one familiar refrain. No, the race issues had not gone away, as immigration, religious extremism, and the global terror threat continued to dominate the fear agenda.

He dropped his shopping onto the kitchen table and picked up one of the newspapers he hadn't yet opened. He flicked through to the letters page, where citizens continued to rail against buses that still didn't come, roads still full of holes, and, depending on how the breeze blew, the rubbish putrefying on the streets that continued to sour the evening *aperitivo*. He tossed the paper aside and set about about fixing himself a decent drink.

***

Rossi looked down from his balcony, his after-dinner sambuca and ice still holding its own against the enveloping evening heat. With the sun down, the city had begun to breathe a little. Traffic was almost non-existent, with only the odd revving *motorino* whining and yelping its horn from some unseen side street. Cut-price tourists, escaped from the throng, ambled about off the beaten track in mismatched summer clothes. Oblivious. Oblivious. Yes, thought Rossi. A state-within-the-state has its own people killed in the name of a perverse agenda and there's nothing you can do about it. Just count yourself lucky it wasn't you getting the bullet or the bomb. After all, these days you got it easy. The days of bombs in banks and train stations were long gone, buried under the rubble of the Seventies and Eighties. Of course they were.

Yana, his Ukrainian girlfriend of several years standing, was already in bed. He had cooked dinner and then they had chatted a little. She had seen, however, that he was distant, newly involved with a case. Tired herself after a busy day in the health centre, she had left him to ponder. Since going back to work full-time in the Wellness Centre, she had hardly had a moment's rest. She lived, ate and slept work now, as if surviving the attempt on her life only a little more than six months earlier had left her leading a charmed life – every day and every moment was precious. She knew it and she was going to make it count and was even talking of expanding the business.

But it still chilled Rossi to the bone when he remembered it all and he still feared for Yana. Giuseppe had taunted him, letting him know in no uncertain terms that he had crossed Yana's path

9

in the dark days when she had arrived in Italy and fallen victim to traffickers. It had unsettled Rossi profoundly. But who else knew Yana's secrets? Who else might crawl out from under a rock and want revenge? Perhaps the snakehead of the trafficking ring who had evaded Rossi all those years ago, thanks probably to a tip-off from a rat in his own Rome Serious Crime Squad, the RSCS.

The same rat who was still on the force now and, though he had his suspicions, remained unknown to him.

And the calls still came to his house or to Yana's when they were together, sometimes months or even a year apart. Sometimes in the dead of night to torment him, or them. No voice. Just silence, a barely perceptible breathing. Someone he knew, he was sure, keeping tabs on him, making sure of where he lived and who he was with.

His thoughts turned to Yana again. The August-induced insomnia had left her feeling jaded, and the combination of heat-disturbed sleep and the effects of her cocktail of medication were wreaking havoc with her natural rhythms. Still she had astounded every doctor that had examined her. It had to be something to do with her inherent athleticism and her Ukrainian resilience or the will to live that he had seen all those years before when he had played his part in freeing her from the nightmare world of drugs, violence and exploitation that she had been sucked into as a naive young immigrant.

Apart from that, all in all, Rossi had to admit he was quite enjoying their, albeit temporary, cohabitation. Perhaps *because* it was temporary. So far, so good at least. He had even proposed the arrangement himself when Yana, having improvements made to her flat, had found herself in limbo. Their busy schedules meant that the time spent together was only ever a few hours in the evening. Yet, he felt it was a start and steady progress in uncharted waters.

He looked towards the Roma hills and the flickering yellow

lights as he sipped on his drink and the rubbish collection truck made its slow, lumbering progress along Via Latina. It was the Prenestina fire that was beginning to occupy his thoughts and perhaps already to obsess him. He knew the signs. He knew too that it had come from on high when he and Carrara had been moved "temporarily" from homicide to arson. Why else, when by anyone's standards they had got concrete results in the Marini case? It was dressed up as something else, of course – we need your expertise on this one, we think you're the men for the job, and all that bullshit. And Maroni, his boss, in his best *don't shoot the messenger* guise, had assured him that it all fell under the Serious Crime Squad remit.

He looked back into the lounge. His phone was buzzing on the coffee table. It was Carrara.

"Gigi."

"Another fire, Mick. Initial reports indicate it could be of interest."

"Where?"

"Parioli."

"Parioli?"

It was one of Rome's more well-to-do suburbs.

"Yep. They think there's a family inside. Nigerians. You'd better get here quick."

The fire brigade were still dousing sizeable pockets of flame in the detached two-storey villa's badly scorched shell. The worst seemed to be under control but it had spread quickly with the hot summer air and a light breeze exacerbating matters.

A large crowd had assembled for the spectacle, but there was no hard fast news on who the occupants might be and so far chaos seemed to be reigning. Rossi and Carrara began to apprise themselves of the situation, only to find that no one could give them a simple, unified version of events.

What they knew was that flames had been spotted about about

11

an hour earlier, and a passerby had raised the alarm. Others had then hammered at the door to rouse the presumably sleeping occupants, but all to no avail. Attempts to kick the door in had also failed.

Rossi walked over to a fountain and splashed his face, trying not to imagine the worst that could be about to greet them when they finally got news about the occupants' fate. As he looked up again, Carrara was returning. He'd got something.

"Registered in the name of a prominent local politician, the Honourable Mimmo Carducci," he said. "But some of the neighbours are saying there's an African family living there, fairly recently arrived."

Rossi pondered the information.

"But no one's been calling for help from any of the windows, back or front," he said finally. They both knew what that meant: that smoke inhalation could have done for them already.

The fire crews were gathered and assessing the level of danger. Nineteenth-century building. No reinforced concrete, a lot of wood in the ceilings. Parts of it could collapse at any moment.

"Family of four. Nigerian asylum seekers," said the chief fire officer.

Behind him a squadron of four men had begun donning breathing apparatus.

"I'm sending them in," he continued, "if there's half a chance of finding anyone alive. But it doesn't look promising."

Rossi put an anxious hand to his face.

Carrara, who had dashed off again, was now concluding a rapid discussion with another local family who had pulled up in a car. There was a lot of nodding of heads, then some cries of either pain or happiness. It was hard to be sure. Then Carrara turned back towards Rossi and raised a hand in what appeared to be a sign of victory and as a signal to call off the search.

"A lucky escape," said Carrara, the relief on his face clearly visible.

The house had been empty. When Carrara had finally spoken to the absent occupant, a Nigerian university professor in exile, it emerged that as the dramatic scenes had been playing out on the street in Parioli he, his children and their friends had been playing blind man's buff in someone's converted cellar in Trastevere where there was no cell phone signal. Friends of theirs had organized a surprise party. The guy hadn't had even an inkling of the plan and they had all left the house at the last minute. The father had seen the missed calls only when he went out for a cigarette.

Rossi tried to rub the stress out of his face as Carrara dialled a number.

"I'm calling the professor now."

The fire crew were removing their apparatus as they awaited further orders. This one at least had turned out for the better and their cold beers would go down a lot easier when this shift ended.

The Parioli fire had now pushed the Prenestina case off their agenda. Rossi and Carrara had driven back to the office in the Alfa Romeo to weigh it all up.

"Initial findings say that the house was torched," said Carrara. "Accelerants and a relatively sophisticated *timed* incendiary device were used. The occupant has been confirmed as being the exiled Nigerian writer and professor – Chini Okoli – and his family, living there as guests of the Honourable Mimmo Carducci, who had given them the run of one of the houses he had in his portfolio."

"Portfolio?" said Rossi sitting up. "What do we know about him?"

"Ex PCI, Italian Communist Party. Now part of the wobbly left-of-centre alliance. Well-to-do Roman family, connections with the university, family law firm. Active overseas in human rights work. The usual story. Seems there was a network of friends of friends in academic circles. They helped out with solidarity missions for Palestine and Brazil."

This was certainly different to the Prenestina fire but whether or not it was connected he didn't know. Racial, maybe, but if they had targeted an intellectual, given the context – Nigeria, asylum seekers – it had political written all over it.

"So, technically, it was a bomb. An incendiary. When can we speak to Okoli?"

"I think he might need a night off first, don't you?" said Carrara.

Rossi nodded but knew he would need to see him as soon as was practicable, to get a handle on any motives, but there were other elements which were already interesting him.

He got up and opened the door of the office's mini fridge. No beers left. He went then to the bottom drawer of the filing cabinet and pulled out a bottle of Jameson's twelve-year-old reserve.

"What have you got?" said Carrara. He could see Rossi might already be onto something.

"First up," said Rossi, pouring a large and a disgracefully small measure for himself and Carrara respectively, "the surprise party. It was so well concealed that any intelligence the firebombers might have had didn't reveal it either."

"Go on," said Carrara, warming to it now. Rossi took a bottle of water from the fridge for his whiskey, a few ice cubes for Carrara and pulled up a chair for himself.

"So, either they hadn't been tapping the phones or they hadn't employed the sophistication necessary to monitor, record, and translate from their private conversations in Okoli's native language."

"Which suggests a lack of sophistication on the part of the assailants."

"Or plain sloppiness," said Rossi. He took a meditative sip on his whiskey and water. It was too hot for it but he needed the kick.

"Improvised far-right aggression?" said Carrara. "A warning by way of a relatively high-profile figure?"

"Or an attempted assassination under the *cover* of a spontaneous race attack."

"Riding on the back of the Prenestina business," said Carrara.

They both considered the significance of their theorizing as they sipped on their drinks. Some unifying strategy could have been behind it. Attacking minorities, blacks, immigrants. That was Nazi-style. It also grabbed the headlines.

"Or what if we're talking some kind of Unabomber?" said Carrara. "A lone wolf carrying out random strikes, varying his technique, leading us all a merry dance as we try to come up with some ideological motive behind it all?"

They both knew the story well. The Italian Unabomber had never been caught. He, and a he it almost certainly was, as far as the psychological profiling went, had terrorized the north of the country for over ten years with random attacks, planting pipe bombs and incendiary devices in public spaces – park benches, beaches, bus shelters and the like. He had caused only one direct fatality but had maimed and traumatized numerous members of the public. He had once booby-trapped a child's chocolate egg.

The theory went that since the last attack some six or seven years before, he had either died, or was on an extended cooling-off period, serial-killer style. That there might be more than one, other emulators, could not be ruled out either. That he might have moved south or spawned an imitator in Rome was also a possibility.

"Perhaps someone with military experience," said Rossi. "Someone with a generalized grudge. PTSD from Iraq or Afghanistan. The race-hate agenda might be right up his street."

"Maybe" said Carrara. "Have you seen this?" he said then, holding up a printout.

Rossi reached across the desk. Another "potentially relevant" incident had come up on the radar from earlier in the evening.

A lot of motorbikes had gone up in flames in a car park in the affluent Prati area and their none-too-pleased and, in some cases, influential owners had already been harassing the local cops.

"No casualties, no homicide," said Rossi.

"But they want answers," said Carrara. He was scrolling through the latest headlines and news on social media. "And those with a bit of weight to throw around are calling for 'deployment of resources, protection of Italian interests. Get the police out of the ghettos and back in the heartlands'."

Rossi was now beginning to toy with the idea of there being some link there too, but knew it was early days. What if someone was trying to sow chaos, stretch their resources? Crazy environmentalists maybe. There were nuts everywhere in Rome, especially when the mercury was rising. He got up and went to the window to get some air. There wasn't much.

"Priority goes to the house fires for now," he said turning back to face Carrara. "Send out some uniforms. Get statements, check for witnesses and CCTV. Then we'll see."

The others would get their precious insurance eventually. He was going to nail the real cowardly scum who got their kicks out of burning working men, women, and children in their beds.

Three

Yana was going in late to the Wellness Health and Fitness Centre, so Rossi had let her sleep. She was her own boss and could do as she pleased, but she had a business head and a work ethic that put others to shame. Plans were afoot for expansion and her hunger was plain to see. He steered clear, not understanding a thing of that world. He hoped they would find a balance, however, as his own obsessive approach to cases was not always ideal for those around him.

He laid the table for them both and then allowed himself a quiet, meditative breakfast before the sun began to emerge from behind the apartment blocks, extinguishing with all its gathering fury the night's last vague hints of coolness. It was relentless, sapping. He lowered the shutter a few notches to keep the heat minimally at bay and then finished his coffee, leaving enough in the pot for Yana. He did a couple of yoga stretches that Yana had taught him, just so as to render the exercise not wholly perfunctory. He was sweating already and headed for the shower.

She was waking as he slipped on his lightest summer jacket.

"Don't make yourself too beautiful," she said through her sleep-infused languor. A strap had slipped off one shoulder of

17

her ivory silk camisole and her smooth body was again calling, siren-like, to Rossi. He knotted his tie as loosely as decency would allow and leaned over to kiss her, his lips straying then along her neck and shoulder and into the warmth of her breasts. As Yana flopped back onto the bed the sunlight fell across her body evoking the promise of long carefree hours. But he stopped and tore himself away.

"Have to go," he mumbled. "Gigi will be waiting." He didn't say where. On a morning like this, when life seemed to burst from every pore of his and their being, it was neither the time nor the place to talk of mortuaries, death, and carbonized corpses. She flopped back down onto the bed. Her strength seemed neutralized, and he couldn't help feeling protective again, even now. A good deal of time had passed since the winter's events but Rossi knew that doing the job he did and having the enemies he had would always mean she was vulnerable. They could always hit her to get to him. Always.

"Don't forget to lock the door," he said then, trying to assuage something of his guilt. As if that action would lock off his darkest and most persistent fears. As if that could stop the worst they could ever do, if they chose to.

He felt tense. The relief after tracing the professor and his family had worn off and he had slept badly, fitfully, in the near-tropical humidity, his thoughts looping as he turned over the various scenarios again and again.

The city was tense too and that same heat wasn't helping. Grievances often rankled in the punishing summer torpor, especially in situations where numbers or circumstances created a critical mass – a crowded bus, a queue in the post office, a traffic jam. People didn't move on with their problems here and in the stifling humidity they could fester. They were oversensitive, their assailed and worn-down egos were fragile. And August in the city was also the time of the forgotten and marginalized – the loners, the rejects; those who didn't or couldn't get away to summer retreats to enjoy the fruits of their year-long labours. They too had their own axes to grind.

Only the other day Yana had dared to remind a dog walker not to let his animal foul the street outside her building, and the owner in question, once he had quickly established Yana's non-native status, had subjected her to a tirade of the most venomous abuse. Racist, misogynist, vile and frightening. A few phrases echoed now in Rossi's mind as he remembered Yana's stunned retelling of the event.

We wanna be the bosses in our own country! ... Italy for the Italians ... Burn the lot of 'em!

In another part of the city, as she stepped into the bathroom, Tiziana Belfonte amused herself by thinking again of the extra touches and final details she might add to a well-deserved holiday she had been planning. She had stayed up late the night before to profit from some of the cooler air that had finally wafted in over the city and onto her balcony. She had been organizing the vacation for months now and had decided to take it in September with a good friend in similar circumstances – happily single, feisty and ready for whatever may come, be it fair or foul.

She was also one of the tribe who liked to work through the hottest months, drawing comfort and real benefit from living in the city when it was at its most arid and deserted. True, the sleep-impaired nights could be torrid and also, being a fairly strict ecologist in her outlook, she didn't use any artificial air-conditioning. Only adding to the source problem, wasn't it? Heating up the atmosphere to keep you cool. It was against nature. The summer heat meant you had to slow down, find natural solutions to combat its toll on the body. As such, she enjoyed these months when an ice-cold shower before breakfast was like plunging into the waters of some imagined crystal lagoon. That would soon be a reality and the thought gave her a frisson of anticipated pleasure as the water rushed against her lightly tanned skin. She glanced at her own reflection in the misted mirror panelling, patting and caressing herself a little with satisfaction. Not bad. Not bad at all considering she'd been doing the daily grind for nearly twenty years now. Ready for action in mind *and* body, whatever the bastards might throw at her today.

And then she shuddered, but not because of the water as she recalled the anonymous note that had arrived just a few weeks before.

N***er lover. Bitch. Whore. We know where you live.

But she was tough, she had to be. But she was human too, and even her skin was only so thick. She also knew that the events of the previous winter – especially the body of the murdered African that she had tried so hard to get identified – still weighed on her conscience. She wondered again what might have become of Jibril, the young immigrant she was sure had some connection to the corpse he had viewed in her presence. But he had just disappeared then and the body had remained unclaimed.

As she thought about it, it stung her conscience and the holiday suddenly seemed like another cowardly attempt to flee her responsibility, an extravagance she did not deserve.

Driving in Rome in August was as close to a pleasure as it could ever get. Traffic was down to its annual minimum and a hint of space could finally be seen and felt. As Rossi looked out at the sky and its default-setting of blue, a little of his tension fell away. The air too felt cleaner, while colourful, carefree, smiling tourists seemed to mop up some more of his previous negativity with their languid sweep through the city. Tradition dictated that the lion's share of the citizenry would be out of town for the whole month and the pervading feeling was usually one of mild and welcome liberation. In the suburbs away from the well-worn tourist trails every second shop had its shutter lowered. *Closed for holidays. See you in September.* But then there was also something final and obstinate about those shutters – like the sealed

20

lips of a witness who will never speak, holding the secrets back, the unstated "Fuck You" if you want an answer. Try as he might to let the spirit of summers past dominate his thoughts, Rossi knew his work was just beginning.

Carrara was waiting under a tree as Rossi approached. He held out his newspaper so Rossi could check the front page. They'd got their story but not all the facts. "A possible electrical fault" was one theory, and Rossi had made sure they kept a lid on the forensics, at least for now. As usual the man from Puglia was looking fit and focused in an apparently laid-back way. The years in undercover anti-mafia work had kept Carrara sharp and adaptable, and family life with kids had scarcely seemed to sap his energy.

"Coffee?"

Rossi glanced at his watch.

"Why not?"

The corner bar was the only one open within walking distance and catered mainly for the skeleton staffs of the nearby public offices and time-killing locals. Most offices had coffee machines on every floor and any employee worth their salt knew which was the best. Some had their own bars too, but there was nothing like leaving the office behind for the dark gunshot of an *espresso* to banish the morning lethargy. Some, however, lingered over a *cappuccino* or a *caffè latte*. There were even those that didn't bother to go back to the office at all, having clocked in, and then went about their daily tasks with complete nonchalance until they saw fit to put in at least a token appearance before lunch.

In the bar there was the usual hubbub and high-octane gossip; at peak times there would be the kind of crush more typical of a British pub on a Friday night than a café at ten o'clock in the morning. Fallen and discarded napkins and *cornetti* flakes littered the floor as Rossi and Carrara edged and nudged their way towards the counter to catch the bartender's eye. Once they had been served their respective *macchiato* and *espresso*, they established themselves at a standing-only table in the corner.

"So, do we have an appointment at the morgue or do we just walk in?" said Carrara stirring his *espresso* with energy. "Lallana will have been already, of course. Do you think they might consider it irregular?"

Rossi stirred a half sachet of brown sugar into his *macchiato*. "We just say we have a wide brief to investigate all acts of arson and we're cross-checking facts. Thoroughness never goes amiss and Lallana's off it now anyway. Maroni's busy with some internal audit business. I say we press ahead until we encounter an obstacle."

Carrara finished stirring his *espresso*.

"But have you got a theory about this or are you going on instinct or what?"

Rossi knocked back his coffee and waited for the rush.

"The more we know the better. I don't like taking the easy way out. All this open verdict stuff. That's a gift to criminals and an affront to investigative police work. We have to eliminate any doubt about this being accidental, which it can't have been, and then find out if there was more than blind racial hate behind it. So we need to get down to the hospital before they've forgotten all about this Ivan guy. He might have said something. Seen something. It has to be worth a try."

"And last night's business? I've had some more info through on Okoli."

"Set up a chat with him. What does he do?"

"Playwright, investigative journalist. Rubbed the government up the wrong way it seems."

"So a target or a coincidence?"

"See what he has to say for himself," Carrara replied. "I'll give him a call." He glanced at his watch. "Should be up and about by now."

He moved away from the babble and noise of the bar.

A slim but strong woman, perhaps approaching forty but easily passing for five years younger, had seated herself at the bar to

Rossi's left. Her off-white summer dress was elegant without being provocative, thus going against the dominant Roman trend which saw the season's clothing often resembling more négligées than daywear. The dress's broad straps framed a rich, evenly tanned rectangle between her shoulder blades.

"He's going to swing by the *Questura* later," said Carrara returning to the table. "Any news on Iannelli, by the way?" he said, recapturing Rossi's attention.

"Iannelli?" said Rossi with a pronounced exhalation. "It's going to be a steep learning curve for Dario. Life under 24-hour police escort. I don't know if he's realized yet how tough it will be."

Dario Iannelli, investigative reporter, Rossi's long-time friend and confidante, and now with a Mafia contract out on his life. He had made it big with his scoop on high-level corruption during The Carpenter case, but had fallen foul of *Cosa Nostra* and had been fortunate to escape a car bomb with his life.

The woman had finished her coffee and, rising from her stool, appeared to make for the exit, but then stopped, as if struck by some sudden realization.

"Excuse the intrusion," she said, moving back and then coming alongside Rossi and Carrara's table. "But I couldn't help over-hearing something. You mentioned Dario Iannelli. The journalist."

"Yes," said Rossi. "Is there anything I can do for you?" he began and reached out to take her hand. "Inspector Michael Rossi. And this is Inspector Luigi Carrara."

As Carrara turned to take her hand, he too was struck by her unostentatious elegance.

"Well, yes. Maybe there is." She glanced around at the chattering clientele. "Could we talk somewhere, in private. But perhaps not in my office. I work at the hospital of legal medicine. The mortuary to be exact."

Four

"If I don't get the job this time then we go, right?" said Francesco. "We pack our bags and leave Italy for good."

Paola replied on the other end of the line with the usual consternation.

"Where?" she said. "*Where* do we go? I mean do you have an idea, a plan?"

Francesco let out a sigh.

"To Spain, to Ireland, or Germany, or anywhere a researcher can make a decent living. Anywhere where they appreciate and value me for my knowledge and experience not just my loyalty and my contacts or my family connections."

It was the old story. She knew it but didn't want to hear it, and he was tired of telling her.

"But what about Mum and Dad? And your mother on her own?" she shot back.

It was true that it would be a wrench, a sacrifice for him too, but he had decided.

"Paola, I've had enough! I'm going to grow old here trying to get a job in the university, don't you see? I want to settle down. I want *us* to settle down and have children. Then we see. And I want you to be able to choose whether or not you want to go

24

back to work, not get thrown on the scrapheap at forty because you've had a kid. If we go abroad you can have that chance."

There was a long pause. He could hear the random noises of a train station in the background. She'd called to wish him well but the conversation had turned sour. But he had to get it out in the open.

"I'll call you later, when it's over," he said, with little real conviction. He wanted to be alone.

He finished his coffee and bit on a breakfast biscuit then went over again the possible questions they could ask him, trying to conjure the unforeseen from thin air, the unseen questions in the envelopes they would proffer him, smiling at him from behind the desk they so loved to interpose between themselves and the mere mortals in the other, real world. The uninitiated, the hopeful, the desperate.

So this was to be the last *Concorso*. He had decided. The *Concorso* or "public competition" was, in theory, an open, transparent method of selecting candidates for positions in state bodies or for publicly funded research projects. You applied, sending off the forms and all the relevant paperwork and then you were called to take an exam. Then you got to the interview, which was when they could do what they wanted.

He had been from pillar to post, to deliver conference papers, often at his own expense, to take low-paid temporary teaching positions in this or that university, to win a research grant, which meant he could live just above the breadline for a year. And then when the money ran out? Back to square one. In and out of offices. Up and down the country. Moving. Moving back. Working for free. This was the life of the researcher who could not count on patronage, or a powerful relative, or a favour due from on high. This was the life of that singular and sorry category of person who was not a *raccomandato* – not "recommended" for a job or a grant. Not useful for someone. Not worthy of being a token to flip across the baize in their feudal game.

25

He didn't want to leave Italy, but he had tasted freedom once and had liked it. For the six month post he had been awarded in San Francisco, after he had completed his PhD, the university had contacted *him*! They came looking for *his* expertise after they had seen his research. They had decided to go to the States together, and Paola had then had to persuade her parents, old-style Catholics that they were, that the cohabitation abroad would be a prelude to marriage. They went. The wedding, however, had remained on hold.

They had not committed themselves to a longer stay as Paola was less keen to tear up her roots in the old country. So they had come back, hoping to make a go of it and use the experience gained to get a leg-up. He had been obliged to make the expected compromises – working for free, waiting, biding his time. But he had believed that it might just be worth it. That there would be an outlet in Italy for his ideas. Now the nagging fear always at the back of his mind had become the simple realization that he had been wrong.

And it could all have been so different. He had done his compulsory military service in the *carabinieri*, the military branch of the police, and had enjoyed it, thriving on its culture of rigour and seriousness and dedication to duty. He'd also been drawn to the increasing use of technology, science, and psychology for the solving and prevention of crimes. So much so that after his initial one-year conscription he had signed on for another one as a paid, working recruit. He hadn't wanted to fall back on his parents again. That would have been the easy way out; whereas he enjoyed a challenge, like when he was in the mountains with his friends and he would head for the highest peaks. He wasn't content with the view of the top from halfway up.

Francesco got up from the breakfast bar in the kitchen and began closing all the windows despite the heat. He was cautious, prudent, suspicious of the opportunist ready to exploit any weakness in their defences. His family had always expected him to pursue an academic career, their view being that the police force and the army were for those who didn't have it in them to go any further. They were also institutions tainted by their association with the "regime". They had been a well-respected and quietly influential family until the fascists had seized power before the war, something which had set in motion their gradual decline towards irrelevance. Yet they had clung on to some of the trappings, the values, the pride, the culture. As for what had actually happened back then, Francesco didn't know the details but, according to his mother, it was something that had continued to rankle, at least for his father, while he had been alive.

Five

They left the bar and walked across the almost-deserted Piazza Verano, the nearby cemetery not visible but always a presence.

"The park, perhaps," she suggested, walking slightly ahead. "There are tables and it's quiet now."

They stopped at a dark green art-deco kiosk and a wide esplanade where cast-iron tables occupied the space under the shade of several tall eucalyptus trees.

"May we?" said Carrara, addressing a white-shirted and tieless employee moving about without particular urgency while a mop in a steaming bucket stood propped against some flower pots. The bar seemed in general disorder with teetering piles of ashtrays and cases of mineral water dumped here and there. His grudging nod of assent meant they were technically open for business.

"The coffee's not the best and gossip doesn't travel well if it's not in a confined space," she commented. "So you can always count on getting some breathing space."

Rossi imagined that it was a commodity she was in need of.

"Here?" he said, indicating the most isolated corner and the cleanest-looking table and chairs. Their new guest gave her approval and Carrara was first to pull out a chair for her.

"Well, gentlemen, I suppose now I should introduce *my*self," she said, placing her light, coffee-coloured handbag on the table. "My name is Tiziana Belfonte. And as I said, I work in the hospital."

"And you have something you would like to tell us?" said Rossi. "With regard to Dario Iannelli."

"Well," she began, "yes, but indirectly. It concerns a murder victim. An as yet unidentified murder victim."

"Do you mean from the Prenestina fire?" said Carrara.

"No, actually. An earlier victim. The African murdered last winter. I have reason to believe Dario Iannelli may be in some way connected."

"Go on," said Rossi. "We know something of the case, among others. It was a busy time."

"Well, it all goes back to the winter and when your colleagues were trying to identify the victim. His body has not been identified or claimed but sooner or later he will have to be buried: in a pauper's grave, if no one comes forward. It's policy I'm afraid and it's all to do with the demands of cost and space."

"The fate of many," said Rossi. "In this day and age."

"Yes." She nodded. "I am afraid so. And not only migrants or foreigners. But the point I want to make is that someone *did* come forward to identify him. At least I thought he would make an identification but, as it turned out, it wasn't to be."

An accumulation of guilt, perhaps, or unresolved doubts seemed to surface now, as her voice began to betray more emotion. Rossi knew the signs. The secret knowledge that could devour the thoughts of the well-intentioned and conscientious, just as it could eat away at the souls of the remorseful. This had been backing up for God knows how long and he wondered what trap she might have felt she was in.

"Could you perhaps clarify what you mean by 'it wasn't to be'?" said Rossi.

The waiter had begun his slow walk towards their table.

"Perhaps we should order something," said Rossi, noting the approach and sensing the need to ease the tension.

"Tiziana?"

"Oh, just water for me, thank you,"

"*Solo un'acqua minerale per la signora,*" said Rossi dismissing the waiter before he could materialize.

"There's no rush, Tiziana," said Rossi. "Just tell me what you remember and then we'll see what we can do. But when you are ready," he added, placing a reassuring hand on her shoulder.

She almost smiled and some of the rigidity in her elegant form softened. Plenty of men had put their hands on her in plenty of other situations, something she neither sought nor appreciated, but she didn't find Rossi patronizing or threatening. He seemed genuine and she was warming to him already.

"My job is very important to me, Inspector. I have considerable responsibility and I am the only woman in my department. I oversee the clerical side of things but I have become a *de facto factotum,* if you will."

"A sort of Girl Friday," said Rossi. "The go-to person."

"It's frequently the way, in the public sector."

Rossi gave a knowing nod. He sensed she didn't have any sounding board in her work life.

"Otherwise," she continued, "nothing gets done and we would be doing a disservice to the citizens we are supposed to be there for. It doesn't go down well with everyone, however, my attitude to work and duty, and I've had to put up with my fair share of bitching."

The water arrived, and Carrara filled her glass but Tiziana didn't drink.

"Anyway, that day, last winter, a young man came – I don't remember the exact date but it's all recorded in my diary. He was African and he said he was looking for his friend who he feared might have been murdered. He had no form of identification and the front office staff had given him the brush-off, while neglecting to inform me of his presence. It was common practice on their part. Trying to isolate me, trying to get me to slip up, withholding information, that sort of thing. However, I happened to be passing through the office – I had come to find a file or something – and I noticed the gentleman still waiting. I enquired as to who he might be and asked him to come with me and then I assessed the situation on the merits of his story. He seemed to have a genuine interest."

"Did he give you a name?" Rossi enquired.

"Yes," she replied. "Jibril. I didn't press him for a surname as I had gathered that he was an illegal, but my conscience would not allow me to throw him out. I could see it in his eyes, Inspector. He was biting back the tears."

"So you let him see the body, at his request?"

"Yes, but I first asked if there was anyone who could vouch for him. I had no reason to believe he himself might be criminally involved. Surely no criminal would go back to see the victim if he had been his killer."

"Stranger things can happen," said Carrara.

"Go on," said Rossi.

"Well, I just felt that I would be more comfortable if there were someone who could corroborate his story. And that's where Iannelli comes in," she continued, with greater composure now.

Rossi knew that what she was saying tallied with his own recollection of events at that time – his old journalist friend's investigation into high-level corruption, the mysterious attempt by some emissary of the powers-that-be to buy him off, and then the attempt on his life in Sicily, which had sent him into hiding and the life under 24-hour armed escort he now lived.

"The gentleman, Jibril, produced a business card – *Dottor* Iannelli's business card – and said that he knew him personally. I assumed that it had come into his possession by pure chance and that he hadn't the slightest idea who it might belong to. The card was professional, of course, and said *Dottor* Dario Iannelli, *The Facet.* Enough perhaps for a naive young migrant to think it could serve as some temporary passport to acceptance. I had also just heard that the journalist had been caught up in an ambush and was feared killed. I didn't take it any further. I assumed it was a desperate last-ditch attempt to circumvent the obstacles that bureaucracy put in his way, and I could only feel pity for him, not suspicion."

"And you then took him to view the corpse, I presume," said Rossi.

"Given the circumstances, I waived normal practice. I followed my conscience, feeling that he and the victim had likely been acquaintances or even relatives. They were, as far as I could see, both of West African appearance and I deduced they could easily have been co-nationals."

"And yet the identification was negative," said Rossi.

"Well, that is the central issue here, Inspector. As I pulled back the cover, apart from the reaction of shock you might expect – you know, of course, how he was killed."

Yes, Rossi knew. His throat had been cut, almost to the point of decapitation.

"The reaction I witnessed was consistent with recognition. I have seen it enough times to be reasonably confident. He was restrained, yes, but when I asked him to confirm whether or not he could positively identify the corpse he gave a firm 'no' and that was that. He then asked to leave and began to get rather agitated. I think he also feared that he might be detained or reported to the police. I let him out through a side door as I didn't want him to have to face the other staff and I didn't want anyone asking me awkward questions. I would be able to manage that better by myself. I've had plenty of practice."

Rossi looked at Carrara.

"So, if he did recognize him, why didn't he say so?"

"As I said, presumably fear of being detained, as an illegal, even if that hadn't stopped him stepping into the lion's den in the first place. He took a big chance."

"Are you sure he was a migrant?" said Carrara. "How did you know?"

"I presumed he was. I suppose from his clothing. I mean he really wasn't dressed for winter. He looked itinerant, tired, and he wasn't streetwise yet, not in the Roman sense. He seemed fresh out of Africa. It was the impression I got, but I've met many such people in my work and in my voluntary activities too. I help out sometimes with a group providing assistance to refugees and migrants."

"So," said Rossi, "Iannelli was or wasn't connected? You said you thought it was a ruse, the business card, a stratagem on his part. What makes you think differently now?"

"I just think that maybe there was something important, something more to it than I first thought. When I heard *Dottor* Iannelli had survived the attack in Sicily and when the stories began to emerge about corruption in the Detention Centres, I thought that maybe their paths could have crossed in some way. I didn't give it serious thought at the time, but later I wondered if I'd been hasty in dismissing it out of hand. And then there was the fire on Via Prenestina. All those people. At least one of them was West African too. Call it intuition or instinct but it has continued to prey on my mind, every day – the thought that there could even be a connection. And when I heard you talking about him this morning, it seemed like I had to seize an opportunity to put things straight. I had thought about going to a police station but I was concerned for my position. I didn't know what to do. It could have come out looking very bad for me. Do you understand?"

Rossi could see she was taking a chance, putting trust in him. It was courageous, a quality he admired.

"Well," said Rossi, "as luck would have it, we were on our way to the hospital to pay a visit to the pathologist. *Our* paths may well have crossed anyway."

His comment raised a more relaxed smile. She had a conscience, he reflected, but she didn't look like someone who put much stock in fate. Compassionate but practical, realistic. She had to be.

"Did Jibril have an address for the person he was looking for?" asked Carrara.

"He gave me one but it was false. I checked it but I let it go. You have to understand how emotional and how trying all this can be. He needed to know and as far as I was concerned there was no ulterior motive, no other reason for his being there. You know, it did even occur to me that they might have been lovers."

"Well," said Carrara, "he was clearly covering all bases if he didn't want to give a real address. He wanted to appear credible without leaving any trail. As you say, probably the illegal immigrant's preservation instinct."

"And *his* name?" said Rossi. "Do you think he gave you his real name?"

"Like I said, it was Jibril, but more than that I don't know."

"Well, it looks like we will have to get on to Dario," said Rossi to Carrara. He turned back to Tiziana; she was taking restorative sips on her water like a witness granted time to collect herself during a cross-examination.

"What you must remember here, Tiziana, is that this is a murder investigation. Anything that could lead us to the killer could help save lives. We don't have reason to believe that there have been other victims but we can't rule it out either. But whoever killed him was ruthless and could do it again. This body was meant to be found. Others may not have been. Your biggest mistake here, if there is one, is not dishonesty or dereliction of duty but simply that of having let time pass. In our job, time is everything. It is a little late in the day."

She first nodded with something like contrition but then rallied.

"What you say is, of course, perfectly true, Inspector, and I realize that I fell short of certain obligations. However, if I hadn't

34

intervened in the first place, if I hadn't set aside normal practice, he would have walked out that door. He was being turned away by my colleagues. I too could have done the same. At least now you have something to go on, even if it is, as you point out, 'a little late in the day'."

Carrara was nodding his agreement while Rossi, taken aback first by the steeliness of her retort, couldn't help then but smile. He sensed he might have the makings of a dependable ally in Tiziana, and allies were hard to come by at the best of times.

"Could you leave us your number, please," Rossi said. "Mobile and office." He slid his notebook and pen across the table. "I think we'll need to be seeing more of each other, Tiziana. But you can rest assured that for now, at least, you have nothing to fear."

Tiziana wrote down two phone numbers, then Rossi slipped the notebook back into his jacket pocket.

"Perhaps we could accompany you to the hospital," he proposed.

"Thank you, Inspector," she replied. "If it's no trouble."

"Not at all," said Rossi. "As I said, we were on our way there."

Six

At the reception area, Tiziana waved them through the security checks despite the burly security guard's evident displeasure.

"These gentlemen are with me," she said. "They are senior police officers."

The additional information seemed to make the necessary difference as the guard acquiesced and went back to studying his phone.

"I think we know the way now," said Rossi.

"Wait," she said, "let me ring ahead first. It will make things easier."

She unlocked a door on her right in the dim, impersonal corridor in which they now stood. "My office. The *back* door."

She emerged a moment later holding out a slip of paper. "Doctor Piredda. First floor, corridor 2, room 209. He's not busy, so ask him as much as you want. He's usually pretty straight up actually. Sardinian."

They thanked her with firm handshakes all round and made their way along the eery passageways. While there was nothing to see, what lurked behind the doors and the nature of the traffic that went through the place was enough to overload the dark side of the imagination.

"Always prefer to come here in the morning," said Rossi. "Gives me time to forget about it during the rest of the day."

"Bad dreams?" said Carrara.

"Bad memories more than dreams," Rossi replied. "I can deal with the dreams. You wake up from them."

Doctor Piredda was sitting waiting, his hands joined on a writing pad in front of him, a clunky monitor and a computer keyboard yellowed to a soiled ivory colour to one side on his sparse, largely unencumbered working space. He reached across to shake hands with them both, his white-coated bulk straining against the edge of the desk.

"A bad business," he began. "And still none the wiser, are we?"

Who *we* was supposed to be, Rossi couldn't quite be sure.

"I went through it all, you know," he continued, "with your colleague. He looked down then at his notes in an open Manilla folder. "Lallana."

"Yes," said Rossi. "He's in homicide, specifically. We, Inspector Carrara and I, are from the Serious Crime Squad. We are investigating acts of arson in the city, and we were wondering if there was anything else that may have come to light in the intervening period. Apart from the identification, of course. Any anomalies, for example? We are fairly certain it was intentional. Could you give us something that might indicate intent?"

Piredda shook his head. Rossi knew the signs: that he wasn't going to stick his neck out on the motive behind the fire.

"Death was due to asphyxiation *in primis*. The absence of oxygen. It would have been relatively rapid, in the circumstances, with the confined space and the volume of highly toxic smoke."

"Even with the windows open?" said Carrara. "It was hot. There were locked bars on the windows but the windows themselves must have been open, for ventilation."

"I think that's beside the point. The oxygen coming in would only have fed the flames further. They would have quickly lost consciousness, in minutes, and the burns would then in a sense have been secondary factors. Horrendous though they were. I'm sure you know that most victims are not actually burnt to death. What's more, they will have been asleep and the chances are they were already inhaling the fumes as they slept. They were, I believe, in all but one case found close to where they would have been sleeping. It was night. You can't orientate yourself in such conditions, and the heat would have been completely overpowering."

"The ethnicities?" said Rossi feeling already that it was going to be a wasted visit. "Age? Nothing you think you might be able to add?"

"I provided my estimates for age, considering a margin of error of around three to five years either way. I also provided the racial profile. Nothing has changed, Inspector."

"You said African. Black African. And North African."

"That is correct. Three black African corpses. One North African. The other victim, of course, was identified by his jewellery. His 'dog tags'."

"Could you hazard a guess as to a country, a more specific region?" Rossi asked. "South or West African? You see we've had very little in the line of witnesses who had even seen the occupants."

"Seems like we've run into a bit of *omertà*," Carrara chipped in. "No one's saying a goddam word."

The doctor gave a weak smile.

"That's more difficult without DNA tests, but I'd venture that the two black Africans were likely sub-Saharan, possibly West African."

"But we could run those tests," said Rossi. "If necessary, and get something more definite on age. It could help narrow the search considerably. It might give us something more to work on."

"Teeth can give excellent results. Carbon-14 dating and crown dentin analysis, without blinding you with the science, Inspector.

38

Of course it takes a little time and it's rather expensive and there are budget constraints to consider. But if it's required ...," he trailed off without appearing to exude any great enthusiasm at the prospect.

Carrara meanwhile had whipped out his phone. He nudged Rossi.

"We're going to have to adjourn, I'm afraid," he said.

"Now, what?" said Rossi. "Another fire?"

"No. Look," he said showing Rossi the screen on his wafer-like smartphone. *Codice Rosso. Tutte le unità.* A red alert. For all units.

"You will have to excuse us, *Dottore*," said Rossi, rising with as much decorum as was possible but already making for the door. "Maybe we can talk about that DNA again soon, but it seems we have a major incident in the city. I think it would be a good idea to alert the hospitals. Perhaps all of them."

Seven

The Libertas Language Centre was on a side street off the road running south away from the centre and parallel with the Brutalist concrete bulk of Termini station. Here, at only two or three minutes' walk from the station's buzz, it was already far enough away from the bars and shops to attract very few tourists. Just beyond the school, there was an improvised stall selling pornographic magazines and videos for the remnants of the pre-digital generation. Staff smoked and idled outside a Chinese wholesaler of knick-knacks and costume jewellery, and there was a knot of middle-aged men chatting intently outside a cut-price Indian takeaway. The language centre served as a focus, especially on hot afternoons in summer, for various nationalities who loitered on the footpath and against the railings on the raised walkway leading further away from the station. Some had improvised a marketplace underneath its slope where, on tarpaulins and rugs, they laid out second-hand clothes, shoes, kitchenware and dated household goods and furnishings.

Olivia Modena had already stacked up her books, the unmarked homework, and the register. The money a non-profit cooperative paid her for the few hours a week she taught Italian to immigrants was hardly worth the effort but she wasn't there for that. She was there because she needed the experience, but also because she enjoyed making a difference. She enjoyed seeing the barriers between herself and the others coming down as their trust in her grew. She took pleasure too from seeing some of those same barriers crumbling between people who would never have had occasion to meet in other circumstances.

For some the dream of making something with their lives was still fresh and real, and their vigour and optimism could be uplifting, especially on mornings when the weight of her own existence sometimes dragged her down. Even when you liked what you did and couldn't imagine doing anything else, getting up every morning, criss-crossing the city and juggling work commitments was draining.

For others it was not so easy. She saw the hope dwindling in their eyes as the obstacles they encountered day after day began to sap their energy and their belief. Work with anything like a decent contract was not easy to come by. For those who worked in agriculture, the gangmaster was king. A call could come in at the last minute and they would be expected at an often ungodly hour to get to the appointed meeting place on the outskirts of the city from where they would be picked up and driven to a remote destination. If they didn't want to accept the going rate it was too late then to turn back. Take it or leave it – there's a queue of workers outside the door. Add to that the back-breaking work under a searing sun for twelve hours or more, and maybe the promise of more of the same the next day. Maybe.

When they weren't working, they were killing time, getting by, and other exploitative figures sought to draw them into criminal and other informal money-making ventures. Drugs, prostitution, the running of prostitution. Protection. Punishments. Contracts. There was always an outlet in a city with a hunger for sex and chemical oblivion that never wavered, and weed and coke were the best earners.

In front of her, in the cramped and stuffy improvised

classroom, her adult pupils were either still grappling with, or else putting the finishing touches to, a grammar test. She was ready to go but knew she would probably end up hanging around outside to chat. In fact, today she *wanted* to chat.

One of the brightest of her students deposited his paper on the mounting pile of completed tests on her desk. As he did so, she raised her hands to indicate to the others that there were ten minutes left and she followed him outside. She knew a little of his story – that he was Nigerian, a Muslim, had come up from Sicily, like so many, that he was without papers but that he had plans.

"So, Jibril," she said, once they were out of earshot, "are you coming to the intercultural picnic on Saturday?"

Jibril shook his head and smiled. A short distance away, Olivia glimpsed the various groups of non-students and occasional or former students who also chose to congregate outside the centre. It was handily near the centre but the police didn't bother them much here.

"I am sorry, Olivia," he continued, placing his hand on his heart, "but on Saturday I must attend to other matters in my community."

"All work and no play," Olivia quipped, "makes Jibril a dull boy!"

He smiled again. "Next time. Next time, I promise. *Farò del mio meglio.*"

"*Bravissimo!* You see? You will soon be fluent! And I will do *my* best," she replied, echoing the promise he had made in near-perfect Italian, "to convince you. And why don't you bring some of your friends?" she added, indicating the tight-knit group itching now for Jibril to terminate his extracurricular discussion.

"If you change your mind, let me know. You have my number, don't you?"

He nodded.

"I will try," he said. "*Arrivederci*, Olivia."

"*Arrivederci*, Jibril."

She watched him walk away and glanced back through the window at the rest of the class as they continued to do battle with their past perfects, subjunctives, and indirect object pronouns. As friends, she and Jibril had already shared enjoyable chats over coffee, but whether there might be more, as yet remained to be seen. She watched too as one of his companions put an arm around his shoulder and squeezed it tightly as the group walked away; the direction, if not the actual destination, known to Olivia and always the same. She picked up his test paper and toyed with the idea of making an early start on the corrections. This one would be easy. The neat, clear hand. Scarcely an error. Even the accents were in place. Jibril was good. No. He was *very* good. And why did he have to be so charming? He was definitely going to be one to watch.

Eight

Paola walked away from Trastevere Station towards the tram stop. A number 8 was already approaching from the direction of the San Camillo Hospital, descending the curve of the long road skirting round the base of the Gianicolo Hill. It had been ages since she'd been there, and she reasoned that she could get home just as quickly going this way and then taking the 3 to San Lorenzo rather than changing trains. Besides it would be nice to have a wander. Easy come, easy go, she always said, when she had time on her hands.

Her fingers toyed with her phone. Francesco would be in there now, with the commission, or maybe still waiting. He would call when it was all over, so there was no point hassling him anymore. She would send a message later just to let him know they had cancelled and that she'd be home early. Perhaps they could do something together, now that the studying was over, regardless of what happened with the damned interview. She took out her phone to write a message.

Hi Mom. OK if I swing by in half an hour? I'm in Trastevere.

The response was almost immediate.

Great. Will be waiting.

She got off at Piazza Mastai, where office couples and homeless alike had taken up their appointed spots on benches around the hexagonal fountain. To the left she could wander away into the winding streets of Trastevere. It was easy to lose yourself there, but you'd soon pop out somewhere recognizable. She passed a shop front and checked her reflection. Early lunchers were filling the outside tables of the *pizzerie* and *trattorie.* Tourists mainly. As they waited, some of their eyes strayed towards her. So, she was looking good. Well, she was a part of the city they had come to see. Better live up to their expectations then and she put an added spritz of elegance into her step.

She continued to walk until she came to Piazza Trilussa. By day, its steps hosted workmen on their breaks and sightseers taking in the scene. The traffic tearing along the Lungotevere, the road running parallel with the course of the river below, was as noisy as a race track. She too was completing a circuit of sorts but at a human pace as the road would bring her first past the Israeli university and then to Ponte Garibaldi.

The narrow footpath along the river was crowded with parked cars randomly slicing the pavement and bullying for space wherever it could be found. She moved into the road to avoid an oncoming mob of students. Her own student days were long gone but she still remembered them fondly.

Back then, she had sent out hundreds of CVs to companies; she too had done *concorsi,* and she had taken whatever work she could find to get a foot on the ladder, to get away from home and eke out an independent existence. Now she sold textbooks for a publishing house, a job nominally related to her literary studies, but she may as well have been selling cars or insurance for all it was worth. Her own literary efforts were gathering dust in boxes or on a hard drive of an ageing computer.

As she approached the university, armed military personnel stood cradling their automatic rifles and scanning the passersby near the entrance. There were bikes outside, chained to the waist-high railings providing an unobtrusive security cordon of sorts. A soldier began waving in an agitated manner at a white jeep that had pulled up.

"*No, no, signora. Via! Via!* No parking here. No parking.

At least someone was doing his job. Paola glanced at the selection of new and innovative bicycles she presumed must have reflected the considerable spending power of the students. One had a sophisticated-looking kilometre counter and all of its expensive-looking lights still attached. Lights, at this time of the year? And risky that, in Rome. If it wasn't nailed down it was a goner.

Her thoughts moved again between the present and the past. This place where they would come on Friday nights and where they used to meet foreigners and students from all over the globe. It was a window on the world, and it had been a time of fun. But that was gone. People were settling down. She thought of the melancholy and so true line from a Joyce story: "Everything changes".

But does it? thought Paola as she passed. *Does it?*

Then, unseen to her and the smoking, chatting students, the seconds on the digital, liquid crystal display flipped from 58 to 59 to 00 and, as the detonator nestled deep in the explosive charge packed into the bicycle frame did its brief job, everything did.

Nine

"... which, over time, would radically reduce our dependence on oil and be a real step forward in reducing levels of atmospheric pollution linked to cancer in our cities and beyond. Besides that, the initial cost would soon be offset both by savings for the consumer and the provider. I have some figures here, if you don't mind."

Francesco began to reach for his briefcase leaning against the leg of his chair.

"That won't be necessary, *Dottor* Anselmi," the president of the commission said before Francesco had managed to extract the relevant file. "Really, time is against us, as always, but it was, I think we all agree, a most interesting presentation. Even if I'm not sure it's what our friends in ItalOil would want to hear," he added, leaning back and laughing out loud. The three other members gave knowing smiles and also nodded their approval as the president craned his neck slightly to make eye contact with each in turn.

The clerk too, who had been hunched over his papers recording the candidates' names and cross-checking documentation and identity cards all morning, would now have his small increment of institutional glory.

"The results of the *concorso*," he announced, "will be published at the end of the week on the university's website."

"Ah, yes, just one thing." The sole female interviewer was scanning the first page of Francesco's CV through her bifocals. "If I may, it says here you are fluent in English."

"Yes," Francesco replied.

"I was wondering, could you envisage overseeing a course, or courses, for the faculty in the *medium* of English? How would you go about organizing, for example, training the stuff?"

"I'm sorry?" Francesco replied.

"How would you train the stuff," she repeated.

"The staff," the president said with careful emphasis and exhibiting only minor irritation.

"Oh, sorry," said Francesco.

It was the one he hadn't prepared for.

"Well," he began, buying time. A helicopter's unmistakable whop-whop overhead and a swirling emergency siren beyond the drawn blinds took everyone's attention hostage for a moment.

"Do go on, please," the president enjoined Francesco.

"Well, I would first assess their competences and then put out a call for the most suitable candidates to fill the vacant positions."

"And the staff not 'up to the job'?" said the bespectacled interviewer.

Francesco knew he had to answer, but he was fumbling.

"They could be moved to positions better-suited to their competences, and then offered training, in the long term, to get them up to speed."

"Ah. I see." She turned to the president of the commission. "I think that really is all now."

"Very well," he replied. "And unless there are any other questions."

But something told Francesco it probably wasn't what they had wanted to hear. And then maybe none of it had been. And his English was better than hers by a country-fucking-mile. Yet she was sitting there.

There was a knock at the door. A minor office flunkey clutching a piece of paper popped his head round. He looked, apart from his general obsequiousness, more than a little shaken.

"*Presidente Bonucci, Dottori, scusate. C'è una communicazione.*"

Allowing his glasses to slide down his nose, Professor Bonucci scanned the note while conveying its salient points. "'Major security alert in City of Rome. Possibility of further explosions. All universities, places of worship, public buildings and schools to remain on high alert until further notice. Senior management to evaluate the situation and assess the practicalities of executing evacuation or effecting security lockdown.'"

He looked up.

"*Dottoresse e dottori*, to use the popular contemporary lexicon, it would appear that we are 'under attack'."

Ten

An entire stretch of the Lungotevere – the one-way road system and footpath following the Tiber's snaking course through the city – had been cordoned off. There were army bomb disposal units and armed personnel carriers, police vehicles with their lights flashing. Black-clad snipers crouched on the roofs of five-storey buildings and on balconies high above onlookers' heads and at the strategic angles of Viale Trastevere overlooking Ponte Garibaldi. The municipal police had rejigged the one-way system so that nothing could pass if not with strict authorization. Even so, an animated discussion had broken out between a plump, wheezing traffic warden and a baby-faced *carabiniere* about the evident breakdown of communication between the various forces. Where all the diverted vehicles were going was anyone's guess. But it was like leaving a tourniquet on the city. It stopped the bleeding but at what cost?

Rossi was standing in the middle of the road and assessing the extent of the bomb damage to the university's facade when an old friend emerged from among a small crowd of uniforms and plain-clothes operatives.

"Well, surprise, surprise! How the hell did you get here?" said Rossi. "You're Italy's most wanted journalist. What happened to the security drill?"

Ever since he had escaped the assassination attempt in Sicily, Dario Iannelli had been living in hiding with a 24/7 armed guard. Collusion between politicians and organized crime in drugs and other profitable businesses had been at the root of his investigation, and it had all come to a head just as Rossi had been closing in on The Carpenter. Iannelli saw complex, sometimes wild, conspiracies everywhere but his insights gave Rossi frequent food for thought. What's more, he trusted him. Rossi's opportunities of seeing the journalist were infrequent now and usually involved first discovering his latest address via a strict protocol and then arranging for a rendezvous in the utmost secrecy.

Dario Iannelli lowered his dark glasses by the required number of degrees to look Rossi in the eyes before opening both arms and giving his old friend a firm embrace.

"Good to see you," said Iannelli. "We weren't far away, in transit, and I managed to persuade the guys here that it was about the safest place I could be in now. Given the traffic chaos, it seemed as good an idea as any other."

He gestured to the civilian desert around them. Only uniforms and hardware to be seen. The other press guys had been forced to wait, but Iannelli had special security clearance.

"My somewhat anomalous state confers the occasional privilege on me."

"So, surviving captivity?" said Rossi then.

"Next question," Iannelli replied, the strain clearer in his face as he fully removed his designer shades.

"Well at least you're getting to stretch your legs," said Rossi, giving him a firm slap on the shoulders. "How are you bearing up?"

Iannelli gave a sigh.

"You can get used to anything, Mick. That's what they tell me, but I have to stay alive."

"Well, I was going to call you," said Rossi, "to see if we might get together, but it seems events have got the better of us."

Iannelli's escort had maintained a discreet distance, but the journalist gestured for them to come over.

"Let me introduce you to my shadows," he said, presenting the four plain-clothes officers of his escort, now his permanent companions. "They allow me 'to live an ordinary life'," he added drily. "Really looks that way, doesn't it?"

"Well, you're still with us, aren't you?" said Rossi.

"No comment."

"So, who's here?" Rossi continued. "Might save me some time if you tell me what you've got on all this."

"More like who's *not* here," Iannelli replied. "Good time to do a break-in, I'd say. It's very Italian, isn't it? You know, the stable door after the horse has bolted and all that."

"C'mon, Dario! Were they supposed to predict this? Is that it?"

"Intelligence? A security plan? This is a prime target in the capital and they managed to put a bomb outside? And the synagogue's just down the road," he added, gesturing across the river to where the four-sided dome could be glimpsed through the trees.

Rossi was looking in the other direction now to the tarpaulins shielding an area around the university entrance of some 60 to 70 square metres, while a wall of ambulances provided further cover.

"So, how bad?" said Iannelli.

"Maybe six dead, twenty plus injured," said Rossi, who'd already had a provisional briefing. "No names yet. It wasn't huge but it was nasty. A nail bomb. It wasn't term time but there were summer schools going on. These places never close now, and everyone was off guard."

"I still say you've got to see these things coming," said Iannelli.

"Well, it's not as if it's the first time, is it? I mean Jewish, Israeli targets."

"They shot up the synagogue a couple of times," said Iannelli.

"But this, this here can only be Islamist. Or be meant to *look* Islamist."

"I see you haven't changed your outlook on the world, Dario," said Rossi.

"Got to keep an open mind on these things, Michael. You of all people should know that."

"Well, perhaps we can be open-minded enough to start with the facts before we go down the rabbit hole of conspiracy theories. No one's claimed it yet. Unless you know something I don't."

Iannelli shook his head.

"Early days. They'll wait. See the reaction then see who wants to take it and how useful it will be."

Carrara was approaching from the far side of the road.

"What's the story, Gigi?" said Rossi. "Not a car bomb I take it, or a suicide?"

"It's a mess but it was no suicide. The AT unit's are on it and Forensics. Working hypothesis of an IED – some sort of large pipe bomb left outside the building. There's a lot of burn and blast damage. Shrapnel wounds. It just depends where it hits you in these cases."

"Any witnesses, CCTV?" said Rossi.

"They're going through the recordings now."

"Who's they?"

"The university president's there. He's freaking out. I think he's more worried about the parents wanting to pull all their kids off degree courses. He's called his press officer back from vacation to work out a PR damage-limitation strategy. Then there's the assorted services, if you like. ATU. Military and civil. I also have it on good authority that there were undercover guys in the building too. They won't confirm but you can put money on it."

"Who are we talking about?" asked Iannelli. Carrara looked at Rossi before getting the nod to go on.

"CIA, maybe Mossad. Whoever they were, they can't have seen it coming either."

"And who's your good authority?" said Rossi.

"The Hare."

The Hare was a hard-to-pin-down figure. An informer, a fixer, an elusive go-between of Boston Irish stock; he had gone native so long ago that his origins hardly mattered and were barely noticed as his information was always spot on.

Rossi gave an approving nod. He knew the way it worked. The aircraft carriers, the Nato bases, the embassies, the multinationals and then the cultural centres. From Italy to Egypt to Lebanon to Saudi Arabia, US higher education establishments were a way of maintaining a presence, keeping an ear to the ground, and a way of shaping politics, culture and business too. You could send recruits there; you could make new recruits there too.

"Any chance of us mere mortals getting to see those recordings?" he said then.

"Maybe, if you're very quiet and sit at the back and don't ask questions. Want to try?"

Rossi gave a nod.

"Dario, how about using strength in numbers? Can your guys create a bit of a diversion or something? I say just flash a badge and keep going. That's my usual approach."

"Anything for you, Michael. Come on. But I'm out of here in five. I don't like getting snapped by the paparazzi, if you know what I mean."

"Well, while you *are* here," said Rossi. "Does the name Jibril mean anything to you? Sicily by chance?"

Rossi was watching for a reaction, but the mention of Jibril didn't seem to stir much in Iannelli, other than his usual journalist's suspicions as to why Rossi might be asking.

"Anything I should be interested in?"

"Just working on a lead," said Rossi. "Or you might say we're clutching at straws."

Iannelli's escort were looking keen to get them off the street, despite the cordon extending around them for a kilometre in every direction.

"Let's go inside and see what we can get," said Iannelli, taking the hint. Rossi followed. The name Jibril was not high on Iannelli's agenda. He would try to jog his memory later.

Eleven

Francesco hurried down the fire escape and out of the university building with some of the other candidates and the various office workers and public servants who shared the ten-storey complex with them. For most of them, the drill provided a welcome chance for an unexpected break, and the bar across the road was already filling up. As false alarms were frequent, few seemed to be giving any credence to the idea of there actually having been a major incident, but Francesco took out his mobile and called Paola anyway. He was sure she would have done the same if she had heard the news; it was the way she was and some of her attitude had clearly rubbed off on him too. But there was no answer.

There was a temporary lockdown in place in the building but hard news was still at a premium. He ordered a coffee, and as he half listened to the gossip and looked up at the rolling news on the small TV in the corner over the fruit machine, fragmentary accounts began to emerge of an explosion with possible loss of life at or near the Israeli university in Trastevere. So they at least were safe, but they had hit somewhere else, another university. Others were watching the screen now and the jocular tone dropped an octave or two. Then he heard a rumble of talk and a few low, hissed "murdering bastards".

When the all-clear came, Francesco darted back into the building to dot the i's and the t's on some outstanding administrative procedures. He exchanged a few quick words with the other candidates, most of whom knew each other in one way or another, either through work or the periodic ritual of the *concorso*. One of the candidates had unsettled Francesco. On his own admission, he'd only been in the university sector for some six months, was much younger than any of the other candidates, and yet seemed to exude an air of slightly embarrassed certainty about "the job" and what it would entail. All the others had CVs stretching back to the beginning of the previous decade and they exhibited the worn exteriors to prove it. But what worried Francesco more now was Paola.

As he stepped back out of the building he tried again and as he did so he noticed her text.

Going to see Mom then on my way home. Had a cancellation. Will ring later. XXX P.

The timestamp meant it must have come through late. Network problems, probably, he reasoned. Everyone calling at the same time. So maybe that was why she hadn't rung and why she wasn't answering either. He tried again. Still nothing. He closed the phone and looked about and thought about getting a bus, and he was just slipping the phone into his pocket when a call came in. "DadP". it said on the ID. It was Paola's father, and he *never* called but Paola had insisted they swap numbers, just for emergencies.

Francesco felt a sudden hot surge of fear as his thumb hovered over the icon. Her dad must be checking too, like he was. He must have seen the news. He took the call.

"Yes," said Francesco, ready to rise to the unlikely occasion.

"Francesco," came the reply, firm, familiar but in a tone he had never heard before. "It's Paola, she's not answering her phone. Have you seen the news? She was in Trastevere. Did you know? Has she called?"

***

Francesco walked on in a daze. After the initial call, there had followed a to and fro of frantic phone conversations as Paola's father had drawn on all his available contacts to get access to the crime scene and confirmation of what had happened. They had hoped that in the initial confusion the story might prove to be the fruit of a misunderstanding, but soon the evidence relayed back to them had been crushing. The formal identification would still have to be made but it was as good as there in black and white.

Was he going in the right direction? What direction? What was the point? She was dead. There was no doubt. Her date of birth. Her height. Her hair colour. It was all there on the card she carried. The identity card they all carried like convicts in their own country. The card that said he was a citizen of the Italian Republic with its most wonderful constitution; the best in the world, so they said. The card they carried so that they could be stopped and checked and identified at any time of the day and night to ensure that they were not enemies of that same Republic, enemies of the *patria*. The card that could be used to trace them to their house, to their staircase, to their apartment so the knock could come in the middle of the night. So they could always be found.

He wandered on up the incline of Viale di Circo Massimo. Past the fruit sellers. Past the teenage tourists playing in the middle distance with joyful abandon in the old amphitheatre. They were climbing on each other's backs, playing at being charioteers, like Ben Hur, the Jewish prince who took on the might of the Romans in this very place. Their cries carried to him as they surged across an imaginary finishing line acknowledging fictional crowds and falling then to the ground in mock scenes of death and slaughter. Then, like parents giving children piggyback rides, they got up again. A joyous resurrection.

He came to the crest of the hill from where he could look down to the Tiber. Behind him and towering above him was the monument to Mazzini, the father of the *patria*. High up in his chair, on his plinth, he seemed to be dozing in old age. Venerable, noble, yet atop his verdigris bronze head, the city's seagulls perched one after another, as if to take their bearings, only then to foul his likeness with impunity.

He had not been able to accept it. He was sure, first, that there must have been a mistake. Any number of women could have the same name. It was a common one in Italy. Paola Mancini. But with the same date of birth? But the details they gave him were final. He and her father had discussed the formal identification briefly, but it was a father's job to identify his own daughter no matter how close they had been. The police said she had not been caught by the full force of the blast but that she had been "unlucky". Already, he was appropriating the lexicon of disaster as his own.

From the Municipal Rose Garden a rich, variegated perfume battled with the acrid summer smog of urban pollution. Good and evil, past and present, youth and age were tearing each other apart now in his own mind too, but beneath the surface. He wondered why he didn't feel tired. He had instead a feeling of bizarre elation as though he had been chosen for something, been elected. Something was telling him that life now would be lived on a new level. The old life, like a bridge collapsing into a gorge, was still visible but gone for good. He moved nearer to the railings and sat down on the narrow wall. An ambulance approached from Viale Aventino, fleeing then past the Bocca della Verità in the direction of the Tiber. Maybe she was only injured. Maybe this ambulance was for her. Flowers protruded from between the railings above his head, and as a sudden light breeze lifted from over the Palatine Hill, it stirred a shower of petals, and he watched as one by one they fell to the ground before him.

Twelve

"So what about Maroni?" said Carrara, stirring his coffee. They were in the university canteen situated on the side of the building furthest from the Lungotevere, where the explosion had occurred. One corner had been transformed into an incident room until the usual suspects had finished clearing up outside and hosing down and gathering the necessary minutiae for Forensics. The university was an imposing building and while the bomb had torn through the soft tissue of passersby and disfigured the facade of the eighteenth-century *palazzo*, its structural integrity had not been compromised.

Meanwhile, inside, all available officers had been charged with interviewing every imaginable person that had been inside or in the vicinity of the building.

"He'll be turning his boat around now, I reckon," said Rossi. "And wherever he is, he'll want to be informed of the facts as they happen. You know he brings a satellite phone on holiday."

Carrara knocked back his *espresso*.

"So I've heard. Prudent man."

"Likes to know. Doesn't appreciate getting ridden roughshod over when he's out of the picture."

"That's a polite way of putting it. Better not to take a holiday."

"Don't worry," said Rossi, "there won't be any for the foreseeable future."

Carrara scratched his head as he recommenced scanning papers and spreadsheets and maps of the building.

"Are you sure there's much point trying to interview all these kids and staff today without proper interpreters?"

"I brought that up already," Rossi replied, "but certain individuals are convinced of their language skills."

"You mean the ones whose evidence then gets torn apart when the lawyers get stuck into them?"

"That sort of thing. Anyway, not my orders, Gigi. The call goes out and we answer. This is one major security shitstorm. You realize there's an international summit coming up, and the word from *very* on high is that they want answers sooner rather than later. It'll be the Americans. You can count on it. They've got a shedload of interests plugged in here."

"But you know as well as I do that the evidence is inadmissible without a lawyer present," Carrara insisted.

"Well, they want 'facts' that might help point us in the right direction. I don't think they're counting on the bomber still being among us. It's intelligence gathering."

"Intelligence? They might perhaps have made a better job of gathering before it all kicked off, especially if they had agents in there."

Rossi nodded.

"And he managed to plant a device without anyone checking? Either the guards were sleeping or they thought it was someone who studied or worked here."

"What did you make of the footage?"

"You mean the footage they *let* us see?"

"You're saying Anti-Terror were being 'selective'?"

"Playing it very close to their chests," said Rossi. "Like in any good story, it's what you choose *not* to reveal."

"But the guy in the hat walking away a minute or so before

the blast? Well covered up for the time of year, don't you think?"

Rossi shrugged.

"Could be anyone. But from what I saw of it, it looked like a bike bomb. There was no other vehicle in the vicinity, no cars, only passersby and students, no visible packages. They should have found a few fragments by now, so they'll be able to put some meat on the bones."

"It wouldn't be the first time," said Carrara. "You can get a lot of plastic inside that tubing. At least a kilo, maybe two. And it only takes one to obliterate a vehicle."

"It was a taster, if you ask me," said Rossi. "Small but nasty. Nails and bearings. But we've got six corpses in there and maybe more to come."

"A spectacular?" said Carrara. "In Rome? That's turning the clock back forty years."

"Well, someone's opened the betting. It all depends if the stakes rise. And who's playing the game. Look," said Rossi, "Bianco's here."

The sergeant was approaching their table with his customary heavy tread now even heavier. He flopped down into a chair.

"Relatives," he said. "In the mortuary. What a fucking job."

He gave them the low-down on things. A temporary mortuary had been set up in a ground-floor classroom. The air-conditioning helped. Despite being August, the road diversions and massive security clampdown combined with a general heat-stoked hysteria was wreaking havoc on the city's traffic. The scene-of-crime magistrate had agreed with the City Prefect to keep the bodies at the scene until things calmed down and until they could get next of kin informed, at least in the case of the local victims. Then they would see to the overseas students.

"Dario's forming his opinions already, isn't he?" said Carrara, waiting then for Rossi's reaction.

"He's going through hell! A guy like him cooped up 24/7 with an escort, as good as living on the run. There are Mafia scum who've got more freedom to walk the streets. The least he should be doing is concocting another conspiracy theory."

"As far-fetched as the last one wasn't? I mean The Carpenter case turned out to be just about as fucked up and twisted as you could imagine. Faked deaths, suicides, triple bluffs. You couldn't have made it up."

"Take every case on its merits, Gigi. Follow the facts until they prove you were right not to believe somebody's wild theorizing, or until what you *do* see begins to eat away at your long-held notions of the rational and believable. Otherwise you lose your direction. There's a place for instinct, for gut feeling but it's the catalyst, not the constituent in the equation. Or the angle; the right kind of lighting that illuminates what you hadn't noticed before."

"So how do you see this one shaping up? Us against the bad guys in a nice straight fight? Do you see a tall dark stranger?"

Rossi gave a nervous look over his shoulder to the tables behind him in the canteen nearest to the coffee machines and the free food. They were all there. Known and unknown. Uniformed and non. Some friends and a sprinkling of well-seasoned foes. Yes, thought Rossi, it took events like this to really shake up the law and order establishment. It was like some sort of world cup and everyone was suddenly going for glory and sensing the opportunity to get their hands on the trophy.

"Or another one where we're watching our backs and wishing we were on traffic detail again?" Carrara added.

Rossi flicked a used sugar sachet into his cup. "I predict interesting, Gigi. That's what I see. As in very 'interesting times'."

Carrara had set up a meeting with Dr Okoli. The professor was waiting in an interview room but without any of the accompanying security. Rossi noted that unlike the usual suspects they had to face across a desk in there, he seemed quite unperturbed by the surroundings.

"So, it seems I am a lucky man," he said with a broad smile as he rose to greet Rossi and Carrara with a powerful handshake.

"I tend to agree," said Rossi as he introduced himself. "We'll keep this as brief as we can, Professor. I'm sure you have a lot to attend to."

Okoli nodded and sat down again. He had the relaxed air of a writer for whom ideas come easily and in abundance. No tortured soul here. Rossi was getting the feeling that this was a man who had probably seen worse on many occasions. Much worse.

"Enemies?" said Rossi.

"How long do you have?" the professor chuckled. "That part of the Nigerian establishment which is corrupt to its rotten core and in cahoots with the petrodollar touting rabble and the foreign 'investors'." He made his own inverted commas for Rossi and Carrara's benefit. "Speculators, predators, depredators of our country would be a more accurate term. But *investors* is what they like to be known as."

He reeled off a list of names. Carrara took notes.

"Some of these people have *form* as they say. Nothing proved, of course. There never is. But take it from me, they would like me out of the way. Ever since I resurrected the ghost of my old friend Ken Saro-Wiwa, when I called for his name to be cleared, for a state pardon and recognition of his innocence, and for his murderers to be finally brought to justice. I went too far for my own good it seems."

Rossi knew the story well. The writer who had championed the cause of the oppressed and exploited in the Niger Delta, where the oil companies and their friends in government were the kings. He had finished up on the end of a rope, widely believed to have been convicted on trumped-up charges. The whole thing stank.

"So do you think they could be pursuing you?" said Carrara. "You may have heard we've had some race-related incidents in

64

the city. Hate crimes we think. Far-right groups targeting foreigners. That kind of thing. Did you receive any threats? Any signs of intimidation?"

The professor listened and pondered for a moment. He shrugged. Non-committal but open.

"Someone let down the tyres on my car once. Someone else lets his dog shit outside my house every day. Maybe the same person."

"That could just be Rome," said Carrara.

"Apart from that," Okoli continued, "the attack on me and my family was out of the blue, gentlemen, but not, shall we say, entirely surprising."

"Did you lose much?" said Rossi. "In the fire. Your work?"

Okoli shook his head.

"Some possessions, but I left Nigeria in rather a hurry, you know. The possessions I had I knew I would not have much chance of holding on to, so I sold or gave away what I could before leaving."

He put his hand in his pocket and took out a USB drive.

"Everything else of real importance is on here," he said. "My research. My sources. I never part from this. They'll have to kill me first if they want it."

Their eyes locked for a moment in understanding before Rossi moved things along.

"We'll see to it that you get the right security. Do you have some work lined up?"

The question had come out spontaneously and was inspired by goodwill, but as soon as he had said it, Rossi realized it made him sound like some sort of fake-casual immigration official.

Okoli smiled.

"I was thinking of selling my body, officer. I have heard it's all the rage among the Nigerians in Rome. Haven't you?"

Thirteen

Rossi stood on his balcony watching the cloudless sky as the sun's first rays began to cancel night's all too brief dominion. It was an implacable scene, like a Cyclops's blank stare. The temperature gauge in his living room had dropped by two degrees overnight. Small comfort. No breeze. Nevertheless, as he drank his cool coffee and looked out at the still-sleeping metropolis, his mind felt fresh, at least for now, and he reflected on what had emerged from the previous day's events.

They had not kept Doctor Okoli long. He had his life to reorganize, again. He had not been able to put any substantive leads their way other than to indicate that plenty of well-protected diplomats in Rome were probably just as likely as any fascist organization to have been trying to kill him. He seemed perfectly credible and their background checks matched his own story. But his final wisecrack about male prostitution had set Rossi thinking more than a little. Okoli had not elaborated, had backtracked even and glossed over it, but the suggestion was that his reluctance might have been because he was working on something and may even have had confidential sources to protect.

Responsibility for the bombing at the Israeli university had been claimed by an obscure, as yet unheard of organization. An e-mail from one of the galaxy of fundamentalist Islamist websites operating from within the safe havens of the Dark Web had been sent to Iovine, Iannelli's Editor-in-Chief at *The Facet*. The organization proclaimed itself the Islamic Caliphate in Europe. ICE. Despite the heat, the effect was rather less than soothing. Iannelli too was able to confirm that it had been received. As for establishing the veracity or other of their claim, that was another story. These days anyone could and would put their name to an unsolved or unclaimed attack, if only for the headlines it would generate, or as a quick shot of publicity for some plan they had hatched.

In this case, the details furnished by ICE did at least tally with what the Anti-Terror Squad had been able to ascertain from their analysis of the damage inflicted, the recovered bomb fragments, and their assessment of both the size of the device and its method of manufacture. There were also enough elements of novelty to suggest a different supply line to that of any known groups operating either in France or the UK where there had already been attacks. Neither was the hardware homemade. Military-grade explosive had been used, hence the compact nature of the device; all of which pointed to a strong possibility of a Balkan connection, as the best-case scenario. But that was reserved information.

Then there was nothing. Rossi glanced down at his empty cup, unsatisfied and wanting more coffee. Where they were now was at that point of heightened and uneasy hiatus which accompanies any terror attack. Saturation news coverage, heavy doses of human interest stories – the near misses, the shattered lives, the solidarity of a nation and the wider civilized world. Security is ratcheted up as the media machine evokes the blitz spirit, encouraging, even lauding it as the irrepressible manifestation of a city or a people's collective character. And yet to the jaded eyes of the cynical, it appears to be some futile attempt to follow the ball rather than get inside the mind of the playmaker and second-guess his next move. Like a gambler always seeing the number he was *going* to bet on coming up trumps for another. It's too late.

Rossi went back to the kitchen, and as he unscrewed the *moka* to make another *espresso* he began to prepare mentally for the day ahead.

In the light of the high-level summit, the City Prefect's office was planning a press conference to put on a united front and allay the fears of a jittery public and business community. The relevant ministers had convened the heads of police, the mayor, as well as the prime movers in the secret services and wider intelligence community, charging them with formulating a new, coordinated response. Without a clear road map, and without comparable past experience to go on, the Minister of State for Home Security had demanded a shake-up. In other words, he was saying they'd been caught napping or looking the wrong way on this one and they'd better get their act together or heads would roll. The blame game again.

Maroni had summoned Rossi and Carrara and a handful of the most promising and senior operatives on the RSCS. Following a torrid crossing, their long-time chief had dropped anchor at Civitavecchia the evening after the bombing, having left Corsica only half-discovered. He was, to say the least, irascible when he finally pinned Rossi down to a telephone conversation. The meet was to be today and he wanted everyone to bring "something worth hearing". Hence Rossi's prompt start with hopes of getting some inspiration in the relative cool and quiet of the early hours.

He placed the compact, bomb-like machine on the gas and stared into the quietly hissing flame.

Maroni was an old hand. He'd been a raw recruit on the hunt for the last cells of the BR, the *Brigate Rosse* or Red Brigades in the late Eighties. Rossi had heard the stories, second-hand, and despite the ambivalence he sometimes felt towards his superior he had to give him some credit for past glories.

68

As was to be expected, he'd suggested Rossi and Carrara drop the arson investigations. "Keep an eye on things, you know. Set up some standard surveillance op, but it's hardly a priority now, is it? I mean, a pyromaniac with a grudge against motorists."

Early release for good behaviour, thought Rossi, *but hadn't Maroni been forgetting something?*

"And the attempt on Dr Okoli's life?" Rossi had ventured, at which Maroni had paused then let out a sigh which Rossi knew all too well. Rossi's consternation had inadvertently betrayed his growing interest in the Prenestina fire and its victims as well as Lallana's apparent reluctance to probe deeper, not to mention the question of the timer, the locked security grilles. "Am I to presume you are trying to tie all that in with the Prenestina fire too?"

"I think it's a possibility," Rossi had replied.

"And who the hell gave you the authorization to dig around there?" Maroni had blurted back down the line.

"Arson's arson, isn't it?" Rossi had countered. "And what if we've got a maniac on our hands who only needs a can of petrol and a box of matches to hold the city to ransom? Sooner or later we could be mourning another massacre."

There had followed another Maroni pause. Rossi had made his point but knew he was up against a brick wall.

"The real point here, Rossi, is that you just can't keep your nose out of another bloke's patch, can you? The case is *closed*. If only you could summon up the same enthusiasm for what you're *supposed* to be doing."

Rossi had let the relatively minor storm blow itself out, judging it wiser to withhold the details of his meetings with Tiziana and *Dottor* Piredda. But he still had to get Iannelli to spill the beans on Jibril, if there was anything to spill. With the chaos of the bombing, and the journalist's reluctance to court publicity, they'd had to postpone their tête-à-tête. He'd get on to him today, after the meeting, if that didn't throw up another mega work fest.

Then there were the handover reports to do, which he hadn't even started. And Yana wanted him to help her get settled back into her flat again.

The sun came up over the rooftops and began to unleash its fury. Rossi felt he had rather too many irons in the fire.

Fourteen

The brothers were sitting cross-legged in the living room of the first-floor apartment in Torpignatarra. Newspapers and other printed materials lay strewn around the flat, on the floor on kilims and the cheap sofa draped with Arabic-style throws. A computer screen showed the fluttering black flags and the looping images of black-clad commandos tramping through dust against a brightly sunlit desert backdrop. Islamic chanting came from the soundtrack as Ali's hijab-wearing wife left the room, backwards, curved over as if with age and with her eyes to the floor, having served the menfolk their refreshments. She closed the door behind her without making a noise. Ali, the Tunisian, unfolded a real black flag and placed it before them then began to speak.

"My brothers. You all know the seriousness of your vow of allegiance to this flag and this organization. As your emir, under the guidance of Allah, I shall take all the final decisions. I am responsible for you but you are all, as I am too, willing to die for Islam in the name of vanquishing the infidel and freeing the Islamic people from tyranny in the lands not yet returned to the bountiful and just order of the Grand Caliphate. I will ask you soon, one by one, to speak your minds. We are all from different lands but in Islam we are one. This is our strength. This, and our faith. Soon, it will be our turn to act. The moment ripens day by day. Look around you my brothers at the iniquity and the filth. And they say this is a religious city. It is a den of infidels. It is a rat hole, a sewer. And the vermin must be expunged. We must crush them until, on their knees, in the blood of their children, they acknowledge Allah as the one and only, just as we have knelt in our own children's blood cursing the unbeliever and the collaborators for their crimes.

"Now, brothers, I ask you to speak. How shall we act? Where must we strike? Share with me the fruits of your wisdom. Who will put himself forward for the supreme and wondrous act of martyrdom and take then his reward in paradise, where he will be served by angels and his fifty virgin wives will attend to him as is his right, as is written by the Prophet, peace be to his name, in the Holy Qur'an."

One of the company raised his hand.

"Yes," said Ali. "Speak, Jibril."

Fifteen

"We've been given a pretty open brief here," Maroni continued leaning forward again over his notes. One document was headed in bold lettering "**Combined Security Committee**".

"CSC want us to approach it *intellectually* and *operationally*, given the abundant expertise we have in both those fields. Which, as far as I'm concerned, means keeping your eyes and ears open and doing proper police work."

He sat back then and looked up, scanning the faces gathered round the oval table in the conference room. He forced a wry smile. "I prefer the operational side myself but as you know I am always ready to hear your suggestions."

"Ah, glad you could make it," he said then as Rossi made his way into the meeting and grabbed a chair, more than a little late. "You know everyone, I'm sure. If not, get acquainted during the break."

Rossi sat down opposite Carrara on the other side of the table.

"I had just been telling everyone here that you're one of our top languages men, but Arabic's not on your list, is it?"

"Not as yet, sir," Rossi replied.

"Any suggestions as to how we might approach surveillance and intelligence gathering on the ground? The question's open to you all," Maroni continued, eying the gathered operatives one by one now over his rimless reading glasses.

"I was wondering," said Carrara, "about the tech side. Is that all in the hands of the usual crew? The Telecoms Police and their, shall we say, 'subsidiaries'? I assume their GIS mapping is going to be central, but what about our role? Do we have any added capabilities?"

"Well you can forget about ClearTech for now," Maroni said, looking to close quickly on that score, "Judicial inquiry's out on that one, as if you don't remember."

Rossi and Carrara remembered very well. They hadn't been able to prove it but, during The Carpenter case, they had found enough to suggest that the outsourced computer forensics had been manipulated to keep them off the trail. Silvestre, an integral part of the RSCS but never one to see eye-to-eye with either Rossi or Carrara, had been seconded to assist ClearTech just before. They didn't think it had been any coincidence.

"The problem," said Rossi, cutting in, "as I see it, and from what I've gathered from Europol, and our French counterparts in particular, is that these groups, the radicalizers and the potentially radicalized, initially get together via chat rooms and forums. They sound each other out first and then they move onto secure encrypted platforms, things like Telegram. There's very little you can do to intercept the coms."

"Well at least you've been doing some homework, Rossi," said Maroni. "But I think our lot are on to that and aware of the limitations of straightforward phone taps."

"If they're any good at all, they hardly even use phones," said Rossi. "They use word of mouth, trust and community protection, couriers."

"So what's the big idea then? I assume you're going to get to your point." The surprise contribution had come from Silvestre. He had popped up at the corner of the table where he'd been slouching, lying low as usual. "I say we pile into the ghettos and stop and search till they're sick of the sight of us. See a car with a couple of Arabs in, we turn it over. Send 'em a message, the murdering scum."

"You're assuming we're dealing only with Arabs then Silvestre?" Rossi countered.

"You know exactly what I mean. Come down heavy on the lot, I say. Show 'em who's boss. Take no prisoners. Flush 'em out of their holes."

"But you use your head first," said Rossi, "like Dalla Chiesa did with the Red Brigades. He played a long game, and he didn't take any innocent lives doing it. If we go in like you're proposing there'll be an exponential growth of home-grown terror."

"All right, gentlemen," said Maroni, "let's keep on an even keel here. This is neither the Wild West nor the Seventies or the Eighties. I was there for some of that and I knew the general, personally. So let's leave it at that."

"You can't go antagonizing a whole community, if you don't want a war," said Rossi unable to resist the parting shot. "If you target them *as Muslims* it will be wholly counterproductive. That's how their recruiters work, telling these kids that their religion is their common bond, regardless of their nationality. We'd be doing their job for them."

"And the government doesn't want the city in a lockdown scenario either," said Maroni. "It's bad for the economy, and God know's it's already on life support. The moment is delicate, gentlemen, very delicate. And there's the Olympic bid to consider. There's a lot of pressure on that front too, I don't mind saying."

Rossi shook his head.

"We need to think like they do," said Rossi. "Try to understand what these young guys want, and they will be young, for sure. Then we can isolate them within their communities, get them to rat on each other once they realize it's in their interests. And we can take advantage of the fact that there aren't any true no-go areas in Rome yet, at least not like in Brussels and Paris. We can still manage this situation."

Inspector Katia Vanessi had raised her hand to speak. New to the team, and the only woman on RSCS, she was an as yet unknown quantity as far as Rossi was concerned.

"Every domestic terrorist act is underwritten by a prevailing sense of social injustice validating if not the means then certainly the end."

Rossi adjusted his position from a half slouch to interested. He could see Maroni was growing impatient.

"Ladies and gentlemen, I get the point but we are not the UN here. We are not delivering global solutions for the hard done by. We are trying to stop Islamist extremists planting bloody bombs in our city!"

But Rossi wasn't going to let it go yet.

"In its day," said Rossi, "the Red Brigades had a wide support base, and they did have a certain Robin-Hood quality, at least initially. But is that the case here? Putting bombs in public places?" he said, letting his own open question hang in the air like incense. "To me, it smacks more of fascism – the disdain for the masses for the advancement of a private agenda."

Katia appeared to have let her attention wander for a moment. Rossi waited, expecting a personalized response that didn't come as she continued to make unhurried but assiduous notes.

She had heard a lot about Rossi and was working out as she wrote how best to comment on his little speech. Yes, she'd heard about his intellect, his unusual background, his barely concealed disdain for authority, and his reputation for getting results, often against the odds. Well, she reflected, dotting a final i on her notepad before laying down her pen – he seemed to be able to talk the talk at least. She raised her hand.

"Well, Inspector Rossi," she said, giving him her firm and confident attention now, "that's a nice little story but, given your experience on the ground, what do you propose we actually *do* about it?"

Sixteen

Jibril wiped the steam off the mirror to make sure he didn't cut himself with the new razor. Olivia had been surprised. Yes. Very surprised. So, she was finding out that he wasn't quite as shy and reserved as she had thought him to be. And he had made the first move. Well, really the first move had come from her and not just the invitation. That had been an open invite. But giving him her phone number as she had a few weeks earlier. Then the other stuff. Picking him out with her eyes every time there was a question that needed answering. She was drawn to him. And he'd let it happen whether he had needed it or not. It was true that she would be part of his cover but he realized he had wanted it too. So, in a corner of his battered heart, perhaps not all hope was lost. Some innocence maybe still thrived. And the others must have known too. But what of it. The class favourite? The teacher's pet? He'd already learnt about that from his own school days in the village and after. Days that had finished so abruptly, so cruelly.

He stopped himself. Have to keep focused. He rinsed and wiped his face with a towel then slipped his shirt on and adjusted the collar so that the chain hung around his neck against his skin just above the topmost fastened button. He smoothed his chin

77

with one hand. His beard was gone but he'd never really got used to having it. When the rebels had first tried to reimpose the old ways on the men in the village, his father and uncles and many others had laughed at their attempts, calling it out as the harking back to some failed distant ideal, their new-found love affair with ideology, with ancient Wahabist rules and certainties.

Yet things had changed somewhat since then, and Jibril had also lived a little in the true believers' shoes. Now that his journey had brought him to the point where he'd understood the need for decisive action, such symbols were only that: symbols and nothing else. He'd made his case and made it well. He had bided his time with the brothers. In his hour of need they had been there for him. This much was true. He was strong, had always been, but embracing his religion and its comforts had helped him to be stronger. He had felt weakness when he had first come to Rome. Fatigue and hunger, but the strength of true brotherhood had quickly lifted him. There were decent, honest brothers who acted in good faith, but there were those, he knew very well, whose minds and hearts dwelt elsewhere. Such was life. But he was taking control in that regard too and the younger ones knew it.

So, as he had explained, first, you had to fit in. Be like those of the country where you are a guest, or be their *idea* of how you should be. Play to your strengths, exploit their weaknesses. Ali had protested strongly and some of the others hadn't been so sure either at first, but as he spoke, building an argument with patient explanation, he had begun to convince them even as he had convinced himself. The more attention you bring to yourself by your difference and your separateness, the more chance they will have of hunting you down, spotting you against the horizon. It was urban camouflage, brothers. Then you could strike unseen when the time was right. But only then. Haste was a fool's game. Our revolution wears no watch, so it can come at anytime, when least they expect it. Let them sweat it out while we, with cool heads and focused determination, construct the perfect plan.

He walked back across the hall into his room and picked up his phone off the nightstand. It was new. New second-hand. A decent model about whose provenance he hadn't been encouraged to enquire. It would give him relative anonymity, linked as it was to a new identity. He would need it for everything legitimate now. There was work lined up, hopefully. He would talk to Olivia about that tonight. She would help and had already proved invaluable as a key to opening the intricacies of Italian society. She was always keen to know how he was "getting on" and whether he was going to get his *permit to stay*. Well, the story he would recount was that he had every intention of making a go of it and she was an attractive young woman with many of the qualities he admired. Somewhere, behind it all, if he hadn't been at war, she might have even truly touched his soul. But he had no time for that. Not now. Not after what *they* had done to him.

Perhaps they made an unlikely couple: an Italian woman and a Nigerian man. A teacher and an illegal immigrant with false papers? But he was also a care worker now, a social assistant. Once that was his identity it would not seem so strange. And that was where he was heading, on a fast track, and there was plenty of work to be had. These Italians didn't lock their old people away like they did in some countries, but instead paid carers to shoulder the drudgery of looking after them. And yet they complained about the numbers of foreigners, the hordes of *stranieri* they had to put up with.

This Christian nation. Love your neighbour, said Christ. But where was their gospel now? When I was sick, did you care for me? When I was in prison, did you visit me? He thought then of Victor, his friend murdered in Rome some six months before. He recalled their many long discussions before they had been separated. But in those days, so much of it was theory while theory had now become practice. Reality now had grown harsh.

"Remember, Jibril," Victor would say, "when the day comes, what He will say to those on his left. 'Depart from me, you who are cursed, into the eternal fire prepared for the devil and his angels'." Well, *they* had killed him – his own Christian brothers – and they would have to pay for it.

"So, my friend," he said out loud, as if someone might be there to hear him, "who is the devil now?"

Seventeen

The atmosphere in the conference room was tense. The press wanted answers, wanted a story, but they weren't getting much change out of the eight-strong panel of stony-faced city officials and law enforcement chiefs facing them in the grand hall of the *prefettura's* renaissance palace. Security was high and the press had arrived in numbers, among them Elena Serena, sent by Iannelli to do the public work he couldn't risk undertaking. She had taken up a position near an exit and had set up a tripod stand with a video camera to stream the whole proceeding back to Iannelli. She had opted to use the local WI-FI but it was just her luck to have found the only spot where the signal was shaky.

"So, we are under attack?" The question came from a staff reporter on *The Post*. The journalists were hammering the same nail again and again, but the panel was resisting.

All eyes turned to the City Prefect, Roberto Cavalleggio. It was his job to guarantee public safety and coordinate between the Home Office and local government.

"As I think my colleagues have already made clear, it was *an* attack," he replied, adjusting and leaning into the microphone almost as if in an attempt to find some shortcoming in the hardware that might distract attention from his own. "A vile and cowardly attack, I might add." He paused, perhaps to weigh his words or to emphasize some greater gravitas. "It is not clear whether this is part of any concerted campaign or an isolated incident. I can say, however, that the police and the security services are working flat out, night and day, to find the perpetrators and bring them to justice."

"What do you know about the level of technological sophistication of the device?" a reporter called out from the back of the room. There was another brief pause as, after comments off mic and various sideways glances, the prefect indicated that the question would be taken by the head of the state police, Fulvio Martinelli.

"From what the forensic police have been able to ascertain so far, it would appear that it was a fairly rudimentary device but lethal nonetheless. It was designed to inflict maximum casualties without requiring a major logistical operation."

Elena looked up from where she had, until then, been jotting random notes. *Rudimentary?* It certainly wasn't the impression she'd had, and she'd got the low-down from Iannelli who had been on the scene early. He had said all the evidence pointed to C4, high-grade military plastic explosive and a high-spec timing device. He and she had kept that to themselves for now, though. From the front row, it was a RAI TV journalist's turn to quiz the prefect.

"We've been hearing from the Police Federation recently that in the last few years there has been a chronic lack of funding for the security budget to face an increasingly sophisticated terrorist threat. In the light of these comments, are you able to provide assurances that the public's safety will be guaranteed? In concrete terms, what is being done?"

An ashen-faced prefect suppressed something akin to a stifled yawn or a sigh as he prepared to speak.

"Ladies and gentlemen," he began, assuming a tone both informal yet recognizably patrician, "as I continue to reiterate, everything in our power is being done. Rest assured," he continued, glancing up at the crowd just long enough for the flashes' brief frenzy, "that no stone will be left unturned and no effort spared. With specific reference to the question regarding our resources, let me say this." He reached for a pair of reading glasses, then taking a sip from his glass of mineral water, he looked down to where he appeared to have a speech of sorts prepared. "Regardless of the resources and hardware at the disposal of its law enforcement personnel, no city can ever be 100 per cent safe, just as no other daily action we take can be in 100 per cent safety. The moment you set foot outside your apartment you are inevitably exposed to risks. You are, incidentally, statistically exposed to a great many more risks within the four walls of your home. However, when you do venture out onto the streets of your city, what we can do and what we are striving to do is to *reduce* those risks, to *contain* them, just as the rules of the road and the actions of the police aim to reduce the number of fatal traffic accidents.

"Yet," he paused and looked up again to deliver the most sententious part of his speech, "there is no single strategy which can protect a city and its inhabitants and its visitors from determined and ruthless terrorists. These are not individuals who can be deterred by the prospect of receiving a fine or temporarily losing their freedom. Their commitment to their immoral course of action is often total. Fortunately, fortunately for *us*, the men and women of the police and the *carabinieri* and the security services are also immovable in their dedication to protecting the people and upholding the principles of the constitution. I should add, however, that the citizenry too must play its part by being vigilant and cooperative. The importance of your contribution cannot be underestimated. Therefore, if you do witness suspicious behaviour, if you do feel uncomfortable, do not hesitate to contact the police. By working together we can defeat this threat to our city and our freedom."

Elena took out her earpiece for a moment and raised a hand to speak, catching the prefect's eye.

"Yes," he said, pointing in her direction, "just one more question *signore e signori*, please."

"As yet there is no name or even a nationality for the attacker. Do you suspect he was part of a cell? Could there be others ready to assume command?"

The prefect shook his head.

"It's too early to say, and so as not to compromise the work of the counterterrorism unit I am sure you will understand that we have to withhold some information."

Elena put back her earpiece and, in a low voice, checked that Iannelli had got what she had been hearing.

They haven't got a clue, Iannelli, concluded to himself from the dull safety of his hideout. *Not a clue.*

A message buzzed on his phone. It was Rossi.

Are we good?

Good for what? he thought, then he remembered. The Jibril story. He hadn't given it another thought. Perhaps he had started sketching out some bigger picture already. Maybe he wasn't really clutching at straws. But he still couldn't see where, if anywhere, he fitted in. He pondered the notes he had been making, as Elena commented on what was happening out of shot on the stream. Iannelli wanted that too. The reactions, the looks, the nudges and smirks. Well, they were already suppressing evidence and, if they didn't have any leads, maybe they were making it *look* that way. Because what they knew was too damned explosive for the public domain.

Well, if Rossi really was onto something he too was beginning to feel things might just be getting *very* interesting.

Eighteen

Rossi had left the meeting and intercepted Carrara before he might be tempted into going straight back to work. The whole thing had dragged on well into the afternoon, and they'd had to sit through a series of presentations on new techniques in crime solving, which were basically the old ones dressed up with Powerpoint and a new English-inspired lexicon. Rossi hated Powerpoint with a passion. He hated the whole culture of the presentation. The chopping up of an interesting topic into disposable chunks, the misspellings and poorly constructed sentences that the presenter then read anyway before handing them a printed handout of the same. Straight in the recycling bin.

Still, he had to admit that Katia's take on things had been fresher and mercifully brief. And not a single error in her slides. So, she was a perfectionist, or just very good at her job. All of which was confirmed from the first glimpse he had managed to get at her CV during the coffee break. Well, she certainly had all the pieces of paper. But know-how? Experience? They couldn't teach you that on a Master's course or a PhD. And she was a classical dancer. The polymaths were coming, he concluded, and she might want to make getting his job another first on her record. He would have to keep her onside and within reach.

He looked down at the small but slightly more visible bulge at his waistline as they descended the stairs. He wasn't overweight but these days when he looked in the mirror in the mornings there wasn't so much to get excited about. When he had been in his thirties and running he had clocked some good times, but he'd let it slip.

"You still keep in shape, don't you, Gigi?" he said.

"Ten kilometres three times a week, gym twice. It's as much as I can manage these days, what with the family."

Should have known, said Rossi to himself.

"How about a drink? I fancy a cooling draught of the Hippocrene. Need to get the cogs whirring."

Carrara smiled. Coffee, or iced tea for him, that was for sure. Well, it was better to have one steady hand, if only for the driving. They got into the waiting Alfa and headed for the centre.

"See you're on that phone again," said Carrara, as Rossi checked it for the fifth time in as many minutes. "Something I should know about?"

"Trying to fix a meeting with Iannelli, but he's playing hard to get," said Rossi. "About this Jibril story. What do you make of it? And Tiziana, the ID on the body?"

"Definitely worth probing," said Carrara accelerating smoothly as the road opened up and then swinging off Via Nazionale and round towards the Quirinale Hill.

"What do you say to parking round here somewhere and having a walk?" said Rossi, as he took in the view across the city that the hill afforded. Armed units were posted in and around the Presidential Palace, the highest point in the centre of Rome and its symbolic apex.

"Put a sniper over there, say, on the top floor of the museum," said Rossi. "Take them out, then move in with a car bomb and it's *buona notte*, good night Rome, isn't it?"

"Not even that," said Carrara, as a pair of deeply tanned South American tourists in hot pants and holding a map sidled up to a professional, but clearly very willing, soldier. "A suicide bomber with a backpack. It's a no-brainer. How do you defend against it?"

"Over there?" said Rossi, indicating a shaded café bar.

***

Rossi took a long welcome draught of ice-cold Moretti. The sun was punishing, but under the awning its power was held at bay. He looked approvingly at the beads of condensation, the glass's ghosted exterior, like a fairy mist. Then, as he traced a vertical line with a finger along its length, the images of the world around him swam into a reduced focus through its narrow amber lens. Carrara could guess what might be coming next. He'd had an idea.

"For now," said Rossi, "'we see as if in a glass darkly, but then face to face'."

"Bible?"

"St Paul. 1 Corinthians, 13:12."

"Meaning?"

"Well, by glass, he was referring to a mirror. They would have used polished metal, bronze or something. But what I was thinking," he continued, "was about the university. We really need to see those images."

"The CCTV?"

"Yes," said Rossi. "But all of it, not just the edited highlights."

Carrara took a sip on his mineral water.

"I assume that means you've got some sort of plan lined up here, Mick, because the counterterrorism boys weren't dishing out favours last time I knocked on their door."

Rossi nodded again.

"Well they wouldn't, would they? It's their gig and highly

87

sensitive first off, but, as Iannelli might have us think, it's also potential raw material for steering a narrative. There's a possible suspect, but they didn't see the guy parking the bike because of the crowds. Someone leaves in a hurry but it could be anyone. Apart from the fact that there's no name or face to go on, they could say whatever they want. That might help somebody. That might help to provide a sideshow while they, or we, are all looking for who did it and trying to predict the next one. Still, how does the saying go? God helps those who help themselves?"

Carrara knew well what it meant.

"Hang on," said Rossi, reaching for his phone again then flicking through to his messages. "OK!" he said. "Well, at least we're in business with Dario. 'His place, tonight. Await further instructions. Dinner will be provided'."

"Need me?" said Carrara.

"No, take the night off," said Rossi livening up and polishing off his beer before it could become even remotely warm.

"Well, how about I head to the hospital, about this Ivan character," said Carrara breaking the contemplative silence that had briefly enveloped them. "While you continue to sketch out this plan of yours?"

Rossi nodded his approval. In this heat, everything was a theoretical yes. He nodded again. "Good call. But get everyone and anyone who had any dealings with Ivan. Find out if he spoke to them. If they're on another shift or if they left the hospital, get their names and contacts and follow it up."

"OK," said Carrara. "So what about Dario? Are you getting anything?"

Rossi gave a half shrug.

"Don't ask me what exactly, but I think he might have sensed something's going on too."

Another, smaller, beer arrived at Rossi's elbow.

"I didn't even see you order that," said Carrara.

88

Rossi smiled and took a sip.

"Dario was on the scene fast, and he saw enough before things got tidied away. So I reckon he's spotted a role for himself in the game, once again. He's ambitious. Very ambitious and when he's involved things invariably tend towards both the fair *and* the foul."

"Have you swallowed a library today?"

A sequence of heavy vehicles and SUVs roared past leaving a trail of diesel fumes. "Especially in Rome's fog and filthy air."

"Your round, Dante?" said Carrara as the waiter deposited the bill.

"Again?"

"Forgot to put money in my purse," said Carrara, slapping his pockets.

Rossi counted out the exact change, this time adding a modest tip. "Now," he said, as if in the full flush of love with the possibilities of phone technology, "let's see if our friend Gab's still in town."

Gab was Rossi's twenty-year-old dope-smoking go-to tech wizard for when the official lines of communication were either too slow or too legal and moral imperatives dictated he could not afford to wait. His fees were nominal as Rossi could guarantee him a steady flow of legitimate clients seeking both his quality and speed. Since their first chance and decisive encounter at a key moment during The Carpenter case, his stock had increased rapidly in value both for Rossi and his own growing list of clients. So a bedroom hobby had turned into a small but flourishing business. As for trust, Rossi didn't ask too many questions but still tended towards the feeling that his consultant had not knowingly been drawn to the dark side. At least not yet.

Another message came in.

"Shit," said Rossi, slapping his forehead in full Neapolitan style. "I'm supposed to be helping Yana sort out the flat. Totally forgot."

"Sure she'll understand, won't she?" said Carrara with more than a hint of irony.

But he could see that Rossi's excellent mood, like the country's credit rating, had just undergone a downgrade.

Nineteen

"Tomorrow," he said. "Promise. I'll put a reminder on the phone."

Rossi had at least turned up at the flat to make good his excuses. She had been holding out since she answered the door to him without even looking him in the face.

"So, what is it this time?" she asked, finally, while continuing to busy herself around the newly painted and still dust-coated apartment with a sweeping brush. "They're supposed to tidy up after them, aren't they? Look at this!" she said indicating a tide of white residue she was pushing down the hallway.

"Dario," said Rossi, feeling self-consciously useless and also knowing that time was running short. "He can't make long-term plans because of the situation, the escort situation. He's moving around a lot again since intelligence got wind of something, so I was lucky, really, to pin him down tonight."

"And what does he have to do with all this?" she asked, shaking more dust out of the ornaments lining the corridor. "He's only a journalist, isn't he?"

"A very good journalist," said Rossi. "And a sharp operator who may have information that could open up a breach in a cold case. Remember the fire at Via Prenestina? The migrants?"

"That's a cold case?" she said. "Wasn't it only a month or two ago."

"Well, it seems they'd run into a wall before we got onto it. No one's come forward. No real witnesses, no names except this Russian guy who hung on for the best part of a week in hospital."

She stopped for a moment to rub the back of her neck and the shoulder muscles. The cerise sports vest she had on revealed warm, honey-coloured triangles of flesh.

"Allow me," said Rossi. "Where's the pain?" He stood behind her and rested his hands on her shoulders then worked his thumbs in small circles into the tense, resistant fibres. As he kneaded the flesh and muscles, they began to soften and then he felt the rest of Yana's body responding. He leaned over her and began kissing her neck. His hands slid down her back, reaching around her waist, moving upwards then, as she half turned towards him and let the duster fall to the parquet.

"I thought you were running late, Inspector Rossi?" she said, softer now and only teasing him.

"Well, I suppose I'll have to break the speed limit all the way, *Signora*," he replied. "So, is it your place or mine?"

Twenty

He'd left Yana dozing in a wild tangle of sheets, her bronzed body forming a startling oblique contrast to the otherwise candid tableau. One hand hung down off the side of the bed, and her fingertips seemed to caress the wooden floor in a frozen, coquettish gesture. A couple of insubstantial silken garments lay in a casual pearly knot on the floor, and the deep red sun was reflecting off the many shuttered apartment blocks opposite, rendering everything in the room a rich glowing amber. Yet, as he'd stood at the door, showered and still exhilarated, while he'd tried hard to resist it, even then he couldn't help thinking of the times he'd seen dead bodies assuming the very same pose.

Rossi put his foot down again. He was running late, and Dario would be jumpy. At the lights on Via Merulana he sent a quick, terse message. He'd only got the address an hour earlier. He remembered that Dario had been in transit the day they had met at the bombing. That was the way it had to be now and he knew Dario couldn't always count on staying in the same location for more than a few days at a time. If local people, neighbours, shopkeepers, or hoteliers realized who he was, he would have to move on immediately, regardless of the plans he might have made. Regardless of the consequences for his stability.

So "his place" was, of course, relative and an ironic reference to his all too real situation. It could be a hotel room, it could be a police station, even a monastery that rented rooms to the public. If he was lucky, he could settle into a small, isolated apartment which would become home for a time. But always with limits. If he had to move, it could be at very short notice, depending on the level of the risk assessment. As such, he carried only changes of essential seasonal clothes, the books he was reading at any give time, his computer. The minimum. So, enforced reclusion had turned a natural hoarder into a minimalist overnight. As such, he had discarded former Luddite tendencies and now treasured his e-reader like a convert taking to his new faith and practising it daily with unfettered zeal.

Balconies and windows, while important for his heightened sensory needs, were also considered high-risk. You could expose yourself, be a target for snipers or for the inquisitive. And people talked. Always. Information had a price tag, too. It was no kind of life, that was for sure. But he'd made the choice by his actions. He had obtained fame rapidly by way of his scoops and had been feted, rightly, for a period, in the media. Yet the gloss resulting from that season spent in the public eye had then begun to fade. The media was fickle, quickly bored, and in some cases, to squeeze extra mileage out of him, the narrative had taken a sinister and cynical turn. *He was only in it for the money; if he was so at risk why had no one tried to kill him again? Was one journalist worth all this expense? He had drawn it on himself; he should have kept his nose out.*

As for Rossi, though weighed down by responsibilities, he knew that, in comparison with Iannelli, he was a free bird. His quarrels with the dark side were, paradoxically, relatively clean fights. But Dario had condemned them with his words and with his ability to sway public opinion. That was the unforgivable transgression for the dark lords who dwelt in the shadows from where they were accustomed to pulling the strings unseen.

Iannelli had dared to throw back the curtain on their holy of holies; he had dared to let in the light.

Rossi parked, turned off the engine then took out his phone. "Here," he typed.

On the other side of the road the front passenger door on a sizeable, but otherwise anonymous, black Lancia swung open, as if radio-controlled. The backup car would be nearby and both would be armour-plated, bombproof, weighed down by their second skins. The windows too would be built to resist the most concerted onslaught of any assassin's bullets. A signal metaphor for the heavy burden of moral responsibility, Rossi reflected. Like some ponderous medal for your achievement in having spoken the unpalatable truth.

One of the car's occupants crossed and approached Rossi's vehicle, all the time making discreet checks on human and vehicular movement. A thin and oblivious stream of traffic, meanwhile, threaded up and down the sun-dappled and tree-lined street.

Rossi got out of the car, and his contact greeted him with a firm handshake.

"*Dottore*, so glad you could make it. Our client is waiting. How was your trip?"

Rossi went along with the necessary pantomime until they had climbed the steps to the front door and then closed it behind them. They took an old-fashioned lift barely big enough for him and the considerable bulk of his dark-suited companion. There was nobody outside the apartment. That would only have aroused suspicion. The door was opened by a less stocky but equally formidably focused-looking member of the team. In the well-appointed but inappropriate surrounds of a mock Regency room, sat Dario Iannelli. He was on the edge of a chaise longue, hunched over some papers and dressed in a crumpled linen shirt and light, casual trousers. A bottle and a couple of glasses were poised to one side, like mute attendant footmen.

He rose to greet Rossi, as the officers comprising his escort

95

briefly converged on each other and then dispersed to make more of the necessary checks at the points of entry or exit. Rossi too got a pat down. Admirable professionalism.

"So, here we are," said Iannelli. "Welcome to my world, Michael. My brave new world."

Twenty-One

"Of course, it's not as if I'm the only one who has to live like this," he said as he reached out to pour another generous measure of whisky.

"I know," said Rossi. "But you did a double whammy, what with the Sicilian encounter and then the local shenanigans, up here."

"But all in its way connected," said Iannelli, raising a mildly admonishing finger and taking a sip as if the liquor were a necessary medicine about which he still held some professional doubts.

"You weren't a whiskey man before," Rossi commented.

"Everything changes, Michael. And everything has changed for me. It's not like I couldn't have seen it coming but reality bites, doesn't it? This is another of my faithful travel companions," he added wryly, patting the bottle as if it were a dog that might just as easily have been feeling the force of his boot.

"It's not your fault, Dario," said Rossi. He could have murdered a cold beer in a bar but knew it would prove logistically tricky. The apartment they were in was Iannelli's new home for now, though he had only arrived that evening. It was a short let and the landlord hadn't even turned the fridge on in advance. So, no ice.

Iannelli recounted how the security checks at his last residence had flagged an individual, albeit well into his sixties, with links to a Roman gang reputedly involved in any number of Italian "mysteries", including the disappearance of a girl near the Vatican, never to be found, as well as unclaimed bombings attributed variously to far-right neo-fascist groupings or anarchist and Maoist revolutionaries.

"So, time to move on, again," said Iannelli, although Rossi perceived in his recounting of the tale something of his verve still emerging, that egotistical risk-readiness that characterized him and others like him. He was a kind of moral base jumper. Had he not weighed up the risks? Well it had to be the buzz. And it was the detail, the preparation required, the ritual, and then the accolades undoubtedly also played their part. There was though something of the wounded eagle about him now as he looked from time to time towards the window, the curtains drawn, the world beyond going on without him. Good and evil, right and wrong were out there in some long-term game at which, if you wanted, you could always be a spectator.

"And it's all getting so interesting now, isn't it?" he continued. "The stakes are being upped as we speak, and I need to be on the ground, getting my sources, finding new contacts. But these days, going out for an ice cream is like conducting a minor state visit." He almost laughed. "It's practically impossible. But I have to sometimes," he added. "I just have to. So, I've become a master of disguise." He laughed and reached for a bag containing some of his props. "Of course, the problem is if someone is watching the apartment. They're no fools, but if I reckon I can slip out and slip back in, where I then go is relatively safe for a time. I'm driving these guys nuts though," he said gesturing to his suited companions.

"Well it's good to see you, Dario. Even if you are, shall we say, not in your natural environment."

He nodded his thanks before assuming a more businesslike demeanour.

"Well, let's hear it," he began. "What is it you want to know about this character, this Jibril?"

Rossi began to recount the details of his chance encounter with Tiziana.

"First things first, did you meet the guy?"

"Yes," said Iannelli. "I did meet a young man called Jibril. He was in the centre for identification and expulsion, the CIE, in Sicily, and we were introduced, by a priest, I don't remember his name. Cristian, I think."

"And you gave him your card?"

"Yes, I generally do. Just in case there's a chance of somebody coming up with the goods. But what's the link?"

"The link is that he may have known the guy whose body was found on the Tuscolana. Remember? Throat cut and a pig's head thrown in for good measure. He, Jibril that is, went to identify the body. At his own risk, I might add, as an illegal, a *clandestino*."

"Yeah, a 'wop'," said Iannelli with a dash of bitter irony. "And to think that we were the guys without papers, once upon a time, in America. We've got short memories, we Italians. Selective ones."

"Well the Sicilians do us proud, at least," said Rossi. "Hearts big as houses."

Iannelli was nodding and allowed a half-smile to break out as a wave of nostalgia washed over him momentarily.

"And Rita?" said Rossi picking up on it straight away. "Or shouldn't I ask?"

Rita was the flame-haired beauty with an unshakable sense of justice who had captured Iannelli's heart in Sicily. And whose father had subsequently put him onto the suppressed dossier that brought him his life-changing scoop.

"No, no. Ask away. It's still on, very much so, but as you can see, the dating arrangements aren't really to my liking." He laughed again. "Trust me to find a beautiful Sicilian girl with a truly modern approach and then it's me who has to bring the chaperone."

Rossi laughed with him now. It wasn't the old Dario but it was close.

"Anyway," said Rossi, "there's something about this guy that doesn't quite fit."

"Go on," said Iannelli.

"Well, he goes there to identify a body, endangering his own freedom. He says it *could* be his friend, and he slips through the bureaucratic hoops and then it turns out that it's *not* his friend after all."

"So, he made a mistake. Where's the rub, *dottore*?"

Rossi took another sip of the bog-standard Scotch.

"Well, Tiziana, my contact in the morgue, says he *reacted* as if he'd seen his brother, or someone he had been very close to, lying there on the slab. He held it back but she knew. She always knows. That's what she does day in day out. You know a story, I know a crook, and she can spot pain a mile off."

Iannelli had left his drink untouched. He was getting interested.

"So let's run through the scenarios. I find that helps," said Iannelli, grabbing a pen and a notepad. "Let's say he is the guy's murdered friend. What would you want to do in that situation?"

"Give him a decent burial. Get him home. Inform his family," Rossi replied.

"But if you're an illegal, with no money, with no guarantee of getting political asylum, at least not quickly. Then what? You know how it works, how long it can take."

"Leave him? To a pauper's grave?"

"Or get your hands on the bastards who murdered him," said Iannelli.

A dish best served cold? A dish that *had* to be served at any cost, be it cold or hot, thought Rossi.

"So that could be on anyone's agenda. It could be the priority. Payback," Iannelli continued.

"Depending on the person," said Rossi. "There are plenty who wouldn't dream of stepping up to the challenge. We don't all want satisfaction, even if we might fantasize about it. There aren't many who have the means and the will to obtain it."

They reflected on their half conclusions as Rossi refreshed both their glasses then went in search of water.

"Where did she say she thought he was from?" Iannelli enquired.

"West African, quite possibly."

"She could have asked."

"Didn't seem the interrogating type. She'll have wanted to win his confidence."

"West African," said Iannelli. "The plot thickens. A whole lot of trouble going on in that part of the world, isn't there? Always has been. The Ivory Coast, Liberia, in the old Niger Delta. Lots of oil, and our boys are there, by which I mean the big players of our petroleum industry."

"West African is pretty broad and, if I follow you, you're saying he could be Nigerian. But I'm logging it all. You know I never rule out any colour, shade, or shape if there's a chance it might fit into some hypothetical final mosaic."

"You exclude at your peril without first having exhausted all the logical hypotheses, right?"

"Correct," Rossi replied.

"But remember it's the Nigerian guys over here who are the main men and pretty mean mothers, the narco boys and the organized crews."

"Tell me about it," said Rossi leaning back into the plush velvet of his armchair. "And they've been taking on the Camorra at their own game of late. They don't settle for a back seat, that's for sure. So, we can't rule it out. But what was your impression of this guy Jibril?"

Iannelli reflected for a moment.

"A bit ballsy, cocky, confident, fancied himself as a leader, I'd say. And probably with some justification. His English was excellent and his Italian was already commendable too, considering he'd only been on Italian soil a few weeks, maybe a month. And he definitely wasn't Somalian or Ethiopian so he'd had no head start."

"Well it certainly takes guts to cross the Med in one of those deathtraps they use, and in winter too."

Iannelli nodded.

"Well," Iannelli continued, "he must have got himself out anyway, and found his way to Rome. And in pretty good time. What were the dates again?"

Rossi reached into his jacket for his notebook. He showed Iannelli the relevant part of Tiziana's testimony.

"That's good going, by anyone's standards," said Iannelli, settling back himself now into the corner of the chaise longue. "So, that's my side of the story. Where are you thinking of going with this?"

"Another sniff around the African communities could be profitable. It's a big job, mind, and I didn't see much willingness to cooperate last time we went looking. And it's all hands on deck for other very evident reasons, which leaves us short of manpower, as usual. I'm also factoring in that Jibril is, presumably, a Muslim."

"Well," said Iannelli, "he didn't give me any obvious reason to believe he was particularly religious. Principled yes. And angry, possibly, with some potential for hard-line tendencies. There was the priest there, as I said, but it didn't get heated or anything. He was contained but simmering a bit. Not an out-and-out fundamentalist, if that's what you're thinking. But if he is a Muslim, it's not insignificant, given the historical moment, shall we say."

"But also important not to let prejudice or emotion have a distorting effect on the logic," replied Rossi.

"Quite the teacher today, Michael."

Rossi laughed.

"Just like to keep my eye on the ball. We're trying to prevent anything big from getting off the ground. There's quite a bit of apprehension knocking around, in case you hadn't noticed."

"You mean from the safety of my cocoon? My 'bacteria-free' environment?"

"I didn't mean you're out of touch," said Rossi, sensing that his comment might have made the tiniest of dents in Iannelli's thick skin. "How could *you* be out of touch?"

Any offence taken was short-lived as Iannelli fired back: "We had a staffer at the press gig. Seems the prefect, was giving it the old 'no stone left unturned' routine. They also came out with this 'rudimentary device' story. That's total bullshit, isn't it? You know it is."

"They may want to keep the lid on certain things for now," said Rossi. "It could be strategic. That's as far as I'm prepared to go."

"What about GIS mapping and tracking? Are you involved with that?"

Rossi shook his head.

"They extrapolate what we need based on requests, or they point us in certain directions, but instinct, intelligence, and plain old on-the-ground work still plays its part."

"Not to mention the grasses," said Iannelli. "Anyone on the payroll yet? And where are they getting the expertise from? You know it was at least a kilo of military-grade explosive."

"I thought I was asking you the questions today, Dario," said Rossi. "Once again it seems we are digressing, and I get the feeling you're an old hand at the game."

Both men managed to smile. Yes, Dario wanted answers. It was in his nature to start a fight to get them, and he couldn't fail to be uptight living the way he now was. But the battle was one in which they fed off each other, needed each other. It was at times like this that Rossi wondered why Iannelli hadn't just become a cop instead. God knows, for dogged determination, not to mention technical knowledge, he could have substituted more than a few of the so-called high-level operatives he'd run into in the course of his career. Perhaps it was the same reason people who love buildings don't study architecture: because they don't want to end up having to build concrete shopping centres paid for by on-the-ground Mafia money.

"So you're trying to solve this Prenestina case in your spare time too?" said Iannelli. "You're going to be a busy boy. Unless of course there's a link," he added with a half-smile. Iannelli was waiting to see if Rossi would give him some confirmation or some hint of a lead.

But Rossi was none the wiser either.

"I don't like loose ends, Dario. And I don't like it when there's even the suggestion that one life might be worth more than another."

"Are you saying these guys got a rough deal? Apart from burning to death I mean."

"All I'm saying is that when a case passes out of the spotlight, well, maybe something tells me to go and sniff around a bit more."

"It was definitely arson though, wasn't it?"

"For me, without a shadow of a doubt, and murder."

"Deliberate then?"

"Maybe meant to be a crude warning, but anyone who gives warnings like that will be happy to have hit the jackpot. Then there was some story about an illegal vodka operation, which could have been a convenient way of making *sure* it went sky high."

"Possible," said Iannelli.

"Right. But Forensics also found the remains of a timer switch, some quick-fix repair job or home-brewing hack. I'm not so sure it wasn't all a set-up, all evidence conveniently incinerated. And that's *off* the record, for the record. The only other opening is the guy who survived for a week."

"The Russian?"

"Yes," said Rossi. "Gigi's stirring up the embers, as it were, but it's a total shot in the dark."

Rossi looked at his watch. It was getting late. Iannelli meanwhile seemed to be weighing up this news of a second front of sorts. He knew Rossi's way of thinking. Lateral, usually, and capable of opening up the most hermetically sealed of cases.

"Well, at least you've got yourself a name, and a description," he said finally. "Keeping it to yourself for now?"

Rossi nodded. His phone was buzzing.

"Keep your ear to the ground, won't you," said Rossi, excusing himself to take the call, and walking first, by habit, to the window, then remembering the role windows could play in getting yourself shot.

"Mick, Gigi."

"Yep."

"Didn't get much out of anybody today. I got more change out of the cleaning staff. Seems there was one other burns nurse there the whole week that our man was in. Very dedicated to her work, according to my source. Saintly type. She's been off duty but comes back tomorrow. It's the best I could get."

"So he never spoke?"

"Can't confirm that yet."

"Did they say anything about DI Lallana? What did he get out of them?"

"Nothing much," said Carrara. "He didn't exactly dig deep."

"OK. I think it might be worth giving this Mother Teresa a proper interview. See you in the morning at the office."

Rossi slipped the phone back into his pocket. It was nearly dark. Iannelli had resumed his reading.

"I'd better be off, Dario," said Rossi, sensing the melancholy descending now like an evening dew.

"Enjoy your freedom," said Iannelli lifting only his eyes first then rousing himself and getting to his feet to shake Rossi's hand.

"I'll be in touch," said Rossi. "Still got the same e-mail?"

"Yes," he replied. "The wonders of encryption and secret ervice IT protection. It all goes through their secure servers and

105

is totally safe and untraceable. They have the advantage of being able to monitor who's sending it to me too, which I'm not so happy about, but it's actually turned out that it keeps me *safer*. And it's spared me a major headache with my contacts list. So this relic of my former life remains," he added with an attempt at a smile.

Rossi emerged from the building's cool interior into the warm, semi-liquid, heavy evening air. He breathed in the scent of jasmine from some hidden garden. A heady Roman night. So this was the price to pay for staying alive, being excluded from life's feast. He wondered if he would be able to live a similar existence. Still, anyone could take a pop at him, if they wanted, and his enemies could be anywhere. It would all be over in an instant. As he walked back to the car a few remembered words from a school poem played like the chorus of a song he couldn't get out of his head. Yes. Another day was ending. How suddenly the evening came.

It was late but Cardinal Terranova had no intention of turning in. Besides, there was work to do.

It was not such a bad life, he reflected, lying gently to himself as he rose again from his desk. But at some stage one must accept reality. Accept. Yes. He looked out of the window although there was little to see in the darkness. He had the gardens, the cloisters, the gentle trickling of the fountains and the silence. It gave him ample time to think and to read and reflect.

Especially when he could not sleep.

Now, he was a retired "man of the cloth". Officially, he had left behind the cleric's life and was free now to pursue his interests and see out the rest of his days in this benign imprisonment. He was not really free, of course. He could no longer come and go as he pleased. But it had been his choice and it had, he supposed, been his fault.

So this was a compromise. He continued to exercise his

considerable power through his contacts, and a select and restricted circle of persons guarded the truth. Mechanisms had been put in place to guarantee that, both now and hereafter. If it were, however, in any way a known secret that he was here, given time, rumours might circulate, as they had about other senior clerics' conduct, sexuality, or financial affairs. Yet "the system" still held up in such matters, although he knew that in this new age, this rising tide of technology was set to sweep away the certainties so long guaranteed by the former *status quo*. It would require a major "repositioning of the brand", as it were, a large-scale overhaul of their practices if they were to maintain the level of compliancy and intrinsic trust hitherto enjoyed.

That though was no longer his task and others would set about it with gusto and diligence. They would salvage what they could, like Crusoe – Protestant though he was – going back and forth to the ship. The prudent and visionary among them would secure the essentials and these would see them through.

Retirement had exerted a rapid and sudden changing effect. So used to a life of fervid mental activity and commitments, his body and mind had now fallen into more natural states. He was simply growing old. It had come quickly and suddenly but that which had been put off could not be held back. His face had changed. No longer wearing the old garb had also changed his appearance as well as his own attitude to himself. One or two relics remained. He conserved in a drawer his cardinal's ring, which from time to time he would slip onto his finger before consigning it once again to the recesses of memory.

He wore it now too, and twisted and caressed it as he reflected.

He was not short of company if he wanted it. His welfare was also attended to by a succession of personnel, social assistants who maintained his apartments and prepared his meals, washed and ironed his bed linen and clothes.

He had been asked if he would prefer male or female assistants. He had chosen the former and even if they subsequently sent females and males in almost equal number – this too was the nature of the market, supply and demand – he had been pleased with their dedication and their manners. Some had been silent and submissive women wreathed in brightly coloured silken saris, ladies from India and Bangladesh, Sri Lanka too, he had discovered. Some of the men, barely boys really, had been long-limbed Africans, and one in particular who came intermittently had reminded him so much of Victor.

What had become of Victor, the Nigerian, he did not know. He would never know for sure and that was how it had had to be. The boy had been his undoing, his weakness, allowing himself to be temporarily blackmailed, vulgar word that it was. But he had learnt his lesson. And Marciano, his blackmailer? His end was no mystery. He had been dispatched, and his associates and family knew better than to bleat. The cardinal knew he had been well and truly cornered then by his enemies, yet he had fought back, and faking his own death to live this secret life now had been a price worth paying. But he also knew that other forces were now afoot. Thus, he was newly on his guard and another plan had to be devised. A plan that would serve other key interests too. Yes, others had put their oars in since then, meddling in affairs that did not regard them. They should have known better. Thank goodness for the "network" which always reeled in the loudmouthed before they got dangerously "vocal".

Yet he still had his doubts. Perhaps he should have taken his own life and ended it honourably when his blackmailer had first confronted him. Instead, he had denied others of their lives so as to cover, in the world, his own mortal sins.

Judas at least had been decisive and, as such, would have deserved to have acquired a sainthood of sorts. The saint of sinners beyond redemption. Some small comfort then for them as they ponder final solutions to their own very personal brand of guilt.

Then he expelled the dark narrative from his mind as if he

were a wayward seminarian and went back to his desk, where there was a letter nearing completion.

... in the event of my violent death and the subsequent involvement of the civil authorities you must do the following as specified here below. (Failure to do so will mean that you too will be in grave danger. A copy of this letter, to be opened in the event of my violent death, is in the hands of trusted individuals who, in turn, have their instructions to act accordingly should you fail to follow to the letter these instructions).

There followed a series of imperative statements, a brief inventory.

He closed the letter in the envelope. Then he reached for a box of matches.

He watched, fascinated as ever, as the flame migrated from the thin, twisted and carbonized limb between his finger and thumb, revitalizing the candle's dead wick in an act of quotidian resurrection. He extinguished it and tossed the charred remnant aside. One life for another. The willing and the *un*willing sacrifice. It was all God's will.

Then he dripped molten blood-red wax onto the envelope and, with his cardinal's ring, was poised for a moment to leave on it his inviolate seal, before he remembered and stopped and put instead its cooling salve to his own lips before sliding it from his finger. He placed it next to the letter and a few other items he had seen fit to collect for the occasion.

Then he rang his bell and waited for "the courier" who would see to everything else, as he always did.

Twenty-Two

Giancarlo Mondo stood in the glass and steel cubicle suspended above the void of the lift shaft. He was like the last link at the end of a taught chain coiled and turning constantly at the behest of an unseen behemoth.

He made another slight adjustment to his tie, tightening the red silk knot against the stiff juncture of the collars of his powder blue, handmade shirt. As on all such armour hanging in his wardrobe, his initials in a darker hue were embroidered at a point on the right below his ribcage.

And a warrior he was. So he had been told and he had learnt to move and to sway and to parry and then deliver the decisive blow as and when an opportunity presented itself. To cut the deal. To cut the right deal. To make sure that all parties left feeling that they had got what they wanted, whether they had got it or not. To make sure that he came away with the prize. To make sure the others didn't get a look in. To exile any lingering emotions to some faraway land where others could continue to fritter away their time on this earth, while he defied time's tyranny by owning as much of the here and now as was humanly possible.

All this, he reflected, had already been achieved. The lift continued to climb. Now he only needed to keep his nerve and, like a tightrope walker, never look down, never look back. Only forward to the goal and then beyond to the next one. It stopped. The doors slid open. He was alone and stepped out, turning right on the soft, yielding carpet, treading with decisive, deliberate steps, dismissing one door after another until he had come to where it would all begin again. He knocked. The door was opened by some unseen hand. Flanked on both sides by two dark-suited and sombre bodyguards, a tall, elegant gentleman in traditional African robes strode forward. He then stretched out a hand laden with gold accessories and gems.

"*Dottor* Mondo, how very, very good to see you. We have been expecting you."

Giancarlo returned the greeting, holding the handshake until he sensed beyond the host's words his host's will as the muscles then began to relinquish their grip.

"Honoured to meet you, President. Truly honoured."

***

Time had passed. Outside, through the tinted windows of the suite it was beginning to get dark. To one side there was Vesuvius, a sleeping colossus, and then the broad, majestic sweep of the Bay of Naples. Small boats traversed it. A few white crests had formed here and there while the island of Capri was a calm, supine, sleeping woman's profile. "Take some time to think it over," they had said as they broke for refreshments. "We have time, for now." Giancarlo knew what time was and what it meant. They had cornered him with an offer promising a quantum leap as far as the plans for his own personal enrichment were concerned. It would project him to the next level and even beyond. But for all their repeated assurances, it was an affair which he wouldn't be in control of. Yes, he would oversee. That went without saying. He alone would give the authorization to use "the channels", the delivery would depend on him, his men, his trusted intermediaries. But he knew he was a link in the chain and not the blacksmith beating it upon the anvil. And he knew that the hand holding the hammer could sometimes stop or be stayed mid-strike and that sometimes it could slip.

Giancarlo splashed his face with cold water from the pristine taps and took a soft hand towel from the neat pile next to it. For a second, he felt like he was in the tiny cabin of the first marine-blue boat he had taken out on that sea. It was an honest, simple wooden boat. It required love and attention, devotion, to make it seaworthy. And it had been his. A boom of laughter came from beyond the wall. Then just as quickly as it had come to him, the image of the boat vanished from his mind. There was work to be done. An agreement had in principle been reached but now he found himself at a crossroads.

He strode back into the lounge and took up his position again. The main negotiator sat across from him as the President conversed with his retinue in a huddle, oblivious, it seemed, but very much involved.

"This was not mentioned in the preliminaries," said Giancarlo turning back to face the official reclining now in an armchair, his tie gone, the top two buttons of his shirt undone.

"This is true," his interlocutor replied, "but it is merely a question of *safe passage*. Guaranteeing the safe passage of this certain number of units can bring you, personally, a conspicuous reward. Look, let me show you the kind of numbers we are talking here."

The figures were dizzying. It would be like turning the poisoned water of the bay into fine wine.

"And everything is already in place, *Dottor* Mondo. The wheels are ready to turn tomorrow, if needs be. Just as soon as you make the necessary calls. You know, in this business, there is a quick turnaround. Prior planning is detailed, meticulous, down to the very last detail and we have our men working on this day and night. They and we identify a route. We are always one or, if all goes well, two steps ahead of our pursuers, shall we say."

Giancarlo continued to listen. He knew what this was now.

"Then the route becomes active and if it there are not hitches we send more and quickly. Then we change. A route rarely has a long life. There are variables, risks. There are informers, checks, rivals and human error. But as you can see the rewards are truly magnificent. Are they not? And then, at some later stage you may like to put your hat in the ring. Grow your capital. But all this will be yours to keep, *Dottor* Mondo. No tricks. No catches. No strings attached."

"And with this, we can sign for the exclusive concession for another fifteen years?"

"You read the contract many times. It has not changed. You are a lawyer, *Dottor* Mondo. You know your stuff, I believe."

For what seemed like the hundredth time, Giancarlo scanned the documentation.

"And the agreed payments to all parties concerned remain the same?"

"As agreed."

"Through the offshores, the pre-established 'system'?"

"And we raise the unit cost accordingly."

"Show me the other papers again," said Giancarlo.

The intermediary reached out and handed him a blue plastic file.

"Of course, for the rest, it remains a gentleman's agreement but as a sign of goodwill we have prepared a down payment, as it were."

Another official made his way, as if on cue, across the room bearing a briefcase which he placed on the glass table. He turned the golden dials of the combination lock then swivelled the case through 180 degrees.

"Open it, please. It is yours."

Giancarlo looked at the oxblood leather rectangle before him and in the hotel's tinted glass saw himself reflected. Your life is one only. Make of it what you will but remember that every action has its consequences and you must be prepared to face them. They were not his words, but the words of one whom he had once considered wise. He placed both thumbs on the locks. They clicked twice. It opened.

***

He stepped out of the office tower in the Centro Direzionale business district and walked across the central piazza. It was night and carrying two briefcases now made him feel rather more self-conscious than he would have liked, quite apart from the matter of their contents. He hailed the first taxi he saw.

"Hotel Rialto," he said and handed over a large denomination bill. "Take the scenic route. As long as you like."

He then took out his phone and dialled the pre-arranged number.

"Giancarlo! Good to hear from you."

"Same to you, Uncle! Are you well?"

"As well as can be expected, as well as can be expected, at my age. And you?"

"Well, very well."

"And the cousins? Tell me, how are the cousins, Giancarlo?"

"All well, very well indeed."

"And were they happy to see you?"

"Ecstatic!"

"And were they pleased with their gifts?"

"Delighted."

"Wonderful."

"And your mother? How is *mamma*? Please, tell me everything about your dear mamma."

"Fine, thank you, Uncle. She sends her love."

"Good. Good. You send her mine too. Now. You must come to dinner with me? It's been so long. Are you still in Naples?"

"Yes."

"Well, drop in, my boy. But don't bring anything. Leave it all to me."

"OK, Uncle, it will be a pleasure for me." He looked at his watch. "I'll see you in about an hour."

"*Perfetto*. See you then."

He put the phone back in his breast pocket and breathed deeply as the taxi sped south on the *lungomare*, homing in on the brightly lit, honey-coloured medieval fortress of the Castel dell'Ovo. The wind was picking up a little, and in the distance he saw a few small, silent waves crashing in against the castle where its sustaining bulk nudged out into the bay. Time to change. Call Giulia on the legitimate phone for family and non-suspect business. They could put as many line taps as they wanted on it but they would get nothing incriminating. Then a shower. A clean shirt. Time to stash away the prize and prepare for round two. Time maybe for some diversion too. After all, he had earned it.

Twenty-Three

"Went home, sick," said the hospital receptionist. Carrara had gone off to make further enquiries and had come back with the confirmation. Exhaustion had been cited and, despite her protests, she had been sent home. Rossi had turned up expecting a routine interview. Time was relative now as no witness to the events of the Prenestina fire could be considered fresh, so a day here or there in this case would matter little. Yet, as they both stood at the desk at the impenetrable distance from their taciturn interlocutor, the same Rossi was becoming irritated and had decided to dispense with the usual niceties.

"Well, if you'll kindly provide me with her particulars we will go directly to her apartment."

"I'm really not sure I can do that without clearance," the bearded receptionist replied in a flat tone.

"You do realize this is a potential criminal investigation, don't you?" said Rossi. "Or are you trying to obstruct it? I can obtain the information anyway, with a phone call to the records office, just as I can have your particulars, in an instant, if I have reasonable suspicion that you are in some way attempting to pervert the course of justice."

The receptionist looked back through the thick lenses of his oversized, red-rimmed glasses. He seemed cemented into his seat and, without altering his posture, put out a hand to reach for the phone, as if it were a comfort blanket that might at any moment be snatched away. He rattled off the appropriate commands and then, after a few clicks of his keyboard, presented Rossi with a handwritten slip of paper.

"Here's her name, address, and telephone number."

Rossi glanced at the note then handed it back.

"You forgot the mobile number."

The omission was just as quickly corrected.

"Thank you," said Rossi, "and good day."

***

"Go straight to her flat next time," said Carrara as they pushed through the swing doors and into the car park.

"Yes," Rossi replied, "but I like to have a witness *in situ*. It helps me to complete the picture and makes it more likely that they might remember the details. Not to worry."

"Where are we going?" asked Carrara

"Viale Marconi, Piazza della Radio. Lucia Rinaldi."

***

Carrara had jacked the air-conditioning up as high as it would go despite Rossi's displeasure.

"Just until it cools down. Then we go for old-fashioned windows open, if you really must. I did say we should park out of the sun," said Carrara as beads of sweat continued to roll down both their faces and he negotiated their way out of the labyrinthine car park. "Is that your phone?" he said, detecting a muted uzzing from Rossi's direction.

Rossi reached round for his jacket that lay crumpled on the k seat.

"Great," he said. "Message from Gab. Out of the city till September. The new computer will have to wait."

"So that's your new code, is it?" said Carrara with an air of gentle mockery.

"Would you rather he said 'let's break into the Israeli university when I'm back from Sardinia? Why isn't anyone available in August?'"

"To be fair, he's not just anyone," Carrara replied. "He's your private hacker and all-round gadgets man. Consider yourself lucky."

But Rossi's day had not been going according to plan.

"Well I hope you've got some bright ideas if this one draws a blank," said Rossi. "Otherwise it's going to start looking like we're becoming ineffective, or irrelevant."

"A cop's only as good as his last collar, is that what you're saying?"

Rossi shrugged.

"We'd better come up with something. When you least expect it, that's when the shit hits the fan. And there's still talk going around of 'changes', efficiency audits, performance-related career incentives and the like. Downsizing. Putting out to grass."

"All talk," said Carrara, dismissing it but knowing that there was always an opportunist ready to step in, especially if it served someone else's agenda.

The telltale point of white light and the faintest of clicks told them someone was looking at them through the spyhole.

"Signora Rinaldi, we are police officers," said Carrara in as reassuring a tone as he could manage. The door was opened by a nervous-looking middle-aged woman, in a green dressing gown and with plenty of slightly greying hair tied back. Rossi first apologized for the inconvenience, then explained the nature of the situation and the relative urgency of matters.

"Thought you were selling something, or Jehovah's Witnesse

she said as she gave a cursory glance at Rossi's badge. "Seen plenty of those in my time. You get all sorts coming in to the burns unit, and all sorts of stories going out with them."

They followed her down the narrow hallway and into the living room.

"Well, can I offer you coffee, officers? Or perhaps something cool?"

"No, thank you," said Rossi, seated now on the sofa in the rather kitsch and old-worldly apartment. Little or nothing had been done to alter the effect it gave of stepping back in time to an Italy without chrome kitchen fittings, parquet floors, or LED spotlights and lowered ceilings. Here was well-worn Formica, and terracotta tiles, a few thin rugs and flimsy-looking single-glazed windows thrown open to allow the air to circulate and let the non-stop traffic noise in. The bulky, once-modern TV was turned down. On a heavy dark wood sideboard, a plaited Easter palm rested against one of several black-and-white framed photos.

"Give me one moment please," she said. "I wasn't expecting visitors."

She came back only a few moments later wearing a light wrap-around flower print dress in place of the dressing gown. Rossi deduced that she had either dressed hurriedly or that the dress had been chosen to deliberately display her more feminine attributes. He tried not to let his eyes stray.

"My mother used to always do the serving if there were guests, but she left us, I'm afraid, not so long ago."

"I'm sorry to hear that," said Rossi, as a large ginger cat made its presence felt at his foot before slipping away again. So this was "us", he wondered. Probably. Hers had all the hallmarks of a life lived in a world on permanent pause, suspended at some key moment in the past. He wondered about her and her late mother, speculating as to when and how they had been left alone.

"So," the nurse began, addressing Rossi, "you wanted to ask

me some questions, I believe. My friend told me you were at the hospital yesterday."

"The cleaning lady?" said Carrara, flicking back through his notes for a name.

"That's right," she said, "My friend, Barbara."

"It's about Ivan, the Russian," said Rossi. "Did he ever say anything? Was he even able to speak?"

She shook her head.

"You didn't see the state of that poor man, the extent of his burns. The pain he was in and the infections, all the strain it must have put on his heart. Any normal human being would have left this world the night he came in. He must have had a great will to live, or a need to hang on for as long as possible. I've seen a lot in my time, Inspector, but when you see someone resisting like he did it has an effect on you. But I told the other officer all that, the last time, when Ivan was still with us and then when he passed on."

She appeared to shudder then despite the heat.

"So there's nothing you can add, nothing you might have remembered in the meantime?" Rossi asked again.

"Only what I told your colleague, like I said. He must have had very strong faith or belief in a higher power. Maybe that's what helped him for so long."

"How did you know?" said Carrara. "How did you know he had faith, if he couldn't speak?"

Rinaldi turned to look straight at Carrara.

"He wore a crucifix. We removed it, of course, along with his identification tags, but I sterilized it and left it near the bed out of harm's way. I thought it might help him to have it near."

"But many men wear a crucifix," said Carrara. "It's just jewellery, usually."

"Was it an Orthodox cross?" said Rossi leaning forward. "With the extra bars, at the top and the bottom?"

Carrara leant back as he saw Rossi warming to the enqui now that it was getting theological.

"Yes," she said. "I believe it did. Well, he was Russian, wasn't he?"

"But that doesn't explain how you *knew* it was important to him," said Rossi.

The nurse appeared to reflect for a moment, as the cat made another appearance at her ankles.

"Well, there was something about it," she said, "and now I think of it, I don't know what it was exactly but it's just that he would try to look at it occasionally, in one of his moments of lucidity. I was there most of the time and at least that's what I remember. I used to watch over him and it was almost as though he was drawn to it. I'd be on one side of the bed and he would try to move his head or his eyes in the other direction, where the crucifix was."

"So he must have had the last rights," Rossi continued. "That would be normal procedure, based on the assumption that he was religious."

"Well, now that you mention it, that's a thing that struck me," she said, becoming more animated. "He got very agitated one day when a priest came round. They're often in, giving blessings, and last rights, as you said. I don't like that lot snooping around at the best of times but this one gave me the creeps. Anyway, off he goes, this one, old fella, and he makes his way over to the bed. I had to tell the priest that Ivan wasn't a Catholic, as far as we knew and that with his burns he hadn't signed any papers, of course. I even showed him the Orthodox crucifix, but he was dismissive of it, said the man would be meeting his God soon enough and it was his Christian duty to give absolution. But Ivan did seem agitated by it. Agitated by him even, by his presence."

"He can't have been able to move much," said Carrara, "with he burns."

She turned to him. "In this job," she said then, as if remem-
ng in a moment a career's worth of memories, "after a while
egin to learn a new language. It's a sign language of sorts.

121

When you're with a person for a long time, even in that state, you'll notice the slightest thing – a twitch, a gesture, or an attempt to move."

Carrara looked at Rossi whose hands were joined as if in prayer in front of his face.

"And you know," she said, "you'd be surprised sometimes what you can hear."

PART II

Twenty-Four

It had been the best part of a month since Francesco had given up on the career he had glimpsed for himself in Italy, the career he had envisioned with Paola, the life they had planned. And here he was with nothing in his hands but the fragments of broken dreams. Dashed hopes like the snarled steel confetti of a bomb blast flung across a piazza. Against the backdrop of such a scene, surely all action was useless. All action? Not quite.

"If we don't move now, then when? If we don't strike at the heart of the Establishment, the powers that be, the blind forces stealing your future, my future, the future of all the young people and of all the disadvantaged, the discriminated, the stigmatized, the scapegoats, *when* do we do it? I tell you, comrades, the time is ripe for action."

Francesco sat at the back, his arms crossed. He had taken another step, albeit a small one, even if his position remained tentative, reserved. The door of the meeting room was near, symbolically and literally. But he had come. On the pressing of his friends, he had agreed to set foot inside the collective. He was not a member. He wasn't a joiner by nature but rather an observer. He was not planning on being a pawn in anyone's game. If he played, it would be his game, by his rules, whether they knew it or not.

"Direct" was the word now on their lips, as in direct action, although no one had dared make an explicit public call to armed struggle. "This was a country at a crossroads, a stalled reality." Not that they didn't have a point and, while it had helped to take his mind off other things, he was also there to make a reasoned choice. Was there no other way in this country? Did attempts to change the order by peaceful political means always have to run into a brick wall?

The speaker touched also on the MPD, derided as a *movement* "put there" to absorb the social tensions and draw off like puss from a wound the anger and vital energies of the populace.

Francesco weighed the words in his mind. He was working. That was true. Not in the job he wanted but reasonably well paid even if with no job security. It was the usual story of renewable contracts, no holidays, no sick pay, minimum pension contributions. But it bored him to go over his own hardships both because it was futile and because it led then to other thoughts feeding into a dark cycle he had to break.

His depression following Paola's death had been bleak. After the funeral he had closed himself off from everyone. Even if they'd had time for him, they had soon given up trying, sucked back as they had been into the all-consuming domestic obligations of their own lives.

And then he had experienced his first moment of revelation. He realized that he had found it easier to fall in with those friends who had hitherto occupied a zone on the fringes of his life, the life he had envisaged as a journey towards a form of bourgeois respectability: the house, the family, the career.

It had started with drinks in the clubs they had frequented before he had met Paola, then pizzas in the old haunts, and before too long he had been tagging along to the odd political get-together at the social club, the *centro sociale*. It had released th pressure for him. It wasn't nostalgia and it didn't provoke melancholy but when he looked in the mirror he didn't see his failure but rather his other, older, untainted self. Perhaps it had been the weight of recent events, and he had heard it said, but he now also saw something else. He saw his father.

Francesco's family, despite its proud and honourable history, had not been one of those families that carefully looked after its silverware and antique chairs. While not bourgeois, they had standing and had exercised some influence not least because of its partisan history. His grandfather had been a dedicated antifascist and combatant for Italian freedom in the 1940s as the country had been plunged into a bitter and brutal civil war.

He had passed on his beliefs to Francesco's father, Maurizio, a mild-mannered but principled individual who had been active in the Communist Party in the 1970s. Though he had never embraced violence, he had never hidden their past either but rather wore it as a badge.

It would, however, cost him his life when a neo-fascist murder squad followed him as he was leaving a Party meeting. He was slaughtered in reprisal for an equally cold-blooded assassination by far-left militants who had firebombed an apartment where a far-right collective had been meeting. Maurizio had been bundled into a car, strangled, then shot in the face and his body dumped on the street in his own *quartiere*, his own area. Francesco had been a baby and he had grown up knowing his father only from stories and fading photographs.

The meeting was breaking up. They would be moving on to the pubs and clubs, getting something to eat, engendering further discussion, but away from indiscreet attention. There were spies, plants and informers to be wary of. It was exciting for some of them, the younger ones especially. But they had never seen an armoured car slicing through a peacefully protesting crowd then bearing down on them, the water cannon toppling grown men like skittles, the tear gas choking you and burning your eyes and throat. And there was always the fear, the feeling of being exposed as if naked, if they decided that today the shooting would start too.

He made his excuses, saying brief goodbyes to friends who were busy in huddles and discussions around the hall.

***

Outside, it had rained. September was here and with it the promise of thunderstorms but still many more long warm days and evenings to come. Summer's extended lease was always a comfort, of sorts, in Rome.

He made his way then towards Porta Maggiore's busy tram interchange, following the towering old Roman walls that dominated the western side of San Lorenzo, and boarded the number 3.

The short journey left him on Via Carlo Felice, off which, on a side street, the family house was located. He had come back to live there after Paola's murder, handing all responsibility for it over to her family. Glad to be shot of them anyway. Let them do with it what they please, and her father, calculating even in grief, had been keen not to lose the rental contract.

There was no sound. His mother was already in bed, and his grandfather too would be sleeping. The care assistants would have been in to see to his medical needs and to give him a sleeping pill. Francesco turned on only a small table lamp in the hall which cast enough light for him to see along the corridor and into his grandfather's room. He opened the wardrobe and, getting down on his knees, reached in under the blankets and spare sheets until his hand touched what he was looking for.

He removed the wooden box about the size of a hefty old leather-bound family bible. He put everything else back as he had found it, switched off the hall light and went into his own room, locking the door behind him. He checked that the blinds

128

were down behind the curtains before switching on his bedside light. Only then did he open the box.

The Smith & Wesson revolver lay nestled inside. He lifted it out, relishing its weight, its solid realness. He had handled guns in the *carabinieri*, and he remembered how a brand-new weapon when handled would shed the occasional drop of oil like a bead of perspiration, like a slow tear to be wiped away.

The simple weapon in his hand had a story, one that ran parallel with the official history of the state and the law-upholding duties of a *carabiniere*. It was the weapon his grandfather had used to fight for freedom and for what he believed in when there was no other choice available. He had taken life with it, he had saved his own life with it too, all so that others might live free from oppression.

The lamplight gleamed on the gun's grooves and on the dark, sleek rod of the barrel, like he imagined moonlight must have gleamed on it when they waited ready to ambush fascists and Nazis in the mountains. Then he laughed to himself – his romantic idiocy. The gun, like their tunic buttons, their wedding rings and their grimly determined faces, would all have been blackened quite deliberately with grease or with handfuls of the very earth they marched upon.

All then would have been as one with the night in which even the slightest glimmer could be enough to get you killed.

Giancarlo's hands were sweating as he put down his phone. He glanced at the time. Working into the evening again. Sweat was glistening too at his temples and running down his cheeks despite the powerful blast of the air-conditioning. It was as if he were running a fever but he wasn't sick, only tormented. He dried his hands on his trousers and pulled open the desk's top drawer then rummaged around for tissues and another pack of dexedrine. He wiped his face and neck and snapped out and popped another couple of pills, sloshing them back with water.

He had first begun to use them as a prescribed medication when he had found his attention wavering in meetings and his ability to recall facts not quite what it might have been. His doctor had given him the once-over, advising him to cut down on his working hours, which he had tried to do but in vain. He had continued to return for repeat prescriptions until the same doctor had written out a phone number and pushed it back across the desk instead, advising him to seek professional help for his substance abuse.

That had been some weeks ago. It seemed an age but it was in fact only a month or so. The job did that to you and everyone in his circle was popping something as if it were the pre-dinner *aperitivo* or the afternoon shot of coffee.

But he had other worries and now he was buying the stuff anywhere he could. Because he hadn't been sleeping much either he was knocking them back just to keep himself minimally focused during his waking hours at the office.

He stared again at his to-do list. It was getting longer by the hour and he had been doing precious little to shorten it. He had put things off, delegated, and buried what wouldn't be likely to surface in the short term. That could be someone else's problem further down the line. It would all come out later, when he wasn't working there, when maybe he wasn't around anymore.

He let out a powerful sigh of pent-up stress and anxiety, enough to let his blissfully serene leather-skirted secretary, Giada, raise her eyes from her keyboard for a second to take note. It was as if she were mocking him, flaunting the gold bracelets and jewels he had made sure she could choose for herself in return for her making his toil a more rewarding experience.

He had already seen every inch of her body in every imaginable position on any number of work-related weekend and late-night escapades. All since he had hired her on a whim after making his life-changing deal with the President. How she had first wheedled her way into his world had all seemed so purely casual, but now he suspected she was there for a reason.

The deal had seen him swimming in cash and comfort, wading through the riches promised for those destined for the mythical next level. The thousand-euro gourmet meals all over Rome and Milan. The private jets. The high-class escorts. It had been a whirlwind, in which, however, his responsibilities had continued to grow like a skyscraper being built at cartoon speed in the eye of a hurricane. Money brought more money and more money brought more risk. There was more to cover up, more to conceal and move around, more of everything. Yes, he had truly arrived.

But all the bling and status meant next to nothing now because he had fucked up and fucked up big time and he could see no way out that was not going to cost him dear.

"Anything I can do for you, *Dottor* Mondo?"

Never use my first name at work. Never call my home. She was sticking to those rules at least.

"No, Giada. No, thank you," he replied and, after a second or two in which she appeared to be studying him for some extra sign, she went back to her slow typing, the tic-tic of her keyboard like water torture against the silence.

He stood up and went to the window, looking back across the city in the direction of his home. He longed now to do ordinary, banal, boring things, to reconnect with his family, to make it work. But he had told Greta, his wife, nothing. It was just the work, he had said, just the pressure. He wondered where she was, and with whom. He snatched up his phone then thought better of it, especially with Giada in the room.

Greta had already stopped working, on his insistence, ostensibly so that at least she could dedicate her time to the kids. But in his absence the cheques were now going to an increasing army of babysitters as Greta began pursuing her hobbies, her dreams, frequenting the chicest of the local gyms, taking courses, spending hours of her evenings making multi-tier cakes for new friends while he ricocheted around the peninsula and flew back and forth to one overseas appointment after the next. But then the photos had arrived.

On his desk.

Him and other women.

Him and other men.

And then the ultimatum. He had been left with no choice but to bring them on board – the bosses, the Camorra. He had grown up with some of them, so they knew him and his family inside out, even though early on in his life he had taken what he had thought to be an alternative route: ItalOil and corporate success. But all roads lead to the same destination when you're rotten inside.

He pressed his face against the plate glass, his breath clouding the clear view, the shadow on the X-ray of his life. And there were only those few centimetres between him and oblivion.

He had put his trust in them as he had no choice and they *knew* he had no choice. It was the merry-go-round of malevolence from which he could not get off.

And then they'd screwed him, hung him out to dry. They'd even sent him back the originals in a sign of some kind of mock chivalric gesture, but it was already too late.

He stared at the city's confusion and saw in it the thousand-piece jigsaw puzzle of his own dilemma. For the hundredth time he tried to analyse, like a balance sheet, the options open to him. He could run. He had funds where no one could reach them – enough to make a start, to begin again. But his family?

Or he could turn himself in, flip, become an informer for the cops and disappear into the other system made for those like him, never to return.

But time was running out.

He sat down and grabbed the mouse then flicked between screens. His old touch had evaded him, but if he could make one big deal and pull it off he could at least meet them on something like equal terms. *I can repay the money, every last cent.*

But the trust, Giancarlo? Can you ever repay our trust?

And how they loved to use their clichés, loved them because they were so true.

Twenty-Five

Rossi was sitting opposite Maroni, who was surveying the paperwork to be forwarded to the magistrate. They had practically caught the student they believed to be responsible for the spate of incendiary attacks on car parks and motorbike stands that had left a trail of destruction but no fatalities. The other fires, however, were still frustrating them – both the Prenestina massacre, which he and Carrara continued to investigate secretly, and the arson attack on Professor Okoli and his family.

Rossi was clutching a ragged copy of *The Post* folded to the local news section. As Maroni studied the report Rossi took another furtive glance. There was a short article about some other sporadic firebombing attempts – molotov cocktails thrown at a social club frequented by Senegalese immigrants and a mosque hit by youths – likely the hastily planned work of a far-right splinter faction. Thankfully none had done any significant damage, but he had also heard how traumatized the victims had been, something that had *not* made the headlines. The *Roman Post* was Torrini's paper, and Torrini had long been a thorn in Rossi's side. He couldn't wait to see Rossi make a false move and if he did it would be front page material.

The Post had also been ratcheting up the hysteria on a regular basis after the Israeli university attack and had fully bought into the anti-immigrant and ICE narratives.

"Well, you got a result there, Rossi," said Maroni looking up over his reading glasses. "I'll give you that, and while we're at it what are you managing to come up with on the other matters?"

"It's slow going, sir, as you know, but patience can bring its rewards." As he continued to read, Maroni's face softened into almost placid tranquility but that didn't mean he had committed himself on Rossi's theorizing about the ideological background. Rossi had already spent some time explaining to his superior how they had laid a trap using some GIS mapping strategies that Carrara had put together, in order to approximate where a possible next attack might come. Profiling had helped too. They had reasoned that the lack of witnesses meant he had been extremely careful and was not a random thrill seeker. He had avoided any areas covered by CCTV, so they had put some covert cameras in a few spots likely to fit the bill.

"But maybe you just got lucky, Rossi. Have you considered that? Putting your surveillance op where you did? Do you ever gamble, by the way?"

"Not anymore," Rossi replied. At least not the gambling Maroni was alluding to. Maroni frowned again.

"In any case, as I said, a result is a result," Maroni continued, leaning back and stifling a yawn, "and it looks good on the percentages." It was getting late and Rossi was also well aware of the ticking clock behind him. "But if this guy really is an anarchist, do you think it's part of any concerted effort or is he just some bedroom crank? I mean he's what," he looked down again at the notes, "twenty-one. A student."

"Says he was making a statement about the petrol economy. Our dependence on oil. The wars waged in the name of the petrodollar. The rights of indigenous peoples. Bit of a mish-mash really."

"And he told you all that?"

"There was stuff in his flat. A thesis of sorts."

"Sounds like a nut if you ask me. You don't think there's any network, do you?"

"He's a *centro sociale* guy. He hangs around with the radical crowd."

"The radical chic too, I wouldn't wonder," said Maroni with an air of evident exasperation. "You know my daughter's gone and got herself one of those hipster-types who goes around on a bike your grandad wouldn't have been seen dead on, and with juggling clubs for God's sake!"

"She'll grow out of it," said Rossi. "Or he will. What are his parents? Bankers?"

"The father's a bloody filthy-rich executive or something, in ItalOil! I'm surprised it wasn't him doing the arson."

Rossi shook his head.

"That would be too much like getting his hands dirty. Leave that to the foot soldiers. But this is no rich kid."

"Well you collared the squirt and that's what counts."

Maroni leaned closer.

"Now, tell me why you won't leave that Prenestina case alone, or is there something you aren't telling me?"

He'd saved the best for last, thought Rossi. Better come clean. A bit. He told Maroni what they'd uncovered, leaving out only what might compromise Tiziana and only alluding to his half ideas concerning Jibril. Maroni heard him out.

"Well no harm in trying, is there," said Maroni. "I'm all for justice being done, Rossi, but don't let it look bad on Lallana. It was his case after all."

Maroni gave him the look which Rossi interpreted as "better not to ask". So Lallana was *raccomandato*, was that it? They were probably fast-tracking him for some ministerial job and didn't want any trouble.

"And," Maroni continued, "I'm also getting a bad feeling about the whole Islamist side of things. Did you see that

Caliphate publication about Italy being the next territorial target?"

"The march on Rome?"

"Looks as if they might be serious about rocking up in our part of the world, like they're doing across Syria and Iraq."

"It depends whether you take it as literal or not. The Koran mentions Rome but it's interpreted in different ways by the scholars. Rome could just be a kind of umbrella term that means the West in general. I think it just fits in well with their propaganda to scare us with the threat of an invasion."

"Well Libya's in our backyard, Rossi. Remember Gheddafi's missile attack on Lampedusa? We could be the next port of call. Now, no one's expecting them to come over in landing craft but what if they target tourist spots? Beaches with kids? They've done it elsewhere, why not here?"

"As far as I see it," said Rossi, "we can plug the holes but it also depends what's going on in the corridors of power. Are we playing a straight hand overseas? What's at stake? What's up for grabs? It's not as if we don't still have a few colonial interests of our own, is it?"

Maroni began to look uneasy.

"Well that's hardly our concern, Rossi. We catch 'em, we stop 'em, we find 'em. End of story. We don't dish out the foreign policy, unless you had forgotten that."

"Of course, sir," said Rossi. *We never get involved. Ever.*

"But it's just like we've run into a brick wall."

Rossi took a sip on his red wine while they waited for the first course to arrive. "But at the same time, I think there could be something behind it all. It was arson. It had to be murder, but why? For money? Drugs? The so-called agent's evaporated and there's no surname for him. The only guy whose name we *have* got looks to have been clean though. So we're back to square one."

137

"You mean Ivan didn't have a record?" said Carrara. "OK, so we've bust a gut trying to find something, but that doesn't prove he was clean. You know as well as I do, he might just have been good, or lucky, or protected, or all three. We can go deeper, if you're convinced there's something in it."

They had already spent days that had become weeks trawling through the minutiae and sifting through half-leads and chasing up rumours and possible contacts only to find themselves left with next to nothing concrete to work on.

"We got his phone records," said Carrara. "We went through his contacts, got the access and read his messages."

Rossi took a longer sip then put down his glass.

"Let's go over it again. He was a petty criminal in Russia, that much we know. Probably enough to get him sent to a gulag over there, but here he won't even get a slap on the wrists."

"That's why they all come here," said Carrara, deliberately provoking his friend. "Get away with murder here, don't they?"

"But seriously, what else can we go on?"

A huge plate of *spaghetti alle vongole* had just been placed before a now very contented-looking Carrara.

"Why does yours always arrive first?" said Rossi as the waitress sailed away without giving him even the outside chance of catching her eye. Carrara was already intent on extracting the succulent molluscs and tossing their stripy shells into the extra plate left for the purpose. Rossi was still thinking as the clam shells clacked against the china one by one.

"I was just thinking about the crank calls, Gigi. Every investigation gets them, right?"

"Of course. But what about them?"

"They're all logged, right?"

Carrara nodded. The time wasters and attention seekers were to cops like hypochondriacs to doctors – blocking the system, distracting the personnel, obstructing the investigation.

"And the letters, the notes, the ones written in hieroglyphics, like the Rosetta Stone, in green biro on the back of a sweet wrapper."

"The tinfoil hat crew?" said Rossi.

"Exactly. Ignored usually, if they're anonymous, but nothing gets chucked, if that's what you're saying."

"In theory, they shouldn't be," said Rossi.

"Yes, then if something outlandish *were* to come out further down the line they could be dug up."

"Right," said Rossi. "And what do you say if we see what there is? Anything's worth a try at this stage."

"For both cases?" said Carrara, swirling another few strands of clam-coated spaghetti into a tight parcel as Rossi's *primo* arrived.

"Better late than never," he said inhaling the unmistakable perfume of *porcini* mushrooms, garlic, and parsley rising from his deep yellow egg *tagliatelle*.

"Worth the wait," said Carrara. "We can get on to it in the morning."

"But *all* the cases," said Rossi. "The bomb, the body, and the fire."

Carrara lowered his fork.

"You don't think they're *all* linked, all three?"

Rossi shrugged. The *porcini* were good. The wine was exquisite. The pasta had been cooked to a perfect *al dente*.

"I don't know," said Rossi, "but I have this thing about threes."

Carrara was making short work of his spaghetti and gave a satisfied smile.

"And first course, second course, and dessert is another holy trinity, excuse the blasphemy. Here's the waitress. What are you going for next?"

As Rossi took up the menu to browse the meat offerings, the TV high up in the corner diverted his attention. The volume was turned down but some of the staff had gathered underneath to watch. Carrara had noticed too.

"What's going on?"

"A shooting," said Rossi as the strapline below unspooled its information. He dropped his knife and fork and motioned to the proprietor to turn it up, showing at the same time his warrant card.

"Looks like university area," said Rossi moving nearer to the screen.

Carrara meanwhile had got out his phone and was motoring ahead with social media and agencies.

A call came in for Rossi.

"OK, OK," he said. "Seen it. Got it," and snapped his phone shut.

"Says here a Professor Bonucci. But, hang on!"

"What?" said Rossi.

"It's been claimed by the *Brigate Rosse!*"

"The what?"

"The *BR*," said Carrara. He began to quote from the news agency website. "A telephone call to *The Post* ... The Red Brigades Proletarian Action have claimed responsibility."

They both knew that the Red Brigades had been defeated and out of action and all their operatives put behind bars some twenty years previously.

"But they don't exist anymore," said Carrara.

"Don't they?" said Rossi, taking a last forkful of his pasta as he simultaneously wriggled into his jacket "Well, it looks like they're back in business. Come on."

Twenty-Six

The body was sprawled across the pavement in a spreading slick of blood just yards from the front door of the apartment block. A bicycle believed to have been his lay on the ground next to him. Carrara and Rossi had to shove their way through the crowds and the police lines holding back a sizeable and growing collection of the curious. They had got there in a matter of minutes but the local police had been alerted first when residents had heard the shots. It had been too late anyway.

"Who's in charge here," said Rossi to the most efficient-looking officer he could find.

"Me, I suppose," he said, introducing himself. "I was first on the scene. We were in the vicinity and heard the shots and when we got here we found this. I called 118 and checked for a pulse but he was already dead."

"Did you identify him?"

The officer nodded.

"His wallet, on the floor with his ID card inside. I thought it might have been a mugging. I radioed in everything."

"Time?"

The officer checked his notes.

"Shots heard at 8.07. We were on the scene about two minutes later."

For Rossi, the priority, as always, was preserving the integrity of the crime scene. The past was crystallized here: what had happened previous to the crime and how it had all played out. He dispatched the available officers in search of material witnesses as more personnel from AT pulled up in unmarked cars. "Anyone who saw anything," said Rossi, "get their particulars and let's try to find some leads. Any vehicles spotted leaving the scene, for starters. Anyone running away," he shouted after them. "And don't let anyone out of these buildings," he added, indicating the three apartment blocks that made up the residential complex.

"How do you think the press got it so fast?" said Carrara as they moved in with care to see the body for themselves before the Forensics team arrived.

"They'll have had an accomplice, probably two or three, watching and ready to send a message. Mission accomplished. They wanted to make the evening news for sure." Rossi was thinking now as he surveyed the scene. Body and head shots, not to the heart as far as he could see but he was stone dead. Twenty minutes after. They would be away, melted into the Roman night.

"I take it they've got blocks up on all the roads out," he said then as he knelt down next to the lifeless body. The slick of blood had stopped spreading now but issued mainly from a neck wound. He'd been shot in the back and in the face several times.

"So, who was he, this Bonucci? What did he do to deserve this?" said Carrara conscious of the past tense he now had to employ.

Rossi shook his head. It was like the bad old days again.

No one inside the building had been expecting him. No one had come yet to mourn, there were no tears or keening, hands raised to heaven, or tearing of clothes. He'd seen that in his day. Carrara would have seen it too during anti-mafia in the deep south, in Calabria and the Neapolitan hinterlands.

The victim's house keys were inches away from his outstretched right hand.

"Any family we know of?" Rossi asked.

Now it was Carrara's turn to reply wordlessly in the negative before adding,

"I heard the locals say they'd seen him come and go. Said they thought he lived alone."

Twenty-Seven

Rossi was sitting opposite Iannelli in the apartment on Via Merulana, with tumblers of whisky and a jug of iced water the only other props on the table apart from books.

"Well aren't you the lucky one," said Rossi. "Fancy being the man given the privilege of receiving the first declaration of the Red Brigades, version 2.0."

The call from Iannelli which had brought him there had come in while Carrara and himself were at the *Questura* trying to piece together the jagged edges of the new development now presenting itself to them.

In times past, in such cases, a journalist would have had to go to a predetermined drop off in a railway station and been directed towards a left luggage locker or an isolated waste paper basket, to retrieve an envelope. This time the newspaper had received an e-mail from an untraceable server.

"Well, for a start," began Iannelli, "it's a bloody world record my being in the same place for more than a few weeks, though I rather fancy that might now be about to change. What with my ever increasing fame, or notoriety. You know they actually sent it to Iovine, but he decided I deserved the scoop. Generous of him, wasn't it?"

"Not sure they'll like that approach to protocol," said Rossi. "But it depends how you look at things. At least now you may be more than a footnote in history."

"That too depends on how 'things' play out. I mean do you think we're heading for another twenty years of low-level civil war and Marxist-Leninist revolutionary terrorism?"

"That's a bit like saying should I bother taking a photograph of my street even though it isn't actually very interesting. In twenty years' time you'll regret not having done it. Any moment could be the beginning of history."

"At least it might take the pressure off me."

"Until they start hitting journalists again," Rossi reminded him.

"Well, let's hope it doesn't come to that."

Iannelli had printed out the declaration which, true to the form of the old BR, combined an analysis of Byzantine complexity of the current sociopolitical moment with a meticulous explanation of the reasoning behind their decision to embrace the armed struggle and sentence to death an academic with a background in labour law liberalization and drafting laws tailored to certain politicians' personal needs.

"I thought I'd tell you first, anyway. Pleased?" said Iannelli continuing to leaf through the pages hanging from his hand.

"Well, it's nice to get a peek before it goes to the counterterrorism boys. Not that they would alter it for the public consumption. All this revolutionary stuff about taking the power back and stopping transnational big business usurping national sovereignty."

"Dread to think."

"So where do you see it heading?" said Rossi, reaching out to take the declaration with its unmistakable, elongated five-point star crowning the first page of text. "We've got them coming at us from all angles now. Islamist, Marxist – who the devil's next?"

"Well, you've got the energy summit at the UN next month,"

145

said Iannelli. "That's high profile. Somebody might like to put something in that shop window."

Rossi handed the papers back and then rubbed his own face. He'd been burning the midnight oil again and now, sitting there with Iannelli, there was something almost monastic about their twin obsessions. Men dedicated to a cause at the exclusion of almost everything else. They had given themselves all sorts of avenues to explore but this bombshell had really sent things flying. He had also let things slip again with Yana since she had moved back into her own place. He knew he had promised some weeks before to set aside a weekend for them both, but the way events were unfolding, it was going to take some sort of miracle. He didn't know how far it could bend before something would snap.

"It's going to be all shoulders to the wheel now for sure," said Rossi, "but I don't see anyone breaking cover for a big one, at least not now when the world's watching. They'll hit when we least expect it or where we haven't massed our forces. At which point," he continued, getting to his feet, "the inspector realized he'd better be catching up with his various lines of enquiry."

As he stood up, a book on the floor under the far corner of the chaise longue caught his eye.

"*Petrolio*," said Rossi.

Iannelli glanced askance and nodded.

"Pasolini's unfinished masterpiece."

Rossi bent down to pick up the weighty volume. Although never finished, it still came to some five hundred pages of notes and work in progress.

"Could have been the great Italian novel," said Rossi. "Our *Ulysses*. What do you make of it?"

"Well, they reckon he was onto something and not just at the artistic level."

Rossi was flicking through the work. There were numerous Post-its and coloured markers at key points. That was Iannelli. No surprises there.

"Like he'd hit the nail on the head?" said Rossi. "This is what we've really become or what we were going to become."

"Prophetic even," said Iannelli. "He saw it all and then knew how to articulate it."

Rossi read a bookmarked passage. It spoke of a postwar petit bourgeoisie that instead of being liberated by newfound affluence had become instead a kind of enslaved homogenized mass, shaped by desires and frustrations and destined for existential oblivion.

"So is that why he was killed?" said Rossi. "So he *couldn't* finish it?"

Iannelli raised his hands in a sign of exasperation while giving a simultaneous conditional confirmation of the probable truth of Rossi's observation.

"He was the one person able to cut this society open and then put it on display and at the same time reach a pretty broad audience. Think about it. Why was Mattei killed when he was? Is it an accident when our leading oil entrepreneur's plane goes down just when he's on the verge of making Italy independent of the USA in energy terms and free to get our oil from whoever we want? He was going to throw off the shackles of postwar dependency on the States. You tell me. And you tell me where we've got to today, fifty years later."

Rossi closed the book and left it down on the corner of the chaise.

"And now," he said. "Where does all this leave us?"

"What?" said Iannelli, picking up the declaration again. "This?"

"Among other things."

"Well, the ground is fertile, shall we say. There are plenty of people out there, especially the young, who just aren't seeing the fruit of their labours. And as economic realities begin to bite harder they all tighten their grip. And all this austerity," he added, getting up now and pacing about. "All this tighten your belts bullshit. It's always the same ones who have to stump up and go without."

"And we end up laying the blame where they tell us to lay it."

"Exactly. First it was the communists – by which I mean social democrats – and now it's the foreigners taking your jobs, then the Muslims, the Travellers and the Roma, and always our friends the Jews."

"The Jews?"

"They always get a kicking when the far-right gets going, sure," said Iannelli. "Especially if they're supposed to be in cahoots with the banks."

"But not the Church? Leave them out of this?"

Iannelli smiled wryly.

"They're always ready to step in. Always. And they can take a hammering, but they'll give as good as they get."

Twenty-Eight

Olivia had been delighted that Jibril was making changes, making waves, and that it was all paying off. She had thrown her arms around him and hugged him with delight. He had been more than a little embarrassed, playing it down and saying that it was only a beginning, that he had other dreams, other plans.

"But that means you can get any job now with a *permesso di soggiorno*. You are free to do what you want."

"Until it expires and then I must go to renew it again like everyone else, queuing up at six in the morning to get an appointment, if I'm lucky, and then paying too for the privilege."

"But all that is in the future," she had said. "Forget about it for now. Live for this moment and we will cross that other bridge when we find it."

We. She had said it. So, did she already envisage that this was going somewhere? Or was it still the collective we of friendship and solidarity? He suspected both in actual fact. She was driven by the urge to do good and to be of use to others and to society. But she was also sensual. He had felt that from the moment they had met in the classroom. For now that was certainly not a problem or him. In fact, it could all fit together very well. He refused to let himself be drawn too much either way. The attraction was real but it was always part of the plan.

He was aware that he had rehearsed his reactions well but experience had shown him what the others had had to go through, were *prepared* to put up with, in order to get that prized piece of paper. The document that said that you weren't unwanted rubbish to be swept back to where you came from. His *permesso*, of course, was a skilfully produced fake. In counterfeiting terms, it was an easy enough document to duplicate, as was his identity card. Careful scrutiny would reveal that but they would give him the time he needed to bring things to fruition. He had seen the bigger picture all right and was growing ever more sure about the importance of striking a blow.

Now as he sat in the flat, the safe house, and began to outline his intelligence strategy, the others listened. He had won them over with his calm authority. He had slowed them down, told them that time was on their side. The longer they kept the infidels waiting the more they would fear what might befall them. Now, with their contacts in the cleaning and care agencies and the cooperatives, they were spreading their net wide and quickly. It was ideal. They and their many contacts within the community were working as domestic servants and everyone could find someone who had access to the homes of the rich or powerful. It was a capillary network and one that required a certain kind of person: either willing, corruptible, needy, or all three.

And as trust grew, so they fanned out even wider. One contact spawned another as like found like. They could listen, observe, collate, collect and he would analyse everything, be it a phone conversation, a letter, the contents of a dressing-table drawer. Word of mouth, handwritten notes passed to intermediaries who would have no knowledge of their final destination, even if caught, questioned, even if tortured. Then they could winnow down the harvest to the essential. So far, in spite of all the pain that never left him, he couldn't believe his luck.

Twenty-Nine

"Well, I'm sure I hardly need to tell you I thought we'd seen the back of all this," said Maroni as he pondered the case notes that had been put before him.

"What do you two make of the briefings then?" he said, addressing first Rossi and Carrara who were with him, and others of the select group of operatives on special secondment from the RSCS, and who were being pulled now in all directions by circumstances which, if not beyond their control, almost defied even their belief. "There can be no question of there being a *coordinated* approach. These groups have nothing in common, surely."

"You mean other than their bloodlust and ideological rigidity?" said Katia.

"Well they're hardly pooling their resources or their intelligence or anything as outlandish as that, are they?" said Maroni, his face betraying his puzzlement.

"One man's trouble is another's opportunity," said Rossi. "Either that or the moment is ripe, shall we say, in more ways than one, and for more than one current of political thinking."

"You call that thinking, do you?" blurted Maroni. "Shooting an innocent man parking his bicycle? A university professor!"

"I meant the thought which goes into constructing the justification for the act," said Rossi.

"What more have we got?" he said turning then to Katia, who he had asked to get hold of the latest information on the gun used. He also wanted to put her through her paces in front of the boss. "Any definite form on the weapon?"

"Almost certainly a Smith & Wesson revolver, rather on the old side, WWII issue, but that didn't have any bearing on the outcome, as it were. So, well maintained. And modified ammunition. Soft tops, hunting type. Pretty much guaranteed to be fatal, even without hitting vital organs, if there's any delay in stemming the bleeding. We got some fragments. Those things deform on contact and rip the shit out of anything in their way leaving a hole you could put your fist in. So, it didn't have to be any ace marksman."

"At least you know those things'll never jam," said Rossi not expecting quite so much detail. He had no idea she was an arms expert too. "And with a sitting target, you've got all the time in the world."

Katia flicked through the printouts she had in front of her. "Ballistics haven't come in yet but I had a look around myself – I have a little experience there. Provisionally they're saying it may have been used in other shootings, some of which, from the Seventies and Eighties, remain unsolved."

She waited a moment for a reaction. Maroni was suitably impressed. Rossi appeared less comfortable.

"Well," said Rossi,. "knocking up some of the familiar faces through the old lines of communication is a definite starter. If someone's dusting off their gear, are they coming back into the game themselves or passing on the flame?"

There was a buzz on his phone. He gave it a discreet glance. Gab. Finally. He needed a breakthrough badly.

Let me know what you want me to do.

Rossi nudged Carrara.

"Well, why don't we get to work on some of these characters

with their heads still stuck in the old revolutionary Marxist days?" said Rossi, hoping to get the proceedings adjourned before Katia had upstaged them on every front. "Where can we get the files?"

"All the relevant files are now on the integrated databases. So, it shouldn't be too much of a hassle. Then it's just a case of cross-checking info and knocking on doors and seeing what they're doing these days. If they've kept their IDs up to date, of course. Or not moved out of Rome. Some characters are already under light surveillance but they're not considered viable threats. At least that's the intelligence I get fed. But see what you can come up with. Among your myriad other duties."

There were knowing looks and nods around the table. Word got round when Rossi was juggling more than one line of enquiry or stepping on other people's toes.

"There was just one thing," said Rossi raising his pen.

"I was wondering if I might take a trip down to the university again, the CCTV."

Maroni let out a sigh of contained frustration.

"You've seen it, haven't you? We all did. They isolated the guy with the hood making a quick getaway. Granted, it could have been anyone or anything. You can take another look at those, if you want more work to do."

"Well, no. I had another idea in mind," said Rossi. "What if someone went back to the scene of the crime? Maybe recently, in the past week or two."

"You think they'd be that stupid? You think lightning strikes twice when international terrorism is involved?"

"Well," said Katia, "they hit the World Trade Centre twice, didn't they? The first one was in 1993."

"And then waited eight years," countered Maroni.

"It's a hunch," said Rossi. "I'll do it in my own time."

"I can get you the permission, I suppose," said Maroni, "Or just ɔ there and say you're investigating a traffic violation or an assault

153

on the Lungotevere or something. I don't see it being a problem," he added, as he began to stack his papers and cast a concluding glance around the table.

"Everyone's got something to be getting on with then, I don't doubt," he said. "Just keep me in the loop."

Rossi allowed himself a half-smile as they filed out of the conference room. Carrara had already begun walking in the direction of the archive.

"Where are you going?" said Rossi.

"To get started on the database," he replied with a look of mild consternation.

"Sod that," said Rossi. "We're going to do some real work. Gab's waiting. We're going to see if there's anything they didn't want us to see."

The university receptionist had just come off the phone again.

"You can ring through directly to Maresciallo Maroni of the RSCS if you want," said Rossi, leaning in close to the window separating them. "Or, if you like, I could call him on his mobile while he's in his meeting with the minister, but I don't think anyone will be very pleased about that."

"One moment," she replied looking flustered now and failing once more in her attempts to find anyone in the right offices answering their phones.

"The key's just there," said Carrara, pointing to a cupboard, remembering from his last visit where the CCTV recording equipment was located. "We'll be in and out in ten minutes. You've seen my badge."

The receptionist put the phone down and then, reaching first for her cigarettes, opened the key cupboard and unhooked the relevant bunch.

"This way," she said as she emerged from behind the glass-screened booth and then descended a short staircase into th basement.

She identified the right key and opened an anonymous white door. She found a smaller key then.

"This one opens the cabinet. If I'm not back in ten minutes," she said, holding it up, "lock the door and bring them back. I'll try security again."

Rossi smiled as Gab produced his laptop and a jumble of accessories and set to work.

"OK," said Rossi. "We're one up here. I wasn't planning on getting access like this. I thought we'd have to get round the head of security first, so I suggest we make hay while the sun shines."

"OK," replied Gab as he hooked up to the system and began tapping away at the keyboard. "It's all on the hard drive. I did my homework on this model. Here's real-time images, the last twenty-four hours."

"They're supposed to delete anything after twenty-four hours unless there's a good reason to keep it," said Carrara. "Like a reported crime. In that case they can keep it indefinitely or until the case closes."

"Which, in my experience, is synonymous with indefinitely," quipped Rossi.

"And then if you want the last seven days' images, you just go through *here*, if they haven't been deleted," said Gab, revealing new worlds of images with lightning-fast finger work.

"Forget about that," said Rossi. "I want the day of the bombing. How many days is that?"

"About thirty-five days ago," said Carrara. "But it could have been deleted, copied or something."

"Nothing's deleted," said Gab, "if you know where to look. Might take me a bit, though."

"Can you do it before she comes back with security?"

"I'll give it a go."

He began typing away again, scrolling through data logs and code. He stopped, scratched his head, then resumed as before.

"What was the *exact* date," he said.

Rossi whipped out his notebook. "August 10th. Late morning."
More tapping, typing followed.

"Someone's coming," said Carrara.

"Stall them!" said Rossi. "Think of something."

Carrara leapt up the steps two at a time. Rossi and Gab heard Carrara's muffled tones.

"Good morning," he said. "Inspector Luigi Carrara, RSCS. I was just wondering, is there another camera at the rear of the building?"

There was a monotone response.

"Is it also connected to this recorder? Is there a remote data collection unit too? There should be. This is a sensitive security area."

The next reply was more curt and the pleasantries brief as two pairs of footsteps then began to draw nearer.

"Nearly there?" said Rossi, looking over Gab's shoulder.

"One sec, I think and ..."

A progress bar was filling but not fast enough for Rossi's liking.

"70%, 73%, 80% ..."

"Just downloading everything onto an external. Nearly there. Got it."

He disconnected the drive and slipped it into Rossi's pocket and then began scrolling in a leisurely way through the time-lapse images of the smoking students and traffic on the Lungotevere.

"So, yesterday was it you wanted, Inspector?"

"Allow me," came the reply as a burly, suited security operative strode into the tiny room.

"Maroni, RSCS," came the reply from over his shoulder. It was the receptionist. "Just had him on the phone. His meeting with the minister must have been postponed," she said with more than a hint of dry irony. "But he's faxing through authorization now."

"And what crime were you investigating, exactly," the security operative cut in.

156

"I think we have seen all we need," said Rossi with a smile. "It was pretty straightforward."

Rossi and Carrara were heading back to the *Questura* and the day job.

"Makes you wonder though, doesn't it?" said Carrara as he guided the Alfa through another tight squeeze on a double-parked street.

"Almost tempted to get out and fine the lot of them," said Rossi surveying more burgeoning chaos. A seriously dressed middle-aged man who couldn't get out of his parking space leant through the window onto his horn until the miscreant parker blocking him in might return. Rossi turned back to Carrara. "What was that you said?"

"It makes you wonder whether that was just a one-off at the university or something concerted, meant to get bigger."

"Well they picked up a guy at Piazza Re di Roma this morning with a portable arsenal in the boot of his car. Grenades, handguns, AK47s. So far he's refused to divulge."

"What do you make of it? Eastern European? Gangs?"

"No, Italian as you or me. I fancy he's had an order come in for hardware and knows where to get it. It'll be Bosnian stuff, ex-Yugoslavia."

"Easiest way in," said Carrara, getting some speed up now as he hit the Via Cristoforo Colombo. "Straight across the border at Trieste, probably in a few discreet cars with reinforced suspension for the weight."

"But who's buying?" said Rossi. "And if he won't talk. He probably doesn't even know."

"Well, it's got to be for something. What about the narcos?"

Rossi nodded.

"Could be. Could be any of them, but it doesn't bring us any nearer."

He fondled the hard drive in his pocket. Gab had left it with hem promising to catch up later.

"What can we do with this?" he said.

"I can take a look if you like," said Carrara. "I'll convert it into a user-friendly format," he said with the hint of a smirk.

"I'm making great strides, I'll have you know," said Rossi, who had his phone out.

"The good lady?" said Carrara.

"Mmm," said Rossi. "Says we need to have *a bit of a talk*."

"Sounds *a bit* ominous."

"Nah!" said Rossi, shoving it back into his pocket and toying then with the hard disk. "The usual story. I've not been around much since all this got kind of interesting."

"Take a night off," said Carrara. "Let me go to work on the footage, and I can get some names out of the files and then tomorrow we head out for a chat with the ex-*brigatistas* and die-hard Maoist revolutionaries. Probably all computer programmers and web designers now."

Rossi reached for his phone again. The thing was he enjoyed it. He liked not having a minute, having to shuttle between the office and crime scenes and trying to come up with answers to questions that he was still trying to formulate himself. He wanted to get back on the Prenestina fire too. There were too many loose ends flapping away in some wind of his own imagining. The Ivan story, the almost esoteric tale about the priest they had heard from Nurse Rinaldi. Then there was the chance meeting with Tiziana and the link with Iannelli that had started it all.

There weren't many who approached things like Rossi did. It was as if he were producing something resembling a work of art and, as such, taking the path well travelled for him was an indication of predictability and thus of defeat. Granted, it wasn't that he could always pull it off, but if he stuck at it, if he believed in it, if he could see something coming together, he thought there might be a moment where a crack might open, a key might fall into his hands. And he didn't want to miss that moment.

"So?" said Carrara as he stopped to park the car outside the

Questura. "Are you coming in with me or going to use that sophisticated communication device to get your personal life back on track?"

"What about yours?"

"I'm a married man, with kids. It's different. She knows I'm a second stringer on these operations. She wouldn't have married me otherwise. Besides, I gave up on the stake-outs precisely for that reason."

"So, it was a condition?"

"It wouldn't have been possible any other way. We both knew. And we knew it was worth it."

"OK," said Rossi, "I'll leave it in your hands for now and take a breather."

"Might be productive," said Carrara. "Where shall I drop you?"

"Think I'll have a walk," said Rossi, handing over the hard drive. "It's a wonderful day, isn't it?"

He was about to get out of the car when he stopped. "I've just realized we have made a major faux pas."

"What?"

"Jibril, the mortuary. CCTV."

"We didn't check it, did we? But wasn't it too far back?" said Carrara seeing that Rossi was kicking himself.

"Gab reckons you can find it, if you know where to look."

"But this is not something we can ask Maroni about it, is it? He's not fully in the picture on this."

Rossi was thinking.

"Get on to Tiziana, if you can," he said. "See what she says. She'll play ball, if you ask me. It's a long shot but why not try."

"OK," said Carrara.

"At least we might have a face to go on."

Thirty

Rossi was sitting back and enjoying the afterglow of good food while pondering another glass of well-chilled *Falanghina*.

"Did you notice the new stuff I got for the lounge?" said Yana as she took another strawberry from the bowl between them. The flat was clean and ordered and had the kind of equilibrium of colour, proportion and style which Rossi admired but could never imagine for himself.

"The cushions," she said, indicating the furnishings, but Rossi's thoughts had returned elsewhere, even if he knew it was a miracle he had actually sat down and had a proper meal with her for the first time in about two weeks. He turned around to look again.

"Nice," he said, trying to distinguish between old and new.

"So," she said then. "Tomorrow?"

Rossi leaned over to take a last strawberry for himself. *Tomorrow?*

"Are we going to go somewhere, stay the night maybe, before the bad weather comes? September's practically still summer."

"Yes," said Rossi. "But *this* weekend?"

"What's wrong with this weekend? I'm taking a few days off, and I thought we could do something together."

Rossi drained his glass. Soon be time to move back to the red wine with autumn coming. He pictured some mountain retreat. A glass of *Montepulciano*. It wasn't that the idea of a break didn't appeal to him. But he wanted to make another push. He realized they might have slipped up with Tiziana and the CCTV, and now they had the footage from the university, time was of the essence as there was every chance that they had already been deleted after the statutory seven days.

"Michael?"

Rossi looked up.

"Michael. I've met someone else."

"Have you?" he said. Her words could just as well have been "Michael, would you like more wine?"

"No. Of course not. But if I had? Would you notice? Or would it make things easier for you?"

Rossi looked at Yana across the empty plates, the knives and forks arranged in the manner which, had they been in a restaurant, signalled that her plate could now be taken away. She had put on a little weight, but in a good way. The days spent in the hospital were long gone. He would have liked to have been able to think about nothing else but her, yet he knew that was not possible. Not now.

"You know I was always there for you, then," he said. "In the hospital."

"And now? I also need you now, Michael. It's hard now too, you know. Normal life is hard. I need to see you more often. I need to know you care about me in normal life too. Not just when I become a part of the case."

There was a buzz from the hallway, where he had left his phone out of harm's way. It would be Carrara. He was able to come in and out of a case. He was full-on when there was work to do but he could separate things. But Rossi knew he couldn't. The phone stopped. He was obsessing about it. It made his head hurt.

"We may not have much normal life ever again," he began,

"if we allow them to do what they want to do, to divide us. To sow hatred. If they drag us back to the old days, days you never saw, we can say goodbye to anything like normality. And it will be worse than then. It could be like nothing we've ever seen before."

"And it's all down to you to stop it happening?"

"I can't *let* it happen," he said.

The phone began to buzz again.

"Answer it then," she said. "Answer it, Michael. Save the world, Inspector Rossi. Then come back for me if you want, if I'm still around."

She stalked off to the living room and turned on the television. Rossi watched her through the hatch knowing – *or believing* he knew – what thoughts were going through her head: that there was the usual mindless rubbish and films diluted to meaninglessness by the constant interruption of streams of advertising. So, this was the normality worth fighting for, was it? He wondered to himself. Wasn't it fucked whatever way you looked at it? All of their lives. In this country. Buy this, buy that. Get the perfect body. Smile the perfect smile. But nobody knows their neighbour. So maybe he was right. Better to dedicate yourself to a noble cause and stick with it.

She flicked over the channels. Rolling news. Rossi walked in and sat down next to her. He hadn't answered the phone.

"Come on," he said. "Looks like there's nothing on."

He reached out to take her hand and pulled her up off the couch. He reached his arms around her waist, then, in a sign of detente in a cold war that he had allowed to escalate, "Let's go to bed."

The room was almost completely illuminated now. The nun who had made the discovery was sitting in a chair in the hallway of the residential wing. Someone had given her a cognac to counter the effects of shock. They, meanwhile, were inside, with the door locked behind them, where the body lay face down on the floor. A knife was protruding from beneath the right scapula. His throat had been cut and blood had spread freely over the terracotta tiles and into the edges of the nearby tasselled rugs. One side of the victim's face was just visible but slightly brown now with drying blood. Patches of pallid and contorted skin showed through, testimony to the violence of his death. There had clearly been something of a struggle, books and ornaments tossed here and there.

"We can't!" hissed the younger of the two priests standing over the body. The voice of the older priest was low and expressed quiet authority.

"We have to."

"Why?"

"Didn't you read it? Don't you understand?" he said, holding up the letter in the other's face. "'In the event of my violent death …' We have orders.The police will be on their way as soon as I call. There is no time. They will ask questions about why we delayed. We can do nothing for him but this. Ours is not to question orders!"

The older priest went to the drawer. It was unlocked. He took from it a hunting knife in a worn leather scabbard, razor sharp, and turned to his accomplice, thrusting the handle of the knife towards him.

"Do it!"

"I can't!"

The older priest looked at him for a moment. In his youth he had eviscerated animals more times than he could care to remember with knives like this one, in the mountains. In Calabria, where hunting was second nature and, for many, often a means to survival. He knew those who had joined with the *n'drangheta* when they were still only boys, initiated by their own families into its obscure and secret rituals. Others had become bandits and kidnappers, out of necessity. They too had used their hunter's skills to quickly and efficiently remove a section of finger, an ear, a nose even, which could then be sent to the victim's family. It was proof of their captivity; it was the essential catalyst to effect the payment of a ransom.

And here he was, the intellectual, the bright hope of his family who had gone up to Rome and risen through the ranks of ordinary priesthood. He knew the rites of Rome, had sworn allegiance to God and his Church, but he had slipped inexorably towards mammon. His duties, his priorities had been bound more and more to this world. His flock now amounted to accounts and portfolios, and the wolves circling it were any of his enemies – the state, journalists, and some paid assassin, most probably, intent on exposing them and inflicting mortal damage. He had been variously a custodian of secrets, a confidante, an adviser. Now he was a fixer, a butcher, cleaning up when necessary where others had fouled the nest, ensuring that the volatile truth might not emerge.

"Give it to me!" he growled.

He took the knife. He was back again in the mountains and, standing over the lifeless body, he yanked up his sleeves past the elbow and then knelt down to set to work, cutting and slicing into the grey, pliant flesh.

"Bring a large plastic bag and towels from the bathroom. Quickly!"

He continued the butchery, the soft kissing sounds of ripping skin and gristle the only accompaniment before he began to dispose of the body parts. He made a cursory attempt to mop up the blood and then concluded by thrusting everything into the carrier bag. He made for the en suite bathroom where he scrubbed his hands with near violence under the scalding water. He removed any traces of red he could see from the bathroom's tiles and snow-white fittings with another towel and threw it too into the bag.

"It's done," he said. Sweat was dripping from his brow. "We must bury all this evidence, first, in the grounds, deep as possible, then burn it when we can. Come with me. And not a word to a living soul," he added. "If you don't wish to meet with a similar end, then this goes with you to the grave. It was an order and orders must be obeyed."

The younger priest nodded in abject abeyance. His life had now been irrevocably changed. He had not been able to look at what the priest had done but he'd heard him and the knife doing their work.

"We saw nothing," said the older priest. "We say only that we surveyed the scene. The sister will be in a state of shock. She was confused and ran straight from the room. Give her more cognac and she'll say what we tell her to say. You are sure no one else saw the body before you came?"

The younger priest nodded.

"Yes. I came straight down from my room."

"Go to speak with her now. Tell her he's been mutilated. He has had the last rights of his Holy Mother the Church. She can thank Christ she didn't see what they did to him."

Yana opened one eye to see light seeping through the shutters. It was morning but how early she didn't know. She reached out a hand and found the bed was empty on Michael's side but still warm. She turned over and glanced at the clock. It was nearly 6 a.m. There were splashing sounds coming from the bathroom. The flush. Then the door opened and Michael walked the few steps down the corridor and back into the bedroom. She could smell the aroma of coffee from him now. He had breakfasted early. He was fully clothed and ready to leave. He sat down on the bed next to her. The night together had been blissful, carefree, timeless and they had fallen asleep where they had collapsed. Now, in the half-light she could see that all that was a memory;

a happy memory, one to sustain them again, at least for a while. His expression was grave.

"Just got a call," he said, as if minimizing its importance. "They think that maybe it's all starting up again. The Islamist thing. They've murdered a priest."

Thirty-One

"Maroni wants to see us later," said Carrara. "He's not in Rome but everything is to go back to him as and when it emerges."

"But for now we try to keep a lid on it?" said Rossi.

"A lid?" said Carrara. "Have you seen how many hacks are outside already?"

"Well, we make it generic, for as long as we can. It's homicide but we're here because of you-know-what and we don't want them to know. Not yet."

"We don't know the motive yet."

"Well anything that *could* be Islamist, we've got to play it down until we plan our next move."

"There's even talk of it being Satanic."

Just to make things a little more interesting, thought Rossi.

"Come on," he said, clearing a path through the various groups of officers who had crowded into the monastery's ground floor.

"A retired Belgian priest. Expert in canon law. Father Joaquim Brell."

The pathologist, Lula, was concluding initial crime scene analyses. She snapped off her latex gloves to shake Rossi's hand.

"We meet again, Inspector."

"And in eerily similar circumstances. What have you got?"

"Suppose you'll want time of death?"

"It could help."

"Yesterday evening, or night, early hours maybe. But late, probably."

Rossi turned to Carrara.

"We got the call in the morning, about six, right?"

Carrara nodded confirmation.

"A nun said she'd heard some sounds, and when she got up she noticed the door open and a light on. She went to check and made the gruesome discovery."

"And what time was that?" said Rossi. Carrara consulted his notes. "She says 'about five', but she's in shock. The abbot who's in charge here says she was rambling, hysterical. She might have averted a massacre, who knows. Remember the Italian sailors who had their throats cut in Algeria?"

Rossi did remember. The Lucina massacre. 1994. Claimed by Islamist militants, while others saw the hand of the Algerian secret services behind an op to discredit the official Islamic opposition to the ruling dictatorship.

"Did she get a good look at the corpse? She assumed he was dead, I take it?"

"She saw the blood, the knife and ran straight out."

"But that leaves an hour," said Rossi. "Did she call?"

"No," said Carrara, "A Father Rénard. Also Belgian."

"Do you reckon they had trouble finding our phone number?" quipped the pathologist. "Or did they think he might come round if he got a bit of fresh air, with a knife sticking out of his back?"

Rossi was rubbing his chin.

"Church murders. They like to keep these things under wraps. Remember the Swiss Guards? But this isn't extraterritorial. They have to call us."

"So they hesitated?" said Carrara. "For a *reason*?"

"Or something delayed them," said Rossi. "If the sister's story is as she said."

He turned to the pathologist.

"Is there anything else, *Dottoressa*? The mutilation for example. They actually removed his face?"

She nodded. "Afraid so. Disfigurement would be the word. Post-mortem, of course."

"Why 'of course'?" said Rossi. "Have you ever seen what narcos and Mafiosi are capable of, to get a confession or for kicks?"

"Not here though," said Lula. She was the youngest pathologist Rossi had ever worked with but he had complete confidence in her despite her tendency to play the odd game of cat and mouse. "There would have been screaming."

"Right," said Rossi. "And someone would have heard it. Assuming the nun's good for her word."

A point to Lula then, thought Rossi. *Fair enough.*

"You don't think it's Satanic? A sect or something?" said Carrara.

Rossi shook his head but without any great conviction. The truth was he didn't quite know what to make of it. He moved away from where the Forensics team were using an array of solvents in their attempts to glean more evidence from the scene. The smell was familiar and characteristic but he thought there was something else.

"Do you smell that, Gigi?" he said, bending down to inspect a rug and the bottom of a drape. Still slightly damp, they appeared to have been doused with a volatile substance, possibly alcohol. Possibly an accelerant.

Carrara looked at Rossi. They each knew what the other was thinking. More of the same? Rossi stood up again.

"How did they get in? Assuming they had to break in. We'll start with the most likely hypothesis."

"A side door forced," said Carrara. "They'll have scaled the wall into the gardens. There's no security. No cameras at the rear. Only one on the intercom at the front."

"So they had an idea of the layout. Anything missing from room?"

"Some drawers were rifled but we have no inventory – there was some ecclesiastical paraphernalia – scapulae, icons, mass cards, and some money."

Rossi looked about the apartment. There were a few tasteful, well-framed paintings distributed judiciously across each of the walls. A couple of watercolours but mainly oils.

Rossi moved over to the far side of the room.

"Something hung here once," he said indicating a theoretical rectangular space on the wall. "You can see there's a gap, and here – these holes. These were for the supports, brackets of some description."

He looked down at the floor and wiped a finger along the tiles. Masonry dust. Somebody had been in a hurry.

"But if it was there, it hadn't been hanging for very long. There's no sign of a shadow. It's just a hunch but it might be worth asking if anyone can at least account for a painting being moved recently or even going missing."

"An art thief?" said Lula enjoying the chance to go beyond her normal brief with Rossi.

"I'm afraid we're getting a bit of a brick wall of silence here," said Carrara. "Not to mention the language barriers. Either French, or Belgian, or Filipino, or very old and not too many teeth."

"And the guy who reported it?"

"Rénard?" said Carrara. "The most coherent so far. He disputes the sister's five o'clock theory. Says the clock in the room was slow. They had noticed the other day but it required a technician to look at the mechanism."

"And is it slow?" said Rossi.

"It would appear to be running fifteen to twenty minutes slow, yes."

"Hardly significant, is it? And had they called the technician? I suspect not yet."

"No."

"These clocks can be notoriously unpredictable," said the pathologist. "We have one in the country."

"We?" said Rossi.

"My father and I. You should pay us a visit some time when we're not working."

Rossi tried not to look overly interested in the proposal, moving on through the litany of checks and steps to take.

"Any fibres?" he asked, hauling his attention away from the young pathologist even if she presented a more than pleasing alternative to the business in hand.

"Lots. His and many others."

"Prints, Gigi?"

The Forensic team were still scanning with their various ultraviolet, infrared lights, and metal detectors.

"Again, plenty. But none on the weapon so far, I'm afraid."

"Seems there were a lot of visitors," said Rossi.

"Care workers and social assistants, cleaners and the like," said Carrara. "So a few interviews to do there."

"Get on to them, ASAP," said Rossi. "I want a statement from everyone and anyone who's set foot in here in the last six months at least."

Carrara gave a nod and stopped a passing uniform. Rossi was still surveying the room. The crime scene spoke. That was the golden rule. It could immortalize the very moment of the crime, if treated with the utmost care.

"How long had he been living here, Gigi? He was retired, wasn't he?"

"According to Father Rénard, over a year."

Carrara had been busy again.

"Compare the statements as and when you get them," said Rossi. "Memory can be deceptive, can't it?"

"You mean when there's a murder?" said the pathologist. "The ˙hock."

"Yes, or when you want to forget about the past, or want the past to be forgotten," said Rossi.

He led Carrara away, leaving the pathologist to collect up her things.

"Did you get a chance to have a look at the university images?" said Rossi. "Even if it has been kind of overtaken by this."

"Had a quick look but there's nothing of particular interest, as far as I can see. Oh, and I've been getting some names of *brigatiste*, *ex-brigatiste*. I've put it all into easily accessible form for you. Browse it at your leisure," he said and handed Rossi a key drive.

Rossi slipped it into his pocket.

"So, where next?"

"You're not so sure about this guy, are you?" said Carrara, knowing when Rossi felt a sliver of doubt, even in the most seemingly clear-cut cases. They were standing in a doorway and Rossi was looking back at the scene.

"You tell me why there was up to an hour's delay. Last rights? First aid? Look at him!"

"The scandal?" said Carrara. "The bad PR? Or maybe they panicked."

Rossi stopped another officer who was trying to squeeze past unnoticed.

"What's the most discreet way out of here?" he asked.

The uniform led Rossi and Carrara back where he had come from, through the narrow wood-panelled corridors and through a side door into the garden and the cloisters. A moss-embroidered marble fountain was at its centre, the water trickling down the green tendrils.

"A good spot for thinking," said Rossi.

At an intersection of the quadrangle there was a heavy wooden door. An elderly retainer sat on a chair next to it and rose to his feet at their approach. He turned a large old-world key in the iron lock, and Rossi and Carrara emerged into a deserted cobbled side street.

"So many places in Rome I still haven't seen," said Rossi. "In all these years. It's inexhaustible."

Carrara nodded.

"How about some breakfast?" said Rossi.

It was nearly ten o'clock and his very early *colazione* had been meagre. He didn't like crime scenes on a full stomach. Just coffee to get him moving. Now, with the worst out of the way, he felt something like hunger again.

***

They turned onto Via Saturnia. There was a bar with flimsy aluminium chairs and tables outside.

"Too early I suppose," said Rossi. Eyeing the menu.

"Coffee it is then?"

"And *cornetti*."

"The diet?"

"Carpe diem."

"Live for today."

Rossi picked up *The Post* from an adjacent table along with the *Corriere dello Sport*.

"Wonder what Torrini will make of this?" he said.

"Depends if it gets claimed or not," said Carrara.

"Early days."

"Can we run all the checks on the victim?" said Rossi. "When he came there, where he was before."

Carrara was already shaking his head.

"Before retiring, he lived his whole life in the Vatican. It's all in there. The paper trail. The abbot had the essentials ready at the scene. Vatican city passport and official residence."

"And no face left to match to it, right?"

173

The waiter deposited two sugar-dusted *cornetti* on the table with the *espressos*.

"Are you saying it's an identity issue here?" said Carrara as he stirred sugar into his coffee.

"I'm saying nothing can be excluded. Including the possibility that our killer was going to torch the place but thought better of it or was disturbed. Who's onto the staff list? The sooner we get the statements the better. He knew where to go and who he was killing."

"Unless it was random. Any priest will do."

Rossi shrugged. A couple of teenage-looking tourists were sizing up the bar's potential.

"Oh to be twenty again," said Rossi. The girl had a chequered shirt knotted at the front and shorts that were *very* short. She was how he might have imagined Yana at the same age, if she'd been born in better circumstances. He knew that her life had not been easy. She'd been lucky back then if there was enough to eat.

"Just going to make a quick call," he said getting up and walking out of the shade and towards the corner.

She was at work and had been following the media circus reaction to the murder. There was rolling news coverage and the main TV outlets were going all out for the Islamist theory.

"Didn't see you on TV yet," she said. "The world and his wife seems to have been there. It took me an hour to get to work through the traffic."

Rossi gave some generic reassurances but felt powerless to guarantee anything. He sat back down. Another call was coming. It was Iannelli.

"Dario," said Rossi. "You've heard then."

"I'm watching it," he said. "But guess what?"

"What?" said Rossi.

"I've got some pictures you have to see. Now."

"Pictures of what?"

"Your dead priest. With a knife in his back and his throat cut. In my inbox."

Thirty-Two

He had moved, to a small hotel out on the Appian Way, one which better-heeled tourists favoured for its large pool and pine-scented remove from frantic central Rome, not to mention its Michelin star. All of which was relative for Iannelli with his one-star freedom rating. Rossi and Carrara had driven straight there and were now sizing up Iannelli's suite. Iannelli was stroking his as yet tentative attempt at a beard.

"Not thinking of converting, are you?" Rossi tried to joke.

"They reckon it's a waste of time but I do *feel* a little more anonymous. Until someone gets a photo of me and then I'll have to think of something else."

He was hooking up his laptop as he spoke.

"WI-FI's not great but you'll see. Anonymous source, of course."

"When did you get it?" said Carrara.

"About one in the morning. I was asleep but when I logged on before breakfast I saw it. Here you go. What do you make of the message?"

Rossi read out loud.

"'Woe to you, teachers of the law and Pharisees, you hypocrites!'"

"The whole text is included below, look," said Iannelli scrolling down.

The image was much like the scene they had witnessed, but the lighting was artificial, the body lying face down, the knife protruding from his back.

"But the face," said Rossi. "It's visible. It's an unholy mess but it's there."

Iannelli gave a look of consternation.

"What do you mean, visible?"

"We've just been there. His whole face had been removed, mutilated. It was unrecognizable."

"He's not in great shape in this one either, is he?" said Carrara, surveying the scene over Rossi's shoulder. Blood had all but obscured the features but there was no doubting that the face had not yet been structurally disfigured in any way.

"So what about the Bible quote?" said Iannelli. "Wouldn't we be expecting something from the Koran if it was an Islamist scenario?"

"They like to show they know their enemy," said Rossi. "Which could also be part of the game. They follow their faith to the letter, while we infidels are, as it says, hypocrites. We call ourselves Christians but we don't practise what we preach."

"Hence the butchery?" speculated Carrara.

Rossi gave a shrug.

"So, it's not some sort of Bible John character?" said Iannelli remembering the scripture-quoting Scottish serial killer who was never found.

"Good memory you've got there, Dario," said Rossi.

"What about the metadata?" said Carrara. "There should be an Exif tag on the picture. Might be useful."

Iannelli shook his head.

"Removed. No schoolboy errors here."

"IP address?" said Rossi.

"They'll have used a hot phone," said Carrara, "and piggy-backed on an open WI-FI. Or, if we're lucky, a no-questions-asked Internet café. We can at least see if they remember a face."

"So, no extra clues," said Rossi.

"Doesn't look like it," said Iannelli. "Think that's your lot."

Rossi scrolled down to the end of the quotation. It was Matthew 23. Christ's reproaches to the Pharisees and the Sadducees. The warning against hypocrisy and the seven wows on the teachers of the law and the Pharisees. He still knew it off by heart after his brief spell as a seminarian.

"He's not having a go at the Jews too, is he, by any chance?" proffered Carrara but Rossi was shaking his head.

"This is a beef with the Church. The Catholic Church. Or meant to look like one at least."

"But why does he take his souvenir photo and then disfigure the body? And then send it to me?" said Iannelli.

"Why don't we blow it up?" said Carrara, moving in to take a closer look. "What programs have you got on this?"

"Be my guest," said Iannelli.

Carrara pulled up a chair, making a slew of windows suddenly materialize all over the screen.

"Give the contrast a bit of a boost, and the lighting. Better?" he said as Iannelli and Rossi watched over each shoulder.

"Much better," said Rossi, his own interest growing by the second as his eyes began to home in on something. "Hang on a minute," he said, staying Carrara's hand with his before he could make further adjustments. The grotesque tableau in front of them had been shot at a fairly wide angle to show the entire body and the room's surrounds. As such, some secondary background detail also featured. "The corner there. What do you see?"

Rossi's attention was concentrated on a triangular shadow, visible but not sharply in focus.

"A picture?" said Carrara.

"A painting," confirmed Rossi.

"Do you recognize it?" said Carrara. "Is it significant?"

Rossi leant back and continued to stare at the image, remembering the space on the wall, the masonry dust, the absence of ny shadow.

"Maybe. I'm sure we could get an ID on it eventually?"

"So was it stolen or what?" said Carrara.

"Possibly. But that's not the point. Don't you see? It's the one that's no longer there."

Thirty-Three

Jibril had taken a seat at the back of the classroom near the fire exit, the better to observe his classmates and so that he had a clear view of the door. Tension was high. There had been a lot of talk, rumours abounded and he, for now, was lying low. His pen strayed as his thoughts came out in contorted, confused doodles on the paper. So, someone had beaten him to it. Well, the holy man's enemies must have been legion. If it really was the priest he had been looking for. But it had to be. The episcopal ring, the purple shoes at the back of a wardrobe, the diary with its "V this", "V that", "V tonight! "; "V back in town. " All the signs had to point to Victor, his Christian friend of several years' standing. His murdered friend.

Jibril had put in time and miles and miles of walking and knocking on doors and asking for help just to get near the guy. He'd known there had to be a link somewhere. Retirement homes. Monasteries. And it had finally come up trumps. It was police work and he had realized he was made for it. Grinding it out, tracking it down, eliminating the impossible until the possible became real. Begging, asking, offering, showing up, being moved on from pillar to post. The Church needed people like him to validate their own existence and yet they often despised him at the same time. Sure we help the needy but don't ask for too much, brother. Know your place in the hierarchy.

He reflected on the relative success of their intelligence, however. In the end, the priest's diary had clinched it. The cleaning girl had really come up with the goods on that one. "Look for a journal, a memorandum," he had told her. "There's always a diary on a businessman's or a politician's desk. Check for anything unusual or repetitive, initials, codes, make a note." And she had found it, salted away where its owner would have believed it was out of harm's way. There were also the times corresponding to the exact period soon after Victor's arrival in Rome when he had made his boasts to Jibril about having made high-level connections, about knowing a cardinal. All that had happened just before his disappearance. And then nothing until his reappearance as a corpse, the one Jibril had seen in the morgue.

Soon after, Jibril had also discovered that the elderly cardinal Victor had spoken about was dead too. He could still remember every word of that telephone conversation the previous winter when he himself had still been in the immigration detention centre in Sicily. It had been their last conversation. Rome had then still seemed a distant dream for Jibril but Victor had given off the air of an old hand in the Eternal City, the metropolis paved with gold.

But even then Jibril suspected that Victor had already fallen into a trap. The friends in high places he spoke about, one of whom was Cardinal Terranova, would not be doling out charity without some comeback. That was the power game. Victor had alluded indirectly to the favours, the requests for male company in exchange for help with his bureaucratic difficulties, brushing it off as an acceptable price to pay, the initial cost of escaping the immigrant's poverty trap.

Jibril laughed silently to himself. So, how convenient it had been for the cardinal to die just when Victor had disappeared. Quite simply, he had not believed this cardinal to be dead at all, and what they had uncovered in the priest's apartment was damning evidence of his suspicions that this now was the cardinal living in hiding, under a false identity. He certainly wouldn't be the first to fake his own death out of expediency when the law and the press were closing in. Jibril had discovered that early on, in his own country. Then you could pop up where you liked when a decent interval had elapsed. There were men of influence with more aliases than they could possibly remember. Jibril himself had settled for disappearing only once. But this priest or cardinal – this man like anyone else – must have had a hand in Victor's death, either causing it materially or having exploited and used him and then failed to prevent it.

"Jibril!"

"Maestra."

He hadn't even heard the question, and today, an eery atmosphere permeated the classroom and the city. A priest killing was a clear sign. It was cowardly, evil, perfidious. And they were laying the blame squarely at the door of the Muslims, what with the bomb now having been claimed by the Islamic Caliphate in Europe. But no one he knew could give any account of it. Except perhaps Ali. He was positioning himself, manoeuvring. He hadn't fully stomached Jibril's assuming effective command of intelligence. Neither had Ali been in favour of Jibril's more cautious methods, his slowing it all down and waiting for the right moment for the symbolic, truly resonant strike, his military approach to winning and fighting another day.

"Mohammed says he is not in favour of rights for the homosexual community. Do you want to comment?" Olivia asked.

"It's not natural, it is against the teaching of the Prophet," came a voice from the other side of the classroom, which Jibril heard distinctly this time. Mohammed was not one of their inner circle but he was religious. They knew each other and something of what they both did. There was no animosity but Mohammed disapproved of his relationship with Olivia, which was now an open secret. If he knew that it was a carefully constructed front, a means to an end, he might think differently, but Jibril could not reveal that. Not yet.

"It is against our religion," said Jibril. "What can I say? If you have a religion you must follow it. You must practise what you preach too."

Olivia's eyes remained glued to him. He knew what she was thinking – that this was not what they had said and agreed on in private, over glasses of wine and while listening to her music. On their first intimate nights together he had told her how he wanted to embrace the West and its freedom. That was why he was here. Live and let live. Each to his own. Love knows no boundaries if it is well-intentioned.

She moved her attention away from him to the whole class.

"Well," she said, "in Italy, it is certainly not a crime and it is not considered immoral, even if our own Church may take a very different view on this. For the state, all are equal and deserving of respect."

After class, Jibril was surprised to see Ali waiting outside chatting with others of the group. Either he was keeping tabs on him or something was lined up, but Jibril didn't ask. Instead he just expressed his surprise to see it had rained a little but it was warm. So, autumn was making a first shy appearance. Jibril made a well-understood gesture towards Olivia who was still trying to come to terms with his seemingly schizoid attitudes. The gesture meant "not now. Not today". Then he joined Ali as the others went their separate ways. They moved off in the direction of Piazza Vittorio, and when they had walked for some minutes in silence, it was Ali who began to speak.

"So, Jibril. Things are moving fast in Rome. We had our people there too you know in the monastery?"

"Of course," said Jibril. "I saw to that myself. Our intelligence-gathering net is well spread. But whoever it was that killed him was brutal but effective."

Ali didn't seem the least bit disturbed that whoever had carried out the operation was unknown to them. He simply revelled in the fact of the killing itself.

"Well, things are afoot, Jibril, and I'm not just talking about today's great news. Bigger things. Much bigger things."

Jibril waited to see what it was Ali wanted him to know. Ali had connections all right, from his time in Turin and Algeria. He had shuttled between the two countries as a child as his parents had squabbled and fought and, finally, practically abandoned him to his own fate. He was also a hothead, an ideologue, dangerous, not highly intelligent, yet he knew how to press the flesh and impress people. It was probably because of his mixture of Arabic and Italian blood. It gave him a certain flexibility, apart from his instability. But he also had delusions of grandeur; that too probably a product of his turbulent duality, his being two things and, by his own admission, "being no one, being nothing". He'd moved down from the north, where he'd rocked a few boats in the mosque with his refusal to condemn attacks against civilians, his outbursts in support of Al-Quaeda, ISIS – though not publicly enough to get picked up on by the services. At least Jibril hoped not. He was useful but a loose cannon. That he knew important people was, however, of the utmost importance to the movement.

"Go on," said Jibril. "What is this news?"

Ali stopped and turned to face him.

"Well, it seems now a countryman of *yours* is keen to get to know more about us. Word has reached him that we are organizing and he wants to be a part of it."

Jibril could see he was glowing with pride now. But Ali's weakness, his Achille's heel, was that he fell all too easily for flattery, allowing his ego to lead him astray. When Jibril had arrived on the scene, he had understood just how gung-ho Ali was, how emotive. He was, in a word, a liability. Hence the change of tack, the low profile, the patient approach. But he knew it could only restrain Ali for so long.

"He says he is an emissary of higher powers, *much* higher powers, where the movement is strong, Jibril. In *your* country. There they are pushing back the infidels who are running scared. Islam is spreading there, like wildfire. And you know wildfire moves quicker than a man can run. They have no answers for our certainties and they fear for their Western-style democracy, that excuse for letting foreign invaders strip their country's resources. You have Boko Haram, Jibril, and it is feared now, too."

One of the older orange trams trundled past, sliding and screeching along the grooves of its predetermined course.

"We are strong everywhere, Ali, if we believe," said Jibril. "We have no fear, of anyone or anything as long, as we have our faith to guide us."

Ali was nodding now like a toy dog Jibril had seen in the back of a car once when he was young. In his white traditional Islamic robes, he looked every inch the fanatic.

"Yes, yes, Jibril. Allahu Akbar," he said, "Allahu Akbar," but having at least the sense to whisper the exclamation.

So, it was perhaps true. What Jibril had heard and hoped for before he had embarked on his journey was, maybe, true. The word then had been that there were high-level figures from his own country using Rome as a base for their operations. Having fled Nigeria, they had blended in with the community, keeping their heads down, and had then taken advantage of the relatively lax security to go about their criminal business. This was big news.

"The message is that soon he may be able to help bring us up to speed. Then we can take the fight into the heart of Christendom – as the Qur'an says we will – with equipment, means, with *weapons*."

As Ali uttered the last word in the list, he aspirated it with powerful satisfaction, delighting in the whiplash of its onomatopoeia. When they were mingling in public spaces to avoid easy detection, their preferred language was English. Passersby paid them little attention, used as they were to tourists and diplomats in the city. But Jibril was still cautious. His burner phone gave him some security. He was sure they were not yet being trailed but he also knew that the deeper in they got, the more likely it was that they would appear on the secret services' radar. It was mathematical, a probability game. They had to remain one step ahead.

He pondered what "weapons" meant? Assault rifles, grenades, explosives, rockets even?

"Through the established channels, Ali," Jibril said, slowing him down. His response betrayed nothing but his usual cool detachment despite the growing realization that this could be a turning point. The chance of hitting harder than anyone had hit the West before was becoming a real possibility. That was what all this meant. But no emotion should cloud their judgement. "He can be introduced through the established channels. But you have at least a name for this emissary?"

Ali looked surprised and stopped, putting a hand on Jibril's arm.

"But are you not curious to know who he works for?" said Ali. He was almost salivating, it appeared, his eyes agape.

But Jibril now believed he knew exactly who he was speaking about. His own dogged intelligence work, his probing and searching, had not been in vain. Its aim had been to identify approachable targets and high-level figures with exploitable vulnerability – but it had also had a secondary purpose: for him, a nobody, an outsider, to get close to the power structures of the Nigerian underworld in Rome, Naples, and Milan. That was the springboard he needed. Little by little he had been building a picture. A snippet of information here, a drug dealer there. Where to find a weapon, who was running the whores. And the drugs, of course. The cocaine. And so, it had all begun to add up and now he could see where the trail might lead.

"Who, Ali? Tell me."

"A man with influence, Jibril," he said, relishing the build up. "A man with a vision for Islam and for the future. Our future. Look around you," he said gesturing to the greying facade of a church that would have once been at the communal heart of the Esquilino district. "People come here to urinate against these walls when they are drunk or to shoot drugs on the steps over there. Look at the filth. Christians can have no respect for God if this is how they keep their shrines and holy places. They have no faith. They can continue to bomb and maim our people in its name but they are the living dead. Zombies," he added, gesturing to the few dissolute and decadent "native" Italians traversing the street as if his verdict were a fact as indisputable as the sun's rising in the east. He had the zealot's certainty all right, thought Jibril. Ardent. Impervious to any idea but his own.

At that moment there was the sound of a strangled squeal of brakes on the damp tarmac. They both turned to see a black BMW pulling up alongside them.

"Ali!" said a muscular and heavily chained black African in dark glasses as the electric window descended to reveal his full profile. "Get in the car. He is here. He is in Rome."

Thirty-Four

"No one in the monastery knows anything about the whereabouts of any painting," said Carrara. "So can we assume it was stolen by our killer?"

"They don't know when it went missing," said Rossi. "Or no one's telling?" he added. "Quite a difference, I'd say."

They were back in the office and totting up the evidence.

"These priests and monks," said Rossi. "How would you describe them?"

"Taciturn. They're a contemplative order."

"Handy excuse, isn't it, but they're rather sphinx-like, wouldn't you say?"

"Comes with the territory, I suppose. I mean they're always going to weigh their words wisely."

Rossi was chewing on a pen and studying a blow-up of the image Iannelli had given them.

"We'll keep this well under wraps for now. Until we've got something on the painting. So who is our resident art expert?"

"Right," said Carrara. "I was getting round to that."

Rossi looked up from the photo on his desk. Just then there was a knock at the door.

"Yes," said Rossi, swinging his feet off the desk.

It was a triumphant-looking Katia.

"I believe you are looking for an art expert, Inspector."

I might have known, thought Rossi.

"Come in," he said resigning himself. "And close the door."

***

Katia had pulled up a chair next to Rossi and was now leaning over the image again with the magnifier, her honey-tanned bare arms giving her the appearance of a driven but rather sensuous archaeologist. She scribbled some notes into a jotter.

"So, art was your first degree," said Rossi. He didn't expect to get much small talk but thought it was worth a try anyway. That was the Italian in him, an instinct. Never give up.

"Correct," she replied without wavering a millimetre. "All set for a museum curatorship or Sotheby's."

"And where did it all go wrong?" said Carrara from the corner of the desk.

She put down the magnifying glass, checked her notes one more time then looked up.

"The Italian disease," she said with a brief ironic smile, clicking her pen closed. "They kept giving the jobs to less-qualified but better-connected candidates. So I jacked it all in, got a job in a supermarket to pay the rent and then took the public competition for the Financial Police and got myself into the stolen artworks department. At least I could use my expertise."

"Pays less," said Rossi. "The Force."

"Hence the opportunity. Anyway, once I began to find out what some people were prepared to do to get their hands on a work of art, I thought I'd get *my*self some more experience and moved onto homicide and organized crime. Talk about butchers and sadists. It's worse than Hieronymus Bosch," she said with an air of levity that put Rossi to shame, considering how queasy he had felt at the crime scene.

Rossi nodded. "The guy who liked to boil his victims in caustic soda? Or the one who sowed live rats into prisoners' abdomens to get them talking? Where was that?" he said in Carrara's direction, "Mexico?"

"Colombia," said Katia. "I can give you the details over lunch sometime, if you're curious."

"Hence the second degree in criminology," said Carrara looking again over her CV, now in his legitimate possession.

"And what do you do in your *spare* time?" said Rossi. "If there is any."

"You mean when I'm not painting or studying foreign languages?" she said.

She was teasing him, he knew it. So he was not the only intellectual on the block. He might have to get used to it.

"Well, I like to keep in shape. Like yourself, Inspector," she added, with a subtle nod towards the bottle protruding from the filing cabinet's open bottom drawer.

"Well," said Rossi, "we do like to think things through over a drink from time to time. When the day is done, of course." He got up and shut it with a casual side-foot. "So, what's the next move on this one?"

She looked through her notes again underlining a few incomprehensible abbreviations and codes then swung round on her chair to face Rossi.

"I'll get on to it. We may be able to come up with some programs that can match brush strokes and samples with a database of stolen artworks. I presume the reason it was subtracted from the scene is because of its value, or because it was hot."

"Or because the killer was taking it back," Carrara chipped in. "We could always see if we can wring anymore information out of the brothers and sisters."

Rossi nodded his agreement.

"At least it will narrow down the search."

"Better to keep them in the dark about what we know," said

Carrara. "They may get complacent. Presuming someone's moved it or stashed it. And they haven't declared it missing. I mean, it's not like you wouldn't notice."

Katia swung back towards the desk and moved in again to study the painting.

"Well, the frame's interesting," she said. "Depends if it's original, but it tells at least a part of the story. It's all a question of cross-referencing data in catalogues and applying your artistic knowledge."

"Do you have a working hypothesis?" said Carrara.

Katia leaned back for a moment, crossed her arms and put a pensive finger to her lips, further enhancing the curve of her breasts beneath her stretch camisole top. She seemed, however, to evince little or no self-consciousness about her own potential for distraction.

"Renaissance," she said. "Italian. Likely a portrait. More than that, I can't say. I'll need time. You think it's important for other reasons, don't you?" she said, turning and looking directly at Rossi. "Apart from whether it was stolen or not, I take it."

She was good. And tough with it. He was trying not to let the attraction get in the way, or get *its* way like some spoilt child jabbering away inside him.

"I think it has to lead us somewhere of interest," he said, letting some of his former reserve melt away. "And maybe right back to the killer."

Thirty-Five

Jibril had followed Ali without question despite some natural misgivings. The closer you got the more dangerous it became, and there was no one who was going to look out for him if these people had even the slightest doubts as to his integrity. They would dispatch him as a security risk, an informer, a spy. Ali, meanwhile, was blissfully unaware. Not to have followed would have, however, only raised suspicions, also putting his life at risk. It was war-zone logic. The fruit of experience. The driver brandished no weapon, of course, but Jibril was certain a shoulder holster was nestling beneath his loose-fitting silk shirt. He had driven them at some speed until the vehicle eventually came to a halt outside a discreet hotel behind Porta Maggiore.

"I've been seeing the sights of this wonderful city," their driver said, breaking the silence and turning round to study them both. "It almost seems a shame to damage it," he added then laughing out loud and showing, as he did so, white and gold teeth in almost equal numbers.

"Come," he said, "we are here." He gave a quick look around, opened the door and stepped out on to the pavement. Ali and Jibril followed him through the plate glass revolving doors and into the lobby of the unostentatious three-star establishment.

191

Jibril had never even set foot in a hotel and to him this already smacked of luxury. The carpets and smells, the subdued tone. He felt out of place and conscious of being inappropriately dressed, as though he had turned up to a military inspection in civvies.

"Wait here for two minutes," said their driver, indicating the creamy-white, low-slung divans in a corner of the lobby. He then ambled towards the reception desk where, after exchanging brief pleasantries with him, the female receptionist reached for the phone. He turned and gave Ali and Jibril the signal to follow again, and they made their way towards the lifts. Jibril tried to show no sign of fear or uncertainty but he knew now he was going to face a test. It was something he had prepared for but, as with all such tests, one could never know what questions the examiner would ask.

The lift bell rang. They stepped inside.

Their driver led them along a corridor and, as he passed young cleaning ladies bending and busying themselves in open rooms, he gave them approving glances. He then stopped and gave a coded rap on a door with a "Do Not Disturb" sign. It was opened by the very same hand as had opened the door to Giancarlo in the hotel in Naples and, as Jibril entered, he saw coming towards him the same imposing figure in traditional dress as had greeted the ItalOil executive.

Such robes, thought Jibril. He hadn't seen an outfit like this since he had left his country, since he had left his village for the city and for the oil fields so many years ago. The President, as he was to be known, reached out a hand to Ali and Jibril in turn.

"Welcome, my friends."

***

An array of non-alcoholic drinks on a silver serving tray and the remains of a light buffet were still on the coffee table between

192

them. Ali had gone off to discuss matters with other members of the President's retinue.

"I must say again it's so good to meet a fellow countryman and a Muslim in Rome," he said first in English. "Where were you born?"

In spite of the preamble, Jibril was not suprised by his directness.

"Near Lagos, on the outskirts, and then we moved, many times," said Jibril. "My grandparents were from the south but things happened during the war and my father and my mother had to flee."

Jibril gave him the name of a shanty village he had visited once. Better always to keep a distance. Though he knew the lie, if discovered, could have him killed, too.

"I don't know this place," the President replied. "It is very small, I imagine. Out in the sticks!" he added, laughing at his use of English.

"So your mother's tongue, by the way," he said, questioning, as he reached out to take more food.

"Igbo. But she wanted us only to learn English. It was languages that divided us, she used to say, so one language will unite us. And when she died, I was young and had no one to teach me. I adopted English. Or you could say it adopted me."

"A philosopher!" the President exclaimed. "And like mother like son!"

A door opened on the far side of the lounge and a shapely, provocatively dressed figure emerged and ambled across. Jibril saw her heels were at least six inches and the white dress, barely long enough to be called as such, gleamed in contrast with her firm black thighs. The President held up a hand in undisguised annoyance and called to an assistant, rattling off instructions in the language of Jibril's childhood. The real language of his childhood.

The assistant produced a wad of banknotes for the escort,

which she examined briefly before tucking them away in a Gucci handbag. She too then addressed the President, who leapt to his feet as if she had managed to reach him with a cattle prod rather than words. Something in what she had said had enraged him. To anyone else who might have been listening, not Nigerian and not from the north, the only comprehensible words would have been "Hotel Incantevole" and they might have remembered seeing the building's late Renaissance facade while walking north from Piazza Repubblica. They would, however, have had no way of knowing she had also said "the same day, same time" and "the same services as usual".

The President sat down again as his suited flunkey ushered the pouting hooker out of his sight.

"But you know," he said, regaining his composure and placing another sweetmeat into his mouth, "your accent, has just a hint of the north, or am I mistaken? Is it possible, even though, as you say, you are from Lagos? Or maybe it is only in my imagination."

"My great-grandmother," said Jibril, was from the north, I believe. I don't know the village. That is the family story, anyway," he said. "And they say she never lost her accent. But maybe it was in the oil fields. There were many friends there with whom I forged great friendships. I'm sure their way of speaking must have rubbed off."

The President nodded.

"Indeed. Friendship. But there are few friends, Jibril. Few real friends. And so you found yourself an orphan, early in life?"

"Yes, my father had died in an accident when I was a baby. He had gone to the Delta for work but he never came back. I followed in his footsteps in that sense."

So much death, thought Jibril. But it was not so unusual in a country where average life expectancy was forty-five.

"And now, after many travails, you are in Rome. I will not ask you to tell me how you came here. Your story is familiar to me. Like so many, I also came to Europe and Rome as a relatively poor man, but with big dreams and now, well," he said gesturing to his staff, "I am respected, feared, and I am rich. I want to use my wealth wisely and well. To promote the Islamic cause in Africa and beyond. To rebuild the Caliphate, that was once great, with only God's laws. But the new Caliphate will be even greater and will stretch from the Atlantic Ocean eastwards to the Gulf and beyond, northwards across the sea to Europe."

Jibril listened. He knew the importance of waiting to be asked to speak.

"You know, of course, how far Arabic Muslim influence reached once? Through Spain across the Pyrenees and into France."

The President gave another satisfied chuckle. "There are many brothers in France, in England, Belgium, Germany, Sweden. We have our men in place throughout the lands of the infidel. We need only give the word and they will rise up in the name of Allah!"

He raised a pointed finger into the air as a warning of coming war.

"Foreign powers have occupied and exploited the Islamic lands for too long, Jibril. We are all victims; we have all been victims. But you and I and your brother, Ali, we are the spearhead of a movement to set things straight. The non-believers fear us because we are strong. But it is our suffering that has made us strong. Our hunger, our historic hunger. We know how to move, how to arm ourselves, how to fight without stint. But most of all, we know, too, how to make wealth out of their very weakness and turn it round to bite them with such venom and force, like a viper in its deadliness."

The President sat back and looked straight at Jibril, like an artist who has completed a canvas.

"What moved you to join the fight for Islam, Jibril?" he asked.

Jibril took a sip of the sparkling water from his heavy blue tumbler and replaced it on the dark smoked-glass table. The discarded metal ring which had sealed the bottle was lying there curled like a piece of shrapnel.

"Injustice," said Jibril, and then after a brief pause, "anger. Revenge. And hunger for change."

"So true," the President replied. "Injustice is like a parasite burrowing into your flesh. It eats at you until you rid yourself of it by purifying action, if no one is willing to deliver justice themselves. And as they continue to wage their wars on our people in order to rob them of their well-being and their resources, forcing them to live like rats in their bombed-out houses, justice will be delivered, in the form of revenge."

Jibril nodded his agreement.

Ali was coming back to join them accompanied by a suited member of the President's staff.

"So, Ali," said the President, "Jibril and I have bared something of our souls to each other. But shall we talk now in a little more detail about our joint venture? What exactly do you have in mind for this city? The *Eternal* City," he added, bringing a heavy hand crashing down on his own large thigh as his laughter exploded then around them and the whole hotel suite.

"Yes, we need something spectacular," said Ali. "An attack on the Christian heart of Europe, and the world. Here we can make headlines like we did with 9/11."

The President grunted his approval.

"And who do you hate, who do you despise the most in the West?"

"Apart from our persecutors, the hypocrites and the unbe-lievers, the cowards and dogs who bomb our people in their beds at night?"

The President nodded and grunted more approval.

"The homosexuals," said Ali, with unwavering conviction. "They are the ultimate affront to Allah. Lower than animals. They are vermin to be expunged from the face of the earth."

"Yes," said the President. "They are an abomination, and yet here they ply their trade with impunity. They even demand the right to marry and adopt children. And they criticize *us*, in my country, of outrageous crimes against them. As if their behaviour is not a crime in and of itself punishable by death."

Jibril was showing his approval too.

"Yes," he said. "They must see the error of their ways. They must be re-educated with decisive force if they are to turn to Allah. The Prophet himself tells us this. That the sword must be used to convert them if they will not convert by themselves."

The President looked at Jibril.

"Do you have brothers, Jibril?" he asked. Jibril paused for a moment.

"No," he said. "Allah did not bless my mother with more than one son. That was his will. I have only sisters."

The President did not hide his sympathy for Jibril and his understanding of his disappointment.

"So, much then rests on your shoulders," he said.

"I have decided on my path in life," Jibril replied.

"And Allah gives us the means, but our destiny is ultimately in his hands. You know the story of the man who tried to escape when he believed Death was looking for him?"

"Yes," said Jibril.

"And how when this man finally rests at his destination, where he believes he is now safe. And who does he find there waiting for him?"

"Death," said Ali.

"Death," said the President. "And the man says 'but how can you be here. I did all I could to avoid you.' And Death replies. 'I was waiting. But really I did not expect that you would get here so soon'."

Jibril had heard the story before but reacted as if the President was a man of wisdom regaling him with his knowledge as few other men could.

The President reached out to pick up his phone. "Now, gentleman. I believe someone else is waiting and also has an appointment to keep."

He punched in a number then spoke rapidly in his own language, a language of which Jibril feigned his ignorance again. His tone was bullying and peremptory, very different to the suave and inviting tones he had used with them thus far.

He paused before continuing, this time in the familiar register.

"So, you have our guest. I trust he had a pleasant trip. Well we shall make a visit to see him. I want to introduce him to two of my friends."

He replaced the phone on the table.

"He too has come early for his appointment with Death."

Thirty-Six

Katia had stayed behind at the *Questura* with Carrara to tie up as many of the loose ends as they could regarding the Brell murder and to get to work on their hunch regarding the picture.

Rossi walked out of the *Questura* into the early afternoon air. It was a warm September day. On the trees, a few of the leaves had begun to fade and contemplate a paler hue of yellow but as yet they remained undecided. There was plenty of summer left it seemed. Bees were intent on their work, moving between flowers like skilled technicians with a mammoth task to complete. *Until they think warm days will never cease.* Keats. It always came back to him at this time of year. *To leave this life unseen.*

At Manzoni, he went down to take the Metro. Then he changed his mind. He would walk. He didn't want to get anywhere fast. He wanted to think now and put his house in order, mentally. It was as though he were juggling four or five objects and a crowd was watching him, waiting for the whole thing to collapse and give them their crescendo of perverse pleasure. Their *schadenfreude*. Or, as the Neapolitans termed it, *cazzimma*.

The fire, the bombing, the Bonucci murder and now the priest. ICE. The mystery of the painting and his nagging doubts about the dynamic of that murder. Why had he been disfigured? Why had the killer not photographed the final draft of his handiwork, the most revolting and most demeaning? The pathologist had to give him some help on that score. As he walked along Via Filiberto, he made a mental note to get back to her; he remembered also the hint she had dropped about her place in the country. The air in Rome had grown stifling again, thick with smog and pollutants and heavy with the charge of accumulated heat. *God knows these radical types going round burning cars and motorbikes had a point*, Rossi thought, as he watched the dense stream of traffic going past, nearly every car with a single occupant and pumping out more filth.

He took out his phone to call Carrara and moved into a doorway to shield himself from the noise while cupping his hand around the phone.

"Gigi, I was thinking about the kid, the arsonist. Have you had any bright ideas? Are you sure he was working alone?"

"We went through his flat, his computer, his hard drives. Looked for all the world like a lone wolf."

"Well, I want him followed for a bit. See where he goes while he's out on bail. It's a shot in the dark but you never know."

"OK," said Carrara.

"And any luck yet on the artwork?"

"Slow," said Carrara. "I'll call you tonight."

Then Rossi remembered one of the other balls he had been juggling.

"And the disk, the CCTV? Did you get a chance yet?"

"Encrypted," said a busy-sounding Carrara. "Gab must have missed something. I sent it back to him."

"OK," said Rossi and dropped the phone into his pocket then just as quickly took it out again to make another call to Yana, but there was no answer. "The phone you are calling could be switched off." *Strange*, he thought to himself. He stopped and contemplated turning round and walking back to the Metro. He could pay her a surprise visit. Maybe something was up. But he was wasting time. He would call Gab and see if he could hurry things along a bit. His phone buzzed. Someone else was calling. Maroni. He decided to grasp the nettle.

"Rossi?"

"Yes, sir."

"Have you seen the news?"

"No. What news?"

"Well get yourself near a TV or something and you tell me what you make of it."

"I'm in the middle of the street."

"Haven't you got Internet on your phone yet, Rossi?"

"I leave that to Carrara," he replied.

"Well some bloody Caliphate crowd, one among the galaxy, have come out with a video and a very specific threat, saying they're ready to march on Rome. The prime minister's taking it seriously and wants every man we've got on the streets to reassure the public. He does not want a 9/11 European style."

"Of course," said Rossi. "We're doing all we can."

There was a pause. One of *those* pauses, thought Rossi.

"Yes," said Maroni, "but *are* you? Are you actually *getting* anywhere, Rossi? Or are you spreading yourself too thinly on your various hypotheses? I mean what kind of solid intelligence have you been picking up? What about tracking all stolen vehicles, vans that could be used for an attack? You know you're the only one who hasn't given me a report yet? And it's been noted not just by me but by higher authorities. And by the way, remember that audit's coming up?"

"Yes," said Rossi, "the internal one?"

"*Was* internal. Now it's *ex*ternal. They'll be counting everything down to the last paperclip. You can thank those well-intentioned idealists in the MPD on the parliamentary commission for public spending. They want to know what we're doing, Rossi. Not just polishing the leather on our seats with our backsides. And I don't think I need to tell you that you personally don't have many friends in high places. Do you hear me?"

Maroni had got a grilling and grillings were hereditary, passed down the line like unwanted Christmas presents.

"We've got an interesting lead on the priest killing," said Rossi.

"Have you, now?" said Maroni. "Perhaps you'd like to give me the elevator pitch over the phone, seeing as I haven't had anything in writing yet."

"I think there could be some connection with art theft. A painting's gone missing."

"Art theft? How do you know?"

"One of the nuns confirmed it, then denied it. I think she was lying to cover something up, or confused. Anyway, I've got Carrara and Vanessi working on it."

So he'd done it. Again. Withholding vital evidence from a superior officer. But Iannelli's video was the ace up his sleeve. And he would need it. Maroni exhaled deeply into the receiver, his frustration requiring no words.

"And what about your cutesy theory about the bomber returning to the scene of the crime? How much time did you waste on that one? And you told them a whole bloody pack of lies putting me in a decidedly bad light, Rossi."

"We're working on that too," said Rossi. "Nothing firm as yet."

There was another loaded pause before Maroni came up with his ultimatum.

"Look, Rossi, you've done some good work for me but you have a habit of going off-piste rather too often for my liking. I'm out of the city for a few days as of tomorrow. I'll be in Bologna for briefings but when I come back I want full reports on my desk for each and every case and something *concrete* that we can go on. And something I can show to my superiors on the Special Ops Committee. They've put a lot of trust in me and they want to see some comeback. Are we understood?"

"Perfectly," said Rossi. "It's only a matter of time."

There was a lull in the traffic as the lights changed up at San Giovanni, and Rossi ducked out of the doorway and darted across the road, heading for the more leafy side street of Via Statilia.

"Well, Rossi, the message we're getting is that time may not be on our side. The services are picking up increased traffic on the net and in cyberspace. But on the ground it looks like we're still chasing shadows."

"Well a shadow can't exist without a body," said Rossi. "And somewhere there's a sun."

"Philosophy again, Rossi?"

"Jung."

"I might have known. The hole in your life, is it?"

"Could be," said Rossi more than a little surprised at Maroni's familiarity with the topic.

"Well start bloody filling 'em in, will you!"

The line went dead. Rossi called Yana again. The phone was switched off. Maroni was right. They had too many half-leads and not a single solid one. They had neglected on-the-ground intelligence work and piled everything into his hunches. He was beginning to feel like the gambler who knows he's getting in deeper and deeper but can't see an alternative to pulling out.

No answer. Engaged. He'd be up to his eyes in work now with his business up and running. Rossi began flicking through the alternatives. He could hardly come out and ask for official help. He had no right to be storing those images, and they could throw the book at him if they wanted.

He pressed on in the direction of Porta Maggiore, deciding to take a longer, more scenic route from there to Piazza Re di Roma and then on to his apartment. Maroni had told him once how in the Eighties they'd spent five months staking out that particular piazza. They'd had a lead on a presumed helper in the Red Brigades who they had followed but then managed to lose. Dalla Chiesa, the general who would eventually defeat the BR, told 'em to stake it out until he showed up again. It was, he had said, logically only a matter of time. Five months, every day, changing squads three times every twenty-four hours until they got him. And then he had led them to the others.

A call was coming in. Gab calling back.

"Rossi."

"*Ciao*, Michael."

"News?"

"Nothing. Sorry."

"What do you mean 'nothing'?"

"Well, I haven't had much time but so far I can't crack it. Look. it's going to take a while. I don't know how long and I'm not sure I can give you the time you need."

"What's it worth to you?"

"It's not the money, Michael. I'm snowed under with work. It's really taken off, and I'm doing it all myself."

"You have to help me out, Gab. This is the last one. Just this one."

There was a pause. Silence.

"I'll try. I'll see what I can do. But I can't promise. It's fucked up what they do in there. It's impenetrable, I got all the files and saved them but I can't open them. I might be able to get at some of it but I can't guarantee you anything."

"Look, just get me something from before and after the bomb. I'm counting on you, Gab."

"OK."

Rossi walked on. The day was not going to plan. As he neared his flat, he dropped in at the supermarket and did the rounds for essentials and a few treats. Comfort food, wasn't it? Except in his case he went for high-quality and expensive treats, whether he could justify the cost or not. What the hell. He dropped more stuff into the trolley. Cheese, Parma ham, a bottle of overpriced craft beer. A bottle of red, a bottle of white. You never know. Fresh fish, *gamberi*, *calamari*. *Cantucci* biscuits. He might ever do a paella. If he could get through to Yana, he could invite he over. If there was time.

There was no mail in his box in the downstairs vestibule, but when he pushed open his front door, an envelope was waiting on the floor. Yana's writing. Inside, there was a note.

Michael. I've decided to go away for a while. I've left Marta in charge of the centre. She's fine with it and will benefit from the experience. I'll be staying with a friend of mine in Bologna. I need to have a break from Rome and everything there and reflect on things. It hasn't been easy finding time to talk to you recently about this and maybe it's my fault as much as anything. We're both busy people. But there you are. I will call you in a while but don't worry about me. Good luck with the investigation.

Love, Yana

xxx

He read and reread it. Then he took out his phone to call her. The same reply. Unavailable. He picked up his groceries and, contrary to habit, began putting things away. He stopped and went over the salient points again. *It hasn't been easy. My fault as much as anything.* So that meant his fault. He could go to the Wellness Centre. Perhaps Marta could give him some clue about how she'd been feeling. But Maroni wanted the reports. Something concrete. He couldn't let a lover's squabble get in the way now. And it was her choice.

He opened the fridge and shoved the fresh fish into the freezer. He left the rest on the table and headed back out.

When Rossi arrived at the *Questura*, Carrara was still there but had just been on the phone to Katia.

"She went off to meet with some expert at the university. Says he's making 'limited progress' with the painting," said Carrara Rossi, who was now slumped and thoughtful in his chair. "So it's still going to be a slow process."

"Did you get anymore out of the nuns and monks?" Rossi asked.

"Quiet as church mice. Seems the whole thing's more than a little bit taboo and they're not exactly courting the publicity."

"Do they want this to happen again?" said Rossi, straightening up now in his chair. "Don't they care that there's some kind of freak on the loose? We've got people being burnt alive in their beds and an elderly priest dispatched like a lump of meat. If he hadn't been disturbed, the guy might even have torched the whole place or killed everyone in their beds."

"There's absolutely nothing to link any of them with the murder."

"But how did he get in? Are you telling me it was just good fortune?"

"It's a lockdown, if you ask me," said Carrara. "They're closing ranks. The casual staff too. They saw nothing, know nothing. They seem afraid."

Rossi was growing impatient. He wanted to rail against something, anything.

"Well, are these casual staff legally resident? Do we know who the hell they are? Have you checked that at least? Or maybe they're scared of being repatriated or of getting their fingers broken? How many of them are Muslims? Do they live in the same areas? We need to go back there and talk to all of them again. From the beginning. All of them."

Carrara could sense the change in his colleague like the electricity in the air before a storm hit.

"Give us a minute, Mick. We've been up to our eyes you know. We're all spreading ourselves thinly at the moment."

Rossi gave the desk an almighty bang with the heel of his hand.

"But it's not good enough! Is it! We're not getting anywhere!"

The noise rang out like thunder.

"You know there's the first day of the energy conferer

tomorrow," said Carrara. "Goes on for a whole week and there will be bigwigs, politicians, and religious leaders coming every day."

Rossi looked up from the desk and the papers arranged without any discernible logic. He snatched up one of them.

"Heads of state from how many countries?" he said as he scanned the document, furrowing his brow as he did so, his eyes burrowing into it.

"One hundred and seventeen, on the first day."

"That's one big security op."

Carrara nodded.

Rossi dropped the piece of paper he'd been reading and rereading as if it were an impenetrable code.

"Yana's gone," he said.

"Gone?"

"Taking a break. From Rome. From me, I suppose. From this," he said, throwing a fistful of documents up into the air. They floated down as if in the mocking after-calm of an explosion.

"Did she give a reason?"

Rossi reached into a pocket and tossed him over the note.

"Right," said Carrara. "Two questions: who's the friend and what are you going to do about it?"

Rossi shrugged.

"It's not like I can give it my full and undivided attention, when we're on a permanent amber alert with likely red imminent. And I haven't even begun to get through my admin backlog."

"So let her get it out of her system?" said Carrara. "The break will do her good."

Rossi stood up and began pacing the office.

"You don't think there's anyone else?" said Carrara.

"Who knows," said Rossi, remembering the throwaway line she'd sprung on him over dinner and then just as quickly retracted. It had been in jest, but wasn't there always a kernel of seriousness inside every joke? "Think I should go after her?"

Carrara was chewing on a pen.

"Don't know. Let it blow over, I suppose. She'll come back when she's ready."

"I notice you didn't say 'running back'."

Carrara shrugged.

"Better knuckle down then, hadn't we?" said Rossi. He picked up a newspaper that had been lying half-read at some lower level of his desk strata.

"Have you seen this guy who wants to send homosexuals to jail for fourteen years," he said, picking up on an inside page column in *Repubblica*. "Or have them stoned under sharia law?"

"So not the Pope then," Carrara quipped.

"No! The new president of Nigeria. The human rights crowd here are up in arms. There's a big demo tomorrow by the Rainbow LGBT Alliance."

"As if we didn't have enough trouble with the Islamists."

"Freedom of expression is sacrosanct, Gigi," said Rossi.

"But it had to be tomorrow? When we're already stretched to the limit."

"It's publicity, maximum visibility. This guy's coming here for other business, to court the government or be courted. Not sure how it works actually."

"Well, if it's Nigeria, they've certainly got the oil," said Carrara.

"Right, so they have the whip hand now."

"It's no laughing matter there though, is it? I mean with Al-Quaeda, Boko Haram, ISIS."

"And ICE," added Rossi. "Our very own ICE."

"Do I detect a note of cynicism, Inspector Rossi?"

"Far be it from me," Rossi began in a mock hyper-defensive tone, "to say that a terrorist organization – that no one's ever heard of before – can put a sophisticated bomb outside the Israeli university and then melt away into the night without a trace. I suppose another black swan moment could be just around the corner."

"We need to be one step ahead," said Carrara. "Remember the school in Russia? Those kids with bombs suspended above their heads."

"Well, we *plan* against such events," said Rossi. "Security exists to ensure it doesn't happen."

"But then when it does happen we're not really prepared psychologically or pragmatically to deal with it and its consequences."

"And we go into a form of denial. Like the 9/11 witnesses who said they saw a light plane not a jumbo hit the twin towers."

"Right," said Carrara. "So are you?"

"What?"

"In denial. It's not like with all this you're trying to say something. About Yana, I mean."

Rossi reflected for a moment. The silence in his life was uncanny. Even if he could go twenty-four hours sometimes without contacting her, this silence that she had imposed on their relationship felt sudden and tomblike.

The conquistadors had thought nothing of riding up in the New World on horseback in full armour, but to the Aztecs they were like men from Mars. Rossi too felt there had been no warning, only the discussion about his attitude the other evening, which he had presumed had been laid to rest.

"I don't know," he said. "These are uncharted waters."

For a second he imagined being on a beach somewhere. Then he got up and went to the fridge.

"Share a beer?" he asked over his shoulder as he hunkered down to get a Moretti. Carrara gave him a wordless negative. Rossi craned his neck round to see he had his head down, suddenly intent on some detailed task. Rossi snapped off the top and took a decent swig. No glass. Carrara was *in absentia*. A thoroughly male approach to affairs of the heart.

He sat down and took another long draught. It was beginning to feel good as he stared at the mute phone on his desk. Then, as if on a whim, he snatched up the receiver and dialled Yana's number. He let it ring well into double figures. She wasn't answering from this one either. Feeling slightly foolish with himself, he thrust it back down.

Then just as quickly he picked it up again and punched in a different number. This time he got an answer on the first ring and, putting it on speakerphone, sat back to finish the still cold enough beer.

"Katia?"

"Yes. Anything the matter?"

"No," said Rossi. "Where are you?"

"In my office. You dialled my office phone."

Rossi mumbled an explanation. Carrara had stopped what he was doing but was trying not to betray his interest.

"OK," said Rossi. "Look. I'm coming over. Fancy showing me what you've got so far?"

"Sure," said Katia.

Rossi left the bottle on the desk, picked up his jacket and breezed out.

"Reports?" said Carrara.

"Later," replied Rossi. "I'll call you."

Thirty-Seven

Giancarlo was sitting in a chair which, in itself, afforded some small comfort. His hands, however, were numb and his wrists were beginning to ache. The muscles at the front of his shoulders and the adjoining tendons were being stretched, Christlike, by his position. He wanted to be able to move his legs too, but each was as one with a leg of the chair, bound to its squared wooden limbs by repeated circlings of insulation tape. Tight loops of rope also held his upper body and wound around his windpipe and wrists. He had to wait until he was untied to be able to urinate, but at least he could still cling to that small measure of dignity.

Then it was back for the same rigmarole again until they had finished for the day – if it was day – and he was returned to his room.

He had hesitated to use the word cell, and had opted for room, knowing even so that if where he spent most of his time was a room it was such only by virtue of its having a floor, a ceiling, four walls and a door. It was no more a room than a murderer was a member of the human race, or a dope dealer was a neighbourhood grocer.

His eyes, of course, had long since ceased to be free. They too were twin detainees and had their own special arrangements, bound as they were behind a soft mocking wall of perfect, inscrutable darkness.

The door into this second room he now occupied would open from time to time and, amidst the boredom of constant monotonous terror, that opening in itself would be an event. An event in the same way that a butcher's swapping the bow saw for the filleting knife is an event, but an event nonetheless. And there would be voices and languages, their assorted owners chopping between them or sticking stubbornly with their one and only weapon of choice. Arabic, English, Italian and a broad jumble of unrecognizable tongues. He feared that the latter were used only when what was being said was not meant for his ears and was thus a cloak covering other vile intentions or possible consequences.

The dominant lexicon was limited. Coke, oil, payment, money, two birds with one stone. Did he, then, represent "the two birds" – both a lucratively marketable ItalOil man and a Western infidel hostage? But was it his death or his captivity that the stone stood for? They hadn't told him other than to say that he was a captive, and then when the film crew moved in he knew that the game was not yet *up* but that it was most certainly *on*. It had already become a tiresome ritual. The jabbering on about all that was wrong with the West. All that while an apocalyptically sharp scimitar was poised below his throat.

Then it would be over and they'd shunt him back into his cell till the next time.

There. He'd said it. Cell. So cell it was. And a prisoner he was then. But a criminal? He had stolen from criminals, true enough, but that was no crime. Smuggling cocaine, liquid cocaine, into the country camouflaged as barrels of petroleum was a crime against the state. These jailers did not represent any state. So he was a player in a private game, an immoral game, an *amoral* game; one in which, however, he had few if any moves available to him.

His error had been greed. Greed at the wrong moment. Bad timing. Everything had been going smoothly, perfectly even, but he had wanted more and it had all seemed so easy. Then the approach had come and it had been to all intents and purposes a business move.

Someone had known. Someone had talked. They had discovered what he was doing and for whom – for the Nigerians. They, the Camorra, had approached him and complimented him first and simply assessed him on the strength of his curriculum vitae as "the man for the job". They had flattered him, tempted him, and he had succumbed – whore that he was. They had piggy-backed on the dope route into Europe and offered him even greater rewards and a slice of the profits, a seat on the board, if you like.

But when he had wanted out, they had played their ace. There was no way out. They had him by the balls, and while it continued to pay they were not going to pass up their cash cow, so he was in it for the duration.

And then the bust.

Even then they hadn't needed to touch even a single hair on anyone's head. It had all been so unexpected, so well planned, such a perfect inside job, and such a slick deception. The police shields and halyards, the flashing lights, the firepower – real or staged, it hardly mattered.

He had escaped with his life, incredulous to his own good fortune but the goods had gone. The Nigerians had lost their biggest consignment yet and *he* had lost it for them.

The approach hitherto had always been the same. The dummy run to check the route, no risk. The next would be a real run. Next time we go big. Maybe one more. Two max. Then checkout. The route closes down for good. We move on to the next one. And so on ad infinitum.

He'd bluffed it at first with the Nigerians. They'd come from nowhere; there must have been an informer; they must have followed him, put a tracker, a bug, whatever. There were crooked cops on board, maybe one of the President's men had sold them out.

Then they'd taken him in. Why didn't they arrest you? No newspaper, no journalist, no nothing. He'd been shafted and he hadn't felt a thing. He'd been ejected from the board in a bloodless coup and nobody had even raised their voice. He hadn't materially stolen from the President and his men. But by his incompetence he had allowed the Camorra to carry out the biggest snatch in the history of Italian drugs wars. All cold comfort. That they might need to keep him alive for their other projects was cold comfort again. The method was everything. Better a bullet than the sliced jugular of a stuck infidel pig.

So, he was friendless. No "uncle" now to help him. First, when Giancarlo had still believed, he had not returned his calls. Then his number had been no longer active.

He thought of his wife, his son. He clung to hope there, not for himself but for them. His humanity existed now only through the hope of seeing them again.

Thirty-Eight

On the way back home Rossi had dropped in at a bar. To think. That was the excuse at least. He flicked through a paper, creased and softened by use until it almost felt more like fabric. He was fully aware that he still hadn't completed a single report but he'd been going over everything with Carrara. He wasn't exactly optimistic but he was sifting and resifting in the hope of finding some small nugget of a clue. He had even thought about talking to Nurse Rinaldi again despite there being nothing solid in her evidence to go on. He checked his phone for her number, but it wasn't saved. He searched through the scraps and old receipts in his wallet and pockets but realized he must have managed to mislay it. He'd have to take a trip over to her house or contact the hospital.

A pang of hunger hit him. How long had he been there? He picked up the menu and as he did so looked around to see what everyone was eating. There had been a generous *aperitivo* menu which he had picked at a little while other diners were clearly making it an *apericena*, an *aperitivo* bulked out into dinner by multiple visits to the buffet table, in lieu of a formal meal. He preferred to go traditional and ordered a *saltimbocca alla romana* with potatoes and salad. And another large glass of *Primitivo*.

Carrara had cited family commitments, which was understand-able, and besides, they now had to just slog it out until something turned up. He was counting on Katia. She at least exuded rigour and knife-sharp intelligence. He wondered whether he should have invited her for dinner but when he'd dropped in she was so absorbed by her task that he had thought it wiser not to. Always better not to mix work and pleasure, but she was making that rule troublesome. Apart from whether it was an infatuation or not, he was just getting to like being around her, but she hadn't given anything approaching a clear sign that it might be reciprocal and he wasn't going to make a fool of himself.

She'd begun by giving him the low-down on her day spent criss-crossing the city, going from gallery to gallery, rustling up archivists and curators and auction house contacts in the not-yet-vain hope of getting a match. The office was strewn, but orderly, with all manner of prints and copies, books and cata-logues. She'd got coffee for them both and had returned to find him taking a longer than necessary look at some erotica and had given him a teasing half-smile, but only that. Then back to the work. The program she had hoped to use had in the end come to nothing. But she at least was optimistic and had promised to ring if there was anything of significance before the evening was out.

He took a sip of the *Primitivo*. Apt name. The primal instincts. The red-blooded male. And it was going down well, a little too well, but his head still felt clear so he asked the waiter to leave the bottle. His food arrived and, despite the circumstances, he began to eat heartily, relishing the sage-scented veal and cured ham combination.

What the hell, he thought, abandoning the Katia rebus for the time being. There shouldn't be anything too demanding tomorrow. He could probably write the first couple of hours of the morning off.

Thirty-Nine

Amal woke with a start. The same dream. This was evil, she knew it, and she had played her part. She looked at the small clock by the bed. It was nearly time. So early and cold now on these mornings. This was Europe, a cold and damp world compared to the home she still remembered well enough despite the years having passed so fast. She got out of bed, dressed and went to the bathroom. She was the first up today. Her father had come in late from work and they wouldn't see him till mid-morning.

She splashed her face with cold water then went to the kitchen to prepare breakfast. Today she had to go back there, to the monastery where it had all happened. They said the police might call again and that if they did, to say nothing if she didn't want to be incriminated, if she didn't want to have "problems". And these were not problems? Waking in a sweat, knowing that she had perhaps allowed a terrible crime to happen. They had told her to get any information and to relay it to the contacts she would meet at the station on the platform at the same appointed times. She thought first that they had only wanted the information so that they could then go there to steal – a lesser evil. An vil nonetheless but they had threatened her. She had told no 1e else and now her only hope was to leave them. She was

217

looking around for other work to be free of them even if in the community it was hard to ever be free of them completely. But she had her Italian friends. Their hold was not so strong; the ghetto was not like Paris or Brussels and she felt not quite so alone when she thought of that. So she had hatched her plan. She had held back the one thing she now felt had been what they really had wanted to hear: an initial and maybe a name. She slipped out and went to find a working phone.

Olivia woke in the half-light. Jibril was worrying her. She felt she had had some revelation, lying there at night and waiting, willing sleep to come. She didn't like what she saw. These friends of his who rarely greeted her or did so begrudgingly as if she were some unfair exception to a rule that made life difficult for them. They had planned to go to an exhibition and it had been his sugges-tion, but then he had given her the sign – the very fact that they *had* a sign – that all had changed. He turned her on and off like a tap. He wasn't using her sexually or otherwise but he had priorities. Priorities which were so far removed and so secret. Secret because she knew nothing and still had not asked.

But now as she lay there knowing sleep might never come, she began to ask herself what the secrets might be.

Yana too had not slept well. The bed was comfortable, hard enough for once, but it was strange to be waking here, neither at home nor with Michael. Tatiana had made her very welcome, and she had been glad to see her. They had talked a lot, caught up, and it had been nice to be part of the family. Part of *a* family. The children were sweet with good manners, well brought up, she thought. Not like so many of those she saw on a daily basis going back and forth to the school near the Wellness Centre, those who verbally abused their parents and whose parents, if they were there at all, allowed themselves to be abused. Always with their grandparents, as far as she could see. Dumped c them. And then when the parents took over, at the weekends and in the evenings, it looked like they had forgotten how it was done.

But what business of hers was that? For her, today was a big day. Of course that was the reason why she had not slept properly. That and other thoughts.

Nurse Rinaldi really quite liked the early shift. Getting out before the traffic, the sun coming up with you as you got ready to face the day. The smell of coffee and breakfast permeated the ground floor of the hospital as she made her way along the all-too familiar path to the ward. Through the windows of the corridor connecting one wing to another she could see the first intrusions of light into the courtyard and the car park and delivery bay. Colder. Not yet autumnal but a few signs were there.

She put a hand into her pocket to search for a tissue but was surprised to find something else there. A card. It puzzled her for a moment and then it clicked. The policeman's card. Rossi. She must have put the same jacket on after Inspector Rossi had spoken to her some weeks earlier and slipped the card into the pocket. He had asked her to call if there was anything at all that she remembered. She stopped at the water fountain and filled a plastic cup. She saw the bin was already half full. She would use the same one until it cracked.

She stood then and sipped at the cool water and then she stopped. Maybe there was something. There had been one other peculiarity but it was just odd, surely. Not of any significance. Still, if he had urged her to call? If he had given her his card.

But no. She took it out again. Detective Inspector Michael Rossi. Office and mobile. E-mail too. No. What could be done now? There was no recycling bin for paper. She popped the card back in her pocket.

"Ah, Nurse Rinaldi," said a young doctor making rapid progress along the corridor in her direction.

"Dottor Sensi, *Buongiorno*," she said.

He stopped in front of her. "Will you join me for coffee or are you duty-bound once more?"

His eyes gleamed with enthusiasm and vigour. He was a very fine man indeed, she thought. And an excellent plastic surgeon. He was heading for great things, so they all said. Perhaps to America.

"Certainly, *Dottore*," she said. "And we can discuss some of the day's duties as we do."

"Work, work, work, Rinaldi. You never stop, do you," he said. "Oh, and by the way. That policeman was here for you yesterday afternoon. Said he was passing and didn't have your number to hand. But he said you had his for sure. He has a thing for you, it seems," he joked.

She fondled the card in her pocket. She remembered the effect her dress had had on the inspector and gave a little chuckle to herself. She thought he had liked her too, but he hadn't seemed the type to try it on. But it was true. Sometimes it didn't matter what you did. Destiny would find you out regardless.

Forty

Rossi opened one eye. His head had been pounding for some time but only now had he decided to break cover. Where was he? He opened the other. At home on the sofa. Thank God. The TV was on the same news channel but turned down. He lowered a leg on to the floor and tried to sit up. A glass lay on the floor, its spilled contents leaving a tacky yellow stain on the tiles. And to think that Yana had been on to him to get a wood floor, parquet. It wouldn't stand a chance.

He felt a pang of relief mixed with guilt as he tried to remember how he'd got home. He must have walked because the muscles of his thighs and calves were stiff and sore. At least the exercise had taken some of the edge off his hangover. Some. He turned round to see the state of the bottle. Still some left in it. He had probably fallen asleep before he could finish it. Small mercy then.

He staggered out into the hallway. The front door was closed but not locked. And his wallet? Still in his pocket. His phone? On the desk. Three missed calls. The sun was well up and was warming the apartment and dazzling him. He headed back to the kitchen for water. Then a shower.

He sat under the powerful jet to conserve his energy as the water pummelled his skull and neck, trying to claw back any significant memories. He must have blacked out then when he had got home. Some fragments were coming back but he was in one piece and alone. He hadn't been robbed. He hadn't been hurt. But he was behind schedule. The doorbell rang once. Then again. He waited. It rang again. He clambered out and, grabbing a towel, lurched towards the intercom.

"Yes."

"Thank goodness you're there. Where have you been?"

It was Katia.

"Sick," said Rossi. "What is it?"

"We've got a match on the picture. Almost certain. Can we talk?"

Rossi pressed the buzzer.

"Come up and make yourself at home."

***

Katia had given Rossi one knowing look and had then made the largest available pot of coffee and following more of Rossi's instructions was now bringing a pan of scrambled eggs to completion.

"Well, I trust this will have the desired effect," she said, eyeing his now more human form. Katia switched off the gas. The heat of the pan would do the rest.

"Here you go," she said, plonking the pan in the centre of the breakfast bar. "Self-service I'm afraid. So, are you ready to listen now?"

"Go on," said Rossi, reaching out to shovel the hangover cure onto patchily buttered toast.

"Portrait of Lucrezia Borgia."

"Certain?" said Rossi.

"As good as."

"So?"

"Stolen."

"Stolen?"

"Went missing from a gallery in Brescia around 1999. Probably an inside job."

"Any suspects?"

"Plenty, but no convictions. Here," she said passing him a sheet of names. Rossi gave them a cursory scan then stopped and almost dropped his fork.

"What is it?" said Katia.

"This," said Rossi, pointing to a name halfway down the list, his mouth still full of half-chewed toast and eggs. "This!"

Katia took the sheet.

"Marciano?"

Rossi was nodding, his eyes almost popping out of his head.

"Marciano!" he spluttered. "He was killed. Don't you remember? The same day in January as the unidentified African on Via Tuscolana, the guy dumped with the pig's head. The same day as Cardinal Terranova. The day after they tried to kill Iannelli in Sicily!"

Marciano had been a local hood, known to Rossi as a pretty much one-man operation who, with hired help, had been working the Eastern European prostitutes and transexuals before beginning to make his move into legitimate sectors – real estate, construction and so forth. He had even been courting contacts in the Church to that end before his untimely end. His death had, however, been painted as a Mafia settling of scores. Rossi hadn't believed it then and believed it even less now.

He was drinking yet more coffee. After the initial elation and the shock of the possible coincidences he was taking it more slowly. Don't get ahead of yourself. Study the facts. Find the link.

"So, a painting possibly stolen by a local hood ends up in the rooms of a retired Belgian priest. It then goes missing from the scene in the immediate aftermath of the cleric's murder. The same local hood, however, had been murdered, decapitated to boot, on the very day that a prominent cardinal departed this mortal coil."

"Nothing obviously suspicious yet. Just interesting coincidences right?" said Katia.

"But worth digging deeper. Why the mutilation of the corpse, for example?"

"Well, if the painting was known to be stolen, by removing it from harm's way someone was covering their tracks. Someone in the Order."

"But that doesn't explain the mutilation," said Rossi.

"That was supposed to be part of the Islamist terrorism matrix. The hypocrisy. Humiliation, denigration. Make sure he's unworthy of an open coffin burial. What do you think? But doesn't sound a bit Mafia if you think about it? Maybe revenge for Marciano?"

Rossi stood up and went to the window, steadier now on his feet. He turned to Katia.

"What if it was to *hide* the face? To remove his identity?"

"To what end?"

"And what if it wasn't Father Brell? What if there never was any Father Brell?"

"Now you're talking," said Katia. "But who mutilated the corpse? Why would a murderer want to conceal the priest's identity?"

"And what if it wasn't the murderer who did it?"

"Who then?"

"I don't know. I just know that it may not be as straightforward as it seems. In fact, I'm not sure I hold with the Islamist motive at all."

"Some sort of conspiracy?" said Katia. "A settling of scores? Underworld scores?"

Rossi was shaking his head. The hangover had matured enough to make his thoughts insightful but not quite incisive. He felt he was close to something now. Closer than they had ever been and he was damned if he was going to let it get away from him.

"I still don't know. I just don't like a lot of the easy assumptions and the possible inconsistencies. There are too many variables here which could go either way. Who killed him? We don't have a single verifiable trace. How did he get in? Why? Who knows something? Did anyone help him? Who took or moved the painting and to where, if it wasn't stolen."

"And maybe it was."

"After the photo was taken? And then he disfigures the face? Pretty cool customer. And why did he want the face to be seen by Iannelli? Why Iannelli?"

"He went to the press. To a free spirit."

"Also someone with a Mafia death sentence hanging over him. Maybe he knows him. And this is his calling card."

Rossi checked his phone.

"Carrara's on his way," he said. "Look, let's see what he makes of it. Oh, and by the way, good work and all that. You've exceeded all expectations."

Katia shrugged.

"When's Maroni in town?" said Rossi coming back to earth with a bump.

"Tomorrow, or the day after. Why?"

"Reports. He wants something he can show to the top brass. Is this any good?"

"I don't think it's exactly what he's looking for but it will show we've been busy."

"He'll throw it back in my face. Say I'm after the Pink Panther next."

"Not the imaginative type, is he?"

"No. A good cop but he's a servant of a higher order, treading a very thin line."

Rossi reached out for his phone and checked through his missed calls.

"You," he said. "Twice. Oh, and a private number."

"Recognize it?"

"Vaguely. Does this mean anything to you?" he said and reeled off a Rome number.

"That's EUR. And only seven digits, which sounds like a hospital"

"Are you sure?"

"Positive. All the public hospitals I know have seven digit numbers."

Rossi sat up.

"Which could be Sant'Eugenio. Where Ivan the Russian was. Where Rinaldi works."

"Rinaldi?"

"A nurse, at the hospital," said Rossi. He held up a hand as he dialled the number. There was a queuing system in operation. He snapped his phone shut and nodded. It was right.

"And where does she fit in?" said Katia.

"Well," said Rossi, "that would be letting you into a secret."

"Rossi and Carrara's little secret, I imagine."

"Something like that," said Rossi. If she wasn't to be trusted, now was the point of no return. Katia shifted to a more comfortable position on the sofa, tucking her legs under her in anticipation of a decent story.

Rossi noted it and made a brief calculation. She was on his sofa. She had practically made his breakfast. She had seen him at his worst and she looked OK with it all. If he wasn't going to be able to trust himself, he was beginning to feel he might be approaching another kind of crossroads.

"Well you've gone and got me all excited now," she said. "So I hope you're not going to disappoint me."

Rossi had given her the low-down, from the fire through to Ivan and his own chance meeting with Tiziana and the subsequent Iannelli link.

"This Iannelli seems to pop up just about everywhere," Katia commented after Rossi had finished.

"Something of a lightning rod, it would seem. Always whe the action is."

"He's got a nose for it."

"He's got a brain for it," said Rossi.

"So, Iannelli meets Jibril, the guy we presume has been looking for his murdered friend. He gives him his business card, including his e-mail address. And whoever kills our Father Brell figure *e-mails* Iannelli the picture of his misdeeds."

Rossi shrugged.

"Probabilities. Coincidence. Iannelli is high-profile, after all."

"And you don't think they could be one and the same person? This Jibril and the priest's killer?"

"For what reason?"

"That's the missing element in the equation."

"If there is an equation," said Rossi.

"Can you see why this guy would want to kill a priest?"

"Rapid radicalization? A jihadist infiltrator? The newspapers love all that."

"Put it in your report."

"Without a single shred of proof?"

The intercom buzzed.

"That will be Carrara," said Rossi.

Katia was on her feet in a flash.

"I'll get it. Give him a surprise."

As she skipped out, Rossi realized he had never seen her like this in any previous work environment. She had always been elegant, courteous, yet deadly serious, a credit to the force and all that. But now.

He roused himself to get the coffee on. His head was showing some signs of clearing, a Godsend as it was shaping up to be an unexpectedly busy day. Rinaldi would be the first stop after they had brainstormed Brell theories and then they would work on Marciano and the painting. Lucrezia Borgia no less.

***

Carrara's look said it all. Very cosy.

"I hadn't been answering my phone," said Rossi by initial way of explanation, "and Katia here tracked me down."

"I've been learning what makes him tick," she said, glancing now between the two seasoned but starkly contrasting comrades and enjoying just a little the sudden disorientation her presence had caused them.

"Heavy night, was it?" said Carrara.

"It got a tad out of hand. Let's say I had a mild blowout, all right?"

Carrara headed towards the kitchen as more coffee began to announce its arrival.

"I notice you weren't too worried about my state or whereabouts," Rossi called after him.

"I told you, I was otherwise engaged," Carrara replied, busying himself with cups as a half-speed Rossi followed to loiter at the doorway. "Non-negotiable family engagements. You should try it sometime. It would do you the world of good to stop going over the case. *And* bringing your work home," he added with a knowing jerk of the head.

Rossi wagged a discreet "don't-go-there" finger.

"Well, regardless of my bad behaviour and your work-life balance, Katia's come up trumps," said Rossi in a self-consciously professional tone. "And we've got ourselves an ID on the painting," he said, smiling through another spasm of residual pain.

"I don't know," said Carrara reflecting on the various hypotheses. "We can see what comes up when we get all the witness statements. The new improved witness statements."

"That sounds dodgy," said Katia. "Not putting words into people's mouths, are we?"

"There are many ways to ask a question," said Rossi. "The trick is getting the right question to get at the truth."

"Like 'was there anything strange recently in the pries*

behaviour?'" said Carrara. "Or 'how would you describe the priest in the last few weeks?'"

"Exactly," said Rossi. "Question one could be an encouragement to *create* something strange, to invent it."

"And question two might let it go unnoticed, even if there was something to report," said Katia. "The chances are they'll say he was just his usual self."

Rossi nodded and sipped his coffee.

"Anyway," said Carrara, "I'm going back to finish all that later. What about you?"

Rossi scratched his head.

"Nurse Rinaldi," he said, remembering the missed call. He called the hospital again and this time was put through to reception. He explained who he was and waited.

"Could you give me ... Yes ... Thank you," he said then killed the call. "She's in theatre for at least another two hours, but is off from this afternoon and tomorrow morning. I'll see if I can catch her at home."

"Going in alone or do you think you'll need backup," said Katia.

"I think I'll manage," said Rossi, brushing off the dig as he remembered first the slightly dowdy single lady who had welcomed them into her apartment in her dressing gown before changing into a rather more revealing number, which in turn made him reflect on his hangovers and their sometimes unpredictable effects on his libido.

And didn't someone once say that no woman can be written off as uninteresting until you've had the chance to be alone with her? Perhaps he would have to put the theory to the test.

Forty-One

They had moved to a safe house. It was a sumptuous villa but where it was exactly Jibril couldn't say. He and Ali had gone the whole journey blindfolded, and they had quarantined their mobiles. He had slept well, as a guest of the President and had sat through a long and sumptuous dinner with him too. Conversation had ranged from the practical to the frivolous but Jibril knew his host was probing, checking, always. He wouldn't trust him. Why should he? He didn't know where Ali was. Officially, he had been whisked off to meet other potential recruits and to aid the President's men in assessing their suitability. Jibril suspected otherwise; that he was getting a similar soft but thorough vetting. A going-over dressed up as an executive break.

In the morning, new Italian clothes had been laid out for him. Nothing showy but of the best quality, so that he might blend in all the better. The President wore whatever he wanted and whatever was appropriate for his numerous appointments or his particular needs. "I have that many identities I need a team to manage them you know," he said to Jibril over an abundant breakfast of fresh fruit and traditional Nigerian foods and specially imported coffee.

"I have a lot of enemies, Jibril," the President said. "I will you openly that there has been a price on my head for years. It is no big deal, as they say."

They were seated in a lounge beyond which a huge window and a view out on to a pool manned by the usual suited security guards. One of the President's bikini-clad wives was traversing up and down, a metronome keeping cosmic time to their conversation. The President himself was taking evident pleasure in describing the elegance and simplicity of his business machine, the machine that would would soon feed Jibril and their cell with the means to make the infidel tremble and beg for forgiveness.

"My wealth, Jibril, is very great. Fill that pool with banknotes of a fairly large denomination and you will begin to have some idea. But my outgoings are many. And wives like that do not come cheap," he laughed as the metronome continued its predetermined course. "But more than this, I have a long list of employees, starting with the companies I collaborate with, the authorities, the police, the judiciary of numerous jurisdictions, generals, customs personnel. The list, Jibril, is endless and grows by the day. Until a name is crossed off, of course. So this, all this that you see, is like some great aircraft which must keep flying, refuelling as it does. I dare not let it touch earth for fear that it may not take to the air again."

He leant over the maps laid on the table between them. "This is but one of our routes and it was a stroke of genius on the part of our logistics man. His only error was to skimp on the intelligence, and that was his Achille's heel." He jabbed a finger onto the map indicating the port of Lagos. "You know these places well, Jibril. How long were you working in the Delta?"

"Nearly four years," said Jibril, "including my time with the rebels. And I saw enough to teach me that my mission lay elsewhere."

"Here, we were able to take delivery of the merchandise. It me on ships which could dock at ports which we had under control. Otherwise we would make the exchange at sea and then, with fast boats, evade the customs police, those of them who were not our friends, and bring it ashore."

Jibril continued to listen. He could see he had at least gained the President's interim trust but at what price? This man saw a transaction in all human affairs. There could be no limits, either ethical or other.

"And then the master stroke. How do you get merchandise from here," he said, indicating the west coast of Nigeria, "to here, Europe? The police in Spain and France and Italy have the most modern means to track consignments, and they are good at their job. It is always *cat and mouse* with the more traditional methods. But innovation too is our *stock-in-trade*."

He looked at Jibril with satisfaction. He shook his iced drink then as if to illustrate.

"We liquify our merchandise, Jibril, and we put it in barrels and everyone thinks it's petroleum. Liquid cocaine. Fifteen days at sea and then it's offloaded in Spain and back on the road in Europe. The free market! We got a lot of merchandise through, until things went a little astray. We were very well up in terms of profit all the same, and the earnings are truly dizzying in this business, Jibril. Vertiginous. But somebody now is paying the price for their mistake. Someone who abused my trust and tried to steal from me."

The President got to his feet then and walked to the window. His metronome had stopped. She was at the poolside now, towelling her firm, lean body and then wrapping a flimsy thigh-length bathing robe about her before stretching out on a lounger. Jibril's thoughts were elsewhere, imagining Olivia. She would be wondering what had become of him. He was wondering too what would become of himself. Yet this was what he had wanted. Being where he was meant that soon he would be within touching distance of his goal. He would have all the means at his disposal. He was close now. It would happen.

"Isn't she just a wonder to behold?" his host said, continu* to gaze at her as if she were a Ferrari behind a showroom window and only he with the wherewithal to possess her. "Can you even imagine that there exist men – so-called men – who cannot find such a sight erotic? Cannot burn with desire in the presence of such beauty? What value can they have, these homosexuals?"

He was not, however, waiting on any response from Jibril. This theatrical performance required no applause. He was hard-wired to a cool and uncompromising hate. A hate as quotidian as eating, sleeping, and drinking. And thus, hardly hate at all.

"Now, we must leave this oasis of pleasures and you will come with me once more. I am going to show you what my money can buy for you and what hardware you will soon have at your disposal. Then we can begin to talk seriously of strategy and objectives and not just of *pie in the sky.*"

Forty-Two

Rossi was drinking more coffee at the bar and going over the memo on the energy conference faxed in from Bologna by Maroni.

"So no specific duties. That frees us up," said Carrara as they stood up and made their way back to the office.

"Wants us to maintain a floating role," said Rossi. "More like someone doesn't want us sticking our noses in, given past experiences. How do you see it?"

"I see it as a no-brainer," said Carrara. "I've got a load of paperwork and you've got calls to make. Let's press on until we get further instructions."

"Yes," said Rossi, "but don't you immediately get the urge to *dis*obey?" he said, stopping mid-step to confront Carrara and give concrete emphasis to his point.

"You mean your inveterate instinct to go counter to whatever *they* ask you to do?" said Carrara.

"Or my hardwired tendency to try to pick up some points even when the odds are stacked against us?"

Carrara rolled his eyes.

"So you want to go down and take a look? Is that it?"

"What harm could it do? Come on. But there's also anoth‹ idea I've been hatching."

"Apart from Rinaldi?"

"Yes."

"What?"

"Who, more like."

"OK. Who?"

"Marciano."

"Marciano? He's six feet under."

"Long overdue though. Or his wife at least. Remember her? Linda Marciano."

"Unforgettable. What's she doing now?"

"That's what I want to know," said Rossi. "If Marciano was mixed up in art theft, fencing goods or whatever, and if that painting is involved, I want to know how *she's* getting to the end of the month. There could be paper trails or at least something to look into. She's probably working that daughter of hers."

"What, farming her out to the highest bidder?"

"That was hubby's line. One of many."

"But not their own flesh and blood, surely!"

Rossi shrugged.

"I have also heard talk that there could be some sort of a media career being lined up."

"Same thing then," Carrara quipped.

"Whatever she's in, it's untapped potential. I think we need to put a bit of pressure on her."

"I'll find her address."

"Got it already," said Rossi.

***

They were waiting in the car.

"As soon as someone comes out we go in. Then we lean on he doorbell."

"Reckon she's there? Even if she didn't answer the bell?"

Rossi looked up to the second-floor flat.

"Windows open. Washing out. Good chance she's up by now. Suspicious souls like her don't leave any openings for opportunist burglars."

"There we go," said Carrara as the front door opened and a mother and buggy began negotiating the step onto the street.

Rossi jogged up to offer assistance, holding the door open so they could then make their way up the stairs.

"We'll say it's a gas leak," said Rossi. "Look." He held up an ItGas photo ID. "These things come in useful when you haven't got a warrant."

"Gas man," said Rossi in his best Roman accent. "A strong smell of gas been reported in the building."

The light coming through the spyhole was briefly occluded. Then the door opened a crack as a dark-rimmed eye and a head of curly black hair made a furtive appearance. The only smell emanating from the apartment was that of skunk weed, and Rossi jammed a shoe in the gap before she could reverse her error.

"Coming through," said Rossi, giving Carrara the cue to add his weight in the albeit brief struggle.

"You can't come in here without a warrant!"

Rossi sniffed the air like an expectant diner.

"More where that's coming from, is there?"

Carrara closed and chained the door.

"We just want some moments of your time, Linda. And then we'll let you get back to whatever it is you do here."

The flat's modern interior was neither in order nor disorder but the heavy smell of dope gave it an air of indolence and stasis. Unwashed breakfast things were still in evidence at one end of the dining table. There were items of clothing and black underwear draped over a chair. Linda retreated into the apartment flicking out her wiry arms to snatch up the more intimate item with understated urgency. She returned then to face the tw officers. Late thirties and holding her own physically, she was wearing denim shorts, flip-flops and a tight vest top.

She sat down at the dining table and resumed where she had left off with a cigarette still burning in the ashtray.

"Legal tender, as you can see," she said indicating with a flick of her wrist the filter-tipped king-size.

"So you had guests, I presume?" said Rossi.

"I have frequent guests. I'm popular. You can sit down if you want," she added, sizing Rossi up as Carrara made an idle tour of the apartment. "You won't find anything, if that's what you think," she said, as Carrara prodded around, picking up vases and other household objects.

"So what are you living on now?" said Rossi. "Now that the breadwinner is no more. I would say I'm sorry, but I won't. He was a worm."

"I get donations," she said, "loans." Oblivious, it seemed, to Rossi's comment. "I have generous friends."

"C'mon!" said Rossi. "What did he leave you? You don't exactly seem to be in dire straits."

"I don't have a penny. *Nullatenente*. 'In possession of nothing'. The flat's mine by right but they can't have it cos I got a kid. As for the bills," she grabbed a handful of papers heaped on the table, "I don't have to give 'em a penny and I'll be fucked if they get any."

Rossi didn't pursue the potential for irony.

"Look, Linda," he continued, "I don't care about the money. Leave that to the residents' association and the courts but don't blame me if they come for your place. And that kid of yours won't be a kid much longer. What I want is information."

She shook her head like a schoolgirl hauled in for smoking and reeking of the stuff despite the absence of proof.

"I want to know what he had got involved in before he was ¬led. The official story is that he was working for one of the l *N'drina* and the Camorra, but I don't buy it."

She stood up and made a few nervous paces first one way and then the other sucking hard on the near butt of her cigarette.

"Either of you want a drink?" she said, without emotion, "because I need one. Now."

Rossi shook his head.

"A little early for me."

"Yeah, right," she said, tutting, and headed for the kitchen. She came back swigging from a bottle of Ceres Extra Strong.

"So?"

"So, what?"

"What was he doing?"

She threw her head back to drink again then reached for her cigarettes.

"Why would I tell you anything? What's in it for me?"

"Well," said Rossi, "next time we pick up that daughter of yours, or bust one of her parties, she might *not* be found carrying 20 grammes of coke."

"*Sei un bastardo!*"

Rossi shrugged his shoulders and looked at Carrara, who could see no reason for such language. Rossi leaned a little closer.

"This is not my usual style, Linda, but we all have to bend the rules a bit to get by from time to time. And if your dead ex-husband hadn't been rumoured to be pimping fourteen year olds, I wouldn't have to stoop this low either. Now, how is your daughter by the way?"

"Making waves. And using her God-given talent."

"Sleeping her way to the top then?" said Carrara.

"She's getting into TV. You do what you have to do to get a foot on the ladder in this country."

"Look," said Rossi, "I only want to know if the deceased was messing in the world of fine art."

She stubbed out her cigarette and finished all but a mouthful of the beer.

"I got a warning, right?" she began. "I was told, in no uncer terms, that if I gave any of you lot a single thing, we would suffer the consequences. Pietro had plenty on a lot of people and, who knows, one day all that might come out. But you can consider it dead and buried, like him. I didn't tell you a word. You were never here, and I don't want to see any of you in my house again because I won't tell you anything else but this: Pietro was moving money around, laundering it, and running rent boys for all sorts. Right to the fuckin' top."

"Where from?" said Rossi.

"I told you. Nothing else."

"Just the country. Were they Italian or *stranieri*? I need to know."

"I don't know. Maybe Africans. *Negri*, right? They all wanted black guys. The big fuckin' bamboo? Now, will you leave me alone!"

"*Who* wanted them?" said Rossi. He knew he was pushing it but he needed more. "Give me a name."

She looked nervous. The arrogance and disinterest had been replaced by raw fear. He knew it. He'd seen it. Yes, he remembered fear.

"Church," she said. "The Vatican."

"That was impressive," said Carrara as they left the building. "All the bad guy stuff."

"We're in a corner, Gigi, and I need to get out of it," Rossi replied.

"So you'd have picked up her daughter?"

"I had to make her think I would. She can't afford that plan to go wrong. She's her next meal ticket. Until she hooks another gangster, she's investing everything in her offspring. Just the thought of that going up in smoke was enough to get her to spill something."

"You believe it?"

"Don't see why not," said Rossi. "There've been rumours

239

aplenty about the skin trade in Saint Peter's barque. And Okoli knew something too."

"Another reason for someone trying to take him out?"

"Who knows?"

"Where next then?"

Rossi glanced at his watch.

"The Energy Conference, lunch, and then Rinaldi. See who's there and then see if it was her who called and if she's got anything to say for herself."

"You don't think she's the attention-seeker type, do you? Likes having cops round for coffee and all that?"

"Possibly," said Rossi. "But it's like panning for gold. A lot of sludge, back-breaking work and wasted time, maybe for that one little nugget."

"Or fool's gold."

"Or fool's gold," said Rossi, in acknowledgment, though not wholly thankful for the levelling comment.

Forty-Three

He was still not answering his phone. When he hadn't shown up for class she had assumed that he had been called for a last-minute work commitment. But in such cases he always let her know. This time there had been nothing. She had planned to use her free time to do some shopping around Termini station and then maybe hook up with Jibril for coffee. Now the idea had lost all its sheen. She looked around as if someone or something might clarify things for her, but the world went on the same, oblivious to an anxious-looking provincial language teacher standing in the middle of the footpath on the main thoroughfare. No one in the class had any news, and neither did they seem to care. She would have asked Jibril's friends but they only ever waited outside for him. Today, there was no one.

She had no rights over him but it was out of character. She began to contemplate her options. Was it too early to go to the police? She knew he was distrustful of them and of authority in general. That he had his documents in order had to be a plus point but she didn't want to become another millstone round his neck. He had escaped the circumstances of his former life – a vague version of which she knew – in order to be free to come and go as he pleased.

But what if something had happened to him? More than once he had alluded to enemies back home, saying that he had escaped from political persecution but without being specific. Who his co-nationals in Rome were she couldn't really say. This much she knew, although the world of Nigerian politics was complex and contradictory. And now there was the battle with the oil companies. For Jibril, they were raping the Delta and its Igbo people, that same people who had been the more progressive, democratic, and forward-looking group and who had then lost out when their opponents seized power. And these were the same opponents all too often involved in complex and profitable double plays with the foreign oil companies. But he had spoken too of the Islamist groups in the north not having a pure agenda. It was confusing. He seemed to be saying so many things and it worried her to hear how intensely he felt about it too. Was he just a jumble of contradictions? Unstable even?

She cut across past the back of the Church of Santa Maria Maggiore and then wandered up the slight incline of Via Liberiana turning right then on Via dell'Olmata. She passed The Fiddler's Elbow pub where a slender, red-haired barman was finishing a cigarette. She thought again about what she knew of that world Jibril had explained to her, the one he had left behind. Exasperation and the orphan's unceasing will to endure. He had been a child when his brother was killed but had been a witness to it. His father had left in mysterious circumstances, perhaps for his own safety, but there was something in the story he had held back from her. He had then renounced his wish to continue his education and go to university, in Lagos or even abroad, opting instead to head for the oil fields, where his own father had worked as an itinerant labourer. He had hoped to find him and find work. He had found only the latter and then as the reality of that life sank in, he had become politicized.

These stories, Olivia remembered, had been like some gre nineteenth-century novel for her, for Jibril had a storytelle skill. She had met few with his linguistic gifts, and the rapidity with which he had mastered Italian was a joy to behold. When he couldn't find a word he would throw in an English equivalent and so the story would continue. How he had begun to doubt the real motives of the political leaders guiding the rebels. He had realized there was a lot at stake and profits could be made. In the name of Igbo independence and to strike a blow against the corrupt national government and foreign interlopers, they sabotaged the pipelines. But there was also a flourishing black market in stolen oil. Rumours quickly became reality when it was clear that certain individuals were consolidating their individual power bases with the capital they had accrued. Weapons and narcotics were both currency and a means to an end.

When things had come to a head, Jibril had had no choice but to head north. He might have taken a tourist visa to Europe but he was also on a list of wanted men and had already changed his identity. Better to take the hard way across the Mediterranean and begin from scratch. She felt now, as once more she played the film of his life, that she was looking for certainties, islands of truth and dependability.

She crossed another piazza, passing another medieval church she had never seen before then walked on through the sudden cool shade cast by the Torre delle Milizie with its warlike, crenellated fortifications. She knew his religion was important to him. He had been brought up as a Muslim and yet he had initially identified with the largely Christian people of the Delta in their pursuit of freedom. He had made many friends, some of whom he had travelled to Italy with or met on his journey. But then in other moments he had railed against the Church, as if those same Christian friends had been secondary, casualties of a hatred towards an institution which he saw as corrupt and even evil. It had been strange too for her to see him behave like a completely different person when confronted with the bigoted views of some of his classmates. Was he not free now to speak his mind? It was not that simple he had told her. But why, she asked, why?

She realized she had been wandering the streets without any destination. She didn't want to go home but she felt alone and confused. She looked up and saw she was in Via in Selci where she had also just passed a police station. She remembered that among her documents she had a copy of Jibril's identity card that the school had requested. If she went to the police to report a missing person? But she didn't even know where Jibril worked. She had never been to his house as he would always come to hers. She had accepted it all, until now. But as she stood there debating whether or not to go in, it was her contemplation of this mysterious nature of his that began to get the better of what she had thought was her reason. What if he was leading some double life? Was she then an accessory to his activity? The friends he had, some of whom she had seen but never exchanged even a greeting with. His absences, and now this disappearance without explanation. She walked on and made her way towards the Metro station. A discordant note now had broken the long melody of her reminiscence. How quickly the happy present could become the troubled past.

Forty-Four

The Traffic Police had placed temporary and permanent cordons at Piramide and the beginning of Via Ostiense and Circo Massimo, as well as along Via Aventino and Via delle Terme di Caracalla to facilitate the arrival of various heads of government and their motorcades. Many had come directly from the military airport of Ciampino in the south-east of Rome, ushered at high speed from the suburbs along Via Ardeatina and then in through the gates of the old city walls at Porta Latina, the police outriders stationed periodically like pressure locks in a hermetic system siphoning their charges from A to B.

Rossi and Carrara breezed in and parked up outside the headquarters to the UNAF building.

"Why here?" said Carrara. "For the conference, I mean."

"*Roma Caput Mundi*," replied Rossi. "Where else?"

"You mean everyone wants a nice little holiday?"

"And the shopping."

"Naturally."

"And it's like Italy's at the forefront in energy saving and efficiency, isn't it?"

"Should be," said Carrara looking up at the cloudless blue sky.

"Can you believe Germany produces more solar power than we do?"

"I *can* believe it," said Rossi. "And we pay them to take our rubbish to their incinerators because we can't get our act together."

Protestors were massing beyond the police lines well away from the main entrance to the UNAF building. There were green associations, radical environmentalists, and various national groupings.

"Who's public enemy number one today then?" said Carrara. "The Iranian president? The Americans?"

"Looks like the LGBT crowd want to pick a fight with our Nigerian friend and his antediluvian attitudes to gender equality. He's even making the Pope look like some sort of liberal in comparison."

Agents posing as journalists were already getting all the close-ups they needed which would then go on file and add to the growing database of possible insurgents and troublemakers. Rossi didn't exactly approve but he was in no situation to make quibbles. He and Carrara scanned the crowds.

Among the very heterogeneous placard-waving crowd there were the old bourgeois liberal lefties who'd spent decades on the barricades as well as an array of younger and more militant *centro sociali* types, gay and straight alike. There were plenty of black Africans too, and their slogans weren't pulling any punches.

YOU DON'T REPRESENT US!
BLOOD ON YOUR HANDS!
WORSE THAN HITLER!

"Don't like their president much, do they?" said Carrara.

"No," said Rossi. "Seems he garners a lot of consensus with the gay bashing. It's a transversal issue. In the north, where they've got sharia law, I'm afraid stoning's the order of the day."

"Just for being queer?" said Carrara.

"Homosexual, Gigi, surely. Or gay."

Carrara accepted the correction with a quizzical look.

"So you've got queer culture but I can't call them queers?"

"It's like if I say a joke about the Irish or the Neapolitans, it's allowed. But if *you* make the joke, it's racism."

"Because I'm from Puglia and you've got mixed ancestry?"

"Right."

"If you say so. I'm not a homophobe, Mick. If that's what you're thinking."

Rossi smiled and noticed a friendly face on the edge of the crowd.

"Roberto!" said Rossi approaching a photographer who was busy checking through his photos on a pre-edit. "Safe to talk?"

"*Vatten!*" said the stocky and prematurely grey undercover cop with mock irritation. He had once been a *falco*, a plainclothes motorbike agent, penetrating the organized crime networks of Naples and Rome, until an accident that had nearly cost him his life. He was sending the images straight back to base via a Bluetooth connection.

"They get these in real time and if there are any faces, we'll all soon know about it."

"Wouldn't mind getting a look at them myself," said Rossi. "For a little side project of mine."

"Another of your way-out theories, is it?"

"I do get the odd result, from time to time," said Rossi, smiling. "Are you getting them at the back too?"

"Doing my best. Look out, he's on his way," he said then gesturing to the fleet of black-clad *carabinieri* outriders heralding the arrival of a series of limos and black security vehicles. "The president of Nigeria."

The crowd noise became focused, tripling in intensity then as the motorcade swept through the main entrance, barely slowing on the curve in to the parking area.

"Didn't get much of a look at him, did they?" said Carrara, relaxing his grip on the Beretta beneath his jacket as the first key moment of tension had passed.

"There was an orange alert out on him," said Roberto, letting his camera dangle by his side, his job done for now at least.

"So what's the answer?" said Rossi. "Do I get the goods or do I have to buy you dinner too, at Rosario's?"

"See what I can do," his old friend replied in thick dialect, as another, more senior, plain-clothed operative drifted past with a walkie-talkie clamped to his jaw.

Rossi gave Carrara the signal and they moved in.

"Get a shot of that, will you, before they leave," said Rossi, indicating a home-made placard tied onto a crash barrier and referring to a pressure group called "List of Shame". It was one of those placards that protestors rolled out demo after demo and it detailed a series of deaths in suspicious circumstances and summary executions going back some twenty-five years. There was a Web address too and a contact e-mail. Carrara snapped it with his mobile while Rossi continued to scan the crowd. He did a brief double-take when he recognized the familiar face of Professor Okoli. They smiled and waved to each other. The demonstrators were too tightly packed for him to get forward but Rossi saw that the prof looked his usual self – content and going about his business.

Behind him, unseen by Rossi and the photographers' lenses, stood Jibril – anonymous, a protestor like anyone else.

Forty-Five

"Here it is," said Carrara coming back from the print room with a list of suspicious and politically motivated homicides in Nigeria for the last twenty-five years, names in alphabetical order and background information to each case. He handed it to Rossi.

"I've sent you a digital copy too. It'll make it easier to search online. And Rinaldi?" he added.

Rossi was already deep into studying the grisly inventory.

They had returned to the office after a working lunch at Rosario's feeling very happy with themselves, if only because they had had perfect *calamari* and a glass or two of very cold *Falanghina* on the terrace followed by homemade *granita* sorbets and fresh figs. But the feeling was fading as they contemplated the gravity and complexity of the task ahead of them.

Need to know what it is that makes them tick, Rossi said, half to himself and to no one in particular. Carrara knew what it meant. Rossi's various threads and disparate lines of enquiry were either on the point of overload or a stunning breakthrough.

"What?" said Rossi.

"Rinaldi," said Carrara again. "We need to see if she's got something."

"Right," said Rossi. "Shall we go? Just give me half an hour with this first."

***

Rossi's attempts to match some of the names he'd picked up from the placard with news stories had so far produced nothing. There wasn't a comprehensive online archive of the media he'd been looking for, but he had got some fragmentary leads. Yet he didn't really know *what* he was looking for. He just *felt* the list was significant. They were on their way to the car but had brought paperwork with them to maximize their productivity.

"And I've got the rest of those statements in," said Carrara, "from the Brell case. I've highlighted anything new. See what you think." He handed Rossi another folder which he leafed through as they headed out of the building.

"Let's go and see the nurse," he said, as he opened the passenger door and tossed the folders onto the back seat of the Alfa.

This time she was ready for the visit, dressed in a dark, knee-length skirt and white blouse, with a string of pearls and matching earrings.

"I've finally managed to track you down, Inspector," she said, addressing Rossi as she brought a tray of coffees into the living room. "I heard you were looking for me but we had another urgent burns admission."

"Yes," said Rossi, finding himself drawn to the curves that the well-coordinated outfit now exalted. "We've been very busy, as I'm sure you will understand. We've been reinterviewing anybody who might be able to help us in our enquiries."

"Well," she said, proffering a cup to each of them in turn. "I did think of something. Unusual, like you said, and I wanted to be of assistance."

"It all helps," said Rossi.

"It has to do with Ivan," she continued. Her lips, Rossi noticed, were delicately glossed and she looked ten years younger. "It was something he tried to say. You will remember I said he didn't say anything. That was not entirely true. From time to time he did attempt to communicate. And he was often floating in and out of consciousness."

Rossi nodded. The nurse smiled, perhaps from embarrassment, as she began again.

"At one point we thought he wanted to drink. There was a jug and a glass next to the bed. And he appeared to be saying '*bicchiere*'. Glass. But because of his pronunciation and because he could barely move his lips, we spent a long time wondering what he was trying to say. It came out as *Vik. Vik-yer*. Something of that nature. You know the way the V and the B can be close, like in Spanish. It was odd and we thought he wanted to drink, but every time he refused the glass we offered him. And that's it really."

Rossi sat there thinking. Not much to go on. He wondered if it hadn't all been a ruse. The attention-seeking. The skirt, the lip gloss, the way she sat now on the sofa, slightly sideways, offering herself even?

"Interesting," he said. "And nothing else?"

"That is it, Inspector. Sorry to drag you over here but you did say 'anything' at all, didn't you?"

"Quite right, Nurse Rinaldi," said Rossi.

Rossi gave a glance at Carrara and collected his folders from the coffee table. He stood up and reached out to shake hands.

"So soon, Inspector? But you have only just arrived."

"A hundred things to do," said Rossi.

"But I'd made a cake."

"I'll be in touch," he said. "If we need to speak to you again."

"Anytime, Inspector."

"And thanks for the coffee," said Carrara.

*

251

"So?" said Rossi when they were back in the Alfa.

"She's definitely taken a shine to you," said Carrara hitting the accelerator before another light changed to red. Rossi was flicking through the pages of the statements again for want of something better to do. There was plenty of bumf and boredom-inducing monotony in them, and he was about to stifle a yawn when something leapt out of the page in front of him.

"Hang on," he said. "Pull over."

Carrara swerved into a slip road and stopped.

"Look at this," said Rossi holding out a sheet. "What is it?"

"A transcript, of a phone call."

"Anonymous? Right?"

Carrara nodded.

"We get a lot of calls," said Carrara. "They're all logged. No use in court though."

"OK. But it says Brell knew 'V'. But what the hell is it?"

Carrara studied the transcript:

CALLER (UNKNOWN): *hello*
Officer: *yes.*
CALLER: *I want to report a crime.*
Officer: *Yes. Where are you?*
CALLER: (*pause*)
Officer: *hello*
CALLER: *Father Brell knew V. He knew him.*
Officer: *Can you repeat please.*

"Some five second phone call from a crank. What does it mean to you?"

"But Ivan," said Rossi, "Ivan said 'Bik-yer', or *Vik-yer*. The B and the V thing. Don't you see? What if it's a name? What if it's a connection."

***

They were back in the office and Rossi was scribbling down names and arrows and dates as Carrara made a heroic stab at catching up with a backlog of paperwork.

"House fire. Ivan. Vik-yer. The priest killing. The letter V from the anonymous call. The priest. The painting and Marciano. The cardinal. A murdered African. The same day. The Nigerians. Maybe the Nigerian mafia. Are you seeing anything?"

"Maybe," said Carrara. "And maybe not."

"Ivan didn't like Catholic priests. Remember his reaction? Marciano was pimping African rent boys, *to the Church*, according to his widow. Doesn't it all add up to something?"

"It could," said Carrara, "but *what* exactly?"

Rossi was racking his brains.

"If there's a link between the Nigerian mafia and their operations with the local Mafia, Marciano among them, and then the rogue elements in the Church, then we might be onto something. Remember there was the Lausanne business, the airplane with Vatican insignia bringing hot currency through. A priest went down for it but every thing pointed to it being an operation that went much higher up to the bishops and cardinals. And we know Marciano's stock-in-trade was money laundering."

"And the Church hierarchy distanced itself pretty sharpish if I remember," said Carrara. "Got some junior dupe to take a fall."

"Well, in one way or another, we could be getting close to whoever killed Marciano and possibly even the unidentified African who Jibril most likely really did know. It's the dates that concern me but, even if I am going out a bit on a limb, maybe the cardinal featured in all that too."

"So what do you propose?" said Carrara willingly pushing aside the report he had been working on and sensing already that Rossi was going more in the direction of hare-brained scheme than procedural orthodoxy. "And this list? Where does that fit in?"

It gave the names of those murdered or who had died in

suspicious circumstances at the hands of the Nigerian authorities. It featured those opposed to the actions of multinationals involved in oil exploration in the Delta, those who had championed Igbo human rights and had sought compensation for damage to the environment and their farms.

Rossi was already going through names and unearthing a promising amount of secondary material.

"It's a shot in the dark," he said, "but it might just give us another element. Another piece in the puzzle."

"If there is a puzzle."

"You don't think there is?"

"Not always. No."

"Do you have an alternative idea?"

There was a knock at the door. It was Katia. She stopped and looked at the two men locked, it appeared, in some sort of stand-off.

"I would say I'll come back later," she began, "but I can't. We've got ourselves a body."

"Where?" said Rossi.

"On the Appian Way. Not pretty."

Forty-Six

There had been no second chance.

"That's why, when you see the videos, they appear so calm. It's lucky for them," said Ali. "And more than they deserve. They should thank their God. They're like dumb animals being led to the slaughter."

The ritual had been played out, as it had so many times before, with the camera and the knife-wielding militant reeling off the rhetoric. Then the film-set paraphernalia would be packed up and the prisoner returned to his solitary confinement. Only, this time, Ali had stepped up to deliver the orations in a mask with, unknown to his victim, orders that these should be their prisoner's last moments on earth. There had been no attempt to disguise his voice, either as a sign of arrogance or disregard for his own destiny. His face being recognized would compromise operations. But putting a name to his voice would take longer.

"How did you feel," said Jibril trying only to show his awe. He had killed too. He had been a soldier but with very different rules. He also realized that until then he had doubted Ali, feeling he was fervent to the point of crazy, mostly talk but perhaps lacking in real courage. But if this was proof positive of his courage then he had been wrong. Was he simply a killer for pleasure, for his own satisfaction? Jibril had seen that in the Delta and had smelt the victims' blood up close.

"I felt strong," said Ali. "I felt powerful."

Yes. Playing God, taking life, can do that, thought Jibril. But he knew that taking life was something he himself would have to do again, and he wondered if his reasons made him any different from Ali.

"You will have your chance, Jibril," said Ali, pumped full of his own importance. Yes, he had regained ground with his fearless actions, his bravery, his decisiveness. Jibril, meanwhile, had been elsewhere, sent to observe the demo as an intelligence operative. That the cell was now under the effective control of the President, no one even imagined questioning. They knew how his reputation preceded him: his need to dominate, his expectation of unwavering loyalty, his celerity when extracting merciless revenge.

The members of the cell had moved to a safe house. There would likely be many other such hideouts and they would constantly be on the move. So, Jibril's old life, albeit his fake life, was over. His job before had only ever been a subterfuge for when he was pursuing his other activities. He now "worked" in a shop in the Tor Pignattara district. "You are on the books, you exist, but you can come and go as and when is necessary," the President's man had told him. "No one will bat an eyelid. They all work for us and they know where their bread is buttered." Jibril had then accepted his new papers from another link in the long chain of command. "Destroy everything else," his intermediary had said before leaving him.

Jibril had taken his once-prized items, his old papers, and placed them in a steel bin. He struck a match and held it to the curled corner of his Italian ID card. Watching the flames take hold, a memory from his own past surfaced, that of his grim-faced father in a fit of anger sweeping up armfuls of books from his brother's room and hurling them onto a fire burning in their yard. Until that sharp remembered moment, Jibril had seen books as sacred things to be cherished, as luxuries even. Yet, his father had burnt them because they had, in his words, been the beginning of his other son's downfall. The Devil himself was between their pages, he had said and only purifying fire could rid them of the shame he had brought upon them.

He thought then about Olivia, knowing he could never see her again. He was wedded to his cause and she had been but a stepping stone to cross the torrent. And now he stood on the opposite bank looking over at the path he had taken, the many stepping stones he carried with him as if they had become a part of who he was, weighing heavy in his flayed heart. But there could be no going back now. He imagined himself looking into the deep, dark forest before him, the different roads through it and which of them he had to choose.

Forty-Seven

The crime scene had been cordoned off temporarily with a squad car blocking access on either side of the busy Via Pignatelli cutting across the ancient, now pedestrianized, consular highway. It was the road that gave captured slaves or returning centurions their first inkling of the metropolis awaiting them as they trod its smooth basalt paving. And all along its length it was dotted with tombs and sepulchres of every description.

The body was lying in a stubbly field behind a dry-stone wall. A couple of unmarked cars had also swung up at the intersection. Forensics had just finished erecting a gazebo to keep the *locus* at least minimally uncontaminated by the warm breeze lifting dust and debris off the surrounding farmland. Carrara emerged, pushing back one of the tent flaps and then giving a friendly slap on the back to one of the uniforms posted outside. He strolled over to Rossi, who was waiting by the Alfa and, for now, just thinking things through.

"They left his ID in his top pocket," said Carrara holding up the document in an evidence bag.

"Decent of them," said Rossi.

"Giancarlo Mondo. Reported missing two days ago after failing to return home from a meeting."

"Phone?" said Rossi.

"Nothing."

"Check his traffic, last place he used it. What did he do?"

"An executive, for ItalOil."

"We know that?"

"He had his swipe badge. I gave them a call."

"What do you make of it?"

"Decapitation?"

"And the rest," said Rossi. "Tortured?"

"Can't say yet but doesn't look good."

"Hardly a mugging gone wrong."

"Jealousy killing?"

"Organized crime, more like. If we're lucky. Maybe worse."

Katia was approaching from her car and holding a printout in one hand. Rossi could see the heading already.

ANSA Press Agency.

"Don't tell me, someone's gone and claimed it."

"Read for yourself?" she said. "Thought I'd deliver the news personally."

The text contained the usual prolix preliminaries about imperialists, multinationals, and infidels. Rossi cut to the chase.

"Islamic Caliphate in Europe. *As an example to others.*"

"And there's a video, for good measure," said Katia. "It'll be airing tonight on one of their recruitment Web channels, aiming for maximum impact and maximum revulsion. The Telecoms guys are trying to shut the site down but it will come out one way or another."

"And go viral," Rossi commented. "We'll need it for evidence anyway," he continued, "so someone's going to have to watch it."

He passed the press release to Carrara and, as he did so, noted the timestamp.

"You must have driven like a maniac," he said, studying Katia for signs of agitation, but she was as steady as a rock, as if she'd been out for a Sunday spin.

"I don't mess about, Michael, when it's serious."

Rossi didn't feel he could allow himself the luxury of pondering whether or not it was a loaded comment.

"And what do *they* want to do?" he said, indicating the secret service operatives who had also rocked up in record time. Too fast, maybe.

"Keeping a lid on it?" said Carrara.

"Who knows. But we're in charge here until further notice. See they don't take any souvenirs."

"I'll hold the fort," said Carrara, "till a magistrate gets here. But what about Maroni?"

"He'll know," said Rossi. "By now. What do you think?"

There was a call coming in on his mobile.

"Speak of the Devil," said Rossi but it was Yana. He stared into his own watery reflection in the obsidian-black display, then let it ring, then let it ring some more. Then it stopped.

"Nothing important then?" said Katia, who couldn't resist the tease.

"Nothing that can't wait," said Rossi, tight-lipped. "Come on, I suppose we'd better take a look at this horror show too," he said, jerking his head towards the gazebo, another monument to the reaper on the road out of the Eternal City.

Forty-Eight

Maroni had cut short his work engagements in Bologna and was coming back to Rome that evening. He wanted everyone on message and with something worth hearing. Carrara had been out and about overseeing forensics and heading up initial background enquiries. How long had the body been there? Had he been killed *in situ*? How had he been tortured and why? Meanwhile, the Financial Police had furnished Rossi with a sheaf of documentation on Mondo's professional movements and personal affairs. He had been a person of interest but there had been no investigation open. Katia, meanwhile, had been chasing up Mondo's managers at ItalOil, those that weren't out of town, or the country.

She held up a cup to offer Rossi a coffee from the office *espresso* machine but he shook his head.

"They're not giving much away," she said. "They're waiting on their security department and their lawyers before they commit."

"Did you get an idea, a sensation?" said Rossi, leaning back in his chair and tapping a pen against a blank writing pad. "Are hey covering up or just playing cagey?"

"Well, for a start, a lot of their security outfit is ex-secret services. Add in the high-stakes with international oil deals and something's going to stink for sure. And *omertà* makes no distinction of race or class. Whatever you say, say nothing, right? They could be thick as thieves and buttoning up until things die down."

Rossi was beginning to sense the familiar feeling of frustration like incipient gangrene colonizing a wounded limb. He handed her some of the data.

"These account movements, these figures. They could be anything. There's no suggestion that they were illicit, is there?"

Katia finished off her coffee and walked over to the desk. She scanned them and shook her head. "Need to find something in cash. Or a paper trail, or even a tip-off. But who's going to stick their neck out?"

Rossi rubbed his eyes. He'd thrown himself into the enquiries with gusto in an attempt to break it by sheer force of will, but now it was as if he had strayed from the right path and night was coming down fast.

"Time to take a break?" Katia suggested. "Look. There's a Sicilian bistro that's just opened. We might get some inspiration over a glass of special reserve *Nero d'Avola*."

The offer was nothing if not tempting. But the consequences?

"I think I'll keep going for a bit more," said Rossi. "And then head home. Early start with Maroni tomorrow."

"All work and no play, Inspector," said Katia. "And I mean that as a friend, Michael."

Rossi looked up. She was smiling. Her eyes were smiling too and brimming with warmth and not a little promise. Though she had left on the safety catch with that final "as a friend", was there still just the faintest hint of some new, slow-burning fire taking hold?

When Rossi left the office it was almost dark. The video of the execution had gone out and made the predictable stir. An Islamist decapitation on Italian soil. It was a first and he could only imagine how it might empower the backlash, how it might polarize opinions.

They had their guys in audiovisual forensics working flat out, but the video had been put together with minimal risk. All it took was a backdrop, a soundproofed room. The assassin's voice through his mask was real, so there was a chance he might be a documented suspect. Another grinding, time-consuming matchup job, but they had to pursue it. They were even trying to match his gait with anyone caught on film or known to them. A long shot but technically possible.

In all the years he had never watched one of these vile executions. The unfortunate, the innocents, the naive, the agents too, probably. He had always jerked his head away as they had been dispatched. There were others who could stomach that stuff but not him.

He pondered calling Yana again. She hadn't called back but there was no chance of his being able to have anything approaching a normal conversation. He slipped the phone into his pocket then turned his thoughts to Iannelli. He had been alluding to something like this all along. That conversation. Back then, it had all seemed so fanciful, hypothetical, but now? He began running through the facts. What did they have? A dead oilman and an Islamist cell on Italian soil. At least that's what it was *meant* to look like. That was the narrative. He looked at his watch and took out his phone. Engaged. He didn't even know where Dario was or what safe house he was currently occupying, but he knew he needed more from him. From anyone and fast.

Forty-Nine

Iannelli's new flat was in the centre of Rome, on a backstreet full of short-stay foreign tourists and bed and breakfasts. He'd been there over a week following developments via media outlets but it wasn't enough for him. He wanted the low-down from Rossi who owed him one after all. They'd sent out for takeaway, and Iannelli had then cracked out the *limoncello* – artisanal, of course, and a gift from Rita, his Sicilian girlfriend. The heavy shot glasses from the freezer were still half frosted as he flicked again through the scene-of-crime photos Rossi had brought. He then slipped them into the envelope before handing everything back.

"Not pleasant," he said, through a thick beard that could have placed him in some other epoch. Rossi noted that he appeared to be adapting well to the new circumstances and had, perhaps in some evolutionary sense, prospered. The most varied of books were distributed at key points about the room – next to armchairs, on the writing desk in the corner.

"How are you going to move this lot?" said Rossi. "If you have to ship out all of a sudden."

"Get them sent along if needs be."

"Screen fatigue?"

"I decided I couldn't completely do without the printed word," he said, picking up a slim volume from the coffee table, his interest elsewhere.

"So?" said Rossi. "What are you thinking?"

Iannelli sat forward a little in his leather armchair. Rossi saw the book was Lewis's *The Middle East and the West*. A seminal work.

"Have you wondered why these terrorists never hit the powerful, try to take out a politician for example? I mean it's invariably the common man, isn't it?"

"Well, Mondo was certainly no politician," said Rossi. "But what if he was still a senior player in some bigger game. Where does that leave us?"

Iannelli looked at Rossi over the rim of his glass as he finished the shot.

"What have you got on him?" he asked slamming it down empty.

"Not exactly transparent in his affairs, but who is, at that level? I mean, they try to cover their tracks but when they're dealing with the ex-colonies, well it's hardly like doing business in Switzerland."

"You mean corruption's an entry on the balance sheet?"

"As good as."

"And you know who foots the bill for that, don't you?" said Iannelli.

"Well, in this case, the government. It's a 51 per cent shareholder. The rest is in private hands."

"So the taxpayer has to stump up, if it's a government company. We all pay. Do you know how much we pay for our energy? Have you ever wondered why?"

"The cost of corruption?"

"Right. And apparently you can heat a house in Germany for a year, with what we might pay in a few months."

"OK," said Rossi, "but are you saying this was or wasn't terrorism?"

"Depends how you define terrorism," he replied. "It could be an end in itself but there's always the effect it has on public opinion. It generates fear, which could also be a *means* – a method of paving the way for a reaction. But for what? Another war on terror?"

"If that's the best way to combat terror, so be it," said Rossi. "If we are 'under attack' it's self-defence, right?"

"OK," said Iannelli. "So if a drug dealer gets his brains blown out on a Tor Bella Monaca housing estate then it's a settling of scores between gangsters. Get over it. But if it's a guy in a suit working for a multinational then it's an attempt on democracy, the clash of civilisations. A bit paradoxical?"

Rossi gave a half shrug.

"If you like. I see what you're driving at. He got in too deep or did the dirty on someone and then paid the price. But ICE claimed it."

"And who are ICE?"

Rossi pondered what he'd so far managed to glean from Mondo's tight-lipped and lawyerdependent superiors.

"He'd just brokered the new lease on the Delta oil fields in Nigeria."

"That's a big fucking deal," said Iannelli. "Deals that size carry a lot of 'extra weight'. Jobs for the boys. Sweeteners." He began using his fingers as he enumerated each point. "Either he knew too much, or he was going to talk, or," he paused, "his conscience might have started functioning again."

For Rossi, the shape was forming now of an unholy alliance: terror caught up with corporate and even state-sponsored corruption. Expediency directly or indirectly admitting no moral limits.

"And who does it suit to have us thinking we're after Islamists?" said Rossi.

"Consider this for a minute," said Iannelli. "Did the Americans in Afghanistan or Iraq really *know* why they were there? I mean *really* know. Maybe it takes all this narrative to convince them they're not just playing meaningless roulette with their lives."

"And you can't do the whole thing with paid assassins or mercenaries," said Rossi.

"Right, because when a terrorist does eventually get picked up, if he's only in it for the money, the narrative falls apart. You can't perpetuate the myth like that, the myth which *attracts* consensus, forms consensus, fosters support in the community – ours or theirs. There will always be true believers cutting throats or planting bombs or, God forbid, blowing themselves up in the supermarket. There have to be, but do they really always know why or for whom? Apart from their legitimate sense of perceived injustice at our hands."

"So who do you think we should be looking for?"

"Isn't that your job?" said Iannelli, leaning back now. "I give you the global picture but you have to get your man."

"Well, one name keeps coming up, apart from the Russians," said Rossi. "What do you know about the so-called 'President'? Our intelligence says he's making moves. He's watched as a matter of course but they can't pin anything on him."

Iannelli's eyes came as close to lighting up as they could.

"The President *never* gets his hands dirty but he's running the coke, the prostitutes, legit and semi-legit ops here, in France, Switzerland, Eastern Europe and back in Nigeria. He's as good as untouchable. He's the oil in the machine. Always there, keeping things turning and he has no ideology except that dedicated to his own self-aggrandizement. You want to catch him *in flagrante*? Well, it's boxes within boxes, Russian dolls, front companies, offshores, dummy accounts, you name it. But no one will shop him, if they want to keep breathing that is."

"And now," Iannelli continued, "our government wants to 'reform' the constitution – to make it easier to go to war. And every time they drop a bomb, launch a missile, or fire an AK47, someone's writing a cheque that someone else is going to cash. War is the motor of the currency carousel, Michael."

It was Iannelli's cynical stock-in-trade, perhaps exacerbated now by the harsh reality of his own incarceration. Rossi wondered sometimes why he wanted these answers that could be so crushing, so cynical. But within it all, within the intricacy of the conspiracy, some detail could provide inspiration.

"Does the letter V mean anything to you?" said Rossi. "Perhaps a name connected to Jibril," he added, explaining his half-theory about Ivan's deathbed ramblings.

Iannelli shook his head.

"My contact with him was limited. I meet a lot of people. *Met* a lot of people."

Rossi was trying again to draw the strands together but he needed more, some confirmation.

"And the picture they sent you? Why did Father Brell have his face removed? For me, that's not Islamist. Something bothers me too about the cardinal who checked out the same time as the unidentified African was found with his throat cut last winter."

"Well, from what I've heard, Cardinal Terranova was no angel," said Iannelli. "There were always plenty of rumours about his business affairs and his predilection for underage Africans. So I doubt that he'll be getting his wings *post mortum* either."

Iannelli gave a dry laugh, and as he did Rossi remembered what Okoli had said, or at least alluded to, in his joke about the skin trade and Nigerian men.

If the cardinal died back then, thought Rossi. If he really did.

Fifty

Yana called again. No answer. She began typing a message but then stopped. She had heard what was happening in Rome. Everyone had. They were talking about it in the bars and restaurants, the papers were speculating wildly, and she knew Michael would be in the thick of the action. So what if she needed to set things straight with him?

She picked up her bag as the Eurostar approached the platform. She had plenty to keep her busy for the five-hour journey, and it had been a productive few days. Milan was a city with potential. A city with pretension, sure, but serious about business. Rome was still Rome and it was going to take a bit of getting used to living up here but she was no Roman. She was no Italian for that matter. She wouldn't be put off by a bit of fog in the morning and there would be plenty of skiing opportunities, something she hadn't done since before the— She stopped. No. There wasn't a word for it. Not in her lexicon. She might have said "accident", but it had been no accident. The attempt on her life? She had shaken off the physical effects in record time, though she still bore some scars. They were harder to quantify and they could continue to do their work, like shrapnel in an old wound.

She took her pre-booked seat and set about getting through

a thick wad of reading material. Another loan. It was doable and necessary. The accountant had gone through the costs, the best- and worse-case scenarios, evaluating her proposals and coming up with price lists. The services they would offer in Milan would be different, fine-tuned to the needs of a more varied and more European clientele. They had factored it all in. And of course, if it was going to be a success, she would have to oversee it all, hands on. It wouldn't be forever and it wasn't as if she was making a clean break, but it would require commitment on her part. A move.

She settled into her seat as the train moved off heading south-wards again, heading home? It was home, it had become so with the passing of the years, but its pull was relative. A call was coming in. She took it.

"Yana!"

"Hi, Sergio."

"Just checking you got your train all right."

"I'm on it now. Thanks."

"Great. No problem. Give me a call when you can. When you've gone through everything."

"I will," she said.

"OK. *Un abbraccio.*"

"Thanks again," she said, mildly embarrassed by his effusive-ness. *An embrace.* It meant nothing. It was only words, here in Milan especially, where it might have appeared well meant but was really business-banter dressed up as spontaneity and warmth. She had to see through the smooth talking and remain objective, focused.

From the opposite side of the carriage, a fidgety businessman in a closely tailored blue suit and who looked about half her age, was eyeing her repeatedly over his laptop. She feigned indiffer-ence with minimal effort, popped her earphones in, then put her head down and got stuck in to her work.

"A sleepover?" said Carrara, "In a church?" They were making their way to the briefing room where Maroni and the rest of the special-unit operatives were meeting.

"Trust me," said Rossi. "It might be the key, to everything. If not, well, we're back to square one but no one ever got anywhere by pussyfooting around, right?"

"Can we talk about it seriously later?" said Carrara double-checking he had brought all the relevant paperwork. "You realize we risk causing a diplomatic incident, again. I mean, two cops in sleeping bags in a basilica?"

"We might not even need to stay. That's the safety option. We could be in and out and no one will be any the wiser."

"You still haven't told me why," said Carrara, as Rossi rapped on the door.

At least they weren't late. Some comfort for Carrara, who he knew would be thinking he was at least partially insane.

Fifty-One

"Address," said the *maresciallo* poised with both index fingers over the keyboard.

"I don't have the address. But it would be on his records. For the school," she added.

The plain-clothes officer looked up at her.

"I'm a teacher," she said by way of explanation. "I teach Italian to adults, migrants. The missing person is one of my students."

"Perhaps you can give us the address later, madam. And the date of birth and maybe even the surname."

The irony wasn't impolite but it had the required effect.

"It's a question of privacy," said Olivia, aware now that she had crossed a line. "Some of our students do not always want to be compromised."

The *maresciallo* looked at her again.

"You do want to find your friend, I take it?"

"Yes," said Olivia.

"Is he in any kind of trouble?"

She hesitated before answering this time.

"I'm worried about him. I think he may have become involved with people. People I don't know."

"Criminals?"

"Like I said, I don't know. I don't know who they are."

"Is he an illegal immigrant?"

"No," said Olivia. "Well he was. He arrived illegally but he managed to obtain an identity card, a *permesso di soggiorno*, everything actually. He had all his papers in order and a job."

"But you don't know *where* he was working?"

She shook her head.

"I didn't pry into his personal life. He didn't really talk about it."

The *maresciallo* slid the keyboard back. She looked genuinely concerned, an intelligent girl, like his own daughter on her own now in Milan.

"Perhaps you could give me the name and address of the school. We can take a look at his records."

Gab was up to his eyes. He had computers running and fans whirring all over the place. Some of the machines had their covers off and various additional bits of hardware and hard drives and chips plugged in to cope with the volume of work he had on. If he'd known he was going to be this busy, he would have employed somebody. Still, he couldn't complain. He had cultivated a business approach that was reaping big dividends. He never turned down a paid job from a new customer; he never missed an appointment; he was never late, and he had abandoned the suit and tie for open-neck shirt and a jumper. Clients were getting wary of the clean-cut types, but they trusted him.

Something beeped. He looked around. He'd almost forgot about that. "Now let's see," he said to himself. Code correct. Entry approved. At last. What a pain that had been and it was meant to be a simple job. He made a few rapid interventions on the laptop and lo and behold, there it was. At least some of it. Now he *would* be pleased. Better late than never anyway. He looked around in the confusion for his phone. Rossi. He would be *very* pleased.

"So you have a name? said Maroni, "and nothing else?"

"Maybe two names," said Rossi.

"Two names? And anything else? An address?"

"We think they could be in some way connected. And maybe even to the fire on the Prenestina. And the Brell murder. Possibly more."

Maroni continued to look along the length of the table at Rossi. Other operatives were playing with their pens, scribbling phantom notes, avoiding eye contact.

"But nothing solid? As in *real*. No material links that could lead us to a potential suspect? Someone we can bring in for questioning about any of the recent events?"

He looked around the room. Someone gave a tension-breaking cough.

"Others here seem to have picked up on the religious fanatics buzzing about down at the mosques, as well as other suspect individuals with criminal records, but this is all you've got?"

"As yet," said Rossi, "but it's a longer play. There's also this President character. The Nigerian."

"What, he's a part-time jihadist as well, is he?" It was Silvestre, revelling in Rossi's public difficulty, unable to resist the chance to twist the knife.

"I think there's a connection," said Rossi.

"I'll talk to you later, in private, Rossi," said Maroni. "Now, moving on …"

Maroni had been called to yet another meeting, thus postponing the tête-à-tête to a later date. Rossi was counting his blessings when a message came in from Gab.

Want to see some dodgy videos? Cracked the code. Let me know.

"For once something," said Rossi half to himself and to a distracted Carrara, who was labouring over more reports and printouts. "Gab's come good on the CCTV for us," Rossi added, attempting to divert his colleague's attention. "What have you got there?"

"Cross-checking database info. Seeing if we can get a match."

"What did you try?"

"Jibril, Brell, Prenestina, that sort of thing."

"And?"

"Nothing."

"So Jibril's an invisible?"

"Not surprising."

"And what if we put in the letter V?"

"Ivan's?"

"V or Vik-yer, whatever. It's worth a try. Could be Russian." Carrara shrugged in half agreement.

"If it meant anything. I reckon she was just after attention."

"Well, we've got the CCTV at least. Think you can tear yourself away?"

"Suppose so," said Carrara.

"You don't sound overly enthusiastic," said Rossi. "You're not happy about my hunch, are you?"

"Not really, no. Especially as you're intent on keeping me in the dark, again."

"I've got an idea and I want to see it through, but if we use official channels they won't give us the time of day. And in the meantime, well, anything could happen."

"Shall we get this CCTV out of the way first?" said Carrara.

Rossi was looking at his phone. A message from Yana.

Back today. When can we talk? Dinner?

He picked up his jacket.

"C'mon then, let's go."

Fifty-Two

Jibril and Ali and the rest of the cell were gathered in the new safe house. A good deal of the posturing and bombast of before was gone now. Talk of emirs and infidels had become somewhat secondary to talk of operations and strategy. Conviction and dedication to the cause was a given. They had stripped down things to their essentials, and the seriousness of their work was matched only by the gravity of the consequences should they fail. Jibril and Ali had undergone a test by fire, an initiation from which there could now be no going back. Their comrades knew it too and could read it sculpted into both of their expressions. They had tasted violence, touched death with their own hands.

"Combat training will be quickly stepped up," said Ali, their *de facto* quartermaster and weapons expert following his rapid full-immersion course courtesy of the President's men in his fortress-like set up away from prying eyes. Samples were laid out on the rug around which they were sitting. The blinds had been closed, the door bolted and a man posted on lookout. The purpose-built cover for a hatch in the floor was poised near the opening, and they had been through the drill in the event of a raid. They were there to play computer games and smoke marijuana. They had cover jobs, they had called in sick – it was all worked out.

Ali produced a map and indicated the localities where they would be heading for shooting practice.

"Won't we stick out like a sore thumb?" said Jibril. "All us foreigners descending on a forest in the Apennines."

"These places are as good as deserted," Ali replied, "and besides, we will be on a Christian retreat," he added, laughing. "There are abandoned quarries too, where we can scarcely be heard. And if anyone does cause trouble, well, we can look after ourselves."

"There will be none of that, Ali," Jibril cautioned. "We use caution, we evaluate the risks and we stick to the plan. Nothing else." The others nodded their assent, while Ali continued to stare at Jibril before jerking his head down then to study the map with overzealous intensity. Jibril wasn't planning on getting drawn into any of Ali's seemingly random fantasies of martyrdom. If Jibril was ever going to pay the ultimate price then it would be on his own terms and only in return for a reward of his choosing.

The recruits began stripping and mounting their weapons, following Ali's lead. Jibril had little need of practice. Back in the Delta, he had been able to do it all with his eyes closed. For a long time he had believed in that cause until he had glimpsed the darker side, the obscured underbelly. The collusion, the temptation, the need for unsavoury compromises with the enemy. Then the spell had been broken. Like falling out of love, it had happened from one moment to the next but it had also left a hole in him somewhere he knew he had to fill.

"And soon there will be the heavy weapons," said Ali. "That's the gear we need to make a real mark, take them on in the open."

Jibril saw again that Ali was set on hastening his own end in a reckless blaze of glory.

"Shall we talk of objectives now, Jibril?" said Ali, turning to his comrade and cocommander. "When our requests for hardware are granted we must be ready to strike."

Jibril saw the fire of almost sexual anticipation in his eyes. He must have lain awake at night imagining what the cell would be able to do once fully operational, like a scientist visualizes the moment when his experiments validate his long and stubbornly held hypothesis.

"We will need to establish a strict protocol," said Jibril. "Access to the weaponry, storage, movement; it all requires planning and we can start by mounting a series of dry runs, dummy runs if you like.

Ali was nodding. He too had followed the training, the main thrust of which Jibril was now passing on.

"Ali, as quartermaster, will oversee the cache, will monitor and guarantee its integrity and, acting on my orders, will distribute arms accordingly. In the meantime, you will each have a weapon for personal defence and cash sufficient to maintain your autonomy."

He then reached behind him for a holdall. He unzipped it to reveal its contents, bundles of currency the like of which none of them had seen before. Yet they were focused. This was the means which funded the cause and the excitement in their eyes was because what they saw made their objectives real and reachable.

"Now you can see that we were right to accept patronage," said Ali.

"Use it wisely," said Jibril, handing out wedges to each, "and discreetly. This is your guarantee, your protection. With this you can blend in and remain a ghost within this city. You need to look like a businessman, you buy a suit, some nice shoes, a briefcase. You want to stay in a hotel to check out a target? You go there and you pay in cash. But you use a decent wallet so no one starts asking questions about where you got it from."

"Little do they know," said Ali, reaching out to take his and holding it up to the others, "that when they pay for their perversions – their whores and their drugs – they are putting down a deposit on their eventual purification by fire."

He looked at Jibril again and then at the others as if wanting their approval for what he was about to say next. Karim and Yusef sat cross-legged, tense.

"We are growing impatient, Jibril. The time has come to abandon caution and perfect planning. No attack can be 100 per cent safe. We wouldn't be here otherwise, because we know the dangers and we accept them."

He took from his pocket his own plans. A grave risk in itself, carrying such papers, but Jibril knew he had said enough for now. "This is how to make a device; rudimentary but effective. Household products, easily obtained. Acetone and hydrogen peroxide."

Jibril knew too. "The Mother of Satan", they called it, as it was undetectable, devastating, but lethally unstable.

"I am working now on its manufacture so we can build stockpiles. It's time we made a mark. Then when the serious weapons come we will *all* be battle-hardened."

Ali's eyes had rested on Jibril, who, unflinching, returned his questioning gaze. Had Jibril let doubts creep in? He was the senior figure, they all knew his military past, but if he had lost his nerve he could be their downfall.

"Where do you propose?" said Jibril before Ali could further feed his doubts. "Where would *you* have us hit? A symbolic target? Civilian? Military?"

"Here," he said, jabbing a finger onto the map of the city before them. "With a timed device, during a demonstration. It will be massive. It will bring us respect, and it will spread fear."

Fifty-Three

It turned out that a scrupulous *maresciallo* had been doing his job properly. His instructions in line with the new security protocol had been to evaluate any anomaly, no matter how seemingly banal. He knew that not all his colleagues would have been so scrupulous but that was the way he was. He'd weighed up the young lady before him as soon as she had begun her story; something in his instinct had told him that she might have been lucky. Lucky to be alive even. Perhaps he'd remembered the time at the airport when they'd shot up the El Al check-in desk, or the naive and trusting Irish girl who had come within a hair's breadth of carrying a bomb onto a plane, duped by her Jordanian boyfriend in the so-called Hindawi affair. As this young lady, Olivia, had revealed her skeletal knowledge of her friend or lover, his suspicions had grown.

He'd left a colleague in the *denuncia* office to continue registering lost wallets and complaints about noisy neighbours, and he had driven to the offices of the charitable association she had indicated. Sure enough, a concerned secretary showed him the class lists and the subscription form. A search then through the police computer revealed what he had suspected – that no such person existed, at least with that name and those particulars. In short, the papers were false. Then there was the address and there had been a match with the name on the police computer. There was an outside chance that the name could refer to a person of interest. It hadn't come up before because the papers were fake and not on any database. Now it had. A conversation with his superiors had been enough for them to pass on the information to the relevant inter-force coordination team and word was soon winging its way in the direction of the RSCS and the rapid response unit.

A call came through over the radio for operatives in the region of Piazza Vittorio, Via Principe Eugenio, 23, flat 7. Name of Jibril. Rossi was onto it in a flash. African male, twenty-five to thirty-five. Possible criminal suspect. False papers. Exercise caution. Advise for backup.

"Perhaps Maroni might give us some credit now," said Rossi. "This could be the breakthrough," he said slapping the siren on the Alfa's roof.

"Do we need that?" said Carrara.

"You haven't seen the traffic yet."

Carrara put his foot down and slewed the car onto the tram tracks.

"Sure about taking this route?" said Rossi, "remember the last time."

"Course I remember," said Carrara, remembering how during The Carpenter case they had narrowly avoided a collision with the number 3. "But this time you're not navigating."

The Alfa was eating up the straight stretch of road between Termini station and Porta Maggiore and even a few disgruntled taxi drivers had ceded them the right of way.

"That's what I call public-spirited," said Rossi.

Rossi killed the siren as they zeroed in on their destination.

"Let's wait a second, which is it?"

Carrara was localizing it on his maps app.

"That one there," he said, indicating a large pollution-encrusted and granite-porticoed entrance.

"Flat number and name?"

"Number, no name," he said, "What about the age and appearance?"

"I'd say generic but close enough to a fit," said Rossi remembering both Iannelli's and Tiziana's descriptions.

"Sure you don't want to call backup?"

"What do you think we're going to find?"

"No idea. I thought you knew."

"A priest-killer? A mutilator? Want me to continue?"

"C'mon then," said Carrara checking his weapon. "Let's go in for a chat."

Rossi pressed a few random buzzers before he got a reply.

"Can you open up, please, advertising."

The lock clicked.

"Works every time," he said swinging the heavy oak door inwards.

"Which staircase?"

"Two," said Carrara, already having found his bearings. "Third floor. Lift?"

"Walk," said Rossi. "Element of surprise."

They climbed the few flights into the dark, groping for a light switch as they did so. It was out of order on the third, so there was only the borrowed illumination from the floors above and beneath.

Rossi nodded to indicate the flat. He had his hand on his Beretta.

"Gas leak?" whispered Carrara. Rossi nodded his agreement.

Carrara rang and then knocked.

"Open up, please, Gas board. There's been a report of a gas leak."

From behind the door there was a babble of foreign voices, some shushing, more discussion then silence.

"Again," mouthed Rossi hanging back, his finger on the trigger, the safety now released.

"Gas leak, open up," said Carrara. "It's urgent."

If anyone in there did open up, but with automatics, he was in the firing line, thought Rossi. It should have been him, not the family man.

There was a metallic rattle as a key turned and more voices, a male, clearly audible this time, before the door sprang open.

Carrara hurled himself forward, and the door chain exploded off the jamb, sending a middle-aged man careering backwards into the hall. As he did so, a plump woman behind him let out a scream to wake the dead. Rossi followed, his weapon drawn. The man was cowering on his back, his hands in a futile protective position.

"Don't shoot, please. We are good people. Please, don't shoot."

Calm returned quickly once Rossi had replaced his weapon, apologized and reached out to help the terrified gentleman to his feet. Carrara began a general sweep of the apartment then returned to give a provisional all-clear before checking the adults' documents. Two small children had remained petrified on the threadbare couch in the living room. The family was African but there was no Jibril here. The father had sat down on a kitchen chair, his wife standing next to him a formidable dark Minerva in her flowing robes.

"We have been living here for one week," she said, in good Italian. "We know nothing of any Jibril. We are honest people."

Rossi apologized again, explaining then the circumstances behind their need for stealth and deceit.

"Do you mind if we continue to look around?" he asked.

The matriarch gave him his wish with a swish of her hand.

"We have nothing to hide."

Carrara and Rossi went through the rooms one by one accompanied by the mildly disapproving presence of the woman of the house.

283

"We have to search the children's room too," said Rossi, sensing her disapproval as he pushed open the door with its cartoon figures and felt-tip drawings emblazoned across it. Carrara waited outside as he lifted the mattress on the single bed and the cot, then reached in to the back of the wardrobe, and checked behind the row of picture books on a shelf. All tried and tested places for stashing drugs, money or weapons. But there was nothing.

Carrara, meanwhile, had moved into the bathroom and after a search of the cupboards and behind the washing machine was fiddling with what looked like a loose panel running alongside the small chipped enamel bathtub. He looked up at Rossi standing now at the door. He gave him a nod. The panel came away with relative ease to reveal a space of around half a square metre.

"Hiding place?" said Carrara.

"Could be," replied Rossi, "but no goodies, right?"

Carrara bent further in and craned his head to look under the bottom of the bath and behind the dust-coated pipes. He shook his head, then, almost as an afterthought, ran his finger along the rough untiled concrete where there was a darkish stain. He rubbed his thumb and forefinger together then sniffed at them. It was a familiar smell. He wiped his finger on a handkerchief.

"Oil, and baths don't need oiling. Looks like it could be weapons-grade."

The former occupants, believed to be three Africans and a Pakistani, had disappeared without trace. A group of men claiming to be friends had subsequently materialized, stripping the flat of all its contents and settling their debts in cash. This, at least, was the landlord's story and Rossi and Carrara could find no reason to believe he was lying, although he was unable to produce any documentary evidence for his tenants. A phone call had brought him there in record time, once Rossi had mentioned the issue of tax returns and prosecution for the unsanitary living conditions. They had taken his particulars, leaving

284

him with a nice sword of Damocles hanging over him as he waited to see whether or when the revenue service would be paying him a social call.

***

"But he *was* here," said Rossi replacing his phone into his pocket as they descended the gloomy staircase. "Some sensitive soul's reported him missing."

He'd managed to get through to Katia while she was at the *Questura*, and she had filled them in over the phone about the tip-off and its provenance. "And now that we've planted our size twelves in the community, everyone will know about it, don't you think?"

"Well it certainly wasn't surgical," Carrara replied.

"We didn't have much choice," said Rossi as they emerged then into the bright September sunlight.

"Where next then? This girl who gave us the tip-off?" said Carrara who'd picked up some of the details of Rossi's conversation with Katia.

"Girl*friend*," said Rossi.

"Well, she must know something. Perhaps we should get on to whoever it was that sussed her out."

"Later," said Rossi. "Give him time to file his report. But aren't you forgetting young Gabriele and his video nasties? And I need to get on to the good people at The List of Shame about politically motivated murders in Nigeria. Something tells me they might have an angle on all this."

"Where first, me lud?" said Carrara.

"The girl," said Rossi after a brief reflection.

"OK," said Carrara. He might have known.

Fifty-Four

The visit hadn't required any subterfuge on their part, and Olivia had shown them in to the shared apartment, apologizing for the mess, which, to Rossi's eyes, seemed non-existent.

"Can you describe these friends?" said Rossi. "Their approximate age, ethnicity, appearance. I believe you said you knew no names. Is that so?"

"Yes," she replied, "I had never met any of his close associates. I realize now I was being deliberately distanced and then when he went with them and said he had work to do, I assumed a woman was not welcome."

"And you mentioned a job, I believe," said Carrara.

"Yes, in the social services. Home help, domestic work and the like."

But Rossi was already shaking his head.

"All a front, I'm afraid. He had no gainful employment, according to records. For reasons as yet unknown to us, he seems to have made up a cover story. One of many, I fear, although it may have been for his own protection.What else did he tell you?" he asked, seeing a way in. "Did he know people working in those jobs?"

She shook her head. "He lived with other Muslim men, several in the same house. He said they prayed together, observed the festivities. It was for company and to save money."

Carrara was looking at Rossi now. They'd seen the flat. The panel under the bath. Rossi was homing in on the other link, the anonymous tip-off about Father Brell, the letter V.

"Did he ever mention a friend?" said Rossi. "A friend whose name might begin with V?"

Again she was shaking her head. Her eyes seemed elsewhere.

"He didn't mention any friends by name."

"Are you quite sure?" said Rossi. "It could be very important. Are you certain he never mentioned a name?"

"Certain," she replied. "I would have remembered."

She put a tired hand to her forehead. Rossi knew the pressure she was under. He knew that since she had reported him missing, the questions must have been coming thick and fast. "But I am afraid for *him*," she said. "Not for what he might have done. I can't believe he has committed any crime. Maybe he owes money to traffickers."

"There may be money involved," said Rossi, "but there could be much more. So, you must help us find him and, if he is caught up in something, we can prevent him and anyone else from getting hurt."

She explained how they had met and how he had stood out as an exceptional student and a charming and polite young man.

"It was my idea," she said. "It was a combination of things, really. A desire to help but also an attraction. He was very kind, interesting. Sensitive."

"And did he ever tell you why he was here, in Italy?"

Carrara got up to answer his phone and strode out onto the balcony.

"He was a migrant. He arrived on the boats and after leaving Sicily he came to Rome."

"But did he say why?" said Rossi again.

"To make a new life. A better life. That's all. He said it was hard in Nigeria, at least for him. He had been involved, as far as I could understand, with resistance groups in the Niger Delta; but he believed he had been doing the right thing." She looked up at Rossi as if seeking his understanding. "But you would, wouldn't you? If you had principles and a desire to see justice. Just like the partisans fighting fascism."

Rossi was still sitting across from her, waiting, listening. Arms and explosives training. Expertise. Battle-hardened. Traumatized even. PTSD. It was beginning to add up. He asked her to go on. "And then there was his family; his older brother who he had seen killed when he was only a little boy. His father had abandoned them and when Jibril's mother died, he said he was an orphan, in all but name."

Rossi was thinking fast now. This was what they had needed – some backstory, more possible links to fill in the bigger picture he had been seeing all along, albeit "in a glass darkly". But they were still no nearer to tracking him down. They had a picture, at least, to go on from the language school records. But where he was and what he was doing and why he had disappeared, were three towering unknowns in the equation. In terms of instinct and probability, however, it was all pointing one way. He was observant, ghettoized in his private life and he had got mixed up in something radical and likely violent. And if the corpse he had gone to identify really had been a friend then that might also have been the instigator, the initiating stressor to set him on a destructive path. He rattled off a text to Tiziana. If they had the CCTV pictures from the mortuary to match it would be another piece in the puzzle.

Carrara came back in and took Rossi aside and out of earshot.

"Got his prints coming through from the CIE in Sicily. And there's a possible correspondence on the database search."

"Great!" said Rossi quietly, careful not to let Olivia overhear and squeezing Carrara's shoulder. As they turned back to Olivia he sensed she knew they had discovered something significant.

"Has he done something?" she said. "Is he a suspect?"

"No," said Rossi, playing it down. "But he is in this country on false papers, and for his own good and his own safety it would be better if he were to turn himself in."

Olivia looked him in the eye, and Rossi held her gaze, unperturbed, serious but not detached.

"You think he's a terrorist, don't you?" she said with more than a hint of accusation. She'd heard what some police could do to those who dared to question their authority or protest their innocence. Jibril had told her of the beatings they had dealt him in Africa as he had made his way across the desert and into Libya. She had felt the scars' ridges too, as she had run her fingers across his back in the dark as he slept.

This officer seemed decent, kind even, but there were good cops and bad cops. And if your face was black, or if Islam was your religion, you might not always get the same chances.

"We have to exercise extreme caution," said Rossi. "These are difficult times, for all of us."

Olivia's momentary outburst of anger, more the product of repressed stress than any real rancour, had subsided as quickly as it had arisen; but there were the beginnings of tears in her eyes now and her expression had lost a little of its firmness.

"Don't hurt him," she said. "He's not a monster. He's not evil. I know he isn't. Promise me they won't hurt him."

Rossi had assured her as best he could. Regaining her composure, Olivia had shown them to the door.

"I think you should go home to your parents or stay with some friends for a few days, if you can," said Rossi. "It's not that you are in any danger at this stage but it might be wise, at least as a precaution."

"But my job?"

"Perhaps you should try to get your school to find you something else for now. I'll have a word," said Rossi, knowing that they would have a financial skeleton or two in the cupboard that they would rather remained undisturbed. He was sure they would see reason and do the decent thing.

Fifty-Five

"So?" said Rossi. "What's the story. I don't know if I can take any more good luck."

They were back in the *Questura* and holed up in the office with the plan to see Gab and his CCTV images temporarily on hold. Carrara had been keeping Rossi on tenterhooks since he had got a call and was now staring at the fax machine and chewing on his pen.

"It's a record of an anonymous phone call. I think it could be worth waiting for."

The machine suddenly sprang into life, spewing forth the couple of pages he had been waiting for. Carrara tore out the sheets. "Male, Eastern European accent, according to the officer who took the call, probably intoxicated, makes wild accusations against, wait for it, the Holy Catholic and Apostolic Church *before* the Prenestina fire."

"A drunken rant then," said Rossi. "We've all seen that before, on a Saturday night. Probably done it myself."

"Right," said Carrara, "But he says, and I quote, 'they killed Victor. The bastards killed him'. And then the line goes dead."

Rossi mused for a moment.

"Nothing else."

"No," said Carrara. "It was the only relevant match. Put it all together and what do you get? Has to be one hell of a coincidence."

"Ivan, the fire, the priest in the hospital, and V for Victor," said Rossi, turning it over in his own mind. "And the officer didn't take it seriously?"

"He took it down in writing. Everyone knows anonymous calls are inadmissible as evidence."

"But are always kept on record in the event of their proving relevant to an investigation," said Rossi, finishing the line from the crime-detection manual.

"What do you think?"

"I think it's adding more fuel to a fire," said Rossi, "and if we can corroborate it further we'll have the makings of something that they can't ignore. Can we find the officer?"

"I'll get on to that now," said Carrara.

"And then put it all together: Marciano and his rent boys serving the city's clergy, at least some of them; the Borgia painting, Father Brell's murder, the mutilation of the corpse; the name Victor or something close to it – from three different sources now. That can't be coincidence. That's a story with a beginning a middle and an end."

"So, our next move is? Do we go to Maroni?"

Rossi was slumped in his chair, his chin in his chest.

"I say we go for the jackpot," he said, raising his head to look straight at Carrara still standing by the fax machine, the pages held in his hand. "Let's take it to the limit. We're one step away from seeing what could be the whole picture."

"It's the sleepover, isn't it?" said Carrara.

"Yes," said Rossi. "And I say we move tonight."

Fifty-Six

When Rossi got back to his apartment it was almost seven o'clock. He had sent Carrara on a mission to find the officer who had taken the anonymous call about Victor earlier in the summer. He had also charged him with putting together a detailed reconnaissance of the suspect cardinal's final resting place, the Church of San Lorenzo in Lucina. There was no post for him and, as the beginning of a tentative fitness drive, he climbed the stairs instead of taking the lift. The key turned in the door. Had he forgotten to double lock it? He pushed it open as silently as he could and with his other hand reached inside his jacket for his Beretta. No breaking and entering. But someone was inside. He heard a chair move in the kitchen.

"Michael."

It was Yana.

"You had me a little worried," he said, replacing the weapon in its holster as he approached her. She never came unannounced.

"I called several times," she said, wiping her hands with the tea towel and putting it down. She'd been tidying, he noticed. "But I suppose you were more busy than usual."

He took a beer from the fridge, and went for a glass, offering her one but knowing she would decline. Then he sat down at the opposite end of the breakfast bar. She looked good. She'd cut her hair, was wearing some new clothes.

"So," he said, "it's been a while. What's up?"

She gave a little laugh.

"I could say the same to you."

"I didn't go off for a week."

"You're always off, Michael."

"It's my work," he shot back. "The case doesn't wear a watch, as we say."

She nodded. She'd heard the spiel before, and there was a time when it was very romantic and exciting and she'd felt the buzz coming off him when he was chasing the bad guys. And she knew at first-hand. After all, he'd saved her all those years ago. So she owed him a lot, she supposed. Or did she? He was only doing his job. No. That was unkind. He'd gone beyond the call of duty and she of all people knew that. But now?

"I have to go away, Michael. For work."

"How long?" he asked, looking straight into her eyes as he took another, longer, draught of beer.

"I'm going to have to move, to Milan. I've decided to expand the business and open another salon. I'll need to be there if I'm going to make it work."

"And your place here?"

"I'll be able to let it out, to cover my rent in Milan. That's the plan anyway."

Rossi finished his beer.

"So, it's all worked out. Congratulations," he said and went back to the fridge for another 33 cc lager. The small ones hardly counted.

"It's early days but I'm optimistic. I'm taking out a loan but the forecasts are good and the business in Rome is looking after itself, so there's no reason why it shouldn't work in Milan too."

Rossi sat down again.

"I'm no businessman," he said, "but it's a risk, isn't it? A loan, with a mortgage already."

"It's now or never, Michael. The loan's almost interest free. I have a client who's been very helpful. And anyway, I'm not getting any younger. And if I want to have a different life someday, well."

A different life. A client.

"What do you mean, different?"

"Children, Michael. A family. Wouldn't you like us to have a family one day? It can't wait for ever you know."

Who was he to get in the way of her dreams, if he even featured in them? But his mind was elsewhere, as much as this was turning him inside out. Something had to give.

"I came here to let you know, in person. Nothing is definite, nothing is over if that's what you're worried about," she said, reaching out now to take his hand. "There isn't anyone else, Michael. It's me. It's what happened to me. The coma. It's made me realize there's no time to lose. Life is a breath. *E' uno soffio*," she said. "And you are always a part of it, but I have to take this chance."

He held her hand in his. She held his hand in hers. They had been through a lot. They would be through more, he was sure, if he wanted to. But he had to let her go without guilt.

"I'd like you to stay tonight but—"

"But you can't," she said taking the well-trodden path again. "I understand. Do you understand?"

"Yes," he said. "I do."

She kissed him affectionately but without passion, as if honouring their bond, and then he closed the door behind her.

***

There was no plan. There never had been one, yet something was unravelling. She was slipping away, further this time, like a boat loosed from its moorings, and he on the bank, the rope running through his fingers when he knew all he had to do was grip. Then something made him remember the e-mail he had forgotten to send to the organization, The List of Shame. He would do it now. And he'd get back to Gigi about the details of the cardinal's final resting place. And then do some more of his own research. It might help take his mind off things.

Fifty-Seven

He had begun to assemble what they would need and took a holdall from the cupboard next to the kitchen. He threw in a hammer, a mallet, the closest thing he had to a mason's chisel and, after a concerted search, found what he knew he had somewhere: a crowbar. He found some blocks of wood too. They'd need those for leverage. A torch, of course, better two. Spare batteries. A rope. Then he grabbed a sleeping bag. Better to be prepared and comfortable. Water. A half bottle of whiskey, half full. A packet of biscuits.

He called Carrara. It was engaged. He'd have to get back to his place to prepare too. He stuffed in another sleeping bag. That would do. He tried again. This time it rang.

"Gigi, what's the story?"

"Got what you wanted about opening times but there's no clear indication on the website of where the tomb is located. We'll have to search around a bit."

"And the rest? Did you speak to the cop who took the anonymous call?"

"Yes, he was a bit hazy but he came up with something once I showed him the transcript."

"Did he say he was Russian?"

"Maybe, but definitely Eastern European. And definitely drunk."

"So maybe the booze had loosened his tongue," said Rossi. "*In vino veritas.*"

"Hope so," said Carrara.

"I've got the lot. I'll pick you up there. Seen anyone around? Anyone asking for us?"

"No. Quiet enough."

"OK."

"But what about Gab's CCTV? Are we getting our priorities right?" said Carrara.

"I still say it can wait. We go for this now and then see the lie of the land. Agreed?"

"Agreed," said Carrara even if he only had half a clue what exactly he was agreeing to.

"OK," said Rossi then gave a final look around the flat. It was cleaner, for sure. The woman's touch was no myth. She was not a myth either, though he sometimes treated her like one. She was real. A pang of something close to guilt or anxiety or both cut through his stomach. He checked his watch. He had to leave now if they were going to gain access to the church by normal means. Then they'd be able to prove what he had been fearing and believing at the same time – that there was an unholy alliance behind at least some of what had been happening in the city, and a conspiracy to keep it all under wraps.

Fifty-Eight

Iannelli got up and stretched then walked over to the window, being careful not to let himself be seen. He didn't pull back the linen curtains. He couldn't, so his view of the world was like that of a blind man, a partially blind man. He thought sometimes he was close to going mad. The only thing that kept him sane was that she was coming to visit him. It kept his spirits up for sure. He looked in the mirror and wondered again whether to rethink the beard. He was starting to look like a fundamentalist, he laughed to himself.

He went back to the computer. He was trying to finish an article for an American magazine. "Life Under Escort." He was not the only one but perhaps one of the best-known because of the dramatic nature of his particular story. He had continued to wonder who had saved his life back then in Sicily, who had called to tell him to jump from his car seconds before the roadside bomb had obliterated it. But he still didn't know the truth. Perhaps it was an agent who had penetrated *Cosa Nostra*. It could even have been the owner of the guest house where he had stayed while investigating the collusion between high-level politicians and crime syndicates. But who could set him free now? The cursor was flashing. He was stuck. He didn't have anymore ideas to push it across the page. He flicked over to the Internet. See what was going on. Not much. Then he opened his e-mails. A few new entries, one looked interesting.

To: D.Iannelli@thefacet.it
From: a friend.
Subject: Rome
Keep this channel of communication open.
Tennessee.

Fifty-Nine

"Right," said Rossi, "we do it like this. We go in and assess the situation. It's a bit of a tourist place but there shouldn't be any cameras or serious alarms. If there *are*, it's your job to take them out."

"I'll do my best," said Carrara.

"I'll leave the bag somewhere safe and then we wander around until we've found the tomb. Then we hide and wait until closing time. Keep your phone on silent."

"I don't think there'll be any signal anyway," said Carrara. "Walls are five feet thick down in the crypt."

"Okay, but we wait until it's closed and empty."

"Escape route?"

"We identify the path of least resistance. Either a side door or a window. Something with a lock we can spring. We can try that first, if you like, while one of us gets on with the other job."

"'The other job'. The grave robbing."

"It's not grave robbing, Gigi. It's establishing the facts. Is there a body there or not? As I told you, I have grave doubts. Forgive the pun."

Carrara did not appear overly placated, however.

"Park over there," said Rossi, indicating a space between a

large overhanging tree and some recycling bins, "it's discreet enough."

"Something less suspicious?" said Carrara as Rossi heaved the holdall out of the boot.

"Its my old kitbag. Saying I look past it?"

"No comment," said Carrara, accepting it and swinging it over his shoulder.

"No metal detectors, at least," said Rossi as they made towards the entrance of the relatively modest-looking church with its classical columns and Romanic bell tower.

There was a trickle of hardcore ecclesiastical tourists in and out of its doors.

"Think we can blend in?" said Rossi. "Perhaps we should have brought a guidebook."

"You know one of the Magliana gang had his funeral here, don't you?" said Carrara.

"I *did* know that," said Rossi, "and I'm hoping it's only a coincidence. Like San Lorenzo *in Lucina* and the 1994 *Lucina* massacre is too."

***

There were no security guards or sextons to worry about, and a quick reconnoitre allowed Rossi to find a recess behind the organ where he could drop the bag. Carrara was coming back down the nave, admiring the vaulted ceiling like a natural and then blessing himself on one knee as he crossed in front of the altar.

"Only one camera," he whispered and half-mimed to Rossi, "On the main entrance. A couple of movement sensors but I can neutralize them before the alarm's set."

He waved some compact electronic device and mentioned something about jamming a signal, something about which Rossi was quite happy not to ask any further questions.

"And an exit?" said Rossi.

"Next job."

Rossi looked at his watch.

"Time to find somewhere to secrete ourselves. Meet you at the Lady Chapel in five," he said, as he laid a hand on Carrara's arm to draw his attention to some finer detail of the *baldacchino*. A black-frocked and sombre priest appeared from the direction of the sacristy. He began to make his rounds, extinguishing candles, straightening chairs and indicating to the remaining visitors that it was time to leave. It was earlier than expected.

"Find yourself a spot now," Rossi whispered. "It's chucking out time." They sauntered off in their respective directions.

Rossi slipped behind a pillar and squinted around it to follow the priest as he shepherded a last few strays towards the exit. Rossi moved backwards to the roped-off area near the altar, stepped across and found a dark space between a stone sarcophagus and the wall. He made himself as small as possible, crouched, and waited. If he were found, it would be embarrassing to say the least. His shaky defence would have to be that it was a stakeout, but that would be useless if this priest was a custodian of the secret he felt this church might jealously possess.

He heard the priest's footsteps going this way and that. Some of the lights went out. So far so good. Then he heard the main entrance door opening and banging shut. There was a rattling of keys, a clunking sound, more footsteps. Of course. It would be closed from the inside, and the priest would retreat through the nave and leave through the sacristy, which gave onto his private quarters. Whether he would return or not was a risk they would have to take. Another door was closed with a key then all was plunged into darkness. A little faint light filtered through some high windows but it would be pitch-dark soon.

Rossi loosened himself from his position then took a penlight from his pocket and went to find Carrara.

He located him by the glow of his phone.

"OK," said Rossi, in hushed tones. "We're in."

"I've been trying to find a signal," said Carrara. "Looks like this is just about the only place."

Rossi took out his own phone. Sure enough, there was a message, from Iannelli.

Something odd has come up. "Tennessee" mean anything to you? Call me.

Rossi pondered for a moment the cryptic note. "It's hardly the time and the place," he said out loud, showing it then to Carrara. "It'll have to wait," said Rossi. "Got a job to do. Which way?"

Carrara indicated the gates that led down to the crypt as Rossi retrieved the holdall.

"Fairly straightforward, don't you think?" he said, sizing up the large keyhole. Carrara had already produced his own box of tricks, and with Rossi's penlight steadied on the lock he set to work.

"So far very good," said Rossi as there was the decisive click. "Easy if it creaks."

They opened it enough to be able to slip through then descended the spiralling marble steps down to the crypt.

"Should be one of the new ones," said Rossi as he scoured the darkness with a more powerful torch.

"Got it," said Carrara who had turned his phone into a searchlight. "All present and correct. Name, freshly chiselled."

"And sealed," said Rossi tracing a finger along the line of smooth white mortar running under the bevelled edge of the marble lid.

He wrapped the head of the masonry chisel in a cloth to muffle the sound. Then he took the hammer and struck the first blow. Fragments shot out in all directions like a small explosion. He struck again and began working his way around. "I'll do the first side then we swap and I'll check the coast is clear," he said as he continued to chip with a steady rhythm.

Iannelli tried again. No answer. Rossi was proving even harder to get hold of than usual. He looked at the e-mail, trying to glean some further significance from it, its few spare details. "A friend." What did that mean? Someone who wanted to help *him*? Could it be the same source that had tipped him off about the attempt on his life in Sicily or even the one who had sent him the photo of Father Brell? "Keep this channel open." That implied further news, updates, even a certain urgency while the sender's address was some gobbledygook made for the occasion.

He wondered if he should pass it on to his own security. Maybe they could trace it and get a lead. Or maybe it was someone who wanted to use him as a conduit for a story. And then the name. "Tennessee." He tried Rossi's phone one more time. Nothing.

Rossi had left Carrara on the job while he made his way through the pitch-black towards the main entrance. He had the lock-picking kit and was going to make a start. It wasn't his speciality but he'd had the training and was no slouch. He tried a few different approaches but to no avail. Leave it to Carrara or try another door? There was the option of going via the sacristy and through the priest's quarters but that was high-risk, even if the locks might be easier.

He took out his phone and made for their reception hot spot. Three bars. Good enough. There were missed calls from Iannelli, who he'd almost forgotten about. He rang back and it had almost rung out when there was an answer.

"Dario, what is it?" he whispered. "I'm in a tight spot right now."

Iannelli explained the e-mail, voicing his various concerns. Rossi began turning over the possibilities. It smacked of the imminent but if something big did come up and a call went out for operatives then they would be in serious trouble and they would have to leave the job half done and their intentions exposed.

"OK," said Rossi, "hold on to it for now. But if you get something else or if they up the stakes and you can't get me, pass it straight on to the RSCS." He reeled off a number for a direct line.

Carrara had finished.

"OK," said Rossi. "The moment of truth." He took out the crowbar and a couple of blocks. "Are you ready?"

"Ready," said Carrara positioning himself with a wedge. Rossi jammed in the bar and leant down hard. The lid lifted and Carrara shoved in another wedge. Rossi moved to the opposite side and they repeated the operation. They'd lifted it by a few inches on both long sides and they moved round to the head end.

"One to go," said Rossi when the sound of sirens made both of them freeze. "Keep going!" said Rossi, "we'll bluff our way out if we have to."

He leant on the bar and with Carrara accompanying the lid sideways and exploiting the momentum, they glimpsed inside the casket at one corner. "A bit more," said Rossi, and they shifted it another inch or two. Rossi shone his torch inside. It was empty.

"Nothing. The empty tomb. Come on!" he said, throwing the tools into the bag and wiping the handles clean of prints as he did so. "And the lock and the gate," he said over his shoulder as they climbed up the spiral staircase and back into the nave.

"What now?" said Carrara, as the sirens came closer and then stopped. Rossi shone his torch around.

"Try and open that side door!" he said, and indicating with the beam. "But stay inside."

Carrara dashed over and set to work as Rossi provided steady illumination.

"Shit!" said Carrara as a slim precision tool slipped from his hand and on to the floor. He grabbed it up and began again.

There were male voices now outside and the dull thuds of car doors closing one after another. A couple of cars, Rossi calculated. His eyes turned in the direction of the main door but the sound of footsteps came to where they were. The outer gate rattled slightly on its hinges as if being tried in a perfunctory manner and then the footsteps appeared to move away. A false alarm? Rossi looked down at the kneeling Carrara who had stopped for a few seconds but was now doggedly concentrating again on the lock willing the definitive click, his instruments in the silence making a delicate ticking sound like a small bird trying to open a nut. Then there was a clanking and rattling of metal as away to Rossi's right and on the far side of the altar the door to the sacristy opened. He could hear a grumbling voice that had to belong to the parish priest they had seen earlier. Torches danced in all directions until the first dim lights in the side chapel flickered on.

"We're police," Rossi called out striding away from Carrara to divert their attention. "It's Rossi and Carrara. RSCS."

There were a few "what the fucks", and other expressions of dismay as a group of plain clothes and uniforms ambled in, and the priest headed towards the panel where the main light switches were located just as Rossi heard the telltale click of lock opening behind him. At the front of the police group was Silvestre. It was not their lucky day.

"Well, well, well," said Silvestre. "This is going to take a bit of explaining, isn't it?"

Carrara emerged from the half-shadows, slipped his tools into his pocket, and made his way over with an air of relaxed detachment.

"We saw a light on and that door behind us there was open," said Rossi.

"So you just happened to be in the area," said Silvestre.

"That's right," and it looks like someone's been grave robbing, said Rossi, indicating the open gate leading to the crypt. "Care to see for yourself. Looks like they were going to make a night of it."

***

307

"All this will have to go back to Maroni of course," said Silvestre as the still grumbling priest locked up the main entrance and the officers stood around smoking and chatting, leaning over the bonnets of the squad cars with their torches to complete the initial paperwork. "Very odd case indeed, isn't it?" said Silvestre. "What with your car being parked up here for the last three hours as well."

"Like I told you before," said Rossi, "in the vicinity. On foot. We left the car here for convenience."

"And someone's made off with a cardinal's mortal remains. Looks like a ransom job, doesn't it?"

"Has all the hallmarks," said Rossi.

"And you wouldn't happen to be in any way involved, would you, Rossi? I mean, you are above suspicion. Incorruptible."

"Which begs the question, how did you happen to be in the area yourself, Silvestre?"

Silvestre laughed. "Don't worry, Rossi. I won't shop you. Not for this one. I'm sure we'll be able to find a way out. It'll be better for all concerned. I just didn't think it was your style, that's all. Thought you were squeaky clean."

Rossi ignored the facile provocation for what it was.

"You still haven't told me how you got here so fast," said Rossi. "Just passing were, you?"

"No," he said. "We got a call, from Torrini at *The Post*, of all people. How he got wind I really couldn't say but I don't think he'll be revealing his source. Anyway, I'd say he'll be wanting to run a nice little story on all this. Check the morning papers."

***

"That was a good bit of work," said Rossi as they sipped on *cappuccinos* in the first bar they could find open. Neither had felt like going home yet and besides, they would have to get their story straight in one way or another. The early hours clientele was a mix of stragglers, revellers and shift-workers. "At least it means our story is feasible if not credible."

"They'll say it was locked and that's why they had to come in through the priest's quarters," said Carrara.

"Well maybe they didn't push hard enough. As I said, it's enough to muddy the waters."

"But Torrini? How the hell did they know we were there?"

"Surprise, surprise," said Rossi. "We're being trailed. Phones monitored. Someone must have fed him. And he'd love to nail me."

"Because of Iannelli, right? Leaving *The Post* to wage his private war on its esteemed editor. Well at least now you know there's nothing there."

"Which doesn't *prove* anything but it strengthens the case that the murdered priest wasn't Brell at all. That maybe no such person as Brell ever existed. That Brell could have been our cardinal instead."

***

The story hadn't made that morning's paper but the headline would be ready for the next. "Top Cop Implicated in Corpse Kidnap." That very Italian of crimes. It was much easier to keep a corpse quiet while you waited for relatives to cough up the ransom.

Rossi had arrived home at dawn and had tried to grab a few hours' sleep. But there were any number of loose ends flailing about in his head. He woke up with a start. He was on the couch, in his clothes, and he felt another sharp pain in his chest. He sat up and tried to get a grip on his thoughts. The church, the empty tomb, Silvestre sneering with satisfaction at his misfortune. And Yana. The loan. The client, friend, financial adviser in Milan. She was moving to Milan. It was temporary. But it was always temporary, at first.

He got to his feet and threw open the window and tried to breathe slowly, but the air felt thick and warm and nauseating. It was already nine o'clock in the morning and the city and its street life had begun without him. He needed peace. Silence. He headed for the drinks cabinet and poured himself some medicine. He drained the glass then leant on the table and waited for it to do its work. Something like calm began to spread through his body and limbs and up into his brain. He went into the bathroom and ran the tap for a whole minute until the water had become cold enough for him to freshen up. Then he brushed his teeth and gargled with the strongest mouthwash he could find. He ran his fingers through his hair, dressed again, grabbed his jacket and keys and headed back out.

Sixty

He hadn't even got as far as the office. The press were there and shoving microphones in his face the moment he opened the car door.

"What do you know about the disappearance of the cardinal's body? Witnesses say you were on the scene. Is it true you've been suspended? Inspector Rossi! Do you deny the accusations concerning organized crime?"

He was almost glad when a staff officer interposed himself between the marauding hordes and hissed in his ear that Maroni wanted to see him "now" and not to even open his mouth to the press before he had "got his arse over there".

"His words, not mine," the officer added in his defence.

He ducked through the gates and into the relative calm of the *Questura*. "Hard at work everyone?" he said as he breezed through the reception area followed by a legion of idle stares and headed for the second floor. A message had come through from Carrara.

Advise you to use the back entrance. Press.

Better late than never.

"So," said Maroni. "This is going to have to be good *signori*."

Rossi and Carrara sat opposite him, both in need of sleep and sustenance. Then he exploded.

"What the hell were you two doing in that church! You'd better have an explanation. Torrini knows. He bloody well told *us*. Your car was seen! You were in there and then this cardinal's corpse goes missing. And now there's a ransom demand. It does not look good, gentlemen! Whatever way you dress it up, this does not constitute gilt-edged PR!"

Rossi glanced at Carrara and then at Maroni.

"Well, I suppose we'd better come clean. On everything."

Maroni had sat back in his chair, maintaining a studied silence as Rossi told him what they had been working on, linking the Brell murder with the missing painting, the Victor story, Jibril, Marciano and his rent boys, and the final crowning glory which was that the cardinal had never been buried in the church crypt at all. As far as they were concerned, there was every reason to believe he had engineered his own elaborate plan to disappear and fake his own death.

"Then someone, we don't know who," said Rossi, concluding his version of events, "finally tracks down Brell, or the cardinal. What they did to his face could have been revenge or it could have been for reasons unknown, but as far as I'm concerned, the Islamist plot doesn't fit. It was a crime, it was personal. We don't have all the proof but what we found last night was enough to give us something approaching certainty."

Maroni sat up.

"We can't go with this. Even if it were true, which, despite the undoubted elegance of your reasoning, I seriously doubt it is, we would be going where angels fear to tread."

That was the abstract. Now for the rest.

"If we went ahead with this, I couldn't guarantee anything. If you want to pursue that line of enquiry, for starters you can wave bye-bye to this job. They will put *everything* in your way. Everything. They will drag up anything that can discredit you. They'll bring pressure to bear on me and on my superiors – in a word, they will create a shitstorm of proportions you can't even begin to imagine. Do you realize what you are saying? The levels of complicity and deceit and perverting the course of justice?"

"And what if it were all true?" said Carrara.

"That's my point," said Maroni. "If it is true, or even a part of it is true, you may as well forget about it. Because if that can happen, think what could happen to keep it all quiet. Think about your lives, your careers, your families. Nothing of any significance happens in this city without someone in the hierarchy having their say."

"And what if it were time that all that came to an end?" said Rossi.

Maroni had his head in his hands, his chubby fingers digging into his smooth crown in a slow sadistic massage.

"We could bury this, as it stands, if you cooperate. I can call in favours; we can pull together. But if not, if we don't bury it here and now, *they* will bury *you*."

Rossi was still holding Maroni with his unbroken stare.

"Torrini's got a hard-on over the whole thing, Rossi – you're not his favourite cop, in case you didn't know. Iannelli's chums are his *de facto* enemies it seems. They'll throw the book at you over this. But if we work as a team on this, we can ride it out."

"How?" said Rossi. "What do you have in mind?"

"Right. The tools and kit were there. Easy, they were left behind. You acted on a tip-off. You went alone and without informing anyone as you didn't want to divert resources from the counter-terror ops, time was of the essence. And you're a maverick, we all know that, and you've got some results over the years, so we can get a few friends to big you up in the other papers. You know the way it works. Sometimes in our favour, sometimes against. Anyway, it peters out. No ransom is paid. No one gets any return on their investment, it all fades from memory, Christmas comes and goes and it's all forgotten."

Rossi gave a shrug as if to say it stank to high heaven but what other option was there?

313

"But if you insist on going after the Church you're on a hiding to nothing – it will drag on, for years, they'll mobilize all their friends in high places, journalists, and you'll end up bitter and twisted and heading for an early retirement and an ulcer."

"Like the cop in Sicily?" said Carrara remembering Tonino and his dossier on the large-scale corruption between the police and criminal gangs and which Iannelli had made his scoop.

"He didn't take on the Vatican. There's a difference. Don't forget they've got two thousand years of experience of this sort of thing. They burnt Giordano Bruno, for God's sake, right here in Rome, in Campo de' Fiori. They would have burnt Galileo."

"If he hadn't retracted," said Rossi. "Even though he was right."

"He made a wise move, if you ask me," said Maroni. "There's only one life. There's no room for blind idealism. If you want to play into their hands, they'll take pleasure in watching you squirm when you're on the griddle. Then they'll turn up the heat."

"You're making a good case for our chucking it all in here and now," said Rossi.

"I'm not saying that," Maroni countered. "As far as this Jibril story goes, you've got a lead. You've done decent work. I've never said you weren't good cops. Foolish maybe and with an incorrigible tendency to keep things from me. Even so, I can see that it's been quite a job. But if he's here, he has to be found. That's worth going for. Can you both live with that?"

Nice and safe. The foreigner. The evil other. *The evil within is always a different story though, isn't it*, thought Rossi. But Maroni was shaping up for something else. The sting in the tail? The bombshell?

"Like I said," he began again, "if you two cooperate, there's a way through the woods on this one but there's a price to pay, at least in the short term." He had his hands clasped in front of him on the desk in the bad-news-but-tough-shit pose. Rossi made it easy for him.

"Suspension?"

314

Maroni nodded.

"On full pay, of course. But yes. Until there's a let up. It will soften the blow for everyone."

"And 'our' lead?" said Rossi. "You know it all now. What are you going to do about Jibril?"

"We'll take care of that," said Maroni. "Have faith in me."

"Is that with immediate effect?" asked Rossi staring hard at Maroni.

He seemed to be turning it over. Rossi knew that suspending them was going to make it easier for Maroni. It was the low-maintenance solution to keep the press off his back and God knows who else, but he also knew Maroni was a cop like the rest of them, despite the insulation of institutional necessity surrounding him. He too had taken some risks in his day to get results, and Rossi was counting now on Maroni's reliving at least some of those moments.

"I could stall them," he said then, "for twenty-four hours. But after that it will be public. And you'll be off. Both of you."

Rossi would take that. A quick glance told him Carrara would too. Twenty-four hours wasn't a lot but it could be enough, if you weren't too worried about sleeping or anything else that smacked of a normal existence.

Sixty-One

So Ali had got his way. Jibril looked on as they laid out and arranged samples of their nearly complete arsenal on a khaki tarpaulin. This was Ali's moment. The others were gathered. Karim and Yusef, by their attentive silence, showing their reverence for his devil-may-care approach. Would one of *them* then plant the bomb? In many ways, they were always going to be the kind of guys who would have drifted into a gang, Jibril was sure, if there had been one for them. But this was not Paris or Marseille. Here immigration was still quite new, had been sudden, and as yet remained raw. The ghettoization existed in places, but it was nothing like in the lawless, forgotten *banlieues*.

The Roman gangs would never admit them into their ranks, into their closed world. And Karim's and Yusef's own communities had not yet shown their teeth or any desire to put together similarly minded criminal outfits. Only the Nigerians, who had come up from Palermo and Napoli, had built well-structured organizations founded on fear, belonging, and *omertà*. And the Russians, of course, the Chinese too, always. The rest were the powerful home-grown clans: the Calabrians, the Sicilians, the Roma gypsies and the Sinti. Karim and Yusef were still green, yet

Jibril could see that they would do anything for Ali, for in him and in his authoritative and dedicated almost maverick professorial role, they had found a brother and a father, respect and glory and value in their lives all rolled into one.

And the equipment had now suddenly become a reality. The cache that had been delivered under cover of a furniture consignment and which they had before them was enough to wreak havoc in a crowded city. "We can take out dozens," Ali had said, as he fondled and caressed the automatic weapons, the easily concealed machine pistols, the assault rifles for "open warfare", as he called it. His fantasy triggered something in Jibril then as he remembered, flickering in his own memory, how he had revered the weapons when he had first begun to believe in a cause. His commanders then had held up the AK47 as a symbol of freedom, a guerilla's crucifix, the power to turn the tables now in his very hands. Ali wanted to turn the tables on the life of rejection and bitterly confused sense of self that at least in part had made him what he was. In the newspaper headlines and rolling TV news he envisaged, he would finally be a protagonist with an identity that no one could question.

Jibril's flashback was neutral, almost comforting at first, but as he watched it, film-like, he also began to feel it mutate dangerously. It was not so far back in the past but he felt already he had lived for a long time and taking life meant living many lives at once. It was a kind of cosmic trap, being the custodian of so much truncated being. And somewhere there, too, was the subdued yearning for lost innocence, the life cut off from him for ever, and with that came the insistent fantasy of ending it all. With an effort he stopped the vision.

Time was short and running out but at least the day and the time of the attack had been set. Ali continued to pick up and put down the hardware, demonstrating with rapid, almost theatrical gestures the finer points of their functioning. The planned training had been cancelled for fear they might be exposed before they could act. Jibril knew he had a whole afternoon but he'd been lucky. Lucky again. He had made sure that much, at least, had gone his way.

Sixty-Two

"So, options?" said Carrara. They'd got takeaway second breakfasts and were in the Alfa, away from prying eyes and ears. The
story had come out and even if the content wasn't damning, it
wasn't good. Torrini would be holding back and using what he
had as bargaining chips, and it had all been couched in terms of
"conflicting reports", and "allegations of", "witnesses are reported
as" and so forth. Rossi dipped his wholemeal honey-filled *cornetto*
into his coffee, splashing part of its contents across the front
page.

"Well, we could use having Katia to give us a hand. She's
proved herself already and I think she's game."

Carrara shot him a glance which Rossi chose to ignore.

"And Gab, remember we've still got something there."

Rossi nodded as the coffee and carbohydrate combination
began to give him the needed boost.

"And I've been doing some thinking about Silvestre," Rossi
said then.

"Keep thinking," said Carrara. "He's a law unto himself."

"Slippery bastard, for sure."

"An opportunist. The worst kind. You never know what he
might have in mind."

"Which could maybe work in our favour," said Rossi. "If he smells an opportunity. His principles are very market-oriented."

"He makes me sick," said Carrara. "He'd sell his own grand-mother."

Rossi nodded.

"Agreed, but we're in a tight spot and I want out. So, shall we get on the road?"

Carrara took his and Rossi's takeaway leftovers, stuffed them into the paper bag they had come in and then tossed the lot out into a waiting bin.

"Not recycling today?" said Rossi as Carrara threw the Alfa into gear and hit the accelerator with more than a hint of gener-alized rage.

Sixty-Three

Ali's plan was simple and Jibril had allowed him to take the credit. Ali had laughed at its simplicity. "We could do this everyday," he had said as he helped Karim to adjust the rucksack to comfortably fit his frame and made final checks to the detonators and the timer which would be positioned inside the main charge at the latest possible moment. "Who says we need military explosives?" he said again. "I'm all for do-it-yourself, you know."

Ali then helped Karim to slip the rucksack carefully off his back, and they placed it carefully in a corner of the room. Jibril watched, knowing that the device, containing litres of The Mother of Satan, was highly unstable. Yet he stood and observed. Ali was on some other plane, the strength of his death wish growing steadily. For him it had to be a simple matter of time.

Jibril knew taking public transport to the destination was a risk as a jolt or a sudden impact could potentially cause the bomb to explode prematurely. He had expressed his concerns about this but Ali had won the day. "Whatever happens is the will of Allah," he had said, closing the discussion.

Only the detonators could be called actual explosives, in that they were ready-made for the purpose. The supply lines out of the former Yugoslavia were bringing in materials every day –

destined either for the criminal gangs of Europe and beyond, or actors in a new political sphere to rival the insanity of the authors of the 1990s conflict which had torn the region and its peoples apart. Ali had picked up his sub-machine gun, was stroking it with admiration.

"Will we all have one of these, Jibril?" he asked.

"If you like it, we can get more," he replied. "Now, let's run through it again," he went on, wanting and needing to know that he had left nothing to chance. Ali took up the narrative.

"We leave the house," he said, "one by one, with the exception of Karim, who will wait here until we are out of the danger zone. We two," he continued, indicating Yusef and himself, "will carry dummy rucksacks, and we will go in different directions. We say goodbye to each other outside, in full view, as if we are going on long journeys." The idea was to confuse any surveillance units and to stretch their resources into trailing three or four possible targets. "Then, when the moment is right, Karim will leave and make his way to the destination. He will leave the bomb in what he judges to be the most effective location but will do so at the agreed time. As soon as he leaves the house the bomb will be live with no option of aborting the attack." He looked at Karim who was listening, his head down, nodding rhythmically. "If you should run into transport problems, you leave the device wherever you see fit. Damage limitation, for us, understand?"

Karim looked up nodded and blinked. He was nervous but concealed it well. He was dressed now in light-coloured ripped jeans and a chequered shirt and wrap-round dark glasses pushed back on his head. A bandana completed the disguise. He could have passed for a backpacker from anywhere. Who would suspect him?

"Are you certain about the call box?" said Jibril. "When did you check it last?"

"It's fine," said Ali. "When Karim has left the target he goes into the department store. He changes and walks out the other door and proceeds to where the phones are. There are several. He chooses one and makes the call and then he disappears but is available if anything should not go to plan. Then you, Jibril, will begin phase two. You and I will be in position, here," he pointed to the map. "Exactly where the fountain is. I can go round and keep moving, but I will be here on the fountain. When the device detonates there will be confusion, a massive rush in all directions but it's my calculation that most will flee this way, north."

"And then I open up," said Jibril.

"Yes," said Ali. "You hit the police first, the place will be crawling with them, and then you mingle in with the crowd and proceed towards my initial position."

"Then you begin firing," said Jibril. "But we agree to target the police whenever possible. We create chaos among the civilians, but we concentrate on taking out the *military* targets."

"Sending the crowds back in your direction," said Ali, without acknowledging Jibril's proviso. He continued.

"We maintain radio silence for twenty-four hours. No one returns to the flat except Jibril, who will keep it under observation, as agreed. Everyone stays at their respective safe address until notified. Everyone has their alibi. Then we sit back and watch as the city and this country begins to wake up from its idle dreaming."

Sixty-Four

Gab let them into his emporium, greeting them with a toothy smile. He had hired out a lock-up garage next to his apartment building and filled it with a dizzying array of hardware. Nonetheless, it had a homely feel, like a man cave, with its scuffed retro leather divan and kitchen corner with a fridge and an old-fashioned drinks dispenser. All the mod cons necessary for a codebreaker and hacker extraordinaire.

"Gentlemen, how may I be of assistance?"

Rossi had a wearied air, his face pale and his cheeks sunken from fatigue. Carrara was already showing signs of mild irritation at the unwanted dose of irony as he tried to rub some of the sleep out of his own eyes.

"All is not well?"

"Could be better," said Rossi looking around for another chair near the computer that he could crash out on. "What have you got for us?" he said, pulling up a wholly inadequate bar stool as Gab sat into his swivel chair and proceeded to rev up his various machines and screens like a pilot preparing for take-off in some cockpit of his own design. The larger of his three screens flickered into life, and Rossi and Carrara looked on as Gab manoeuvred his rollerball mouse.

"This is all gobbledygook," he said racing through the frames before stopping, shifting the images then stopping again. "Here," he said, and turned to them both, "this is all I could get. The blast knocked out *one* of the cameras though, not both, so that's the first thing." He clicked and let the black-and-white images run. It was reasonably coherent time-lapse, students coming and going, a large concentration remaining, frustratingly, not right next to but in a direct line between the camera and where they believed the device had been planted.

"Not much to see so far," said Carrara. Then there was the flash, confusion and smoke and then a few more seconds before the video cut out. Rossi did not seem impressed either. Gab, however, was clicking around again.

"Nothing much there, you'll agree. Now, take a look at this *enhanced* version," he said as he let the images roll for a second time. This time the scene was zoomed out slightly. The far bank of the Tiber was now more visible, cars and vans could be made out passing slowly on the one-way system. "Look there," he said, drawing their attention to a detail, a shadow to all intents and purposes but moving. He made some more adjustments and the camera eye homed in a little more. It was grainier but had assumed a recognizable shape. The blast again and then the shadow, which Rossi and Carrara could now see was a human form. It appeared to raise something and lower it and, as if nothing untoward had happened, left the scene at walking pace.

"Show me that again," said Rossi, getting up and going in closer for all it was worth and studying the images frame by frame now. He reached out and rewound the images himself a third time as Gab surrendered the controls. Rossi looked at Carrara.

Carrara was still staring at the screen, his face as pale now as Rossi's.

"Somebody keeping an eye on things?" said Gab. "Could it *her*?"

'Fifty-fifty," said Rossi, sipping on an uncharacteristic can of something fizzy courtesy of their host. "Maybe sixty-forty it's her, even if she is supposed to be dead. But whoever it was, it wasn't any Middle-Eastern terrorist."

"Unless they were working for Middle-Eastern terrorists," said Gab. "But you're saying it wasn't her who went into the ravine back in the winter? In her four-by-four. It was a set-up?"

Again they watched the morsel of film they had before them.

"Long hair, binoculars, no surprise. It could all be adding up," said Rossi.

"What about DNA?" said Carrara. "Let's prove it beyond a doubt."

Rossi shook his head. He knew there would be genetic material conserved from the postmortem on the body found in the ravine, the body they had initially presumed beyond any doubt to have been that of Marini.

"How the hell do you propose we get a sample?" said Rossi. "We can't just barge in and say we think things might not have gone quite as we said they did back then when we were hunting down The Carpenter. Do you mind if we run some tests? And it's really not the right moment for that kind of explaining, with Silvestre probably caught up in trying to frame us."

Carrara was rubbing at his dark stubble and grimacing at the fix they had found themselves in.

"And you can bet we were watched," said Rossi, "and tracked when we went into the church to check out the cardinal's tomb. The chances are we'll be watched now. We can't afford to step out of line. Besides, we'd have to get a sample from Marini's father or her son. Again, how do you propose doing that? More unfeasible bureaucracy, more deception, and time is, shall we say, decidedly against us."

"So we just err on the side of caution?" said Carrara. "We accept that Marini could be alive after all and she might well have had a hand in the university bomb and whatever else."

"We have to entertain that as a real possibility," said Rossi don't know what her objective is, but either way, someone was coordinating that attack. It's there to see. Italians planned the bombing, obtained the hardware, planted the device, confirmed its success and then waited for the fallout."

Carrara and Rossi stared again at the images, willing some other clue to emerge that might give them a competitive edge.

"But gentlemen," began Gab again, "I was almost forgetting. This is indeed your lucky day."

"Are you quite sure about that?" said Carrara.

Gab smiled back. Rossi seemed to have half a concealed smile on his face too.

"Remember a small matter of some encrypted computer files I managed to filch?"

"The Marini files?" said Rossi. He had long since given up all hope of getting anywhere with them. It had seemed like a gift, at first, as The Carpenter case had been drawing to its dramatic conclusion and, beginning to suspect Marini could be either knowingly or unknowingly caught up in a double play, he had got Gab to hook up to her computer via a WI-FI hack. They had copied the files but as yet they had remained uncrackable.

"The ones you said were like trying to open a walnut with your toes?" said Carrara, recalling Gab's past attempts and frustrations.

"Yes, indeedy."

Gab reached behind him for a smaller laptop.

"Well, in the face of extreme adversity and with no end in sight, I called in the FDA?"

"The FDA?"

"Final drastic action. I decided to resort to the Alexandrian method," he said, pulling up a new file. "That is Alexander Magna. Alexander the Great."

"Meaning?" said Rossi, intrigued now as much as he was turbed by the lingering images still before them on the screen.

"Meaning that instead of trying to open it with my toes, I stood on it."

"The Gordian knot," said Rossi.

"Exactly. Not very scientific but effective in its own way."

He spun the laptop around to show them the fruits of his labours.

"As you can see, the results were not particularly clean, but there is some usable data, possibly in some sort of code and there's fragments all over the place. Still, better than nothing. I basically dropped a bomb on it."

"Anything else?"

Gab shook his head.

"Well she was no amateur, that's for sure."

Pages of text and figures and random characters, it looked impenetrable.

"Can you do me a printout?" said Rossi. "It can be my cross-word for the next five years."

"Or while you're suspended," said Carrara.

"Thanks for reminding me," replied Rossi, taking the wad of sheets, folding them and tucking them into his jacket pocket.

"And get us a copy of that film, Gigi," he said. "I love night-mares."

Sixty-Five

His grandfather's passing had been very quick in the end. The last, irreversible decline had begun some weeks before, happening in stages, fatal increments of physical change, and though none of them had wanted to acknowledge that fact, they knew he had begun to die. Francesco had been there when it mattered most. His employers had not been fully sympathetic, so he had taken sick leave and unpaid holiday in order to be around as much as possible. He didn't know if he had a job to go back to. He hardly cared.

He was the man of the house now and had been for some time. He had looked after bureaucratic problems, had helped his mother with the medical paraphernalia and financial matters. He had been a good son. They had both done their best to make sure that it was a dignified end for one who had held dignity to be the bedrock and foundation of humanity. He had always been a sharp dresser but without being showy, as a mark of respect for himself and for those he might encounter. Then they had upped the dose of morphine and, in line with his known if not legally sanctionable wishes, they had eased his passing.

Family had come, old comrades from his partisan days, some party members. All had paid their respects. And now, as they faced the task of moving on, Francesco and his mother stood in the newly emptied room, unable to forget that this was where his soul had left the world never to return. They would always see his face, feel his presence, his room-filling voice and charisma. His habits, some good and a few bad. But his reputation was assured, his small place in history guaranteed. As a *partigiano* from the earliest days of the war he had followed his conscience and served his country. Now there were his old clothes to sort out, his papers, the newspaper clippings, the books he had read and reread. Then she stopped from her folding and filling of boxes and from the back of the wardrobe brought forth the rectangular wooden case. She opened it and turned to Francesco. Inside lay the Smith & Wesson pistol, on its side, as if in a long, historic sleep.

"Take it, Franchie," she said, holding it out in front of her. "This is yours now. Remember what it means."

Rossi and Carrara were doing their homework in Rossi's apartment. Carrara was shaking his head and pacing the floor as Rossi, slouched on the sofa, continued to pore over the printouts with the numbers and codes that had come from the Marini files Gab had managed to crack. He had the semblance of a man banking on identifying something in them that could point to hidden motives or figures involved in recent events, willing it to emerge.

"So she's not dead?" said Carrara.

Rossi didn't look up but continued to study the printout as he replied.

"Who the hell do you think it was then? Long hair, right height. Unmoved by an explosion that she seems to be waiting to happen. Do you reckon there are many secret service operatives like that? And then the tip-off to Torrini or Silvestre or both to try and frame us in the act of grave robbing."

"Anyone could be watching our every move, though," sa Carrara, wanting to dispel the scenario now taking shape bef their eyes. "If we were getting close to knowing something, knowing the wrong things. Take it back to the day of the bombing. They were already clamming up and closing ranks. They wanted it all to themselves from the beginning."

"Tell me something I don't know," said Rossi, circling now with a red pen and joining up ideas scribbled in the margins.

He sat up, as if a shock had gone through him. Carrara sensed the change in a flash.

"What is it?"

"Might have something here," he said springing to his feet. He thrust the page he was studying under Carrara's nose. "Look. Here and here and here," he said. "The same sequence of letters and numbers. SLVSTR. 2K. 4K. 2K."

"Silvestre?"

"And the numbers?"

"Two thousand? Four thousand?"

"Payments," said Rossi. "Payments. We just got lucky."

Iannelli too had something to puzzle over. He sat at his desk staring at the new message.

And that was it. Again, it would have been sent via an anonymous server, a nonsense address, but how sure could he be that this was a tip-off? He reflected that there might be a plan to hand over information. Perhaps a meet or a drop off. And what if it was a hoax or a trap to get him out in the open?

What to do? His thumb hovered over the call button. Pass it on to Rossi, or anyone in the RSCS for that matter? Rossi hadn't got back to him yet about the first one, and on reflection, he was beginning to think he had perhaps been hasty about that. He had heard of Rossi's predicament through the grapevine. He was mildly amused by the cloak-and-dagger circumstances of Rossi's being caught almost red-handed but he would have bet his ycheque on the whole thing being a set-up to discredit him get him off the case. Or if he had been where he was alleged

331

to have been that night then there had to be other good reasons. Interesting reasons, if Rossi was involved. So, he would hold fire. Wait and see if there were any developments. After all, the message said "today" and he wasn't going anywhere. He could wait.

"But we don't *know*," said Carrara. "I mean, they're just random numbers." He had taken a seat on the sofa as Rossi paced the apartment in front of him.

"Right," said Rossi. "But do you think he's not getting looked after by someone?" He seemed to be formulating a plan now. "What if we put it to him that we know he is? This is too much to be a coincidence and, considering the rest of it, if this came from Maria Marini's files, which it did, and if that really was her in the CCTV footage, if somehow she is still alive and staged the whole car crash and if that wasn't her body in the ravine. If all that is true then maybe she is pulling the strings on this one and dog-handling scum like Silvestre. He probably doesn't even know who he's working for and doesn't care. He could be taking a few grand here and there, following orders to keep an eye on us, and this could be the proof."

"So we take him down?" said Carrara. "It's hardly going to stand up though, is it? A lousy printout with a few letters and numbers. A cock and bull story so outlandish that we wouldn't even get the time of day before they'd kicked us out."

"No," said Rossi waving an admonishing finger. "We keep this in the family. Just us. And we pay him a visit."

He reached for his address book, and then flicking through stopped and held it out for Carrara to see.

"You get on to this guy, while I look up Silvestre. He's an old friend. Just give him the name and tell him I sent you. He'll do the rest."

Rossi scrolled through the contacts on his phone.

"How are you going to persuade him to meet?" said Carra

There were the beginnings of a smile at the corners of Rossi's mouth.

"Let's just say we intimate that it's definitely in his interests."

"Offer him a bribe?"

"Of course."

Sixty-Six

"Here," said Rossi, indicating a rough track which led off the wider dirt road they had been walking through the park. The path climbed and wound through some oaks and poplars thinning out then at the entrance to what appeared to be a tunnel or a cave carved into the reddish-ochre rock that formed the hillside.

A place of my choosing. No clever shit. Nice and friendly, right? Rossi had agreed to Silvestre's conditions, all the "demands" and had given him every impression that it was he who was calling the shots. Carrara, meanwhile, had been onto Rossi's contact in the Financial Police.

"Old irrigation channels, I believe," said Rossi. "There's a cave network. They used to use them for mushroom cultivation. They like the damp and dark."

"And mushrooms are parasites too," said Carrara. "Fitting, wouldn't you say?"

Carrara shone his torch into the pitch darkness. And flicked the safety on his Beretta.

"After you," said Rossi, his weapon already live.

"Thanks," said Carrara. "I take it that it's not 100 per ce‑ safe."

Rossi pointed to a rusty and half-concealed sign.

334

They penetrated deep into the tunnel and its sudden other-worldly cold. The rectangle of light from the entrance behind them began to diminish and outside of the torch beam was total blackness.

As they followed the dusty path in search of some sign of life, Rossi was beginning to wonder whether they might not be walking into another set-up. No one knew they were here. Their phones would give no discernible signal. A convenient tunnel collapse and they would already be in their own graves.

"Picked a nice spot, didn't he?" said Carrara.

"Yes, he did," said a voice from the gloom. Silvestre emerged in front of them carrying his own torch. "This way gentleman," he said and continued along the tunnel until it opened out into a modest gallery hewn from the rock. He hung his torch on a hook in the wall above their heads so it gave a more or less even illumination.

"Come here often?" said Rossi looking around at what was evidently a meeting place for practitioners of any number of illicit or questionable activities. Silvestre ignored the comment.

"Now if you'd kindly let me frisk you gentlemen for any thing you might have forgotten to remove and then I think we can all relax."

Carrara and Rossi obliged him, despite their distaste. Silvestre lifted their weapons from their shoulder holsters but left them with their phones.

"Well, your mobile's fucked here," said Silvestre. "Transmitters, phones, all useless. I thought coming down here would *simplify* matters. He flicked the safeties and tossed the weapons behind him onto the ground.

"So, how can I help you, gents?" he said then, lighting up a arette but not offering.

"We want you to back off," said Rossi. "Call it quits on this about the church."

Silvestre blew out a cloud of smoke that hung between them, going nowhere in the clammy air.

"Why should I?" he said. "It's the truth."

"Right," said Rossi. "Like someone just *happened* to see a light on inside and came to investigate."

Silvestre shrugged.

"Well, the truth will out, as they say. At least once there's been *a full and thorough investigation.*"

"We know you got tipped off," said Carrara. "And we know you sold out long ago."

Silvestre felt sure enough of himself to smirk as he drew on his cigarette, as Rossi cut in again before Carrara might lose his cool.

"And what about if we make it easier for everyone," said Rossi. "Save a bit of strain on the public purse. How about we have *no* investigation?"

He reached inside his jacket pocket and took out a slightly bulging envelope. Silvestre's eyes followed its brief trajectory until it halted in front of him in Rossi's outstretched hand.

"Of course," Rossi continued, "I would rather you just made it clear to everyone that the door was open after all the other night."

"And risk perjuring myself?"

"And this is less risky?" said Rossi indicating with a terse movement the envelope in his outstretched hand.

"You will check you haven't left anything behind before you leave," said Silvestre flicking ash from his half-smoked cigarette and turning away as if he had concluded matters before then wheeling round. "And then when we meet again."

"What do you mean, *again*?" said Carrara.

Silvestre drew on his cigarette, the tip flaring, diabolical in the half-light. Paranoiacally cautious, cynical, he still hadn't take the envelope.

"Well, this is the down payment, right? The beginning

fruitful collaboration. And I could use some regular help regarding certain 'consignments' coming into the capital."

Carrara's muscles were twitching with a spontaneous desire to show Silvestre whose fists were in control, but Rossi put out a knowing, calming hand.

"Naturally," said Rossi. "Naturally. Silvestre has a legitimate point. Oh, but wait a minute."

He turned to Carrara and drew back his hand holding the envelope.

"Gigi, I thought I told you to bring the one stuffed with cash."

Carrara was shaking his head. Silvestre's arrogant and detached expression began to change as he watched Rossi open the envelope and remove the papers inside.

"What is *this*?" Rossi said with mock theatrical surprise. Silvestre was staring now at the sheets in Rossi's hand. "Payments made to Silvestre, by a certain agent Marini. Two thousand, four thousand."

He looked up at Silvestre.

"Need I go on? Or do you want me to mention the offshore account? The Swiss bank? They're not so anonymous anymore, you know. But it seems you spend it as fast as you get it and that has come to not a few people's attention."

Despite holding the whip hand in the cave, Silvestre had begun to look like the lion tamer in the ring without his chair. He backed off a couple of steps.

"You can't prove a damn thing, Rossi!" said Silvestre exploding then within his taught wiry frame and pointing an enraged finger at his accuser. "You haven't got a shred of proof! You're bluffing!"

"Try me," said Rossi, "and our friends in the *Guardia di Finanza* will be down on you like a tonne of bricks. At best you'll be under investigation, suspended. Worst-case you're looking at scandal. Maybe jail."

Rossi held up the pages.

've even got the dates. When she handed it over. It's all here.

So, I got lucky for once. Now, about those doors the other night. What exactly happened? It looks to me like there was a right royal mix-up, wasn't there?"

It had been another busy day at the office of The List of Shame. There had been calls from every quarter it seemed – messages of solidarity, the usual familiar litany of abuse and death threats. They didn't come in equal measure but it at least it meant they were making waves. The demo had got plenty of press coverage, and they'd picked up good exposure on the Web too. That was where much of it was happening now. Things got liked, shared and with a bit of luck could go viral. The young especially were instrumental. It was they who could influence and bring about change, create a critical mass of opinion and then what they had been struggling for so long to bring to people's attention would look suddenly startlingly normal.

As Ginika sifted through the remains of a to-do list of sorts, she came across an e-mail she had printed but hadn't got round to following up yet. Inspector Michael Rossi. He had heard of the organization, had seen them at the demo and now he was making enquiries about a certain Jibril, and that crook who went by the name of the President. Well, she certainly knew about his murderous business. Who didn't? It was people like the President who profited from the bigotry, who *fed* the bigotry. Did she know anything about any killings in the past? The enquiry was vague but it was all to do with a very important ongoing investigation and anything might help. He had left a phone number too. Well, she said to herself and looked up at the clock. She had a few minutes and there was no time like the present.

Sixty-Seven

As they emerged into the sunlight from their subterranean rendez-vous, Rossi's phone was hit by a tempest of backed-up messages and missed calls. Iannelli, Maroni, Katia, Yana.

"Who's first?" he said, stopping to flick through and prioritize them.

Carrara too was getting bombarded.

"*Guardia di Finanza*," he said, holding up a hand to signal to Rossi he understood its importance with regard to Silvestre and his cash movements. For a few moments he listened as a quizzical look began to spread across his face.

"But nothing?" said Carrara. "You're sure? OK, thanks anyway."

Rossi just watched and waited.

"The GdF have got nothing on Silvestre," said Carrara, the phone hanging idly in his hand.

"Neither have I," said Rossi. He went on ahead as Carrara followed, looking on as Rossi passed the bins at the entrance to the park and tossed the envelope and printouts into the recycling in. Rossi turned round.

"Won't be needing that anymore," he said. "It was a set-up," explained to a still puzzled-looking Carrara. "I didn't have a

339

thing on him. Gab was in on it and we made the whole story up."

"It was all bullshit?"

"Afraid so," said Rossi. "Saved you the trouble of lying. You looked thoroughly convinced though, and he fell for it hook, line and sinker. It was a bluff." Carrara was dumbstruck. "I had no other option," Rossi continued. "Given the time constraints. But I knew he was up to something and then, after seeing the video footage, well, I took a gamble. Marini's still pulling strings, we get followed and rumbled. He's the man on our tails. There had to be some little sweetener in it for him somewhere."

"So the code wasn't cracked?"

Rossi shook his head.

"Uncrackable, so far at least. Gab's never seen the like of it. I told him to put on a little show when we came round. Which also got me thinking and not just about why someone didn't want us to make the link with the cardinal."

"And perhaps you might let me in on these other thoughts of yours," said a more than slightly disgruntled Carrara as they approached the Alfa.

"I will," said Rossi. "I promise. Now, where were we? I think we'd better get straight on to Dario. I'm sure Maroni won't mind waiting. And he should be in for a pleasant surprise if Silvestre knows what's good for him."

Rossi called Iannelli, who answered on the first ring.

"OK, Dario. I think we need to meet," said Rossi, after listening first to Iannelli's general preamble and then scribbling down some notes and the new address. He closed the phone and turned back to Carrara.

"Well," said Rossi, "things appear to be hotting up on the anonymous e-mail front. Dario's got another message and another name. He passed it on to Maroni."

"And what does he make of it?"

"We'll find out when we speak to him. But not yet."

Iannelli too had got lucky. He was in one of the new top-floor apartments overlooking Piazza Vittorio in Rome's Esquilino district. The original six-storey building had been bombed out during the Second World War and, for as long as Rossi could remember, had remained a ruin, until the council and developers had got their act together and restored it to something like its former glory.

"The place belongs to a friend of a friend," said Iannelli. "He's in the States for a month and I get to stay. A perk of my situation, shall we say."

"Very nice," said Rossi opening the blinds just enough to be able to admire the view over Rome's biggest piazza, which, from above, was now a vivid, leafy emerald rectangle. "Too high up to see the rats."

"The least of our worries," replied Dario. "Come and look at this," he said, indicating his laptop on the glass-topped dining table in the centre of the room. "I feel like I have turned into a middleman. What's next in your humble opinion?"

Rossi leaned over to look. The message was as chilling as it was terse.

Something big. A major incident. Central Rome. Soon.

"And signed 'D. H.'," said Rossi as he turned away from the screen to think and gaze out over an imagined city. "They're both writers," said Rossi. He wheeled round to face Iannelli and Carrara who had flopped into the white leather sofa and armchair respectively. "D. H. Lawrence, Tennessee Williams." Two trams were approaching from opposite directions on the street below and ringing their bells in a sign of warning. "A streetcar," said Rossi. "*A Streetcar Named Desire*. Rome's full of trams. What if that was the reference?"

"So you think it's a code?" said Iannelli, fascinated now and intrigued at being in on the very investigative process itself.

"The terminus is just down the road behind us, at Porta ηggiore," said Carrara reclining, enjoying the comfort. "And η the station, Termini."

341

"But trams traverse the whole city," said Rossi pacing in front of them. "If they do something on a tram we can't defend against it."

"Fill them with agents," said Carrara. "As many as we can spare."

"But low profile," said Rossi. "That's the trouble with a tip-off, if it's to be believed. If we show our hand, they can get cold feet and abort the whole op. Or improvise. If we're talking about a device, they might dump it anywhere."

"If it's real," said Iannelli.

"That's a chance we'll have to take," said Rossi, sitting down next to Iannelli on the sofa. "What did they say when you relayed the info?"

"Nothing," said Iannelli. "Maybe they didn't put much store in it."

"Maroni knows most of it now, though," said Rossi. "I gave him the full spiel. But he's not having anything to do with more controversial theories."

"And what would they be?" said Iannelli feeling he approaching the inner sanctum of another Rossi intuitio

"Off the record, Dario, naturally,"

"Goes without saying," he said, rising then and wa to open the doors to an elaborately inlaid cherry drinks cabinet under the window. "Drink anyone?"

Carrara desisted. Rossi was a given.

"Even got your own personal tipple here, Iannelli as he produced a halffull bottle of James and a couple of weighty crystal tumblers that c as handy weapons.

Rossi gave Iannelli a brief summary of had so far brought them, omitting only revelation the CCTV images had throw their entrapment of Silvestre.

"How do you see this?" said Rossi. deal somewhere, I can feel it."

"The way I see things," began Iannelli, arranging the glasses on the table, "you've got a cell, or maybe more than one, out there, and your man Jibril's involved in some capacity. Whether he and whoever he's fallen in with was behind the university bomb or not, I don't know. As I told you, I nurse my own theories on that front. There's a lot going on geopolitically. There's always the chance someone was sending the Israelis a warning shot. And I don't hold with the idea that attacks on these targets are always fanatics hitting the Zionist oppressor. I think other stuff could come into play. Deals. Weapons. Defence systems. Even cyber stuff, software, encryption technology. The Israelis are players in that game. Maybe someone wants to muscle in."

"Encryption?" said Rossi.

"Just a thought," said Iannelli. "A client who didn't pay up or keep their part of the deal. They could have had other interests on the side."

"Are you referring by any chance to the esteemed rector of the Israeli university in Rome?"

"You said it."

"So he's got form?"

"They all have," said Iannelli, pouring a couple of decent measures of whiskey. "In one way or another. Either it's property deals, currency capers, cover-ups, making sure someone gets his precious degree even if he can only sign his name. I exaggerate, of course, but not that much."

"And it's worth a bomb?" said Carrara.

"It was relatively small," said Iannelli. "Military-grade explosive though. Remember that little omission?"

"So a wholly private matter?" said Rossi.

"Which takes the lives of a few innocent bystanders, a detail if there are under-the-table multimillion dollar deals at stake. And if you don't mind me extending the metaphor, we could well be on two completely separate tracks here and the trams have very different drivers."

Iannelli headed to the kitchen and came back with water for the whiskey.

"What's happening in the city in the next couple of days?" Carrara called after him. "In terms of high profile, big crowds, political gatherings."

"There's at least one demo planned for Friday," said Iannelli, returning and then scanning his diary lying open on the table. "Two actually. Students protesting against the public sector cuts and there's the LGBT cross-party alliance for equal rights. That's going to be big. It's national. All the progressive groups, the left, a smattering of enlightened conservatives, the *centri sociali*, even ANPI, the partisans' association."

He poured water into Rossi's drink and handed it to him.

"And much, much more," said Rossi, taking a first sip, "all for the amazing price of—"

"Could be targets. Could be nothing," said Iannelli. "No way of knowing unless our oracle decides to speak."

"I wish he could be a little less oracular and a bit more time and place and method," said Rossi savouring the smooth Reserve.

"And blow his cover?" said Carrara. "If this is an inside man, then he has to hold back, like we said. Too much detail and he compromises himself."

"So we get drip-fed the information. Unless it turns out to be a nasty joke," said Rossi, pondering the bitter possibilities along with the whiskey. "And, if you are the vital line of communication in this, I suppose it means we're going to have to make you a deputy, Dario."

"Swear me in," he replied raising his glass in his right hand for the oath.

"You'll need to hook up with Gigi here. If and when you do get any further news, put them straight through to him. It means 24/7 though."

"I hardly sleep anyway," said Iannelli knocking back his drink

344

neat in one. "It won't cost me much to have my ear open for a notification."

"What about a radio link?" said Carrara turning to Rossi. "At least on these demos. Dario's in a perfect spot too. We've got a strategic position here."

"That can be arranged," said Rossi. "We can go via your bodyguards. Where are they, by the way?"

"I told them to take a couple of hours off," said Iannelli with an air of detachment mixed with the mild recognition of his own carelessness. Rossi said nothing but sized up the apartment's sniper vulnerability in the vast expanses of thick glass, on its north and east facing sides, albeit shielded for now by blinds.

"Shouldn't you be somewhere safer?" said Rossi, indicating the windows.

Iannelli smiled.

"Bulletproof," he said. "I didn't tell you who the place belongs to, did I?"

Rossi shook his head.

"Well, that's because I can't."

Sixty-Eight

"Franchie?"

"Yes,"

"Are you on, for tomorrow?"

"Yes."

"Good. Where do we meet?"

"Piazza Repubblica. It's going to be a great day."

"Definitely."

"For freedom."

"For freedom. For liberty."

"Liberty, equality, fraternity. We need that in Italy," said the voice crackling on the end of the line. "We need a revolution in Italy. That's why things don't change."

Francesco knew the well-worn dialectic but went along with it all the same.

"Not like in France."

"Exactly. They take it seriously there. They shut the whole city down. They shut the country down. And what do we do? We go on a march if the weather's nice, smoke a joint and go home, and then complain about everything. Am I right?"

"Too right," said Francesco. "It's an important cause, for everyone."

"Like slavery, like votes for women. The fight goes on, brother."

"I'll be there."

"And be ready," the voice said.

"I'll be ready," said Francesco.

"*Hasta la victoria, compagnero!*"

"*Hasta la victoria!*" echoed Francesco, feeling foolish as he did so, as the line then went dead.

There was so much to do and so little time. There had been innumerable visits to lawyers' offices, phone calls, video calls. Then there was the bank, the accountant. The contracts to finalize. The small print Yana insisted on reading and having explained. She wasn't taking any shit from guys in suits telling her to trust them and that it was all a formality. She had to know. She had squeezed the life out of them, made them earn their salaries. She laughed. They would be sick of the sight of her soon. What if she was a *rompi-palle*, a ball-breaker? She didn't give a damn.

She was leaving on Friday. She checked her tickets. Termini. Roma-Milan. The day after tomorrow. And Michael and she had not parted on good terms. Parted in the sense of leaving. Not leaving. What did she mean? She didn't know herself. She felt bullied by the vocabulary. They hadn't left each other; it was a hiatus. A distance caused by circumstances but bridgeable. She preferred that image. The torrent below, the two banks, and the two of them ready to start building again. But what if they lost the will to build, and moved on, each on their own side of the divide?

The clock was ticking. There was so much to do and Marta needed more help than she had envisaged. She was good but she lacked some basics. Too late to go back now. She would manage. She looked around the flat. Most of the essential stuff was in boxes, both the things she would bring and that which would remain for now. She was glad she wasn't a hoarder, unlike someone else she knew.

Olivia still couldn't quite believe it. The school had given her a couple of days off "to get herself together". The inspector had explained everything, they'd said, so she wasn't going to be fired. There was plenty of in-business work they wanted her to do. It wasn't the same but a job was a job, though it would mean taking the train every day to the offices of the multinationals where more or less enthusiastic foreign executives were intent on learning the beautiful Italian language.

But she still felt the gaping hole of absence. There had been no news from or about Jibril and now that she had confided in her friends, they had advised her to forget.

She crossed the strangled, blaring traffic and skew-whiff vans and buses and doubleparked Smart cars on a rubbish-strewn Via Marsala then delved into the great echoing cathedral of the station. Today, as every day, its impersonality and swift-flowing change washed over her, but today it was as if she were a rock in its stream. The glowing shop fronts, the fashion models, those real and those larger than life in the posters above her head, the whole kaleidoscope of colour and sound that had once transfixed her could not breach her consciousness.

She stopped still, staring into space. She didn't know what to think. Commuters and travellers bumped into her or gave her funny looks but she didn't seem to care. She was trying not to think at all, to feel nothing, to be as impervious as a stone to all her fear.

Sixty-Nine

"Well," said Maroni, "it seems Silvestre's memory has been playing tricks on him."

"Really?" said Rossi from the other side of the desk.

"He says there was a mix-up, that there was a side door open after all. 'A breakdown in communication' as he put it. An easy mistake to make, I suppose," his suspicious gaze fixed on Rossi and then on Carrara.

"I'm just glad it's all been straightened out, sir," Rossi replied. "So we can go back to thinking about what to do next."

"Yes," said Maroni. "And guess what?" He held up a piece of paper.

"An anonymous ransom demand. For the safe return of the mortal remains etc, etc."

"I have the feeling that one might drag on a bit," said Carrara.

"And then be quietly forgotten, maybe," said Rossi.

"Whatever does happen, it's the least of my worries, gentlemen. I am rather more concerned with the living at this moment in time. Now, tell me what it was you wanted to see me about."

"The tip-offs. And Iannelli," said Rossi.

"Go, on," said Maroni. "I'm all ears."

'We think it's genuine."

349

"And?"

"Well, we think an attack might be real and possible, imminent even. And we have a hunch about targets."

Maroni was shaking his head already.

"The alarm hasn't changed. If anything, it's come down a peg. There's been nothing from intelligence to suggest any heightened risk or specific targets. The alert remains high but that's the new reality, isn't it? Let's face it."

"Don't you want to see what I've put together, at least?" said Rossi. "We can present it to the security committee. You can present it."

"And look like the bloody idiot if it goes tits up?" said Maroni. "I don't think so, Rossi. Thanks for the offer and all that. Let's have it then. Your hare-brained scheme, number whatever it is."

"If these tip-offs are genuine we need to heed them," Rossi began, "and I'm sure there's a code."

"A code?" said Maroni.

"The names on the e-mails. Tennessee. D. H. They're literary references."

"Literary?" Maroni snorted. "You sure this isn't more wishful thinking on your part, Rossi? The frustrated intellectual."

"I'm convinced," said Rossi, absorbing the body blow. Maroni looked rather less certain but was giving him the benefit of the doubt.

"So what do they *mean* then, Rossi, in your interpretation?"

Rossi took a map of central Rome from the folder and began to outline his theory.

"The tram, the number 3, goes along here, past the Colosseum, where the Christians were thrown to the lions, by the way. And then here, near the corner, there's a bar called the Rainbow."

"The Rainbow?"

"It's the title of a D. H. Lawrence novel."

Maroni was staring up at Rossi.

"Do you seriously believe all this?"

Rossi continued, oblivious.

"We step up the undercover presence on the line and around the area."

"And divert resources from the major basilicas and the station and the underground?" countered Maroni. "We haven't got unlimited resources, Rossi. And we can't play follow my literary leader without having something more concrete from intelligence. Are you out of your mind? And you expect me to go before the commission with this? It's more than ridiculous. It's comical. D. H. bloody Lawrence! Do you think our man is some errant man of letters with an exploding copy of *The Divine Comedy*? Do me a favour, Rossi, for the love of God! Go out and do something real for once. And tomorrow we want you both on general surveillance, as per usual when there's a demo on. Those students are looking for trouble. So make sure they get some if they step out of line."

"Am I allowed to bring in your daughters if they get involved," said Rossi, unable to resist a barb.

"They'll be there over my dead body," said Maroni.

Seventy

"I suppose that's what you might call short shrift then," said Carrara as they wandered back to the office where Katia was working over case notes and suspect profiles.

"Burning the midnight oil again," said Rossi. She checked her watch.

"A normal working day you mean?"

Rossi slumped down into his chair. Maybe his theory was forced. Outlandish, inappropriate.

"You told him about the oil stain, under the bath?" he said to Carrara, who had taken up a similarly despondent stance. He nodded.

"So, the previous occupants might have stored some guns there. It still doesn't give us anything solid to go on."

"But we're looking for Jibril."

"Not exactly easy. He'll be in a safe house, sticking to crowded places. Moving at night. Public transport."

Katia looked up.

"Oh, there was a call for you, Michael. An African lady." She looked down at her notes. "From an organization called The List of Shame. Says she might have something for you and could you drop by tomorrow."

Returning to his apartment alone, for Rossi, was, as a rule, comforting, but tonight was different. Yana was going the next day, and he wouldn't even be there to say goodbye. Everything was on standby again. The two demos, his own concerns, the threat hanging over them and the city. The night was heavy and warm, as if a storm were coming, but the sky was clear. From his balcony he looked away to the hills and beyond the hills to the stars. In Milan, she would see the same sky and the same sun and moon. He wondered if she would feel alone or free or a combination of the two, just as he did now.

Yet at the same time, guiltily, he was experiencing something that was a little more than professional admiration for Katia. Maybe it was just her enthusiasm for the job, her all-round lack of cynicism that had been like a breath of fresh air that was tugging now at the first cobwebs of his early middle-age. It was cowardly, he knew that. When the going gets tough, what do we do? Jump ship? No. At least not like this. But there was a magnetism he could not deny.

He turned his thoughts back to the job. He, Gigi, and Katia would be in and around the centre the next day. Over dinner they had discussed strategies, his theories, the codes or possible codes in the messages. Iannelli was hooked up to Carrara's account. If an e-mail warning came through to Iannelli, Carrara would get it too, in real time. But with no specific target, they had decided to roam and circulate. Rossi and Carrara were going to cover an area from the Colosseum to the Esquilino Hill with a direct line of communication with uniformed reaction groups.

He went back in and poured himself a nightcap, but a modest one. He would need a clear head in the morning. They had talked weapons too. He took up his own automatic, spread a cloth on the table and began stripping it down. He cleaned it, oiled it, and then slipped the components into place. Then he took the magazine and one by one cleaned and reloaded the shells. A soldier cleans his gun. It's his best friend. All the clichés, but true.

He went over to his cabinet and opened the secret compartment with a key. He selected a second weapon. A revolver. Backup. Gut instinct told him he might need it.

***

Rossi woke early with a start, in bed and not in his clothes. His head was clear. He got up and looked in the mirror. Tired, yes. Exhausted nervous energy would keep him going now. He showered and dressed and headed out to meet Carrara for breakfast at the office. He too was looking sharp despite the efforts of the past few days, weeks even. He was poring over a map, identifying blind spots, potential targets, ways in and out, simulating worst-case scenarios – the suicide attack that preyed always on their minds. The coordinated, multiple attack. The Metro hit. Even the dirty bomb, but intelligence, thank God, had not indicated that any such apocalyptic outcome might be on the cards. Not yet.

But a piece was missing from Rossi's puzzle, if there was a puzzle. The List of Shame. He dialled again. This time they answered.

"I'm sorry, Inspector, but the lady who would deal with these matters is not here right now. Can I ask her to call you back? I do know she has been looking into your query."

"Can you tell her that any information could be of the utmost importance," said Rossi, "And to call me on my mobile phone as I will be out of the office all day."

He thanked her and put the phone down.

"Shall we go?" he said.

Seventy-One

The day was fine and the crowds were making the best of the very generous leftovers of a Roman summer. Rossi and Carrara were cruising in the Alfa. They had been circulating and stopping periodically to reconnoitre on foot. Katia too was busy with a squad of uniforms in the east of the city. Demonstrators, meanwhile, were converging on the centre. Rossi and Carrara were descending along Via di San Giovanni, in the direction of the Colosseum, at no more than a brisk walking pace.

"There's the Rainbow," said Carrara pointing at the bar with it's hand-painted sign.

"Suppose we'd better take a look," said Rossi, "and see if we can grab a bite while we're at it."

They parked the Alfa, made a quick sweep of the bar then took a table on the footpath. They ordered sandwiches and settled back to gaze up at the Colosseum's mighty bulk while trying to fit in as best they could among the LGBT+ crowd.

"Think how long that's been there," said Carrara.

"Only an earthquake could bring that down," Rossi replied.

Rossi had almost allowed himself to settle into the near-fection of the scene. It could go on like this for ever. This was Eternal City, after all. Eternity. The never-ending. How small they were in the grand scheme. He watched the crowds strolling by. This was certainly one of the perks of the job – the sun, the food, the views. The worries were there, big as houses, but for a moment, they had shrunk to the size of the plastic memorabilia on sale at the side of the road. Carrara's phone buzzed Rossi out of his shallow daydream.

"There's an e-mail."

Rossi's heartbeat began to accelerate as his colleague focused and flicked through the screens.

"Iannelli. A message. It says 'Termini'." Carrara was looking up now at Rossi.

"Is it signed?" said Rossi.

"'Oscar'."

Oscar, thought Rossi. Oscar. The Rainbow. Tennessee. And then it clicked.

His radio crackled into action in his inside jacket pocket.

"It's Maroni," he said, pressing the earpiece harder to his ear against the traffic noise.

"Rossi! Where are you. We've got a situation here! And you'd better move fast."

Rossi snapped into action and thrust a twenty onto the table.

"Termini station," said Maroni.

"We know," said Rossi into the mic in his sleeve cuff. "We're on our way."

"It's a bomb alert," said Maroni, "and Iannelli may or may not have saved the day."

"We're on our way," said Rossi again as they broke then into a fast jog back to the car. "What do we know?" he asked into the concealed mike as they neared the Alfa.

"A rucksack, red, unattended."

Maroni sounded solid, clear, the years of experience showing through. "We got a phone tip-off too. We don't know if it's rea but it was detailed, so we treat it as real. OK. *Very* real. The pla is swarming and they're evacuating already but police prese is minimal. We have to man the conference at all costs. It's going to be chaos but get there and find it. Fast."

Carrara surged through red light after red light, criss-crossing taxi lanes and tram tracks until they swerved onto the pavement under the station's grey, overhanging bulk.

"They're going to hit the demo," said Rossi.

"But it said the station," Carrara shot back.

"They're hitting both," said Rossi. "It's the code. I'm sure of it. We go the back way," he said as they leapt then from the car and cut through a security barrier and onto the tracks, racing in to the station along one of its forgotten platforms and avoiding the bedlam that had broken out at the main entrance.

"It could be out in the open; it won't be in a bin. It'll be too large," Rossi shouted.

"Toilets?" said Carrara.

"Checking them now," said Rossi. "Get those uniforms there," he said beckoning to a group of local police. "That leaves the forecourt, the shops, the platforms."

At the station proper, the evacuation effort was underway but ragged and confused. Some tourists were shaking their heads and laughing, refusing to take it seriously, others were protesting about missed trains and the language barrier wasn't helping.

"Get out of the station!" Rossi boomed. "This is a bomb alert. Leave now!" he shouted as he physically propelled a middle-aged couple towards the piazza. More uniforms were streaming in as Rossi and Carrara darted in all directions giving orders. Katia had arrived too and began marshalling station staff on the platform.

"Stop all trains coming in!" she said to a passing official clutching a walkie-talkie. "Keep them out!"

Carrara had a radio clamped to his ear. He signalled to Rossi. "Suspect package," he said, "by the news stand, main course."

"Let's go!" said Rossi. The station was something like half-empty but the situation was critical. The tube trains below were still disgorging hundreds of passengers who, largely unaware of the danger, were being siphoned up on the escalators as officers attempted to divert the flow into the relative safety of the piazza.

A bright red rucksack was propped against the corner of the abandoned news stand. A cordon of police was fanning out and officers were hand-gesturing to the public to get back. A stout-looking *carabiniere* came sprinting up to Rossi and Carrara.

"Any news on the bomb squad?" said Rossi. The place was buzzing with police of every description.

"They're on their way," he said, panting after his exertions.

"But the tip-off said fifteen minutes," said Rossi.

"If we can trust it," said Carrara.

"Just evacuate," said Rossi, "as far away as possible."

He watched as a lone figure emerged from behind the news stand, pushing a shopping trolley filled with plastic bags and oddments of every type. It was the station's resident bag lady, blissfully unaware or unfazed by the drama now unfolding. Time seemed almost to stop as she tottered around on the bare fore-court, the lone actor in a piece of absurdist drama. She looked up for a moment at the confusion before her then dropped her head again, shaking it in disbelief.

From a safe distance officers continued shouting and gesticulating to her to leave, but she carried on regardless, noticing the rucksack and going right up to it, where she stopped and began to undo its straps. Rossi stared for a second as the tall and once-handsome lady, now a mass of matted curls and ragged ill-fitting garments, started to poke about at the top of the bulging backpack. He stared for a second more; then, as if exploding out of the starting blocks, he ran straight towards her. He threw an arm around her waist, catapulting her onto the trolley and sending them and careering across the white-flecked marble floor away towards t other side of the station like some bizarre pair of ice dancers

The last few officers had gone through the main doors when the shockwave flung them on to the pavement.

As the smoke cleared Rossi got to his feet. The powerful odour of the unwashed had been substituted by the all-pervading reek of explosives. Amidst the alarms and the tinkling of falling masonry and glass, he began to hear a first few coughs and splutters from the direction of the news stand. It was gone, disintegrated. Then he saw limbs moving through the debris. The living, he thought. The lucky.

And now for the dead.

Seventy-Two

Checking first that the bag lady was uninjured, he picked his way through the rubble towards the blast scene. An officer had been killed outright, his uniformed body motionless on the forecourt in an expanding pool of blood and dust. The injured list would be long, but a quick evaluation suggested that none was in immediate danger.

"Thank God it wasn't a nail bomb," said Carrara, prematurely aged by a coating of white dust but otherwise unharmed. They had been lucky. This time. That was for sure. But as the saying went, *they* had only to be lucky once.

"This isn't over," said Rossi, scanning the zone around them. "There's going to be more."

He called to Katia who had just applied a tourniquet to a uniform's badly bleeding leg. He had been watching her hands – they were steady as a rock as she took a lipstick and wrote a big "T" in plain sight for the medical personnel.

"Stay here," Rossi said, "and coordinate."

She nodded back. She was doing it already. She'd shed her jacket and she tapped the Beretta in her shoulder holster. Rossi's ear were ringing, and through the dust he indicated the main entra in the direction of Piazza Repubblica and broke into a jog.

"How do you know?" said Carrara, checking his own weapon as they began to run through the crowd.

"The code," said Rossi over his shoulder to Carrara. "They're all gay writers. Tennessee, D. H., Oscar. That's the message. They're going to hit the demo too."

Jibril was moving through the crowd of protestors who had begun running and trampling all before them – the weak, the slow, the young – as soon as the blast hit. He had seen the explosion but now he was moving fast, weaving, homing in. They wouldn't start until he did but they would be growing impatient, their nerves stretched to the limit. Ali would be uncontrollable.

Jibril's eyes were scanning the crowd. He had to see them first. As if by providence, in answer to his jumbled prayers, a gap opened in the mass of people in front of him and there they were: Ali and Yusuf, side by side, ready to begin.

Seventy-Three

Rossi's phone was ringing. He was sure it could only be Maroni, but the ID said "unknown caller".

"Inspector Rossi?"

"Yes," replied Rossi as he and Carrara headed for the piazza.

"I'm calling from List of Shame. Can you talk?"

"We have a situation here," said Rossi. "If it's quick."

"It's about your query. Well, it seems that there was no one called Jibril connected to the President and no one of that name involved in a suspect death."

Rossi's hopes fell. He had been sure there was a link with Jibril.

"Is there anything else, about the President?"

"Well, it took some searching but we believe the person you refer to *was* responsible for the death of a certain Banjoko, a promising literature student. He was was lynched by a mob for being gay."

Rossi's interest was heightened now. The literary connection, it had to be.

"The so-called President," she went on, "was implicated in the killing as the prime instigator. I'm sure you know he is a very nasty piece of work."

"Banjoko?" said Rossi. The name itself meant nothing but he remembered what Olivia had told them.

"Did this boy have a brother by any chance?"

"Yes, I believe there was a family. Several sisters and one brother, but much younger."

"A name?" said Rossi.

"No, I'm sorry," she replied.

"Thank you," said Rossi. "You have been most helpful."

He shoved his phone into his pocket. "The hotel," he said to Carrara. "He's heading for the hotel."

Jibril sank down on to one knee and unzipped his bag in one swift motion. He took out the weapon wrapped loosely in a jacket. Ali had spotted him, his hand too, inside his own sports bag, poised on the trigger. So this was it. Ali waited for Jibril to begin, as had been agreed, as the crowds in fibrillation scattered in all directions.

On the battlefield where Jibril had faced his enemies only the quick survived. But Ali's realization of what now awaited him was not quick enough, Yusef's even less so. As Ali's eyes met Jibril's, his expression changed from glee to surprise to rage as Jibril swung a fraction to his left and squeezed off a rapid couple of rounds with a sniper's accuracy into Yusef's right shoulder and another then to shatter a knee. It all happened in a fraction of a second as he sealed Ali's fate with three pummelling shots to his body, knowing that had he let Ali live he would only ever have taken more innocent lives. As he fell backwards onto the fountain, his weapon flew from his flailing hand and he crumpled to the ground.

Jibril yanked the magazine out of Yusef's weapon and tossed it far into the fountain. He dropped his bag and ran on then through the crowds, heading for the Incantevole Hotel.

"Automatic fire," said Carrara. "From Piazza Repubblica."

He grabbed his radio. "Reports coming in of shots fired in

Piazza Repubblica area. Can you confirm. Over. Possible multiple casualties. Suspect seen moving in the direction of Piazza Barberini."

"Come on," said Rossi, his ears still whistling from the blast. "He's heading for the Incantevole!"

They sprinted through the piazza littered with every form of human detritus. There were the walking wounded who had been crushed in the stampede, bleeding from cuts sustained from broken glass, some groaning or gasping for air. Wallets, trainers, shoes, bottles, cans and backpacks of all descriptions were scattered around as some of the protestors who hadn't run cowered behind improvised barriers while others stood zombie-like looking about themselves in shock. Smoke from the explosion hung in the air. The traffic in and out of Piazza dei Cinquecento had ground to a halt. Sirens wailed as ambulances nudged forward in fits and starts along the strangled streets, striving to reach the injured.

"Police!" shouted Rossi as he and Carrara tried to barge their way through the sea of stunned demonstrators still barring the way to the central fountain. He could see a body on the ground and blood spattered across the flagstones. He was dead. Another figure, splayed next to him, was alive but being watched by a crowd of nervous but vigilant onlookers, as if he were a poisonous snake coiling to strike. Rossi strained to try to make out what was happening and glimpsed the injured terrorist's hand crawling towards his jacket. His movements were laboured and he was using his left to get to the weapon he couldn't reach with his shattered right arm. But Rossi and Carrara were too far away to get there in time. Both had their weapons drawn but neither could get a clear shot as figures zig-zagged back and forth in the line of fire.

"Police! Get down. He's armed!" Rossi shouted.

A bearded figure then lunged forward and hurled himself towards Yusef just as he had freed an automatic pistol from its holster and aimed it at the crowd. In the confusion at close quarters, Yusef lashed out and struck his assailant a powerful blow across the face with his weapon before losing the brief battle decisively as his hand was slapped down onto the pavement. The weapon skittered away on the flagstones and as it did, the others piled in, pinning Yusef to the ground.

"*Dis*armed," said a cool voice as Rossi finally fought his way through, holding his badge out in front of him like the gorgon's head as Carrara followed with his gun drawn ready for a possible third assailant.

The bearded young man who had spoken turned to look up at Rossi.

"His weapon jammed. I was lucky."

He had a gash in his head but he would make it. Their prisoner's face, meanwhile, was locked in a rictus of rage but he too would live. Rossi frisked him then tossed a pair of cuffs to the leader of the ragged bunch from the *centri sociali*.

"Good bit of work there. What's your name?" he said.

"Francesco," came the reply.

Rossi turned to Carrara who was still scanning the immediate vicinity for other threats.

"Stay here, Gigi, and call for backup. There could be others mixed in with the crowd. But I think we found today's hero."

"Just doing my duty as a citizen," said Francesco, and through his pain, there was the hint of a smile.

Rossi looked up. The Hotel Incantevole was about another fifty yards away. He raced towards the entrance, extending an arm clutching his ID as a leather-clad cop also drew alongside on a motorbike. Rossi could see it was a female officer but he was already bounding up the broad stone steps leading to the lobby. As Rossi saw her in the dark reflection of the doors and she saw him, some fine needle of doubt pricked his subconscious. But the cop stood her ground and gave him the reassuring nod he needed and set about blocking anyone else from gaining access to the hotel.

"The President," Rossi shouted, as he threw open the glass doors and barrelled towards the reception desk. "Where is he?" Which floor?"

A Latino chambermaid was sitting at the foot of the stairs, clearly in a state of shock.

"Fifth floor," she said. "Black man, with a gun."

Rossi leapt up the stairs two at a time until he was below the fifth-floor landing. There was a trolley thrown at a strange angle outside an open door. Inside, a burly, suited African was writhing slowly in agony, semi-conscious on the floor. A quick glance at his bruised face and blood-soaked trousers told Rossi all he needed to know – that he had been immobilized by an experienced but not ruthless hand. Another door led presumably to the bedroom. He heard mumbled voices and then a patter of stockinged feet as a leggy, scantily clad hooker ran out screaming and flew down the stairs like an ill-clad long jumper.

"Jibril," Rossi called out, "don't shoot. I know everything now." As he advanced, he could see the gunman pointing an automatic at the huge, naked figure on the bed. "Jibril, I know they had Victor killed. I know about your brother too. If you shoot, I'll have to shoot you."

Jibril had scarcely moved a muscle. Rossi edged closer.

"Drop the gun!"

Jibril went left then in a slight arc to a position where he could turn to hit Rossi and hold the President pinned where he was.

"He came here with his whore," said Jibril in a cool detached tone. "That was his mistake."

He raised his voice then to address the glistening bulk of the unmoving figure on the jumble of silken sheets.

"I heard her speak. Remember? She spoke in the dialect. My old dialect. And that's when I knew I could have you. *See you at the Incantevole, same day, usual time.*"

The President was biding his time, weighing the situation. He didn't lack experience but the odds were stacked against him.

"That was sloppy," Jibril continued. "But now I am going to tell you the story. The story of who I am and why I am here. Jibril is the name I took when I left my country, the name of a brother I never knew who died in infancy."

Rossi moved slowly, positioning himself so that the double doors flung almost fully open would allow him a clear shot at either or both of them. Jibril looked quickly across at him. Rossi thought for a second of his radio. His sleeve mike had been torn out at the station when the bomb exploded. Carrara would have already called for backup at the piazza but if they arrived here now it could endanger his life. He thought about calling them off but even moving to use it or just a crackle of static could be enough for Jibril to let fly.

"But maybe you remember a young man called Banjoko," said Jibril. "Well, he was my brother, back in the village, a long time ago."

A flicker of recognition crossed the President's gleaming sweat-drenched face. He knew that his odds of survival had lengthened considerably if this really was who he claimed to be. He gambled.

"Your brother was an animal. A degenerate. He got what he deserved."

"He was an artist," Jibril hissed back. "An intellectual. But you had him killed to build your own popularity through hate. I was young then and understood little but I've always felt it on my skin, always had to hoard those images against my will. But later I learnt of your role in that mystery they kept from me. I discovered why my brother was killed, and when I did I swore to keep the flame burning. But I knew it had to be a cold flame, otherwise it would have consumed me with hatred. Still, I have never let that flame go out."

The President risked a minor movement, a repositioning of his weight that might give him a sliver of an advantage.

"I saw then but in a glass darkly," Jibril went on, "but *now* I see face to face. You know where that comes from, big man? The Bible. A friend taught me that. My good friend. But he is dead now, killed by hypocrites who profess to follow another religion. So many hypocrites. So many liars. Well, I swore vengeance for my murdered brother and I swore justice for Victor too. But somebody got to his killer before I could. The fake Father Brell had Victor killed, the cardinal whose other enemies dealt him the justice he deserved."

Rossi held his stance, arms rigid with cramp, but he dared not move suddenly.

"And with some detective work of my own, we found his secrets – the cardinal's ring he couldn't bear to be without, the diary with his coded references to my friend. But I had no intention of killing him. The only vengeance I sought and seek now is justice, an admission, and penance fitting for their crimes."

He reached into his jacket pocket and took out a compact tape recorder then placed it on the bed.

"Now, you will confess your sins. If not, you *will* die. I give you the chance you denied to others. Confess to the murder of my brother, to the crimes you have committed here, your drug trafficking, the killing of the oilman, Mondo. Ali has paid the price already, and I gave him his wish – to die a martyr with a gun in his hand. So be it. The wages of sin is death, too. But now, the choice is yours."

Now Rossi had heard it all. The last piece in the puzzle was falling into place.

From close to the window onto the street there came then an almost deafening boom that shattered the silence as some rogue demonstrators exploded a paper bomb firework in the street below. As the glass shook, it was enough to distract Jibril for the fraction of a second necessary to allow the President to throw himself from the bed. He grabbed a weapon and squeezed off a desperate burst of automatic fire. Jibril fired twice, but a sash of bullet holes leapt through the mattress and across the wall and his body. Rossi threw himself clear and onto the stairs. Crawling back he edged into a firing position on the floor.

"Don't move or you're a dead man! Drop the gun!" Rossi shouted.

The President released his weapon and pushed it across the floor. Rossi got to his feet and advanced. Jibril's now lifeless corpse was slumped against the wall, the tape recorder still turning on the bed. Rossi kept low and approached. He clicked it, the wheels froze and he slipped it into his pocket.

The President had taken hits to the shoulder and upper chest but would live. *He* would.

"Backup needed at the Hotel Incantevole," said Rossi into his radio. "Medical units."

"You can cancel that!" said a muffled voice behind him. A female voice: one he knew.

"There's a gun at your head, Rossi. If you make a false move you will be the next dead man here. Don't turn around. Cancel it."

Rossi waited a second or two then countermanded the request.

"Marini," said Rossi.

"That is not the name I go under these days, Inspector, but yes I am who you think I am and I have indeed had a hand in the recent events." She pressed the muzzle hard into the nape of his neck, and he heard the familiar creak of bike leathers. She lifted her visor with a click. The cop on the motorbike outside. It was her.

"We will take care of this little mess. You can have Jibril but I think this other gentleman will be needing private medical care and his own trusted doctors. Besides, he knows far too much and we still have a lot of business to finish. But all things considered, today things went moderately well for us."

"Not enough deaths for you?" said Rossi.

"Like I said," Marini replied. "Moderate success. It soon adds up and it will help to get the ball rolling for the bigger projects. We need to get involved in another war you know, Rossi, in our backyard, the Middle East, North Africa. We don't have to lead it, just as long as we can join the party."

"Libya? Is that it?" said Rossi. "Or Egypt? Syria? You want to get a slice of the pie now that it's shaping up to become a free-for-all."

"If there's a gap in the market it gets filled. Besides, the economy needs the boost and what happens in Rome has to happen *here* in order for us to profit from it over *there*. And over here the mob likes to know who its enemy is. It keeps everyone polarized, nicely at loggerheads, makes it all black and white and easy to manage."

"So you just let things happen and give a helping hand if it serves your purpose, and get in our way when we're trying to save lives."

"We let the narrative build, Rossi, and the terror threat brings everyone onside sooner or later. The President here helps us get the funds moving, and he has a certain *gravitas* within his own community. Then we make sure the sweeteners go to the right people. Call it seed capital before the bigger earners come in."

"And you want to murder students, kids and couples at demos so you can keep the tension at the desired level."

"Well, you never know when a real threat might arrive. So, it's best to be ready. Militarized. Keep the plebs on their toes, right?"

Rossi's hand crept to his jacket pocket where the tape recorder was. He pressed what he thought was the record button.

"You hit the university didn't you?"

There was a pause then before the unexpectedly wrong-footed Marini answered.

"Let's say that was more of a private matter and the way events played out dovetailed nicely with other pressing demands."

So Iannelli had been right. The Israelis must have got mixed up in some sort of deal.

"I know you had the cardinal killed too," said Rossi. "If it really was the cardinal you wanted us to think it was."

"And why wouldn't it be?"

"Well, I'm not entirely convinced any corpse went missing from that church. Was that another of your double bluffs? Nice bit of work, putting the blame on the Muslims for the butchery in the monastery. And who's got their hands on the Borgia painting? Two birds with one stone was it? Cheap at the price."

She rammed the gun harder into Rossi's skull and clasped a gloved hand over his mouth. He could smell her, feminine despite it all.

"Don't expect me to tell you every fucking thing, Rossi. There wouldn't be any surprises otherwise, would there? Jibril had his private revenge agenda and even if he was getting too close for comfort we were able to piggyback on his zeal, let's say. Was it Father Brell or Cardinal Terranova he was planning on hitting, before someone got there first? I'll leave that one hanging, Rossi, like the Prenestina blaze. Like the Reichstag fire back in the day. Perhaps it was the communists after all."

She released her grip over Rossi's mouth, the gun still jammed at his skull.

"I don't see any mystery there," said Rossi. "Ivan knew Victor had been involved with the cardinal before he was killed. Okoli knew about the skin trade too. Perhaps he got a warning, did he? But Ivan knew what they were prepared to do to keep it all quiet, and he paid the price for not keeping his mouth shut. By the way, did you send that priest to the hospital to check Ivan wasn't going to make it, or to finish him off?"

He smelt her and the leather and felt her breasts pushing firm against his back. Her finger was on the trigger. He felt it tense, the mantis winding up for the ultimate of hits.

"And how is Yana, by the way?" she said then with surprising softness. "I hear things haven't been great recently between you two. I hear a lot, actually. Do you think those phone calls that come are from her lovers or from someone else?"

She knew where to hit Rossi. He knew when to cut his losses.

The President was dragging himself up on to his feet. A sorry figure but alive.

"Leave by the fire exit," she said, letting Rossi go then as suddenly as she had grasped him. The President began to struggle into a bathrobe. "There's a car waiting," she said.

"You think you can get away with this?" said Rossi.

"Of course," she replied. "Why wouldn't I? We write the fucking script."

The next thing Rossi remembered, Katia was looking down at him and Carrara was slapping him about the face.

"Who hit you, Mick? You've been out for a good while," said Carrara.

"The tape," said Rossi. His head was pounding. "In my pocket."

Taking the cue, Katia fumbled in the pocket of the jacket now slung over a chair and found his keys, the revolver, and all the usual junk.

"What tape?" said Carrara.

"Doesn't matter," said Rossi, "I'll tell you later."

Seventy-Four

Inspectors Rossi, Carrara and Vanessi were sitting in a bar overlooking the station.

"Well, at least we averted a massacre. That's all I've been hearing for the last few days," said Rossi as he sipped on a non-alcoholic cocktail.

"We were lucky the gun jammed," said Katia.

"And lucky that those guys made sure he didn't get the chance to put it right," said Carrara.

"That wasn't luck," said Rossi, "that was courage."

"And what if it was meant to jam?" said Carrara. "I mean, Jibril could have been sabotaging the whole operation as it was being set up. He might have knobbled the weapons too. It was all a means to an end for him."

"I think he was counting on taking them out, with the element of surprise, but the best laid schemes o' mice an' men..."

"Quoting again?" said Carrara.

"Well, you didn't do too bad yourself, Inspector," said Katia.

What sense would being a police officer have had otherwise? Of course, he had thought, in a split second, subconsciously. Perhaps somewhere deep down he'd even seen it as a way out, whatever might have happened. So he was thinking of himself?

Or had he done it to avoid having to deal with the guilt? Yana said once that he was in love with danger, that he couldn't live without being on or close to the edge. He would have to accept that it was an aspect of his nature which had played no small part in her decision to leave.

"Well, talk about a dish best enjoyed cold," he said, changing the subject for them and for himself.

"He didn't get what he wanted though, did he?" said Katia. "Even if it was taking the law into his own hands, the President got away."

"And there was no material proof that would hold up in any court," said Rossi. "Besides, he killed Jibril in self-defence. In Nigeria, he would scarcely be considered a criminal for what he did back then, if it could be proved."

"And Mondo, the fake Father Brell, the newly resurrected Marini," said Carrara. "You still think we were right? All that was choreographed too?"

Rossi nodded but was reflecting also on his own escape. Perhaps it had been too public or the President's being there had made it too dangerous for her to kill a cop. She was a psychopath but she'd played it safe. And after all, she was officially dead and he was in no position to say otherwise, trapped as he was in that parallel world he had been drawn into.

Katia looked from one to the other with a quizzical expression. They were speaking in some secret language now it seemed.

"Perhaps we should let her in on some more reserved information," said Rossi. "For what it's worth. You can keep a secret, can't you?"

Carrara gave Rossi a nudge.

"Here he is."

They all looked up as a tall, rangy and bearded figure approached across the piazza. He was carrying a light attaché case and was wearing a jacket and tie despite the heat. He made his way deftly between the crowded tables in rather different circumstances to when Rossi had first laid eyes on him during the melee in Piazza Repubblica.

"Glad to see you could make it," said Rossi, rising first to shake his hand and pulling out a chair for him. "Let me introduce you to the team."

There were handshakes all round.

"Now, Francesco," said Rossi, "what's all this about you wanting to become a police officer?"

Seventy-Five

"... and how is our 'Lucrezia'?" she asked.

"Safe and sound. Under lock and key. As for my trinkets?"

"Safe and sound too. 'The Courier' did his job to the letter. So, when shall we arrange the handover?"

"At a moment of your convenience," he replied. "When things have settled down."

"Settled down *for the time being*," she replied in a tone of mild, subservient rebuke.

"Quite. Yet, you know I feel quite lost without my cardinal's ring. Even if I cannot flaunt it any longer."

"Well, it was crucial, for our gambit."

"As was the diary. And the letter. Strokes of genius and a great *Victory*, one might say," and to underline his irony he almost laughed.

"It was enough that all the props we planted were noticed then withdrawn from the scene," she said. "Out of the way of other prying eyes."

"It's as well they were not subtracted by the spy in question. They were wise enough not to raise suspicions."

"Well-drilled, yes. But not wise enough to know that we were tracking their every move."

"And yet they came quite close."

"They managed to cause us some inconvenience."

"One cannot stage-manage *everything*, my dear. No doubt you had the now-deceased African on a short leash."

"As soon as he began courting the journalist, Iannelli," she confirmed, "we never let him out of our sight. That's secret service training for you. Don't give them an inch. We're good at that in Italy. It's why terror attacks are usually on *our* terms."

"Yet one cannot know their every move, their every thought."

"A more decisive outcome might have served our interests, in terms of a body count. But we shan't complain."

"One lives and learns," he said. "The best laid plans ... I see you spared the inspector, however, to fight another day."

"For now," she said. "He's become something of a hero, so one must tread a little more carefully and our sometimes friend the President would have been a witness. I hardly need to tell you about honour among thieves. Besides, Rossi is in many ways more useful alive."

"Well, tell me *Agente Marini*! Do tell me this. How does it feel to be immortal once again?"

There was a pause as a cloud of exhaled cigarette smoke enveloped the receiver and her lips moved just a little closer.

"I believe, *Eccellenza*, I could put that very same question to you."

Epilogue

Olivia stood for a moment on the pavement outside the organization's offices. The day was fine, infinite in its way, with a blue sky that seemed to have no limits. She looked at the names on the intercom. A couple of weeks had passed. She had kept as low a profile as she could have expected to. Of course, her name had come out in the press, she had been questioned, earmarked as a witness in forthcoming enquiries, a trial. They had caught one of the others. He had talked, Rossi had told her, and the police were hunting for Karim, the only other fugitive.

She pressed the button for The List of Shame and waited.

"Yes?" came the reply.

"It's Olivia."

"OK. I'll be down in a minute. Coffee?"

"Yes," Olivia replied.

She had left her teaching job and decided to take up the offer of working for the NGO. Ginika had been very kind to her but also practical and optimistic about her future. They had agreed first to work together to find Jibril's family and to bring his body back to Nigeria. Then they had set about seeing what they could do to set up a side project to discover the identities of the other men killed in the blaze that had engulfed the Prenestina flat.

They were also working to secure an identification for Victor, tracing his family, sending for DNA. Only that morning, the bodies of a mother and her child – immigrants lost overboard – had been washed up on the shore, some miles down the coast from Rome. They were still holding onto each other, locked in a last embrace.

She thought again about Jibril. Had she really known him? She had met with the psychologist, Doctor Fusca, to speak about such things. Had Jibril cared about her, loved her even? It had felt good at the time, it had felt natural and real until his disappearance. Or had she only ever been a pawn in his game, some greater strategy being played out around her and over which she had no control? She knew things could never be the same but change would always come, in one way or another. Accepting change would help her move on, the doctor said. But who could she trust now? She trusted Inspector Rossi, Carrara, and Ginika. They had been kind to her but then Jibril had been kind too. She had thought it through time and time again and had come to her own conclusion: she did not believe that he had been evil. He, like so many, like she herself now was, had been a victim, with every right to feel bitter and cheated, damaged by this world and its weary ways.

Acknowledgements

I would like to thank my family, in particular Graziella, Denis, and Liam for finding the time to read an earlier version of *A Cold Flame* and providing some invaluable suggestions. Sincere thanks also to my agent Ger Nichol and my editor Finn Cotton for their continuing dedication.

KILLER READS

DISCOVER THE BEST IN CRIME AND THRILLER.

SIGN UP TO OUR NEWSLETTER FOR YOUR CHANCE TO WIN A FREE BOOK EVERY MONTH.

FIND OUT MORE AT WWW.KILLERREADS.COM/NEWSLETTER

Want more? Get to know the team behind the books, hear from our authors, find out about new crime and thriller books and lots more by following us on social media:

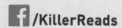 /KillerReads   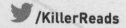 /KillerReads